I Dream of Darcy

The Complete Novel

Andrea David

Artesian Well Publishing

Contents

About This Book

Elizabeth Bennet refuses to sit idly while her sister pines for a lost love. Certain that Bingley will renew his addresses if only he and Jane are reunited, Lizzy travels from Hertfordshire to London to track him down.

A chance encounter brings her face to face with her nemesis, the disagreeable Mr. Darcy. Lizzy is certain he is responsible for parting Jane and Bingley in the first place. Though furious with him for the pain he has caused Jane, she is touched by the brotherly affection he shows towards his own sister, Georgiana.

Lizzy and Georgiana soon strike up a friendship that gains Lizzy and Jane invitations to the best *ton* events. As Lizzy and Darcy are thrown more and more together, he tries to deny his growing ardour for her. But when an earl begins courting her, Darcy realizes he must act. Will the mistakes of the past get in the way of their future? Or will Our Dear Couple find their way to lasting love?

This sweet Regency romance is a standalone novel of 100,000 words. It includes kissing but no on-page intimacy.

Learn more about Andrea's books by joining her newsletter or visiting her website:
www.AndreaDavidAuthor.com

Author's Note

I hope, gentle reader, you will forgive some liberties I have taken with the timeline. While the book is set in 1812, Byron's poem "She Walks in Beauty" was not published until 1813.

Also, while some sources say the waltz was first danced at Almack's in 1812, others give later dates.

Chapter 1

In the slanting light of a January morning, Elizabeth Bennet breathed the crisp air. With a wool pelisse to protect her, she did not mind the cold. The blue sky and open countryside seemed to stretch on forever.

The shopping trip to the little town of Meryton with her sisters had been productive. In the dressmaker's shop, she had scoured the latest fashion magazines for ideas. Resisting the temptation to order a new gown, she bought some notions to update her old ones instead. She wanted to look her best for Mr. Wickham at the next assembly.

She had hoped she would see him in the village, where his militia regiment was stationed for the winter. Only two of the officers had passed by the shop, however. Her youngest sisters had gone outside and flirted with Denny and Sanderson for a full ten minutes before Lizzy went to round them up.

Now, they were heading home to the manor house at Longbourn. Cheerful birdsong played in her ears, and the wide gravel pathway crunched beneath their feet.

She liked bringing up the rear because it allowed her to keep an eye on fifteen-year-old Lydia. The baby of the family, she was a girl of high spirits. Her adolescent ways too often influenced Kitty, the second youngest.

Mary, the closest in age to Lizzy, was of no use in supervising her siblings. Her mind was full of books and music. While she had much enthusiasm for these pursuits, she unfortunately had little taste. Their mother's lax parenting style and love of gossip had incited Mary to quiet rebellion. But she had veered too far, turning rigid and pedantic.

Mary walked determinedly, carrying her newly purchased sheet music. Meanwhile, Lydia tried to wheedle Kitty into sharing her new length of blue ribbon. "But it would look so pretty with my sprigged muslin," Lydia said, "the one with the diamond pattern. You know that I would share with you, if I had bought some ribbon."

"I know no such thing," Kitty protested. "You never share with me, and you constantly wheedle Mama to let you have my things. I bought the ribbon for an old bonnet I am freshening up. I do not have enough to spare."

"I am better at making up bonnets than you are. I'll do it for you if you let me have the leftover ribbon."

"I want to do my own."

And so it went for the next mile they walked.

Lizzy had learnt long ago to ignore their squabbling. Neither of their parents had the resolve to put an end to it. Lydia did whatever their mother let her get away with, which was quite a bit. Of the five sisters, Lydia was the most like her mother in temperament. But she had inherited their father's cleverness. It was not a good combination.

The eldest sister, Jane, was in London. She had been staying in Cheapside with their aunt and uncle Gardiner since the start of the new year. Even after just a fortnight, Lizzy longed for Jane's company. The sweetest and most sensible of the Bennet clan, she was a balm for Lizzy's soul. If Jane had a fault, it was that she was *too* good, seeing the best in everyone. Even those who did not deserve it.

But Lizzy refused to let sadness interfere with her walk. She loved being out of doors, especially on a clear day. The trees might be leafless, but the structure of the grey branches had a beauty all its own.

They reached the cobbled drive too soon for Lizzy's preference. Now she had no more excuses for ignoring her sewing, for which she had little talent. But as her papa liked to tease, she ought to do something to earn her keep.

In truth, with the entail on her father's estate, she might have no choice but to earn her keep if she did not find a suitable husband. She sighed at the thought of Wickham. There was no hope in that quarter. Neither of them had fortune enough to make a marriage possible.

Stepping inside the house, melancholy settled over her again. If things had gone Jane's way last autumn, the eldest Bennet sister would be enjoying London with her new husband. Jane would be happy, and the family would be saved from ruin.

Outside forces had interfered, however. Jane's hopes had been cruelly and intentionally dashed.

Fury rose inside Lizzy whenever she thought of Jane's last letter from Caroline Bingley. That upstart granddaughter of a tradesman thought her family too high and mighty for the Bennets, who had been landed gentry for centuries. Not that Lizzy cared two shillings for rank. The effrontery of it burned.

She took a deep breath to calm her nerves. Joining her mother in the front parlour, she picked up her sewing basket.

While Lizzy worked, her mother prattled about a disagreement with the cook. Mary tried out her new music on the pianoforte in the conservatory, missing as many notes as she hit. Somewhere in the house, Lydia and Kitty continued squabbling over bonnets and ribbons.

In the window seat, Lizzy sighed. She loved her family, but she longed for quiet.

More than that, she longed for Jane. Nursing a broken heart, her eldest sister had seemed despondent in her last letter. Lizzy had wanted to hie to town that very day on the mail coach.

But Lizzy had little hope of leaving the environs of the village of Meryton at that time. If Jane were not in London, Lizzy would not even wish to go. The Bennet family lived comfortably in the country. However, a season in town for five daughters was beyond their means. Mr. Bennet had no sons, and Longbourn would go to a distant cousin upon his demise.

The family economized where they could.

Lizzy carefully cut the ribbon and lace she had purchased to lengthen the sleeves of her best gown. It was a white muslin with a soft damask pattern, one she saved for special occasions. She took care with her needle, to avoid damaging the delicate fabric.

The activity cheered her. She hoped for a ball at the assembly rooms soon. That would break up the monotony of a dull, dreary January.

She had not been long at her work when her aunt Philips was shown in. Her mother's sister had married a lawyer in Meryton. Her situation in the village made her privy to gossip before it reached the nearby estates.

On this day, it was clear from her manner that Mrs. Philips had a fine piece of news to share. Upon her arrival, Lydia and Kitty gave up their quarrel, and even Mary came to join them in the parlour. Hill the housekeeper set out the tea tray and some jam biscuits.

"Why, sister, what do you think?" aunt Philips began, her tone grave. "Have you heard the news about Miss King?"

Miss King was a young woman of about twenty—the same age as Lizzy. She had not lived in Meryton long. A few months prior, she had come to stay with her uncle, but had attracted no particular notice. At least, not until she had inherited the fine sum of ten thousand pounds.

"Miss King is not unwell, I hope?" Lizzy asked. She did not count Miss King a particular friend, but Lizzy had no reason to think ill of her. Lizzy would not wish any misfortune to befall her.

"On the contrary." Mrs. Philips tapped a finger to her lips a moment, as if pondering her next words. She gave Lizzy a sorrowful look. "Miss King is engaged—"

"Engaged!" cried Lydia. "That awful, freckled thing?"

Lizzy glared at her sister, aghast. Lydia was already out in society, but her manners could have used an extra year or two to develop.

Neither mother nor aunt appeared to have the breath to scold her, however. The next moment, Mrs. Philips continued with her story, giving Lizzy a significant look. "Yes. She is engaged...to Mr. Wickham."

Silence descended on the room as Lizzy's stomach dropped to the floor. Wickham, marry Miss King? Though tears did not prickle her eyes, she could not deny that the news made her chest grow heavy.

She could not fathom it. Wickham had never shown the girl a moment's interest before. Rather, he had singled out Lizzy from the day they had met, paying her his attentions at every assembly.

He had been clear from the beginning that he was penniless apart from his officer's pay. The salary of a lieutenant in the militia could barely cover his own expenses, much less those of a wife. He had not misled her in any way.

Still, Lizzy felt all the humiliation of the moment. No, she could not attribute her discomfort to a broken heart. Yet she was mortified that her favourite had attached himself to another. Especially without warning.

All eyes turned to Lizzy, and heat rose in her face. She knew what the ladies of her family were thinking—that she must feel thrown over by him. In fact, she felt no such thing. He had never been hers, and she had known he never would be.

The fault for *that* fact lay squarely on the shoulders of one man. Mr. Fitzwilliam Darcy had ruined all of Wickham's hopes.

Darcy had sojourned at nearby Netherfield Park the previous autumn. Nephew to the Earl of Matlock, he was a landowner of considerable fortune. At eight-and-twenty, he was as pleasing in his physical features as he was black of heart. Though tall and shamefully handsome, he wore a haughty air. He seemed to consider himself above all his company.

And he had struck a blow against Wickham that had left the poor man destitute.

Was it any wonder Wickham found it necessary to marry a

woman of fortune? Lizzy herself had no dowry at all. She had been cautious with her heart. Marriage to Wickham was an impossibility.

No, Lizzy had no choice but to marry a man with the means to support her. She was also determined to marry for love. Under the circumstances, she had resisted falling for Wickham's considerable charms.

Still, word of his engagement was a jolt—if only to her pride. And everyone in her family knew it.

She pasted a placid smile on her face. "What happy news," she said. "I hope they will be as happy as they deserve."

Her female relations continued to stare owlishly at her. It was at moments like this that she missed Jane the most. Jane would have comprehended the irony of her statement. Except for her father, no one else in the family understood Lizzy's sense of humour.

She picked up a raspberry biscuit and passed around the plate. The others resumed their gossiping. She did her best to ignore them.

After aunt Philips had gone, Lizzy found herself alone with her needlework at last. A half hour of quiet ensued before the housekeeper brought her a letter.

"This came for you in the post, miss." Hill curtseyed, then withdrew.

Lizzy expected it to be from Jane until she saw the handwriting. It belonged to her aunt Gardiner, the wife of Mrs. Bennet's brother. Some years younger than her husband, she was a favourite with her nieces.

Curiosity piqued, Lizzy tore open the envelope. She read eagerly at first, then with ever-increasing concern.

Dear Lizzy,

I hope you will forgive this letter. I do not wish to worry you, my dear. We are all well here, and I trust the same is true at Longbourn.

Jane's spirits, I find, continue to be low, even after two weeks in town. I had hoped that shopping and entertainment would distract her from her troubles. But in truth, I can hardly coax her out of the house.

She lives in fear that we will run into Mr. Bingley. She says she cannot bear the thought of seeing his indifference. I tell her such a thing is unlikely, as we travel in different circles. Still, we might see him at a public place like the theatre or a museum. So we generally remain home of an evening.

Mr. Gardiner and I are content to avoid the crowds of the ton *during the season. But Jane is young and beautiful. For her to pine away seems a terrible waste when so many respectable young men are in town this time of year.*

I have done my best to cheer her, to no avail. I am convinced that you are the only one in the world who can manage it. Will you come to London, Lizzy? We can send the carriage for you on Thursday, if that would be convenient. You would be a great comfort to us all.

Your affectionate aunt,

M. Gardiner

The words made Lizzy want to cry. Poor Jane! She had the kindest heart of anyone in the world, and Charles Bingley had broken it.

Mr. Bingley was a good friend of Mr. Darcy. Lizzy suspected that Darcy had schemed against Jane. Without warning, Bingley had quit Netherfield and settled in London for the season.

Lizzy knew not how Darcy had persuaded Bingley to abandon Jane. Darcy had made it no secret, though, that he considered the Bennets beneath him and his friends. Without Darcy's interference, Lizzy was certain Bingley would have asked for Jane's hand.

Pacing the floor, Lizzy balled her hands into fists. The more she thought about it, the more infuriated she became. Jane loved Bingley. He could give her the financial security she needed. Should she lose that happiness because of a heartless scoundrel like Darcy? It was insupportable.

Lizzy had secretly hoped Jane would run into Bingley while

in town. Thus, their love would be rekindled. There was no hope of that if Jane refused to leave the house. If Jane would not take the initiative on her own, then perhaps she could use a sisterly push.

Before discussing it with her mother, Lizzy decided to secure her father's permission. She did not doubt her mother's love for her. Yet their dispositions diverged so wildly, a stranger would not have thought them related. Lizzy was all her father's daughter.

So she waited until after dinner that evening and approached him in his study. Sitting in front of his desk, she explained the contents of the letter from her aunt.

"It is bad enough with Jane gone," her father complained. "If you go too, I shall not hear two words of sense spoken together in this house until you return."

And whose fault is that? she wondered. He had chosen his wife for her beauty rather than her wit. He had been utterly indifferent about his daughters' education. If he heard nothing but gossip and talk of the latest fashions while she and Jane were gone, he had no one to blame but himself.

"Papa, I cannot bear to think of Jane suffering—"

"A broken heart is a common enough thing. I daresay she will meet another young man soon enough, and drive away all thoughts of Bingley."

Lizzy jumped to her feet. Did her father have so little concept of how dire the situation was? If she and her sisters did not marry well, their choices in life would be extremely limited once he was gone.

"How many more men of five thousand a year is she likely to encounter?" she asked him, tamping down her fury. "She is two-and-twenty. There will soon be talk that she is on the shelf."

"Oh, I think we have some years before we have to worry about—"

"If you die tomorrow," Lizzy said more insistently, "my sisters and I will be destitute. We will have to live off the largesse of Mama and her two hundred pounds a year. How will she support six women on such a sum? Mary and I will have to become governesses, and Jane a companion to an elderly widow."

Being a governess was out of the question for Jane. No married woman would hire someone of such beauty into her household. As for the youngest sisters... Lydia ought not to be out of the schoolroom herself. And Kitty—well, she was as ignorant as a girl could be despite surviving seventeen years on earth. She was too much under Lydia's influence, and Lydia was under no one's influence at all.

Her father did not meet Lizzy's eyes. She could not endure the silence. He was supposed to be the head of this household. "Is that what you want for your daughters, Papa? Is it?"

He looked properly chagrined, for once in his life. Lizzy hated to remind him of how he had let his family down. He rarely liked to think about it on his own—or take any action to rectify the matter. Sometimes, however, it could not be helped.

"If you think a trip to London necessary," he said at last, "I will not oppose you."

Her spirits lightened, and the tension in her body eased. Wearing a bright smile, she leaned over his chair and kissed his cheek. He smelled of brandy and cheroots.

"Thank you, dearest Papa. You will not regret it. I am certain I can reunite Jane and Mr. Bingley. Perhaps filial affection made him malleable enough to quit Netherfield. But think how much more pliant he will be in the face of violent love."

With that certainty in her heart, she patted her father's shoulder and went upstairs to her packing.

Chapter 2

Darcy's eyes scanned the ballroom, taking in the crowd. The dark suits of the gentlemen contrasted with the pastel confections of the ladies. Their silks shimmered in the candlelight from brass wall sconces and crystal chandeliers. Hothouse flowers in pink and yellow and purple fragranced the air.

"What about her?" he asked Bingley in a low voice, lifting his chin in the direction of the Earl of Greymore's youngest sister. She was petite and blonde and exactly Bingley's type. "Lady Cressida Marlowe. A very pretty girl."

Bingley turned in the young woman's direction. "Quite so," Bingley said with a nod. "Though not as pretty as..." His voice trailed away in a sigh. As it always did when he spoke of Jane Bennet, even if he did not say her name.

Darcy gritted his teeth but endeavoured to maintain a placid expression. Bingley's obsession with Miss Bennet was trying, but his pain was real. His attachment was deeper than Darcy had imagined.

It had been six weeks since they had quit Netherfield. The wound was fresh, but not so much that Bingley should still be in this state of melancholy. It pained Darcy to see his friend's usual high spirits so dampened.

"Come, Bingley, this is not like you. The best way to forget one female is to seek out the company of another. I must see you dance."

"Forgive me. I shall leave the breaking of hearts to you

tonight." He clapped Darcy's shoulder, then bowed and headed to the card room.

Darcy watched after his friend in frustration. He himself had no more desire to dance than Bingley did. But his cousin, Lady Arabella Fitzwilliam, had just come out. He wanted to make sure she was never without a partner.

And if he were honest with himself, he had another reason as well. Like Bingley, he was striving to forget one of the Bennet sisters.

Darcy had expected to erase Miss Elizabeth Bennet from his mind within hours of the journey from Netherfield. But as the days had stretched into weeks, he continued to burn for her. Though she had not the exquisite beauty of her elder sister, she had an animation Jane lacked. Her face was lively and pretty, and her figure—

Darcy forced himself *not* to think about her figure.

Instead, he looked for Arabelle in the crowd. Spotting her standing with her mother and her sister Nerissa, he headed in that direction. Before he had taken many steps, Lady Greymore cut into his path, her daughter on her arm.

"Mr. Darcy, how wonderful to see you in town so early in the season. You remember my youngest daughter, Cressida?"

"Of course, ma'am," he said graciously, despite his irritation. "Lady Cressida, how good to see you again. Are you enjoying the ball?"

"I am, I thank you, sir. It is quite a squeeze."

He gave her a soft look. "I assure you, once the season is in full swing, you will look back and smile at considering *this* a squeeze."

He was about to excuse himself when Lady Greymore said, "Cressida has received permission to waltz. She is the most graceful dancer I ever saw. I assure you, sir, a gentleman's toes would be quite safe from her."

"Mama," Cressida scolded, her expression unusually serene for a girl making her come-out.

Darcy had no desire to ask her to dance. Though as pretty

as any young woman in the room, she was all of seventeen. If Darcy were to court a woman, it would be...well, a *woman*. One who could offer intelligent and spirited conversation. Cressida hid her wit behind a demure silence.

Rather like Jane Bennet.

Which raised the question: What did Bingley really know of Miss Bennet? Her mother was the crassest sort of fortune hunter. According to Bingley's sister Caroline, Jane had felt no deep attachment to him. She had only been following her mother's instructions in admitting his attentions.

And Caroline ought to know. She had been Jane's confidante while they had been at Netherfield.

Lady Greymore, by contrast, was no adventurer. Cressida's dowry was ample, if the rumours were true. She would make an excellent match for Bingley, and help him to put Jane out of his mind.

It would not hurt Darcy to dance with the chit and get to know her better. She was the sort of girl he would like his sixteen-year-old sister Georgiana to emulate, once she came out. And Cressida's brother the earl was unmarried. An alliance between their two families would be most eligible.

Good heavens. Now he was thinking like a society maven. No, Darcy would be in no way suited to playing matchmaker for his sister, when her time came. He would leave that up to his aunt, the Countess of Matlock. Or better still, his own wife.

He startled at that. For indeed, Darcy had no wife. But when the thought had flitted into his mind, he had pictured none other than Elizabeth Bennet.

Impossible.

In truth, he did not object to the lady herself. She was lovely and well mannered, and she aroused all the appropriate feelings in him. And, sometimes, inappropriate feelings. She would make a fine bed partner.

Do. Not. Think. About. That.

The problem was entirely with her family. Her mother was the embodiment of foolishness. Her youngest sisters were wild and ungoverned. Even her father had a droll disregard for propriety, which could not help embarrassing his relations at times.

Darcy could not imagine aligning himself with such a family—no matter how delightful Elizabeth Bennet was.

And as he had told Bingley, the best way to forget one woman was to spend time with another. Lady Cressida was a lovely girl. She might well have a brain in her head if he could remove her from the scrutiny of her mother. So he capitulated to that woman's machinations. "Lady Cressida, have you a partner for the waltz?"

"I do not, sir."

"Then I would be most happy to escort you."

They made their way to the dance floor. Lady Cressida, as it turned out, *did* have a brain in her head. She was young, to be sure. But her manners were lovely, her French fluent. Her interests included botany and geography.

"I long to travel to Italy one day," she said, "to see the art and architecture of Rome and Florence and Venice."

"Perhaps you will, once Bonaparte is defeated."

"My brothers complained about the war denying them their grand tours. They had to travel to such far-flung lands as Scotland and Ireland. And those quaint little villages in Wales where everyone has the same surname."

She had perfected that tone of ennui expected of the *beau monde*. Yet the sparkle in her eye carried a hint of satire. She was all propriety, and yet…there was nothing bland about her. She had the self-possession of a cat, and the air of mystery, too.

It seemed there was much more to Lady Cressida than she would ever show in public. But she was barely more than a child, and after the waltz, he returned her to her mother.

He went looking for Arabelle again. Just as he spotted her, she was approached by a worthless young man named Rolf Peabody. His brother, Viscount Wayne, was an old friend of Darcy's cousin, Colonel Fitzwilliam. About thirty, Wayne was newly married and had an untarnished reputation.

But Peabody was well known as a rake. According to rumour, he had left Oxford in disgrace two years earlier. His father, still alive at the time, had hushed up whatever the scandal had been.

Darcy did not have to rely on gossip. He had seen enough with his own eyes to form an opinion. He did not want the cad anywhere near Arabella.

In a handful of strides, Darcy crossed the room. "Where is your mother, dear cousin?"

Arabelle looked up at him with wide, brown eyes. "Oh, Darcy! I did not see you there. Mama is helping Nerissa." In a whisper, she explained that her sister's waltz partner had stepped on her hem. Two inches of lace had been torn from the fabric.

"Ah," he replied. "If you are not engaged for the next set, I would be happy to be your partner."

"She is engaged by me," Peabody said cheerily. "I have come to claim her."

Tall and blond and broad-shouldered, the man wore a wolfish grin. He was easily capable of overpowering an unwilling female. But they were in a bright ballroom with dozens of prominent guests. Darcy set his jaw but nodded curtly.

If Peabody had already secured the dance with Arabelle, Darcy would not make a fuss about it. But once the dance was through, he would warn her to stay away from the rogue in the future. Surely the countess would not have approved of Peabody as a partner if she had been there to prevent it.

Darcy would not let Arabelle suffer the same heartbreak his sister Georgiana had. The previous year, Giana had been duped by George Wickham. Darcy had once considered the man his closest friend. But Wickham had attempted to elope with Giana for the sake of her dowry, a sum of thirty thousand pounds. If Darcy had not discovered the truth in time...

His gut clenched, and pain rose in his chest. The possibility did not bear thinking about.

He and Wickham had grown apart during their years at Cambridge. Wickham's dissolute lifestyle had threatened to stain Darcy's reputation by association. Things became worse when Wickham's gambling debts began to mount. Even Darcy's generous allowance was insufficient to cover them. Darcy could not continue protecting his old friend forever.

That, apparently, was an unpardonable sin. Darcy let Wickham suffer the consequences of his own actions. Wickham never forgave him. He seemed to regard Darcy as his personal bank account—with unlimited funds available for withdrawal.

Before he had died, Darcy's father had asked his son to look after Wickham. Being a man of honour, Darcy fulfilled the obligation. He considered the matter settled.

Wickham did not. He had squandered every penny and come looking for more. When Darcy refused, Wickham's resentment burned. He sought his revenge by targeting Georgiana, the person Darcy cared for most in the world.

Darcy had done what he thought was right when it came to Wickham, but the cost to his family might have been enormous. Had there been another way? Might he have salvaged his friendship with Wickham, if he had acted differently?

The thought had haunted Darcy for a year now, ever since he had rescued Georgiana. It was time to let go of the past. He could not change it. He had done the best he could.

Shortly after the break in his friendship with Wickham, Darcy had met Bingley. While Bingley shared Wickham's amiable nature, that was where the similarity ended. Wickham used his sociability to manipulate. Bingley was the most ingenuous person Darcy knew.

Which, unfortunately, made him easy prey.

In the past week, a new worry had surfaced in that area. Caroline Bingley had told Darcy that Jane Bennet was in town, staying with her uncle in Cheapside. Bingley's sisters were determined to keep the information from their brother.

Darcy agreed with them—Bingley was greatly attached to Miss Bennet, much more than she to him. But how would Bingley respond if he learnt of the deception? Was Darcy risking their friendship, now, too?

Darcy had taken Bingley under his wing at university. Bingley had started at Cambridge when he was sixteen. Though academically precocious, he was far too trusting for his own good.

For seven years, Darcy had protected the younger man from those who sought to take advantage of him. Darcy would not let Bingley make the worst mistake of his life by marrying a penniless woman who did not love him.

Yet Darcy's stomach tightened at the thought of losing another friend—this one of far greater worth than Wickham. Though Darcy was a man of some consequence, he allowed only a few people into his inner circle. A rift between himself and Bingley would be a blow indeed.

The music ended, and Darcy looked around for Arabella. When he spotted her, he strode determinedly in her direction. Peabody was escorting her towards the terrace, but Darcy would not permit that.

When he caught up to them, he said to Arabelle, "I believe my dance is next."

Her eyes challenged him. "Is it?"

She was right to be sceptical, as he had not secured a dance with her. He had planned to swoop in when she needed assistance, as she did now. Except that Arabelle had no concept of the danger she was in.

He offered his arm, and she took it without protest. They made their way through the crowd of perfectly groomed lords and ladies. In the crush, they were bombarded by the competing scents of powder and cologne and potions of all kinds. The room was growing warm from the heat of all those bodies.

When they reached the dance floor, Arabelle said in his ear, "I did not need rescuing."

"Rolf Peabody is the most dangerous man here tonight. Simply spending time in his company could harm your reputation."

She raised her brow, a sardonic half-smile on her lips. "What nonsense. His sister Priscilla is my dearest friend. Rolf and I played together as children."

"You are hardly more than a child now."

"I am seventeen," she said with a scoff.

He looked at her askance. "You have just made my point."

Sighing heavily, she looked away for a moment, then turned and met his eyes. "Darcy, do not be tiresome. I have four older brothers for that."

"Let us stipulate that you have reached the age of young womanhood. You must agree, then, that Peabody also is no longer a child. He is a man of one-and-twenty. He knows more of the world than you. Perhaps you do not understand the potential harm a man like that can do to an innocent."

She rolled her eyes, a habit the countess had been trying to rid her of. "I am not as ignorant as you suppose. If Rolf tries to kiss me, I shall rebuff him as I ought."

"He is larger and stronger than you. What if he refuses to take no for an answer?"

She gaped at him. A moment later, she pressed her mouth into a thin, tight line, anger flashing in her eyes. "That is an awful thing to say. Rolf would not do that to me."

Darcy had reason to disagree. He had once caught Rolf doing that and more to a housemaid. If Darcy had not intervened, the man might have brutalized her.

But Darcy could not tell that sort of thing to a gently bred young lady. Instead, he said, "Promise me that you will not allow yourself to be alone with him."

"Of course. I understand how it would harm my reputation to be in the company of a man unchaperoned."

"You were about to go outside with him."

Her brow narrowed. She looked as if she wanted to slap him. "The terrace is well lit. Couples are continually stepping outside to take the cool air for a moment. It is January. No one would meet for a moonlight tryst in the garden in this weather."

Darcy did not like it, but he could not argue with her. Besides, it would do no good. He had made his point, and any further words from him would only serve to antagonize her. Fortunately, he could count on her mother, father, and seven older siblings to support him.

What would he do when Georgiana came out? He was the only family she had left. The Fitzwilliams could wield a certain amount of influence over her. But she did not care for their opinions as intensely as she did for his.

Yet he held no illusions. An adolescent girl could not be counted on to obey her elders without argument.

Thankfully, she had done exactly that when he had separated her from Wickham. He had told her everything—well, everything except the worst of Wickham's womanizing. She had accepted his word that the man's interest had been in her dowry. It had been a blow, after she had thought him in love with her.

Darcy might have fallen into the melancholy the memory usually brought. The Scottish reel distracted him. Arabelle had learnt from the best dance instructors in London. It was a pleasure to see her pretty face so full of laughter and life. The sprightly music created a jolly mood.

A fierce love for his young cousin welled up in Darcy's chest. He protected his own—whether Arabelle or Georgiana or yes, even Bingley. No one would take advantage of them on Darcy's watch.

Not even one as lovely and unassuming as Jane Bennet.

Chapter 3

Lizzy's eyes darted around the interior of a bookstore in Mayfair. Black-painted shelves rose from floor to ceiling. They housed tomes ranging from novels to ancient Greek texts. Lizzy could have spent all day there, but she had a mission.

Her companion, Sally, was employed by the Gardiners and acting as lady's maid to Lizzy and Jane. She was about twenty with ginger-blonde hair and a slender build. Sweet and amiable, she raved over how pleasant it was to look after the sisters during their visit to London.

Sally's words *might* have sprung from a hope of being hired permanently for a more prestigious post. And in truth, Lizzy wished they *could* bring another lady's maid home with them to Longbourn. Yet, she believed Sally truly cared about Jane's welfare. Sally had confided to Lizzy that she sometimes saw tears in Jane's eyes, while Jane pretended to be fine.

The persistent sorrow Jane showed brought an ache to Lizzy's heart. Jane and Bingley had clearly been in love. And while Bingley was young—perhaps three-and-twenty—he was independent. He could marry whomever he pleased. If he wanted Jane, he should have her. His sisters should have no say in it.

So that morning, Lizzy had put a plan into motion. And Sally was a willing partner in her scheme.

Lizzy told her aunt she wanted to spend the day shopping. Meryton did not offer the variety of potions and perfumes that could be found in town. But her reason for travelling by hackney coach all the way to Mayfair was more…complicated.

Jane had learnt from Caroline that Bingley was staying at Darcy House. Lizzy had come to find him, even though she did not know where Darcy House was. If she found out, it would be scandalous for a single young woman to call on a single gentleman. But if she could somehow manage to run into Bingley…

Lizzy sighed. It was not a *good* plan. But it was better than wasting away in Cheapside, hoping Bingley would magically appear at the door. She might overhear something, or catch sight of someone she knew. At any rate, she could not be idle when Jane's heart was breaking. She had to do something.

A few patrons milled about. Lizzy recognized no one, overheard no names of acquaintances. That was not surprising. She was hardly a member of the *bon ton*, though she did have a few connections. She sighed, thinking perhaps it was time to move on to another shop.

She stopped, though, when she spotted a copy of *Lyrical Ballads.* It was a book of poetry by Wordsworth and Coleridge. The romantic sentiments might appeal to Kitty. Lizzy suspected that Kitty would not be averse to reading more—if Lydia were not always distracting her from serious pursuits.

Lost in her musings, she barely noticed that the door to the shop had swung open. Then, a familiar voice captured her attention. Her stomach jumped. Darcy! She quickly turned away from him to avoid discovery.

"Oh, look!" a female voice cried. "It is the latest by Mrs. Hunter."

"*That* you may get from the circulating library," Darcy replied. "Such a book has no place in the library at Pemberley. What about a collection of poetry? I have been searching for a first edition of *The Lady of the Lake* by Walter Scott."

The young woman replied in a teasing tone. "Forgive me for thinking of what I might enjoy reading. Not of what would best adorn your library shelves."

From the ensuing conversation, Lizzy guessed the young lady must be his sister, Georgiana. Lizzy had never met the girl. She dared not look to take in Miss Darcy's appearance. The voice, however, was airy and musical, like a bird's.

"A woman cannot be called truly accomplished," Darcy said, "unless she improves her mind by reading."

The girl tittered. "You mean like a certain lady you knew at Netherfield?"

Lizzy startled at that. Who could they be speaking of? Caroline Bingley seemed the most likely candidate. But she had not been a great reader from what Lizzy had observed.

Lizzy's maid approached. "There you are, miss. I lost sight of you."

In a low, conspiratorial tone, Lizzy said, "The tall man who just came in? That is Mr. Darcy. I do not wish him to see me."

"Mr. Darcy! We've been trying to get information about him all day. Would it not be easier to talk to him?"

"I do not wish him to know I am in town. He may endeavour to keep me away from Mr. Bingley."

Sally looked at her, brows furrowed, tilting her head to one side. "Why would he do that?"

"Well…" Lizzy sighed. *In for a penny, in for a pound.* "I told you of my suspicion that Mr. Bingley's sisters were responsible for parting him and Jane. Mr. Darcy may also have played a role. I have no proof, but he has always looked upon my family with disdain."

Sally's eyes widened. Then, she shook her head. "I cannot imagine it! Miss Bennet is kindness itself. And to see her so full of sadness over her gentleman…well, as I said before, I shall be happy to help put a smile back on her face."

Lizzy was grateful for Sally's support and discretion. At least…she hoped she could rely on the maid's discretion. Sally would not *lie* to Mrs. Gardiner, and Lizzy would not want her to. But she believed the maid could be counted on not to gossip.

Darcy and his sister headed up the tall spiral staircase. Lizzy seized the opportunity. She and Sally made their escape, stepping into the grocer's next door.

Her plan was to watch the Darcys' carriage and follow at a safe distance on foot. As far as they could, at least. That would give them a sense of the direction in which the Darcys were headed. It was ridiculous, but Lizzy did not know what else to do. She had to find Bingley and let him know Jane was in town.

Then, if he did not call on her, so be it. At least Lizzy could be sure it had been his choice to abandon Jane. For now, though, she was convinced he had been pressured into it. By someone —or some*ones*—who did not have his best interest at heart. Until she knew for certain, she could not let it go. Not when Jane's future was at stake.

At the grocer's, Lizzy stood amidst the spices and the jars of delicacies, looking through the window. She soon discovered that she could not find a good position for keeping an eye on the bookshop door. So she and Sally stepped outside to cross the street for a better view.

The rain overnight had stirred up the dirt, but no matter. Her boots were sturdy, and the morning had dawned bright and clear.

Except...while they had been in the bookstore, the sky had grown overcast. Lizzy looked up at the clouds, surprised at how ominous they had become. She held out a gloved hand and caught a few drops. She took Sally's arm, checked the street for safety, and quickly started across.

Too late. The sky opened up.

Picking up their pace, they half-walked, half-ran to the other side. Lizzy's straw bonnet did little to protect her from the wind-blown droplets that pelted her face. The January air bit her exposed skin.

She and Sally huddled under an awning, shivering. Tendrils of curls had escaped Sally's bonnet and were plastered to her face. Lizzy was sure her own coiffure had fared no better.

Their pelisses were soaked, and their petticoats must be two inches deep in mud. Lizzy did not dare step inside one of the fashionable establishments. They would drip all over the floor.

The two women had to escape the cold, though, before they caught a chill. Lizzy looked around for a hackney, but could not see one.

The next moment, from behind her, an arm hauled her up into a coach, and Sally right after her. Too surprised to register fear, she looked about in wonder. By the time she could get her bearings, Darcy was seated on the bench across from them. She stared at him, shock stealing her voice.

His hat and overcoat were damp, but he was otherwise unruffled. Though as handsome as ever, nothing amiable showed in his features. He looked at her with piercing dark eyes, his gaze feral. As if he would sooner roast her over a fire and serve her for dinner, than hold a conversation with her.

Then he should not have lifted me into his carriage.

Next to him sat a young blonde woman. She was everything he was not: light where he was dark, smiling where he glared, petite and delicate where he was tall and broad. They did have one point of commonality, though. Her features were as even and pleasing as his. If indeed this was Miss Darcy, she was lovely.

But the next moment, Lizzy's mortification overcame her. She and Sally must look a fright. It was not the first time Darcy had seen her with muddy petticoats. She looked up at him, her cheeks heating.

Under the intensity of his gaze, her thoughts all stopped together. Something electric passed between them, though she could not have said what it was. This man had ruined Wickham. Had possibly destroyed Jane's hopes with Bingley. And yet, with his eyes fixed on her, she could not look away.

With aristocratic hauteur, he finally spoke. His words were clipped and precise. "Miss Elizabeth Bennet. We meet again."

∞ ∞ ∞

Darcy could not steal his eyes away from her. The hint of pink that rose in her cheeks was quite appealing. She seemed to struggle for speech a moment before sputtering, "Mr. Darcy."

He could not help finding satisfaction in discombobulating her. He had been discombobulated *by* her since leaving Netherfield.

"I thank you, sir," she added. "We might have caught our death without your kindness."

"Not at all." He could not take his eyes off her. He was staring, and it was abominably rude.

She would think him mocking her appearance. What he was actually thinking was far worse. He would like to peel her out of those wet clothes and...

What a beast he was! He had just taken this woman into his care, and he was imagining doing wicked things to her. He could not help himself. Her bright eyes and the sensual curve of her lips reached inside and grabbed hold of him. The sensation was like nothing he had experienced before.

He put the thought out of his mind. "Is there somewhere I can take you?"

She cleared her throat delicately. "Our destination is my uncle's house in Gracechurch Street. But that must be an hour away in this weather. I can hire a hackney—"

"Nonsense. I will take you to Darcy House until the sky clears. You will be quite safe there in the company of my sister and her companion."

"Mr. Darcy!" She glowered at him a long moment. Then, the practicalities seemed to dawn on her, and her rigid posture softened. She did not give up the fight entirely, though. "That is too kind. I could not impose—"

"No imposition at all." He called his instructions to the driver, and the next moment, the carriage was underway.

"Miss Bennet," he continued, "may I have the pleasure of introducing my sister, Miss Darcy."

"How do you do," Elizabeth said with a nod, her voice courteous, yet bearing a hint of exasperation. Apparently she did not appreciate his taking charge of her. But he was not about to let her travel an hour in a hackney wearing those wet clothes.

"Miss Bennet," Georgiana's angelic voice said, "my brother has told me much about you."

"About me?" Elizabeth stared, eyes wary.

His face heated. "Georgiana—"

"Oh yes," his maddening chit of a sister continued. "I have more than once heard him praise you as the prettiest woman he met during his stay in Hertfordshire."

His chest tightened at his sister's impudent words, yet he dared not scold her. It would only bring more attention to her inappropriate statement.

A tantalizing blush flooded Elizabeth's cheeks. "Surely you must be confusing me with my sister Jane."

"Indeed I am not!" Giana insisted. "It is true that Mr. Bingley has done nothing but sigh over her these six weeks. But when my brother speaks of Miss Bennet, *he* is speaking of Miss Elizabeth."

Elizabeth's eyes widened at him, but she quickly turned away.

Setting his jaw, he gave his sister a brief disapproving look. She rolled her eyes at him and smiled.

"What brings you to town?" he asked Elizabeth.

She eyed him a moment. "I am visiting my aunt and uncle," she said noncommittally.

He knew from Caroline that Jane had come to London to stay with her relations. No mention had been made of Elizabeth, though. Was there anything to that?

He supposed Caroline *might* have known the information and kept it from him. She had made no secret of her own interest in him as a marriage prospect. He could hardly have missed the jealousy she had shown towards Elizabeth.

Though he liked Caroline, there was no warmth in her. And after the way she had schemed to separate Bingley from Jane, she was not the sort of woman he could bind himself to.

Had Elizabeth been of superior birth, she might have

tempted him. As it was…well, it was unthinkable.

And yet, with her so close that their knees nearly touched, he *was* thinking it. He was thinking about the gauzy white bed curtains in the chamber at Pemberley that would belong to his wife. He was thinking about her perched on the mattress in her night rail, her dark hair loose and flowing around her shoulders. He was thinking about his hands gliding along creamy skin, her flesh shuddering beneath his touch.

He had no right to imagine such things. She was a gentlewoman. She could never be his except as his wife, and he was determined she would never be that. With that scheming mother of hers, he would be a laughingstock.

Thankfully Giana interrupted his improper musings. "Miss Bennet, will you introduce me to your companion?"

He turned to her and stared. In the past year, his demure sister had developed a new level of confidence. He had been afraid that Wickham's betrayal would make her even more timid. It seemed to have had the opposite effect. There was a new determination in her. A determination to follow her own principles, rather than deferring to others.

Not that she had become defiant. She obeyed him as a girl of sixteen ought, as he was twelve years her senior and also her guardian. She had, however, grown more accustomed to stating her own opinions. And to his delight, he had found them worth listening to.

Elizabeth cleared her throat, looking from Giana to the maid. Then, she said, "Miss Georgiana Darcy, may I present my lady's maid, Miss Sarah Jones."

"I am pleased to meet you, Miss Jones."

"Oh, please, ma'am, you must call me Sally. That is…not that I expect you to address me at all, of course."

"It does seem rather silly, though," Giana said. "The four of us in such close quarters, and three of us acting as if one of us does not exist. But perhaps when we get home, my brother will scold me for my impertinence."

"Not at all," Darcy said. "I hope that you will always

feel comfortable treating another person with kindness. But the proprieties exist for a reason. Miss Jones might be uncomfortable, being asked to converse with those of a different station."

"La, sir," Sally said—even though she had not been introduced to *him*, he thought with a smile—"my mother would laugh to hear you say that. When I was at home, she was always scolding me for speaking out of turn to my betters."

"Sally is a gem," Elizabeth said. "I wish I could take her home to Longbourn."

"The Gardiners are good to me, and truly, Mrs. Gardiner is the salt of the earth. But I do love looking after the Miss Bennets when they come to town."

Giana perked up at that. "Are your other sisters also in London?"

"Sally is speaking in general terms," Elizabeth said quickly. "It is not unusual for myself or one of my sisters to come to London after Christmas. It is rare, though, for more than one of us to come. My parents, it seems, cannot spare us."

"But they will have to spare you soon enough," he said. "It cannot be long before you are married—you and your eldest sister, at least."

Elizabeth gazed at him in astonishment, and the full impact of his statement crashed into him. What had he been thinking, to express such a sentiment? His words had seemed to rush from his heart to his tongue without stopping to consult his brain in the matter.

Elizabeth's reply was quick and incisive. "Why sir," she said, "did you note someone holding a *tendre* for Jane or me while you were in Hertfordshire?"

He pressed his lips together, confounded by her words. Because of course he had. Bingley had been besotted with Jane. He still was. He was as ridiculous as a man in love had ever been.

And if Darcy were honest, he himself held a *tendre* for Elizabeth. Not that it mattered. He would get over her soon enough. By the time summer came, and he travelled back to Pemberley, she would be nothing more than a memory.

At the moment, though, she was gazing at him as if she expected an answer—her eyes all innocence, her mouth wearing a clever smile.

And dash it all, that expression made him want to throw her over his shoulder and carry her up to his bedroom at Darcy House. What demon had brought this woman to London to torment him?

By some happy stroke of chance, they pulled up in front of Darcy House. Thus he was spared the necessity of a reply. The footman put down the step, and Darcy helped the ladies out.

Despite the pouring rain, his hand lingered on Elizabeth's a moment longer than it should have. Even through gloves, he felt the fire of her touch. It quickly spread from his fingers to his loins.

He gritted his teeth as the four of them rushed towards the shelter of the house. Standing under the portico, he sucked in a lungful of cold air to quell his desire. The rain showed no sign of letting up. He did not want his driver or his horses making the round trip journey to Cheapside in this weather. It would take an hour and a half, possibly two.

And he was not about to let Elizabeth pay for a hackney while his coach sat idle. No, she would ride in comfort and have a proper footman to accompany her.

The butler greeted them. As a footman stepped forward to help with the coats, Darcy instructed him instead to add some wood to the fire. Miss Bennet and Miss Jones needed to warm themselves. They were both shivering in their damp clothes.

Elizabeth divested herself of her bonnet, but did not surrender her pelisse. "Will you not take off your coat, madam?" he asked her. "Surely you will warm faster that way."

She gave him a demure look—one which, he was certain, did not reflect her thoughts. She said, "I am afraid I might not be presentable without it, especially in the company of a gentleman."

Darcy immediately understood her. His cheeks cooled as the blood drained from his face. He recollected the tendency of muslin to turn transparent when wet. The thought of the fabric clinging to her body...

He swallowed hard, then cleared his throat. "Yes, of course. I shall leave you in my sister's capable hands." With that, he bowed and made a quick departure. This new vision of her tucked itself into his imagination to further torture him.

Chapter 4

Upstairs, Lizzy watched as Miss Darcy rifled through her closet. The chamber, painted a pale green and trimmed in cream, was large enough to sleep Lizzy and all her sisters. The four-poster bed was canopied in silk and carved with an exuberant floral design.

"I have grown since last year," Georgiana said, "and my brother has bought me a new wardrobe. But I do have some older dresses that might fit you. Ah, here we go."

She laid some pretty muslin day dresses on the bed, whites and pastels with delicate designs. They had clearly come from the finest modistes, and showed no sign of wear. Georgiana must have outgrown them before she could wear them more than a few times.

"Miss Darcy, you are all kindness," Lizzy declared. "But really, we shall be dry soon enough—"

"I shall not hear of it!" Georgiana said, looking at her with astonishment. "In fact, if these dresses fit Sally as well as I think they will, she may keep them. For you, Miss Bennet, they might be a bit tight in the bust—"

"Oh, I can let out the seams, Miss Darcy," Sally said. "It won't take but five minutes. And then I'd like to style Miss Bennet's hair, if you do not mind. We want to remind your brother of how pretty she is at her best."

Georgiana laughed at that. "By all means. But if the novels are correct, gentlemen find a lady to be just as enticing when she is wet with rain as when she is dry."

Lizzy's cheeks warmed. "Do not get carried away, Sally. Mr. Darcy and I are no more than passing acquaintances. I overheard him tell Bingley that I am tolerably pretty, but not handsome enough to tempt him."

Georgiana gaped. She covered her mouth with a hand and gazed at Lizzy with wide eyes. Dropping her hand, she cried, "Surely he did not say so!"

"I promise you he did. He may have thought me out of earshot, but his words were plain."

Georgiana eyed her in consternation. "But...that sounds nothing like Darcy. He has been all compliments when speaking of you since coming to London. And in his letters from Netherfield, he commended you as the sort of woman he would like me to befriend." Her eyes glistened and her cheeks pinked.

Georgiana's words perplexed Lizzy. Was it possible that Darcy had praised her to his sister? No, there must be some misunderstanding. But with Miss Darcy looking to be on the verge of tears, Lizzy put the thought aside.

"Do not distress yourself," Lizzy said hastily. "My family and I laughed over his remark. It is a great joke that he noticed me at all. I could never aspire to a man like your brother."

Georgiana's head tilted to one side, a look of befuddlement in her features. "But...your father is a gentleman. My father was a gentleman. Why would you think my brother is above you?"

"Your uncle is an earl, and mine is in trade."

Georgiana drew her brows, still wearing a look of sadness. "Does that matter so much?"

Elizabeth stepped forward and took the girl's hand. "Indeed, you must have the kindest heart in the world if you can ask that question. But your brother and I... There is nothing between us, I assure you."

"Oh, but there must be! He says you are the cleverest woman he ever met. And you play the pianoforte with such feeling, he would rather listen to you than anyone. I have been so eager to meet you. Now that I have, I think you and I could be great friends. I hope you will call on me in the future, and that you will not mind if I call on you."

From the corner of her eye, Lizzy could see that Sally was about to burst. Could Lizzy have hoped for a better outcome when she had departed Cheapside that morning? She had not only discovered the direction of Darcy House. She was standing inside it, with Miss Darcy asking to be her friend.

And yet, could anything be worse? No matter how Lizzy despised Darcy, his sister was as sweet as she could be. Lizzy could not exploit this girl to forward the scheme of reuniting Jane and Bingley.

In truth, Lizzy like Georgiana. Had her brother been anyone else, Lizzy would have been eager for a friendship between them. What was she to do?

Fortunately, Sally came to the rescue, holding up a gown to Lizzy's front. "This pink one quite suits your colouring. I should be happy to wear the green, if Miss Darcy does not object. It is almost exactly the colour of my eyes."

"Then you must keep it," Georgiana said.

"But ma'am, I could not be so bold—"

"I insist. All these gowns are to be given away, as I can no longer wear them."

Sally curtseyed. "Then I thank you, ma'am. You are very kind."

At last they got down to the business of changing out of their wet clothes. While Lizzy dried by the fire in her petticoat and stays, Sally altered the pink gown. She let out the seams and added some patches of fabric to accommodate Lizzy's more gracious bosom. When she finished, the dress looked as if it had been made for Lizzy.

"You see!" Georgiana replied. "Darcy will find you irresistible now. *Tolerable* indeed."

While Sally attended to the drying clothes, Lizzy went downstairs with Georgiana. Tea was served. Darcy joined them in the drawing room a short time later. He halted when his gaze met Lizzy's. After staring a long moment, he bowed, then sat on the other side of the room.

Lizzy looked down at her skirts, smoothing them, though they were not in fact creased. Whatever Georgiana might have thought, Darcy despised Lizzy as much as she did him. His eyes glared with disapproval, as they did every time he looked at her.

Why did that thought make her so dreadfully unhappy? She wanted nothing to do with the man.

For a moment, Lizzy had been seduced by the Darcy of Georgiana's imagination. The loving brother who was smitten by a pretty country girl. A man wealthy enough to erase the spectre of poverty haunting Lizzy's family.

But Georgiana did not know the Darcy of Hertfordshire. The one who had denied Wickham his inheritance. The rogue who had separated Jane from the man she loved. Lizzy could not let herself forget about *that* Mr. Darcy. Even if she was enchanted by his sister and grateful to him for saving her from the pouring rain.

She forced herself to speak boldly. "I heard that Mr. Bingley is staying with you."

"Yes," Darcy said, but made no further comment. He turned towards the window.

"I believe he went to his club this morning," Georgiana said. "Darcy was kind to take me shopping when he might have been with his friends."

"I see enough of my friends," he replied in an even tone.

Georgiana beamed at him. There had been no hint of warmth in his voice, and yet…she had perceived his words as a compliment to herself. And Lizzy supposed they had been. Darcy clearly loved his sister. Adored her, probably, despite his reserved manner.

The thought was unsettling. She had not wanted that insight into Mr. Darcy's heart. It was better to think him cold and unfeeling, because that made it easier to dislike him.

The tea tray came, and Georgiana served with the grace

of a hostess ten years her senior. The three of them passed a pleasant repast of sandwiches and pecan biscuits together —much to Lizzy's consternation. Darcy watched Georgiana, seeming ready to step in if she faltered in her duties as hostess, but she never did.

And Lizzy noticed the oddest thing. The way Darcy looked at his sister... It would have seemed like haughty disinterest, if he had looked at anyone else that way. But now it seemed the opposite. Like detached interest. Evaluative, but not unkind. Curious.

His expression disconcerted Lizzy. He had sometimes looked at *her* that way in Hertfordshire. She had thought him mocking, but she could think that no longer. He was not mocking Georgiana.

In the company of his sister, the proud Darcy metamorphosed into something different. Kind Darcy. Affectionate Darcy.

Lizzy did not want to see that new man—could not afford to —because it was too easy to like him. It was too easy to be in his presence and forget the harm he had done to people she cared about. Too easy to notice—Heaven help her!—that he was by far the handsomest man she had ever known.

And then, the worst thing happened. He smiled. In all the time he had been in Hertfordshire, not once had she seen him smile. A sweet boyishness came over him. He looked at his sister with so much delight in his eyes that Lizzy's heart melted a little.

Do not think of his sister, she warned herself. *Think of your own sister. Think of how he has wronged her.*

Any man could like his own sister. There was no great show of character in that.

Suddenly the grand drawing room seemed too small, too close, too intimate. She never should have accepted the invitation to wait out the storm here. Instead, she should have asked a footman to call a hackney, and been on her way.

Rising, she excused herself to check with the maid about the condition of their clothes. After a brief conversation with Sally, she concluded they could leave as soon as the rain let up. When she returned to the drawing room, Darcy was alone, standing at the window.

"The storm has died down," he said, "but it is still forbidding outside. You are welcome to stay as long as you like—"

"My aunt will be worried." Lizzy could not stay in this house one moment longer than necessary. She was already obligated to this man for his hospitality, and that was the last thing she wanted. "You have been most gracious, but I should return home as soon as possible."

"Naturally." He spoke lightly, but something like disappointment registered on his face. She must be imagining that. Surely he could not wish for her company?

He held her gaze a moment, his eyes intense. She grew hot all over, as if he could see through her shift. She was acutely aware that they were alone but for the footman just outside the open door.

Her breathing turned ragged. She wanted... She knew not what she wanted. Looking into those dark eyes, her defences faltered. Some strange magnetism flowed between them, and her lips began to tingle. If his fixed stare was any indication, he was suffering from the same affliction.

Then, he stiffened, as if remembering himself. Squaring his shoulders, he seemed to make a resolution.

"Miss Bennet, my sister spoke too freely in the carriage. If you suppose there has been gossip in this house about you and your sister, then I apologize. I assure you that has not been the case."

His words astounded her. How could he make even an apology sound insolent? "Of course not," she countered. "No more than there has been gossip about you and Mr. Bingley at Longbourn."

He coloured, and some emotion flickered across his face. Anger, perhaps? But he schooled it. He stepped closer, though not in a threatening way. He was almost conciliatory. "I do not deny that Bingley and I have mentioned your names. However, my sister is young and rather fanciful—"

"I beg you, Mr. Darcy, do not concern yourself," Lizzy insisted. She could not have this conversation with him. It was humiliating.

And yet... He was not exactly standing aloof. They were so close their hands might brush together. "I have not misunderstood the situation," she explained. "I have already disabused your sister of any wrong notions she might have about you and me."

He made no reply. Rather, he looked—affronted? Was that possible?

"And regarding Mr. Bingley," Lizzy continued, "it is not as if Miss Darcy revealed a great secret. Anyone with the gift of sight might have deduced that Mr. Bingley was besotted with my sister."

"And anyone with the gift of sight might have deduced that she did not return those feelings."

Lizzy's ire rose. Her jaw tightened, and her hands clenched into fists. Never in her life had she slapped a man, but at that moment, she was tempted.

"How dare you pretend to know my sister's heart?" she cried, struggling to keep her voice low. "Mr. Bingley might not have declared himself, but his every action towards her held a promise. And then he abandoned her without a word."

"He owed her nothing." His tone was cold, but his eyes burned with fury.

Lizzy struggled to remain civil. "He courted her for two months—yes, courted her," she insisted when it seemed he might protest. "His honour was involved."

"His honour!" He straightened to his full height. "Do you mean to say that in your part of the country, a little flirtation passes for an obligation?"

"It was more than a little flirtation." She refused to back away from his intimidating stance. She wanted to plant him a facer, but instead, forced herself to lower her voice. She did not wish the servants to hear, or worse, Miss Darcy.

She continued, "Mr. Bingley distinguished my sister whenever they were in company. He sought her out and remained by her side as much as propriety allowed. He *pursued* her. If I did not like him so well, I would question his motives."

"What are you suggesting?" Darcy raged, his expression dark.

"You know precisely what I am suggesting."

His voice was barely above a whisper, but his tone was intense. "Bingley is not the sort of man to abuse a young woman."

"Of course not. If he were, I would be happy Jane were rid of him. As you seem to be happy he is rid of *her*."

Darcy's eyes widened. He stepped back, raking her with his gaze. She felt the look as if it were a touch, as if his fingers ran over her bare skin. A frisson of electricity pulsed through her, but she fought it.

He leaned towards her, an open palm facing upwards in a conciliatory gesture. "I was alarmed on his behalf. He was acting without thinking through the consequences."

"Risking an alliance with a woman beneath him, you mean."

He stiffened again, and his jaw worked. Finally, he said, "I do not think your family beneath him, Miss Bennet. The man is three-and-twenty. He is not yet established. He has the fortune to marry, that is true, but he has no home to speak of. I have seen him in love before, and I daresay I will see him in love again."

"That is the most callous thing I ever heard." Although in truth, her father had said something similar. Were all men this obtuse when it came to love?

"He created expectations," Lizzy continued, working to keep her voice even. "Do you think Jane indifferent to that? Do you think her spirit was not crushed when he—"

"Miss Bennet?"

She startled and turned at the sound of the familiar voice. Bingley stood in the doorway, staring at her. The fight drained from her, and her head grew light.

Bingley looked so changed, she could hardly believe it. His lean build had turned gaunt, and the mirth was gone from his features.

What had he overheard? Did he realize they had been talking about him—about Jane's feelings for him?

Bingley stepped towards her, wearing an intensity in his eyes she had not seen in him before. "It is good to see you again. What brings you to town?" His voice was strained. As if the social niceties held a deeper meaning that could not be put into words.

A headache formed behind her eyes. Too much had happened too fast. She had gotten exactly what she wanted— Bingley was here. She could tell him Jane was in town. It would take all of five seconds.

But at that moment, she could not go through with it. What if his mind had been turned against Jane? What if Darcy had convinced him Jane was indifferent?

Lizzy was not ready for this. Today had been a scouting mission. She had not prepared for confrontation. Before acting, she must learn the new landscape.

And for some reason—she did not know why—it was suddenly important to her that Darcy be the one to tell Bingley the truth. She wanted to give Darcy the chance to redeem himself on that point.

Perhaps it was for Georgiana's sake. Perhaps Lizzy wanted the brother Georgiana clearly adored to deserve her admiration. Whatever the reason, Lizzy could not bring herself to say the words.

Anger and confusion pounded like war drums in her head. "Mr. Bingley, the pleasure is mine, I assure you. However, I must beg you to excuse me. Miss Darcy has been kind enough to shelter me from the storm, but I fear I have overstayed my welcome. I must return home before my uncle sends out a search party."

"Will you be in town long?" Bingley asked eagerly.

"Some weeks, I think. I hope you will call on me in Gracechurch Street the next time you are in the City." She gave him the house number. "We can catch up on the gossip from Meryton. I have much to tell you."

"Yes, I—I look forward to it." Bingley smiled brightly.

Oh, yes. He was eager for news about Jane. All was not lost in that quarter.

"I shall hold you to it, then," she said sweetly. "But it appears the rain has slowed, and I must go."

"Allow me to send for the carriage," Darcy said.

"Thank you. I shall fetch my maid." With a brief triumphant look at Darcy, she turned and headed for the stairs. She could not stop a sly smile from breaking across her face.

Mr. Darcy would not thwart Jane again.

Chapter 5

Lizzy and Sally entered the Darcys' coach to find rugs for their laps and hot bricks for their feet. Two footmen accompanied them, standing protectively on the running boards. Safe from the weather, the ladies sat cushioned on the luxurious leather squabs.

"La, ma'am!" Sally cried as they got underway. "Surely Mr. Darcy must be in love with you!"

Lizzy stared, wondering what in heaven's name could have provoked such an outburst. "On the contrary, he gives me disapproving looks whenever we are in company."

"I admit, he does scowl quite a bit—but for all that, I would rather say they were admiring looks. And those things Miss Darcy said! How he praised you and recommended you to her. If he is not in love now, then he is in a fair way towards falling in love, if you would encourage him."

Lizzy shook her head. "He was kind today, I grant you. In Hertfordshire, he treated me with nothing but disdain." Lizzy could not help smiling. She had not realized Sally was so fanciful.

"But those letters he wrote his sister!" Sally shook her head, her forehead wrinkling. "He may not have shown it, but I daresay he liked you well enough. Maybe he is shy."

Lizzy scoffed at that, and had to cover her mouth with her hand to stifle a laugh. Darcy, shy? The most arrogant man she knew? What nonsense!

But she would not be so unkind as to say so. Instead, she let the subject drop.

Despite the lingering dampness in their coats, the ladies were kept comfortably warm. The muddy roads hampered their journey, but they reached Gracechurch Street within an hour. The rain was no more than a drizzle when they alighted.

Aunt Gardiner welcomed them with relief, as predicted. Sally took the shopping packages upstairs. Meanwhile, the ladies of the house settled into the drawing room. As they awaited dinner, Lizzy recounted the events of the day. Jane grew quiet at the mention of Darcy's name.

"I am surprised he acknowledged the acquaintance," aunt Gardiner said. "You and Mr. Wickham described Mr. Darcy as proud. Yet he invited you to his home to wait out the storm!"

"It was less an invitation than a kidnapping," Lizzy joked. "He hoisted us into his carriage without waiting for permission."

"I suppose that is forgivable in the drenching rain," her aunt said.

"Oh, I am not complaining. It was undoubtedly a kindness. And I confess to being as surprised as you are by his solicitude."

Lizzy stole a glance at Jane. She appeared engrossed in her needlework, though Lizzy was sure she hung on every word. How much could Lizzy tell her?

Pouring tea, their aunt said, "Perhaps he is more of his father's son than you have been led to believe." Mrs. Gardiner had lived in Derbyshire for a time, not five miles from the Darcy estate at Pemberley. While she had not met Darcy's father, the man had been much admired in the neighbourhood.

Her aunt's words brought a sudden pang to Lizzy's heart. Might she have judged the son too harshly during his stay in Hertfordshire? That afternoon, he had not shown the pride she thought his defining characteristic.

Yet despite his kindness, he had been as sullen and disagreeable as usual. And she could not forget his affront to Jane.

She smoothed her skirt, still wearing Georgiana's dress. "Miss Darcy is quite amiable. She asked if she could call on me here."

Mrs. Gardiner blinked a moment, then sipped her tea. "Do you think Mr. Darcy will allow it?"

The question surprised Lizzy. It had not occurred to her that he might not.

Her aunt continued, "I remember what you said at Christmas. How did you put it? That Mr. Darcy would not consider a month's ablutions sufficient to cleanse him of Cheapside?"

"Did I?" Lizzy asked the question knowing that she had. She felt ashamed of those words now. Darcy had been gracious to her that afternoon. Even after their spat, he had made sure she and Sally rode home in comfort.

"Perhaps," said Jane, "Mr. Wickham has been deceived in Mr. Darcy's character after all."

Lizzy looked over at her sister. She had set her needlework down. Jane's nature was to find the good in everyone. She had not taken Wickham's denouncement of Darcy to heart, as Lizzy had.

Wickham had good reason to despise the man, after the loss of the living promised him. Suddenly, though, Lizzy found herself wishing to hear Darcy's side of the story. The man she had seen today with Miss Darcy had not seemed disloyal. But could anything absolve him of guilt?

She put the thought out of her mind. It was of no consequence, after all. She had not gone to Mayfair for Darcy's sake but for Bingley's.

It was time to raise the subject with Jane. She feared how her sister might react, but it had to be done.

Gathering her courage, Lizzy poured herself another cup of tea with a lemon slice. "You may recall Miss Bingley's last letter. She mentioned that her brother is now staying at Darcy House."

Jane's eyes were all astonishment for a moment. Then, she

schooled her features to their normal placid expression. "Did you see him?"

Lizzy answered carefully, "For a very few minutes. He returned there right before I left. He was as amiable as usual, but his spirits seemed dampened. I did not mention that you were in town. I wanted to speak to you about it first."

A long silence ensued. Despite Jane's serene expression, Lizzy knew her sister was deeply affected. "Surely he already knows," Jane said at last. "Caroline would have told him."

"Why would she have told him?" Lizzy objected. "She made it clear that *her* desire is for him to marry Miss Darcy. Your presence in town can only hinder that scheme."

Silence reigned a long moment, emotions electrifying the air. Lizzy was angry at Caroline's duplicity and at Jane's continuing blindness to her friend's betrayal. But she could not say as much. Jane must be in turmoil, wondering what to believe about Bingley. And whether there could be any hope of a reconciliation between them.

Gently, Lizzy said, "I gave Mr. Bingley the direction here, and invited him to call. He seemed pleased at the prospect."

"Lizzy, how could you!" Jane cried, her face crimson. "You know I do not wish to see him."

Lizzy set down her teacup. "You are afraid he is indifferent, but I assure you, he is not. He is eager for news of you. I believe nothing would make him happier than to see you again."

Jane drew her brow, but she made no protest.

Aunt Gardiner said in a pensive tone, "We had better call on the Darcys the next time we are in Mayfair. Their kindness today must be acknowledged. Lizzy, have you an idea what Mr. Darcy's favourite sweet might be?"

Appreciating her aunt's devious suggestion, Lizzy considered the question a moment. "I seem to recall Miss Bingley remarking on his preference for lemon cake. It was always served at Netherfield."

"Excellent! I shall have Mrs. Hastings bake one for him. Even if he and Miss Darcy are not at home when we visit, we can all leave our cards."

Jane did not seem to share Lizzy's appreciation for the scheme. Bunching her skirts in her fists, she fretted. "Even if we do, it is unlikely Mr. Bingley will see them."

"Miss Darcy will mention it to him," Lizzy said. "I have no doubt of that."

"But why would she?" Jane asked.

"She showed no sign of harbouring Miss Bingley's ambitions. She seemed to consider Mr. Bingley more a brother than a suitor. In her situation, she could aspire to a viscount, or even an earl."

Jane did not reply. Mrs. Gardiner said to her, "You seem reluctant, my dear."

"I do not wish to get my hopes up." Her eyes glistened. "Is it not unseemly to pursue a man who left the county to escape my company?"

Lizzy rose and sat on the couch beside her sister, taking her hands. "I would agree, if I believed escaping your company had been his intention. It seems to have been his sister's design. He was planning to come to London for a day or two. The rest of the family followed and persuaded him to stay. Who knows what machinations they used?"

Jane stared. "You cannot believe they did anything underhanded!"

Lizzy wanted to scream. She kept her voice as calm as possible. "That is precisely what I believe. Miss Bingley wants to marry Mr. Darcy. She made that clear in Hertfordshire. A match between her brother and his sister can only help that along."

"Lizzy," aunt Gardiner warned, "you may well be right. But let us not jump to conclusions. If Miss Darcy wants to further her acquaintance with you, then we may have the chance to learn more facts. Let us be circumspect until then."

∞∞∞

The following morning dawned clear, with no hint of the storm from the day before. While Giana and Bingley chatted over kippers and eggs, Darcy read the newspaper. Or perhaps it was an exaggeration to say he *read*. He had been staring at the same paragraph for five minutes, and had no idea of the sense of it.

He could not put Elizabeth's fury out of his mind. They had passed a pleasant afternoon until the final quarter-hour before she left. And the fault for their altercation had been entirely his own.

Part of him held fast to the rightness of his own position. Her sister had accepted Bingley's attentions, and seemed happy to receive them. But she had shown no indications of love. None at all.

But what did Darcy know of love? And what did he know of Jane Bennet?

He had to admit to himself that Elizabeth likely understood her sister's feelings better than he did. Which was something of an annoyance. He had been so certain he had seen the right of the situation. Had congratulated himself on it, in fact.

And he was still not convinced that he was wrong. Elizabeth had not said that Jane loved Bingley. Only that her hopes had been dashed when he abandoned Netherfield.

That was no revelation at all. Darcy had not doubted she would be disappointed. However, he had not seen evidence that her affection matched Bingley's. He did not want his friend throwing himself away on a woman who did not love him.

And of course, there was much to object to when it came to the family. The mother was ridiculous, the father careless, and the younger sisters positively feral. None of which seemed to matter to Bingley, though. His fortune had been made in trade, and he was not a stickler when it came to manners.

Darcy, by contrast, descended from the aristocracy. His maternal grandfather had been the Earl of Matlock, a title now held by his uncle. Darcy could not marry into the Bennet family.

And where had that thought come from? There had never been any question of a match between himself and Elizabeth Bennet. No matter how deliciously enchanting he found her.

Matrimony had not been on his mind when he had scooped her into his carriage the day before. That had been a simple act of charity. He could not leave her wet and bedraggled in the rain.

The image came to him, unbidden, of helping her out of her drenched clothes. Of unpinning her hair to let it dry by the fire. Of running his lips along the curve of her neck, tasting the drops of water on her skin...

"What think you, Darcy?" Bingley asked.

Darcy looked up to find Bingley gazing expectantly upon him.

Darcy realized with dismay that his thoughts of Elizabeth had distracted him. He had lost the thread of the conversation. "About?" he asked in an even tone, setting a mask of distant calm onto his features.

Giana tittered. "Why, brother, I do not believe you heard a word we said."

"I was reading the newspaper—"

"Yes, yes," Giana said. "I am surprised that the sound of Miss Bennet's name did not startle you from that pursuit."

He scowled. "What of Miss Bennet?"

"We are thinking of calling on her this morning. Will it be proper for Mr. Bingley and me to go together, if Mrs. Annesley accompanies us?"

Darcy eyed them in consternation. He should have foreseen this. Naturally, Bingley would want to call on Elizabeth. She had invited him, after all, and he had happily acceded. Darcy could not allow it. Not without warning him Jane was also in residence. Seeing her would give him a powerful shock.

But in fact, Darcy did not want Bingley to see Jane again—not yet. He wanted to learn for himself what the nature of her feelings were. Caroline had insisted that Jane was nothing but a fortune hunter, and Darcy had been happy to believe it. That position aligned with his own wishes. He did not *want* Jane to be in love with Bingley.

But what if she was? Elizabeth's passion the day before had suggested it. Meanwhile, the six weeks since leaving Netherfield had cooled none of Bingley's ardour. He was mooning over the eldest Miss Bennet pathetically.

Would Darcy let his own aversion get in the way of Bingley's happiness? If his friend did not share Darcy's scruples, why should Bingley *not* marry Jane? She was an angel. Even Caroline had said so.

The connection would not, of course, raise Caroline's prospects. And that was something of a pity. She was a woman who *ought* to marry well. Her fortune, her manners, and her intelligence almost ensured she would. But if her brother made an alliance with a noble family, it was almost certain she would do the same.

Darcy thought again of Lady Cressida. She would be a much better match for Bingley than Jane Bennet. He must find a way to prevent his friend from visiting Gracechurch Street.

He buttered a toasted muffin, feigning insouciance. "Georgiana, I shall not have you cultivating friends in Cheapside. It is a great distance to travel for a social call. Arabelle can introduce you to some of *her* friends—"

"You are forbidding it?" his sister asked, her voice a combination of shock and outrage.

"I think it for the best, yes."

"Good heavens, Darcy," Bingley said sharply. "You are as bad as my sisters—talking as if Miss Elizabeth were beneath you."

"Not at all. She is perfectly respectable."

"She is more than that," Giana said crossly. "She is kind, intelligent, and very pretty. It is plain you admire her."

Darcy's cheeks heated. "That is not relevant."

"It is highly relevant." Smiling slyly, his sister spread a dab of strawberry jam onto a scone. "You do not wish me to visit Miss Elizabeth because you are tempted by her."

"Nonsense."

"You are!" Bingley's coffee cup clinked as he set it a little too firmly into its saucer. "Is that why you were so eager to leave Netherfield? You were afraid if we stayed longer, you might end up making Miss Elizabeth Bennet an offer of marriage?"

"Oh, Darcy," Georgiana cried, "how splendid that would be. It is time you married, and Miss Elizabeth is lovely."

Darcy rolled up the newspaper. "You have only met her once."

"But that is why I wish to visit her again this morning. To get to know her better. And Bingley wants to hear news of her family—"

"It is out of the question, Georgiana." Darcy thumped the paper against the table. "I forbid it."

Bingley looked at him with a steely expression. "You cannot forbid *me*. If you and your sister will not accompany me, I shall go alone."

Darcy stared at him a moment, speechless, before blurting, "I do not think that wise."

"Why not?"

"What if the news from Longbourn is not what you wish to hear? What if Miss Bennet has a new beau?"

Bingley reddened. "Then it is better to know sooner rather than later."

Darcy berated himself. He was engaging in deception, and that was beneath him. Judging from Elizabeth's words the day before, Jane did *not* have a new beau. And Bingley would not appreciate any subterfuge.

Darcy straightened the napkin on his lap. Finally, he looked up and squared his jaw. "If the two of you wish to call on Miss Elizabeth, then I shall go with you. But I must warn you," he said, gazing at Bingley, "that Miss Bennet is also staying with her."

"Jane?" Bingley's words were like a prayer. His expression changed to one of astonishment, followed by fleeting joy, and finally, a pain so sharp it stole Darcy's breath.

"But—Miss Elizabeth," Giana sputtered, "she mentioned nothing of it yesterday. At least not in my hearing."

"Nor mine," Darcy concurred. "I got the information from Miss Bingley."

Bingley jumped to his feet. "Caroline knew of this? And did not say a word to me?"

Darcy refrained from displaying any emotion. "Consider, Bingley. Caroline warned you away from her, believing you deceived about the lady's affections. That was why we left Hertfordshire in the first place. You cannot expect that your sister would tell you Miss Bennet is here. Do you wish to fall prey to a fortune hunter?"

Bingley set his hands on the table and leaned forward, looking at Darcy intently. "Jane is not like that."

"Her mother is. How can you be certain that the daughter's motives are pure?"

Georgiana gave her brother a withering look. "You cannot base your opinion about Miss Bennet on anything Caroline says. Caroline does not want Miss Bennet to marry her brother because she wants *me* to marry him." Giana gave Bingley a merry look. "She says so every time I see her."

Darcy stared at her. He had not imagined Caroline's machinations had extended so far. "I beg your pardon?"

Giana took a dainty sip of tea before continuing. "She goes on and on about how lovely it would be if we were sisters. How once I am out, Mr. Bingley can propose. It is nonsense, of course. I have known him since I was a little girl. We are like brother and sister. But she hopes that *one* alliance between the families will lead to another. She is utterly transparent."

The words struck Darcy like a blow to the gut during a match at Gentleman Jack's. He knew that Caroline had designs on him. That was as nothing to him. But if she wanted Bingley to marry Georgiana… Perhaps more was behind her schemes than Darcy had believed.

He turned to Bingley, who looked as surprised as Darcy felt. "Were you aware of this?"

Bingley sat down heavily in his chair. "Not at all. I would have put a stop to it if I had. I do not need my sister's matchmaking services, nor should Caroline impose on Miss Darcy in such a way."

Darcy scowled and looked at his sister. "You are not suggesting that Caroline would lie to her brother about Miss Bennet's affections for him?"

The prospect of such duplicity bit at his gut. He had placed his faith in Caroline's assessment of Jane. If Caroline had been motivated by self-interest—

The heat of shame washed over him. Elizabeth's fury from the previous day plucked at his conscience. Had she been utterly right, and he utterly wrong?

Giana rested her hands in her lap. She pressed her lips together a moment before speaking. "I would not wish to distress Mr. Bingley by accusing his sister of deceit. I do not know what she is capable of. I find it ironic, though, that she accuses *Miss Bennet* of fortune hunting."

It took all Darcy's skills, born of a lifetime of training in proper etiquette, to keep from laughing aloud.

Wearing a scowl, Bingley tapped his fingers on the tabletop. "Caroline has always had her little schemes, but I had not thought her capable of *this*."

"Let us not make hasty conclusions," Darcy said. "We do not know how much of what Caroline said was true and how much false. If you decide to renew the acquaintance with Miss Bennet, I hope you will be circumspect."

"*If* I renew the acquaintance?" Bingley cried, incredulity written in his wide eyes and open features. "I shall do so directly. Did you doubt I would?"

Darcy could not say he had. But Georgiana's revelation had shone a new light on the subject. One thing Darcy knew for certain: He would not be Caroline Bingley's pawn. It was time he found out the truth.

Chapter 6

In the front parlour of the house on Gracechurch Street, Lizzy set down her embroidery. She walked to the window, needing to stretch her legs. Jane sat at a table with her watercolours. Aunt Gardiner worked at her escritoire on the morning's correspondence.

The January day was grey and cold and looked like snow. Restless, Lizzy hugged herself, waiting for something to happen. Her success the day before had only made her more eager to reunite Jane with Bingley. She wanted the ordeal over with. Jane's unhappiness and her own anxiety were wearing on her.

But a few days at least would need to pass before they could go back to Mayfair and pay their respects to the Darcys. She hoped Mr. Darcy would not be at home when they arrived. Seeing him again could only serve to further discombobulate her.

Through the window, her gaze rested on the side garden. The yew hedge offered a show of green in the otherwise dreary January landscape. Part of her missed the wide vistas of Longbourn. But she also enjoyed the more varied entertainments of town.

Not that she had much opportunity to engage in the pleasures of the London season. She had convinced her aunt that a night at the theatre would be good for Jane, so tickets had been procured. A dinner party was planned with some of the Gardiners' friends, with an evening of music to follow.

But Lizzy longed for a ball, for a chance to dance and perhaps even meet an eligible young man. She did not need someone of wealth and family. Her only requirement was to marry for love. An army captain or a clergyman would suit her perfectly.

Her rebellious thoughts, however, wandered to Mr. Darcy. How changed he had seemed! In Hertfordshire, he had been cold and standoffish. In his own home, he had been warm and gracious. Pleasant, even.

Until their argument. She was more convinced than ever that it had been Darcy, as much as Caroline, who had separated Bingley from Jane.

How *could* Darcy have suggested that Jane did not share Bingley's affections? Jane had not been as effusive in her manner as *some* women were. But that was not in her nature.

Her signs had been more subtle. The colour rose in her cheeks whenever Bingley was near. She had accepted his attentions to the exclusion of others. Was that not evidence enough?

The trouble was, for all his officiousness, Lizzy had *liked* the Darcy of yesterday. The entire time she had known him, his every action had confirmed her initial opinion of him. He had shown himself to be a proud man above all his company. Until yesterday.

The thought disconcerted her. Her mind kept wandering to memories of other interactions between them. Had signs of this new Darcy, this kind Darcy, been there all along?

He had disdained her at the ball where they had met. Of that there could be no doubt. His behaviour had been abominable, his slight of her ungentlemanly. And from that moment, her opinion of him had been fixed.

He had behaved with perfect civility towards her the rest of his time in Hertfordshire. She had to admit that much. Lizzy had never gotten the impression that he was inwardly laughing at her, as she did with Caroline.

He *did* have the annoying habit of staring at her with that intense gaze of his. She had always assumed he found her wanting.

Yet on the night of the Netherfield ball—the last time she had seen him before coming to London—he had asked her to dance. Apparently he had found her handsome enough to tempt him *that* night. He had not asked any other women of Hertfordshire to dance. He had reserved that honour for Bingley's sisters.

And Miss Darcy had said her brother had spoken of Lizzy in complimentary terms. But why? The situation was a muddle, impossible to decipher.

Mrs. Gardiner rose and stretched. "Girls, I have been thinking about when we should call on the Darcys. I think it would be best to wait until two days hence. We can go to Mayfair to—"

The sound of the doorbell interrupted her. Uncle Gardiner was at his place of business, so it seemed likely that the visitor had come to see the ladies. Jane and aunt Gardiner took their places on the couch, and Lizzy returned to her chair.

A minute later, the housekeeper announced their guests. "Mr. Darcy, Miss Darcy, and Mr. Bingley."

Lizzy's mind went blank a moment. When she recovered herself, she realized she was staring, transfixed. Bingley was *here*. Darcy had brought him. Good heavens!

The most dreadful anticipation tightened her stomach. She was not ready for this. Certainly Jane was not. They had returned the visit so soon! That must speak of an eagerness on Bingley's part to see Jane again. Poor Jane must be overwhelmed at the sight of him.

Lizzy found her voice and forced herself to make the necessary introductions. Jane, her cheeks tinged with pink, did not quite make eye contact with their guests. She seemed unable to speak beyond a simple greeting.

Mrs. Gardiner ordered some refreshments. She said to the housekeeper, "Do bring us some of the cake that Mrs. Hastings baked this morning." The servant dipped into a curtsey and stepped away.

"How kind of you to call," Mrs. Gardiner said, motioning for the visitors to sit.

"My sister was most eager to return Miss Elizabeth's visit," Darcy said, taking a chair next to Lizzy.

"It was less a visit than an imposition on your hospitality." Lizzy smiled at the siblings and trained her eyes away from Bingley. He had sat in a chair cattycorner to the couch and was looking fixedly at Jane.

"Not at all," Darcy said in response to her words, and showing equal determination not to spy on Bingley and Jane. "It was nothing."

"Nothing to you, perhaps," Lizzy replied. "It meant a great deal to my maid and me."

He gave a civil nod. "Happy to be of service."

The tension in the room was thick. To ease it, Lizzy said, "Mr. Bingley, perhaps Jane will consent to show you her watercolour. She has been working on it all morning."

"I would be delighted!" Bingley cried.

Looking wary, Jane led him to the table, where they could talk in relative privacy if they kept their voices low. Lizzy's shoulders relaxed.

She turned to Georgiana. "I understand you have a talent for the pianoforte."

"I cannot imagine who told you that!"

"It was Miss Bingley," Lizzy said, wanting to be clear on that point. "She was all compliments towards you, as I recall."

"Oh! Then I am not surprised," Georgiana said. "She is quite kind to me. As she is to Darcy." She gave her brother a look and a coy smile.

"I profess," he said, "I have never heard her say a word about you that was untrue. You do play the pianoforte quite well, and the harp, too."

"Do not believe him, Miss Bennet. I *do* enjoy the pianoforte, but I am a perfect novice on the harp."

Lizzy gave her a polite yet heartfelt smile. "I hope to have the pleasure of hearing you play one day, so I can judge for myself."

"I would like that!" Georgiana beamed. It was odd how the girl seemed exceedingly pleased by Lizzy's cordiality. Did Georgiana not realize that she herself was the one of higher rank? That she was the one paying Lizzy a compliment by taking such notice of her?

True, the two had developed an easy camaraderie the day before. Lizzy would be happy for the girl's friendship. With Georgiana, however, the attachment seemed to go further. She seemed unaccountably awed by Lizzy.

"Perhaps you can dine with us one night soon," Georgiana suggested. "I can play the harp while the gentleman drink their brandy. I shall not be quite as afraid that way." She turned to her brother as if looking for reassurance.

"That is a fine idea," Darcy said. "If Mr. Gardiner does not mind taking his family out for a long drive through the city on a cold January night."

Georgiana squeezed Lizzy's hand. "My brother is right, of course. I should have been more considerate about the distance. But I do hope your uncle will let you come."

"I would like that." Lizzy's mind worked, hoping they could manage it.

The housekeeper entered with refreshments, then quickly withdrew. Mrs. Gardiner poured the coffee. "Mr. Darcy," she said, "I hope you will compliment us by trying some of this lemon cake. It is a new recipe, but I believe it has turned out quite well."

Lizzy's mouth watered at the sweet, citrusy fragrance. The light pound cake was a confection of lemon zest, poppy seeds, and a sugary glaze. The ladies of the house had each tested a bite when the cake had first cooled, and all had named it a success.

Mrs. Gardiner served Darcy a slice on a dessert plate of fine Delft porcelain. He raised a small bite to his lips with a fork, then took a sip of coffee. "My compliments, ma'am," he said. "That is quite as good as what Mrs. Nicholls served at Netherfield."

Mrs. Gardiner looked to Georgiana. "I would be happy to pass on the recipe if you would like."

"Oh, please do! My brother is ever so fond of lemon cake. And this—it is as light as pastry."

Lizzy smiled warmly. Her aunt had asked the cook to test the recipe for the family to try, before the planned trip to Darcy House. Lizzy was glad. None of them had imagined Darcy would call, and so soon.

Bingley must have encouraged the visit. Had Darcy told him Jane was in town? Or perhaps Caroline had.

Not likely. A renewal of Bingley's addresses to Jane would spoil Caroline's plans. She hoped the marriage of her brother and Georgiana would lead to one between Darcy and herself.

But what would Darcy's motive have been in bringing Bingley here? The day before, he had seemed convinced of Jane's indifference. It flustered Lizzy to think there might be some goodness in him, when she had so many reasons to dislike him.

Wickham. She must remember Wickham.

And that gave her an idea. How would Darcy react to the mention of Wickham's name? Would guilt show in his face at his consciousness of having wronged the man?

She embarked on the plan before she could lose her nerve. With an air of perfect innocence, she said, "Mr. Darcy, have you heard the news? Your old friend George Wickham is engaged to be married."

Georgiana let out a gasp, then covered her mouth with her palm. A flush covered her cheeks.

Lizzy pressed a hand to her chest, conscious of having made a terrible *faux pas*. When she turned to Darcy, he had paled. The muscles in his jaw worked.

He gripped his sister's hand, not meeting Lizzy's eyes. His voice was clipped and stern as he said, "I had not heard that."

Lizzy's stomach sank. More was going on here than she had imagined. Darcy did not appear guilty at all, and Georgiana seemed horrified.

"Miss Darcy, forgive me," Lizzy said. "You look unwell. Allow me to get you a glass of sherry."

Aunt Gardiner, however, was a step ahead of her. She approached the girl and proffered a slender glass of yellow-gold liquid.

Georgiana took a delicate sip, followed by another. Her face returned to its normal colour. "Thank you. I am fine now." She set down the glass and turned to her brother, who laid a protective arm around her shoulders.

Lizzy's mind raced. Miss Darcy must have known Wickham when she was a girl. Had she felt a *tendre* for him?

That explanation might account for *her* expression, but not her brother's. He would not have allowed a match between Wickham and Georgiana. But his features did not show a cool disdain. He was pained and angry.

What had Wickham done to this girl?

The thought struck Lizzy with a force that stole her breath. Surely Wickham could not have wronged Miss Darcy in any way. He was as amiable a gentleman as Lizzy had ever met.

Yet something had occasioned Miss Darcy pain. Lizzy hated herself for having reminded the girl of it, whatever the cause might have been.

Darcy rose soon after to take his leave, Georgiana and Bingley having no choice but to follow suit. They had not stayed above twenty minutes. Bingley looked disappointed, Georgiana disoriented. Darcy's manner was curt though not precisely discourteous.

Lizzy flinched as the front door closed behind them. Her mind grew ever more bewildered and perturbed. She dared not confront the swirling questions. Despite the discomfort of the previous minutes, she did not wish to think ill of Wickham. Not based on the disappointed tears of a schoolgirl and the resentment of her older brother.

Yet she could not escape the possibility lurking at the back of her mind. Her stomach tightened. Perhaps everything she had believed about the history between Mr. Wickham and Mr.

Darcy had been a lie.

∞ ∞ ∞

On the trip back to Mayfair, Darcy formulated a plan. He could not allow Wickham to take advantage of another young innocent. But how to prevent it?

He and Giana called at the home of their uncle and aunt, the Earl and Countess of Matlock, on Berkeley Square. The earl was at the House of Lords, but the countess was at home.

The brother and sister were shown into the drawing room. Their aunt and Lady Arabelle were sitting with Colonel Richard Fitzwilliam.

The colonel, the second eldest son, was close in age to Darcy. The two had been friends all their lives. Darcy's father had seen fit to name the two together as Georgiana's guardians.

Darcy pondered a moment how best to raise the subject at hand when Giana spared him the necessity. "Oh, aunt!" she cried, sinking down on the couch and throwing herself into the countess's arms, "Wickham is engaged!"

A hush fell over the room a moment while the Fitzwilliams absorbed the news. Lady Matlock patted her niece's back. "Well, my dear," the countess said at last, in a dry tone, "it is not the first time, and I doubt it shall be the last. Who is the lady?"

Darcy took a seat near them. "I met her uncle in Meryton," he said, "a Mr. King. He is in trade there, and has some shipping interests in Liverpool. I do not recall *Miss* King, but Bingley says she is an amiable sort."

"He says that of everyone," Richard observed wryly, turning the page of the newspaper he was reading.

A rare sense of annoyance towards his cousin rose in Darcy's chest. "Even so, I doubt she deserves to be taken in by a blackguard like Wickham."

"Arabelle," the countess said, "could you take Giana—"

"No," Georgiana said. "I shall not be sent away like an empty-headed child. I am the one Wickham wronged. I shall not allow him to take advantage of someone else the way he did me. Something must be done. Miss King cannot marry him."

Darcy rubbed the bridge of his nose, fighting back a headache.

"Come, Darcy." Arabelle passed him a plate of petit fours. "Have some refreshments, and let us discuss this like adults." She picked up the teapot and poured him a cup.

"You are seventeen." He took a delicate yellow cake and passed the plate to Giana.

"I have made my come-out," Arabelle said. "That makes me an adult."

He looked to his aunt, but she offered him no support. She said, "I have never thought it possible to preserve a girl's innocence by preserving her ignorance. The best way to protect her against roguery is with the truth. Besides, Georgiana has confided in Arabelle. She probably knows more about the facts of the matter than the rest of us."

"Darcy," Giana said, "you must put an end to this engagement. Go to Mr. King—you and Colonel Fitzwilliam."

At the mention of his name, Richard set down his newspaper and gave the matter its proper attention. He was a man of action, better suited to the battlefield than the drawing room. The opportunity to strike against Wickham would appeal to him. He had launched into a murderous rage when he first learnt of the attempt to elope with Georgiana. Now that the chance to avenge her was upon them, he would not balk at it.

"Tell the man the truth about Wickham," Georgiana continued. "Mr. King will take your word for it. You and Richard are men of consequence. Wickham is nobody."

Darcy looked at her intently. His nature was not like his cousin's. He preferred to think through the cascade of possible consequences before acting. Of course he wanted to protect an innocent young lady from Wickham's schemes. But that was not the only consideration. "The more people who know,"

Darcy said to his sister, "the more your reputation is at risk."

"The secrecy has already harmed Miss King," Georgiana insisted. "I shall not let it harm anyone else. It is time for the world to know what a blackguard the man is."

Lady Matlock cleared her throat. "I have given much thought to this. It might be better if the truth came out now. If Giana waits to make her come-out until she is eighteen or nineteen, any whiff of scandal will be gone."

Arabelle raised her chin with the proud self-confidence of an earl's daughter. "No man worthy of her hand would reject her simply because that scoundrel tried to elope with her."

"It is not as if he compromised me," Giana said. "We were never alone together, not for a moment. Mrs. Younge was always in company with us."

Darcy rose and paced. Inwardly, he swore at himself for trusting Mrs. Younge as his sister's companion. The woman had clearly been in league with Wickham all along. She abetted his scheme to gain access to Georgiana's dowry. To her fortune of thirty thousand pounds.

The moment Georgiana had confessed her plans to elope, his sense of control had dissolved. His sister was no longer a child. She was nearly a woman, with her own thoughts and desires. The idea that he could not protect her raised bile in his throat.

He eyed her resolutely. "I shall not have your name on the tongues of gossips. The colonel and I can go to Hertfordshire to speak with Mr. King and swear him to secrecy. No one need be the wiser."

"Darcy, no!" Georgiana cried. "You must expose Wickham. Talk to his colonel, at least. Inform the men of influence in the town to keep their daughters safe from him. Otherwise, you might save Miss King, only for him to destroy another young woman."

Her lovely pale-blue eyes beseeched him. He could not refuse her. "Very well. We will speak generally about his character, however, telling the full truth to no one but the uncle. Will that satisfy you?"

"Yes." Giana's face lit up. She rose and kissed his cheek. "Thank you. If you are able to save Miss King, then what I suffered was not in vain."

He stood and enfolded her into a tight embrace. Dread washed over him at the thought of how he had nearly lost his dear sister to that villain forever. But she was safe now, and wiser too. No one would harm her again.

Chapter 7

Silence fell over the house on Gracechurch Street. The visit from the Darcys and Mr. Bingley had been an emotional twenty minutes. As aunt Gardiner made careful inquiries of Jane, Lizzy tried to listen. After all, this was why she had come to London—to reunite Jane with Bingley.

But her mind kept wandering. A sick feeling rose in her stomach, a creeping sense of dread. She could not stop thinking of the expression on Miss Darcy's face at the sound of Wickham's name.

Jane's gentle tone recalled Lizzy to the present. "I am sorry to say, Mr. Bingley knew nothing of my being in town until this morning. His sister did not mention it."

"And you see," Lizzy said triumphantly, "the first thing he did when he learnt of it was to call on you."

"Not exactly," Jane demurred. "He and Miss Darcy had been planning to call on *you* before they learnt I was here."

"Even so," Lizzy countered, "that must have been for your sake, on Mr. Bingley's part at least. He wanted news of you."

"Perhaps." Jane sighed. "It was kind of him to call."

"It is more than kind. He is besotted."

"Lizzy," aunt Gardiner warned, "let us be more prudent. Mr. Bingley cares for Jane—that much is clear. Until he proposes, we should assume his heart is yet to be won." She turned to Jane. "Did he mention why he left Netherfield so abruptly?"

"He meant to come to town on business only for a day or two. Then the others in the party followed him. They convinced him to stay in London to celebrate Christmas with the rest of his family. And now, with the height of the season approaching…"

Her voice trailed off. It was all preposterous. Lizzy fought the impulse to say so aloud. It seemed obvious to her that Bingley's sisters and Mr. Darcy had intended to separate him from Jane.

Rage boiled inside her as she thought of it. The past two days, Darcy's kindness had distracted her. She must not forget the arrogant, selfish behaviour he had shown in Hertfordshire.

And yet…he had told Bingley the truth. He had brought him to see Jane.

"Did Mr. Bingley seem himself?" Lizzy asked, her mind still preoccupied.

"Yes," Jane said, "except that he is more restrained than usual. But every bit as kind."

"It is possible," Lizzy suggested, "that Mr. Darcy has given him reason to question your motives."

"How do you mean?" Jane asked, stiffening, her face turning ashen.

"When I spoke to Mr. Darcy yesterday, he seemed to doubt your affection for Mr. Bingley."

Jane stared in open-mouthed horror. "You spoke to Mr. Darcy of my affections?"

Lizzy's cheeks burned. "Mr. Bingley is a man of fortune. Mr. Darcy does not wish his friend to be taken in by an adventurer. I warned him, however, that he was in no position to judge your feelings."

Jane nodded, that answer seeming to satisfy her. In truth, Lizzy had been too open with Darcy about Jane's sentiments. In the heat of her anger, she had been unguarded.

But perhaps that had been for the best. Bingley had come. And now, Lizzy was sure, Jane would win him at last. It could not be otherwise.

∞∞∞

After dinner that evening, Darcy and Bingley took their brandy in Darcy's study. They closed the door for privacy. Darcy examined his friend's face and was relieved to see the lines of tension gone. His normal animation had returned to his eyes.

But was it only a temporary reprieve? Darcy had observed little of Miss Bennet during the visit to Gracechurch Street. It had been too brief, and his attention had been diverted elsewhere. What had possessed Elizabeth to mention Wickham's name?

From what Darcy had observed, Jane Bennet had been deeply affected by the sight of Bingley. Had Darcy been mistaken last autumn, in construing her calm demeanour as a lack of affection? Perhaps her feelings were too intense to show outwardly.

He decided to take a direct route to discover Bingley's thoughts on the matter. "How did you find Miss Bennet?"

His friend tapped a thumbnail against the crystal glass in his hand. "Skittish as a colt. I shall need to win her trust again if I want to discover what is in her heart."

"Then you will not rush into anything?"

"No," Bingley conceded. "I say, though, Darcy, I can see no hint of fortune hunting in her. She is as artless as they come."

Darcy swirled the rich amber liquid in his glass. "I have not seen art in her, but neither have I seen passion. That might be due to a natural reserve. Still, I would hate for you to throw yourself away on a woman who does not love you. Especially when she has neither family nor fortune to offer as a consolation."

Bingley set his jaw but said nothing.

"I imagine," Darcy continued, "you will tell your sisters you have seen Miss Bennet."

A sly smile broke out over Bingley's face. "I have something in mind for my sisters. But I cannot put it into place until you return from Hertfordshire."

Darcy eyed him curiously but did not press the matter. Instead, he asked, "You will not mind staying with the Hursts while I am away?"

Bingley could not remain at Darcy House with Georgiana there. Not without her brother in residence to serve as chaperone. Mrs. Hurst, the elder of Bingley's sisters, lived with her husband on nearby Grosvenor Street. Caroline was staying with them, as Bingley often did while in town.

Bingley raised his brows. "As it happens, I have some matters to discuss with my man of business in Cheapside. It may take two or three days to get through it all. For the sake of convenience, I believe I shall stay at a hotel in the City. That will save time over travelling back and forth to Mayfair each day."

Darcy eyed him pensively. "It would be a pity to spend your evenings alone at a hotel."

"I have some acquaintances in Cheapside. Perhaps I can prevail upon them to invite me for dinner." A bright smile lit Bingley's features.

It was a clever scheme, Darcy thought. Mrs. Gardiner would be happy for Bingley to spend his leisure hours at her home. And it would afford Bingley time to observe Miss Bennet. With his eyes open this time, to gauge her feelings for him.

Darcy could not be easy at the prospect. He had hoped for his friend to marry a lady of the *ton*, to elevate his standing. The current state of affairs was a disappointment to say the least.

Since departing Netherfield, however, Darcy had begun to feel guilty. Bingley had been miserable. The man's happiness was more important than who his in-laws were. If Bingley made his home in Derbyshire, near Darcy's seat at Pemberley, all the better. Bingley would not need to spend time with his wife's family above once or twice a year.

This of course assumed that Miss Bennet was as attached to him as he to her. Darcy could not countenance the match otherwise. Even Elizabeth's fiery passion would not persuade Darcy. He would not allow his friend to be duped.

Elizabeth. She was another issue. A match between Bingley and Jane would put her more and more in Darcy's path. He wanted nothing so much as to forget her.

The season was just beginning. He had dozens of other women to choose from. He *would* put Elizabeth out of his mind.

∞∞∞

Lizzy arose the next morning feeling troubled. Though she could not remember her dreams, they had unsettled her. Something she could not name nagged at the back of her mind.

A letter from Lydia in that day's post did nothing to soothe her. As usual, it was half exuberance, half nonsense. There was little in the way of actual news. The missive was mostly a lament of the courtesies Mr. Wickham was showing towards Miss King. Which, in Lydia's estimation, the lady did not deserve.

The engagement to Miss King had surprised Lizzy, had dismayed her even. He was exactly the sort of man she had pictured herself marrying. Amiable, intelligent, courteous, and charming. A match between them was impossible given their current financial states. Still, some part of her had hoped something might come his way.

That hope was gone now. He was engaged to Miss King —though he had never paid attention to her before the inheritance. But then, given his financial state, he could not have courted a woman without a fortune.

Yet...he had courted Lizzy. There was no other word for it. He had preferred her above all other women in the environs of Meryton, and had done naught to hide it.

He had not misled her—he had been clear that marriage between them was impossible. But a natural attachment had grown between them...had it not? Or might he have had other motives?

Lizzy did not like to consider that possibility. And yet, she must. Miss Darcy's powerful reaction to hearing of his engagement suggested something untoward. Something more sinister than Lizzy had considered Wickham capable of. What did she know of the man apart from what he himself had told her?

At Longbourn, she would have explored the meadows to escape these overbearing thoughts. Here, she felt fenced in. She rose and went to the window. The day was grey but dry. A walk out-of-doors—even on the dusty streets of London— might do her good.

Thankfully, she had an excuse to go out. She had an errand to run in preparation for that evening's dinner party and musicale. After breakfast, she and Jane walked to a nearby shop to fetch their shoe-roses.

The streets were not crowded, but a steady stream of people strolled along the pavement. They were mostly of the merchant class. An occasional lady or gentlemen in fashionable dress could be seen.

Jane's spirits were light, and she stopped at every shop window to admire the wares. But Lizzy could not escape the blanket of sadness that had fallen over her. What did it say about Wickham that he had courted Lizzy until learning of Miss King's inheritance? Was he an unabashed fortune hunter? Had he—heaven forbid!—sought Miss Darcy's fortune? The girl was only now sixteen!

"It is most vexatious," Jane said, "that Gracechurch Street is so far from Mayfair."

Lizzy nodded. "It does make visiting difficult. Perhaps Mr. Bingley could be prevailed upon to return to Netherfield."

"Perhaps, when Parliament breaks for Easter. But I suspect Caroline will want to come back afterward, once the Season is in full swing."

Lizzy gave her sister a sideways glance. "I do not believe I said anything about Caroline accompanying him."

Jane let out a delicate laugh. "Oh, Lizzy. But you must see the advantage in my remaining on good terms with Mr. Bingley's sisters."

"If you can manage it." Lizzy stopped at a shop window and eyed a pair of white kid gloves, finely made with buttons at the elbows. "Given that Miss Bingley has not called on you in all the weeks you have been in town, one cannot help but wonder..."

"My letters might have been misdirected," Jane said.

Lizzy looked up at her, arching her brows sceptically.

Jane's cheeks tinged pink. "If she does not call in the next few days, then I shall have to call on her. Which would give us an excuse to visit Miss Darcy while we are in Mayfair."

Lizzy nodded pensively as they turned to walk again. "What think you of Miss Darcy?"

"She is lovely. Her manners are nothing like her brother's."

"Strange, that. From something Mr. Wickham said, I had expected her manners to be precisely like her brother's."

A faint breeze ruffled the blonde curls that peeked out beneath Jane's bonnet. "Perhaps we have been too ready to believe Mr. Wickham. We have no assurance that Mr. Darcy is entirely to blame for the rift between Mr. Wickham and himself."

Memories nagged at Lizzy's conscience. "Mr. Darcy once said that Mr. Wickham's manners enable him to make friends, but not necessarily to keep them."

Jane spoke with some feeling. "You may recall that last autumn, Mr. Bingley spoke to me on the subject. He assured me Mr. Wickham had treated Mr. Darcy abominably."

Lizzy well remembered that conversation. She had been loath to change her opinion of either gentlemen in question. No evidence had been presented one way or another, only innuendo. "Mr. Bingley had no first-hand knowledge of the events himself. Nor could he remember the details."

"That is true. But we have only Mr. Wickham's word that the fault lies on Mr. Darcy's side."

"And the evidence of their behaviour," Lizzy insisted.

"Has Mr. Wickham's behaviour truly been so commendable, and Mr. Darcy's so bad?" Jane spoke with unusual force. "Mr. Wickham disparaged Mr. Darcy to anyone in Meryton who would listen. Yet Mr. Darcy forbore to respond in kind. And as soon as Miss King inherited her fortune, Mr. Wickham turned his attentions from you to her. Those are not the actions of an honourable man."

Lizzy's eyes burned, and she swallowed the knot in her throat. Why was she holding on to this notion that Wickham was all he had seemed—all she had wanted him to be? She had been pleased by his compliments, but in the end, the man had spurned her.

Wickham had not disguised his mercenary intentions. He had even spoken to her of the need to marry a woman of means, to make up for his own lack.

Had she been so blinded by her dislike of Mr. Darcy, that she had denied the clear evidence against Mr. Wickham?

Mr. Wickham had liked her. Mr. Darcy had not. Based on no other facts than those, she had trusted one man over the other.

What a lowering realization! Yet she could no longer deny it.

She pulled out a handkerchief and dried her eyes. The softness of the white cotton offered some comfort. "We must find out the truth about Mr. Wickham. We cannot allow Miss King to marry a scoundrel."

"But how?" Jane asked. "Mr. Darcy has always been reticent where Mr. Wickham is concerned."

Lizzy folded the handkerchief and returned it to her reticule. Her mind was such a muddle at this turn of events, she could not think clearly. "Perhaps we can find out from Miss Darcy."

"Oh, Lizzy, that cannot be a good idea. The mention of his name distressed her so that she needed spirits to revive her."

"Mr. Bingley, then? He might have more information, the next time he calls."

Jane smiled, likely in response to happy thoughts of her beloved. "If he calls."

"Surely he will! You cannot doubt it?"

Jane did not reply, but the joy in her expression said more than words could.

∞∞∞

After their outing, Lizzy and Jane handed their bonnets and pelisses to the footman. Sounds of laughter came from the drawing room. The light tones of Mrs. Gardiner's voice were followed by the happy tenor of Mr. Bingley's.

The young ladies exchanged quick smiles, then scurried to join the little gathering. "There you are, girls," their aunt said, pouring tea. "I told Mr. Bingley you would not be long."

He stood and bowed in Lizzy's direction, then kissed Jane's hand. "How lovely you both look after your walk in the fresh air. I hope it is not too forward of me to call again so soon. I am in Cheapside to visit my man of business, and I thought it would be pleasant to stop in and see you again while I am here."

"You must not stand on ceremony with us, Mr. Bingley." Jane motioned him to a chair as she and Lizzy took their places on the couch. "We are neighbours in Hertfordshire, so that must permit us some liberties. I feel safe in speaking for my aunt, and saying you are welcome to call as often as you wish."

"I am delighted," Bingley responded, his face flushed and happy. "In fact, I shall be staying in this part of town for the next few days. I have taken some very comfortable rooms at the Golden Griffin."

Lizzy raised her brows but fought the urge to give Jane a significant look.

"Why, Mr. Bingley!" aunt Gardiner cried. "I hope you are not planning to dine alone. You are welcome to join us this evening. We are hosting a little musicale."

Lizzy admired her aunt's aplomb. Somehow, when *she* extended an invitation to a young gentleman, it sounded gracious. When Lizzy's mother did the same, it sounded dreadfully overbearing. Perhaps the difference lay in knowing how welcome the invitation would be.

"That would be splendid!" Bingley declared. "I have been

longing to hear the Miss Bennets play again."

"Perfect," Mrs. Gardiner replied. "I shall ask the Richardsons to bring their daughter Susannah to round out the table. She is not out yet, but she is a sweet girl of fifteen. She sings quite prettily."

With the details of the evening arranged, Lizzy raised a cup of tea to her lips. The scent of bergamot revived her senses. She said to Mr. Bingley, "What will Mr. Darcy do to entertain himself while you are gone?"

Bingley chuckled. "Darcy can look after himself without me. Most of his uncle's family are in London. The countess prefers to travel with her husband. She comes to town with him when Parliament opens."

"They sound devoted to each other," Lizzy observed.

"Quite so." Bingley's expression suddenly turned grave. "Darcy does have other plans, though, while I am away. He has travelled to Hertfordshire with his cousin, Colonel Fitzwilliam. They will be back in a day or two, after they speak to Mr. King."

Lizzy let out a gasp. Mr. King! That news removed all doubt. She could no longer deny that her favourite was an adventurer.

Jane, sitting next to her on the couch, took her hand. "Then it is as we suspected. Mr. Wickham is..." Jane hesitated a moment before continuing delicately, "He is not what he appears."

Bingley shook his head. "I do not know the particulars. Darcy has not volunteered them, and I respect his privacy too much to ask. But the facts are plain, are they not?"

Lizzy turned to stone at his words. Wickham must be very bad indeed if Darcy and his cousin were taking the trouble of travelling to Meryton.

Bingley placed a chocolate biscuit on his plate but did not take a bite. "Caroline had mentioned some gossip from Hertfordshire a few weeks ago. She said Miss King had inherited ten thousand pounds. I did not think anything of it, until Miss Elizabeth mentioned the engagement. Not once during my time in Hertfordshire had I seen him speak a word to her. His sudden interest seems telling."

"I confess," said Mrs. Gardiner, sitting nearby, "I must agree with you. He appeared an amiable man when I was at Longbourn over Christmas. Looks can be deceiving, however."

"You do not suppose that he..." Lizzy swallowed. The picture of Miss Darcy's sweet face would not leave her.

She jumped to her feet, unable to say the words. Rubbing her hands together, she paced. She could not keep still.

Had Wickham tried to...to seduce Miss Darcy for her fortune? That gentle, innocent girl? It was unimaginable! But given the expression on her face the day before...it seemed the most likely explanation.

Lizzy's face cooled, and her head grew light.

Mr. Bingley came and helped her to a chair. Sitting beside her, he spoke in soft tones. "Forgive me, Miss Elizabeth. Wickham treated you ill, imposing on you as he did. Darcy and I ought to have warned you earlier that the man was not to be trusted."

"Miss Bingley warned me. Mr. Darcy, too. I did not believe them. Wickham had filled my head with lies. He said the most spurious things about Mr. Darcy. To protect his own reputation, I imagine, should Mr. Darcy try to expose him. What a fool I was!"

Bingley pressed her hand. The kind gesture endeared him to Lizzy further. Even if he had no fortune at all, he would still be a fine match for Jane. He was a good man—something more rare than she had realized.

"You are no fool," Bingley said to her. "Wickham is a master manipulator. I daresay everyone in Meryton was taken in by him."

"Poor Miss King," Jane said, a catch in her voice. "Her heart will be broken."

"Indeed." Bingley turned to the elder Miss Bennet. "I have no doubt that Darcy and the colonel can convince her uncle of the truth of the matter. She will be saved from him, at least."

"Thank goodness for that," Lizzy said, but it was cold

comfort to the hollow feeling in her chest.

Chapter 8

Darcy and Colonel Fitzwilliam entered Mr. King's place of business in Meryton. It was a cramped office, the desk piled with papers. Darcy wondered how the man managed to keep the lamp from setting it afire.

Darcy had barely made the introductions when King blurted, "Thank heavens you are here. I was about to hie to London to seek you out. Did your steward contact you?"

Darcy raised his brows in confusion. "My steward?"

"Yes. You must have heard that my niece is engaged to Wickham. I assume that is why you have come." King's suit was rumpled, his waistcoat barely containing his ample midsection. He pressed a handkerchief to his balding pate.

"Indeed it is," Darcy said. "But what does my steward...?"

"I wrote him when I learnt that Wickham was the son of the previous steward. I thought to seek confirmation of Wickham's good character. I had assumed that since he is an officer, he must come from a respectable family. But the report I received from your steward left me quite alarmed."

"Ah," Darcy said, the exclamation speaking volumes.

"Unfortunately, the account I received contained few details. Not enough to persuade my niece."

"No. My steward is a man of discretion."

King shook his head, looking utterly miserable. "I know nothing of serving as guardian to a young woman. I have been a bachelor all my life. But with the death of her grandfather and her maiden aunt, I am the only relative she has in the world. She relies on me for her future happiness, and I have made a bungled mess of this. I just learnt that Wickham had not shown the slightest interest in her until she came into her fortune."

Brushing his fingers through what was left of his hair, King swore. As a businessman, Darcy had thought him quite astute. But this worry about his niece had left him looking grey and worn.

King continued, "She is not one known for beauty. It is easy to see how Wickham's compliments could turn her head. But she is sweet and kind, and deserves a husband who will treat her well."

"I am sorry to say, sir," Darcy replied, "that Wickham is not that man. He is a heartless fortune hunter. He has a history of trying to charm an innocent young woman into a marriage that would benefit only himself."

King sank into his desk chair, wearing the look of one whose worst fears had been confirmed.

Darcy continued, "If you have any doubts, Colonel Fitzwilliam here can back up my claim. He has first-hand knowledge, as I do, of a similar scheme. The girl was not even out of the schoolroom when Wickham convinced her to elope. Fortunately her brother discovered their plans and was able to prevent it."

Pale-faced, King stared at them. He slowly recovered himself as his mind seemed to reach some conclusion. Determination replaced the tiredness in his features.

Tapping his fingers on the desktop, King said, "Well. It seems I need to check on my interests in Liverpool. I believe a trip to the coast would do my niece some good." He rose and shook the hands of his visitors. "Thank you, gentlemen. I am in your debt."

"Not at all," Darcy said. "I should have exposed Wickham when he first came to Meryton. I intend to make amends for that today. I would appreciate your discretion about the details of our conversation. I shall not ask you to keep the substance of it to yourself."

King nodded, looking troubled but resolute. The visitors took their leave. Darcy had a few more calls to make. He was eager to get them over with quickly.

∞ ∞ ∞

Darcy and his cousin handed their reins to a groom at Longbourn. "If we wish to speak to Mr. Bennet," Colonel Fitzwilliam asked, "then why are we calling on *Mrs.* Bennet?"

Walking towards the entrance, Darcy breathed the fresh country air. Red berries dripped from the holly bushes flanking the portico. He turned to his cousin.

"So she can pepper us with questions about Bingley. If we do not make it easy for her, she will devise some scheme and throw the entire household into an uproar. If we grant her an interview first, we can then have a quiet and rational conversation with Mr. Bennet."

"I see," the colonel said, though his drawn brows suggested he did *not* see.

Darcy grinned. "You will understand soon enough."

The housekeeper led them to the front parlour. Mrs. Bennet sat with her three youngest daughters, arranged in an elegant tableau. It could not have resembled their state before the visitors arrived. Not if Darcy knew anything about their dispositions.

Kitty and Lydia wore sweet smiles instead of shooting each other cross looks. Mary held her sewing serenely in her lap, rather than holding a book to her nose. And Mrs. Bennet was silent.

The housekeeper announced the gentlemen, and Mrs. Bennet invited them to sit. All the while her eyes watched the door, as if she expected Bingley to enter behind them.

"Mrs. Bennet, may I present my cousin, Colonel Richard Fitzwilliam. He is the second son of my uncle, Lord Matlock.

He is unlikely to inherit, however. His elder brother, Viscount Astridge, has three healthy sons."

The colonel gave Darcy a stunned look at such a gauche introduction. Mrs. Bennet seemed all gratification. "Well, it is a compliment to be sure, to have the son of an earl in my parlour! But to what do we owe the honour, Mr. Darcy? We had heard that two gentlemen had arrived at Netherfield this morning—"

"Yes, Colonel Fitzwilliam and myself, as you see. We had some business in Meryton, and Bingley kindly offered us the use of his home for the night. He himself is in London, visiting his man of business in Cheapside. I believe he intends to call on your eldest daughters while he is there. We saw them yesterday, and I am happy to report they are both well, along with the entire Gardiner family."

Mrs. Bennet beamed, clearly satisfied by this report. With all her questions so efficiently answered, she seemed to have little to say.

Miss Lydia, however, filled the silence. She asked Richard, "If you are a colonel, why are you not wearing your regimentals?"

"My regiment is under the command of my lieutenant colonel for the winter. I shall join them again in the spring."

She nodded. "I do love a man in a red coat."

Mrs. Bennet spoke to Richard. "We are most fortunate to have Colonel Forster's regiment wintering here in Meryton. Although they are the militia, not the regulars. So perhaps you do not know Colonel Forster."

"I met him today," Richard said.

"And you know Mr. Wickham," Miss Kitty offered.

The colonel grew silent and looked over at Darcy. Then he turned back to the ladies and said, "Indeed I do."

"Oh, that's right, you do!" Lydia cried. "Have you heard he's engaged to Miss King? More's the pity, too. I'm sure he would have been happier if a *pretty* girl had inherited ten thousand pounds."

The colonel seemed confounded a moment, then quipped, "I have no doubt he would."

"Mrs. Bennet," Darcy said, unable to endure this interview any longer, "is your husband at home? We wish to have a word with him."

They were shown into Mr. Bennet's study. He seemed none too pleased at being interrupted. Yet he was courteous enough to offer cigars and brandy, which they declined.

They exchanged niceties. Darcy assured the man that his eldest daughters were in good health. Then, they got down to business.

"I assume you have heard about the engagement of Miss King to Mr. Wickham."

Bennet wagged his head sadly. "I cannot escape the chatter that spreads in our little town."

Of course Bennet *could* have avoided that fate, if he had not married the town's most determined gossip. Darcy refrained from pointing that out, though.

"My cousin and I have informed Mr. King that Wickham is known to us as a fortune hunter of the basest kind. As you are a man of influence here, we thought it best to tell you as much."

"In case one of *my* daughters inherits a fortune, before the regiment leaves Meryton?"

Darcy's answer took the form of a wry smile.

The colonel added, "Miss Lydia is precisely the sort of girl Wickham likes. Young, energetic, and not nearly as worldly as she herself would like to believe. I have not known him to trifle with a gentlewoman of modest means. But if his pursuit of Miss King is thwarted, I cannot say what villainy he will proceed to."

"I appreciate the warning," Bennet said with a nod. "I shall keep my girls well out of his path." Then, he looked Darcy full in the face. "Mr. Wickham has been open about the rift between you and himself, sir. To hear him tell it, though, the blame falls entirely on your shoulders."

"Then he is a liar," the colonel replied coolly.

Bennet raised his brows and sat back in his chair.

"I did the best I could for him," Darcy said. "My father

wished him to take orders. Wickham chose not to. So when the living at the rectory became available, instead of the position, I gave him a lump sum payment. It should have been enough to live off of for the rest of his life, if he were frugal. Or he was free to pursue some other occupation, if he wished to supplement the income he made from the interest. Instead, he squandered the principal. When he demanded more money from me, I refused."

Bennet nodded thoughtfully. "I see. I cannot say I am surprised. Poor Lizzy will be, though."

Darcy's face heated at that. "Yes. As I recall from the ball at Netherfield, she did seem to favour his version of the story."

"Did you tell her yours?" Bennet asked.

Darcy bit his cheek. "No, sir, I did not."

Gripping the arms of his chair, Bennet straightened. "You offered her no evidence and made no overtures of friendship. Yet you expected her to take your side, simply because you are the son of a gentleman, and he the son of a steward."

Darcy thought about that a moment. He had been fond of old Wickham. He did not consider himself *better* than the man. But Darcy's reputation was above reproach, while George Wickham's...

The realization hit Darcy like a punch to the gut. He and Wickham had both come to Hertfordshire unknown to the residents. Wickham had endeavoured to make friends, ingratiating himself. Darcy had stood apart from them, above them even.

Of course Wickham was believed. Of course Darcy was doubted. He had expected their reputations to follow them. Instead, he should have taken steps to build his reputation anew.

He had behaved like a complete ass.

"You have the right of it," Darcy conceded. "I ought to have been more circumspect in my behaviour. I should not have allowed the good people of Meryton to be taken in by a blackguard like Wickham. For such he is, sir. I have known him all my life, and once called him friend. He has shown himself a man not to be trusted."

"Who else have you discussed this with?" Bennet asked, his eyes acute, finally responding to the gravity of the situation.

"Colonel Forster, of course. Mr. Philips, Sir William Lucas, Mr. Long. Do you recommend I call on anyone else?"

"I believe that will suffice. We can pass on the information as needed, to protect the young ladies of the town from Wickham's greed."

"I would also suggest," the colonel added, "that the tradesmen remain wary of allowing him to buy on credit. That is always a problem when it comes to militia officers, but especially men like Wickham. He almost certainly took his current position because he had run out of funds."

"I see," Bennet replied. "And here the townspeople have afforded him the courtesies of a gentleman."

"It has been many years," Darcy said, "since I have considered him such."

Bennet eyed him coldly, and Darcy felt the shame of his own silence the previous autumn. He should have been more forthright then. Instead, he had let his family pride give Wickham berth to hoodwink the citizenry of Meryton. At least now, Darcy had interceded. He hoped it would prevent any irreparable harm from befalling the townspeople.

It was cold comfort, when he considered how he had allowed Elizabeth to fall under Wickham's spell. Why had he not seen it before? Wickham had spun his web of lies, and she had believed them. She must think Darcy a most dishonourable man indeed. And even if he was determined to forget her, it pained him that she thought of him that way. Somehow, he must change her mind.

∞∞∞

The Gardiners' dinner party that evening was one of the

liveliest Lizzy had attended. Her aunt and uncle's friends were prosperous tradespeople like themselves. They had extensive knowledge of foreign cultures and current events.

During the meal, they talked about commerce in the New World. The wars for independence from Spain were disrupting trade. Hearing discussions about exotic places like Paraguay and Venezuela excited her imagination.

To Lizzy's surprise, Mr. Bingley was as well versed as any of the guests. He knew much about the business that had created and continued to support his wealth. Lizzy's opinion of him grew, and Jane...

Jane's eyes wandered to him every minute, and her soft smile did not leave her lips. It warmed Lizzy to see her sister contented and in love. Despite the disappointments of December, January brought new hope for a happy ending.

After dinner, Jane seemed to wait in the drawing room with increasing impatience. The gentlemen spent more than an hour talking over their port. Bingley was the first of them to join the ladies. He went instantly to Jane's side. She blushed in response to the light in his eyes, which focused itself entirely on her.

A sense of satisfaction rose in Lizzy's chest. She had accomplished her goal of reuniting the two. While the battle was won, though, the war was not over.

She could not help but feel some of her mother's anxiety. Bingley must not be allowed to escape this time. Lizzy would stay in London until he proposed, to make sure he came to the point.

While a few of the gentlemen lingered in the dining room, the pianoforte was opened. Mrs. Gardiner encouraged the youngest Miss Richardson to play. The girl seemed nervous —better to get it out of the way. Despite her youth and inexperience, she acquitted herself well. The sound of her sweet voice lured the rest of the gentlemen to come for the entertainment.

When her turn came, Lizzy took to the instrument with

practiced ease. She played a familiar Beethoven sonata. It made her think of ripples on a moonlit lake, or fingers stretching towards a lost love. She was no great proficient and lacked the ambition to become one. But she immersed herself in the magic that seemed to pour from her when she became one with the music.

She stumbled over a few notes but thought she hid it well. The piece drew out such emotion in her, she could not help but play with passion. She hoped that fact made up for any lack in technical precision.

The audience's appreciative applause said she had not embarrassed herself, at least. Next up, Jane played and sang some Italian love songs. Bingley watched in rapt attention. When she finished, he called "Brava!" and escorted her from the piano to a secluded corner. He spoke animatedly, and Jane was full of smiles.

Lizzy's heart swelled at the sight. How could Darcy have believed that Jane was indifferent? It was clear to anyone who knew her—

But then, Lizzy reminded herself, Darcy did *not* know her. Not as anything more than a passing acquaintance. The thought quelled Lizzy's enthusiasm. An objective observer might notice that Jane spoke little, that she rarely laughed.

It was true that Jane met Bingley's eyes and nodded. She leaned towards him and gestured animatedly with her hands. She seemed lost to the fact that anyone else was in the room. Bingley clearly felt encouraged by her attention. Yet Lizzy could see that Darcy, from a distance, might not perceive how engrossed Jane was.

But what right had he to make a determination of any kind? Especially as he himself did little more at balls than stand and stare. Based on that behaviour alone, one might think him a man of small intellect and no conversation.

But that was not Darcy at all. His manner masked the true man. Lizzy had never met anyone more intelligent. He simply did not deign to speak.

Jane, however, *did* speak to Bingley—at least, when she could get a word in edgewise. Bingley was a talkative man, and she a good listener. Did that not bode well for them? Must a woman chatter on constantly to be a good companion?

Silence could also be a virtue—a fact Lizzy had learnt all too well growing up at Longbourn.

That evening as they readied for bed, Lizzy and Jane discussed the evening's events. "I shall try not to be *too* happy," Jane said, "but Mr. Bingley did seem most attentive."

"Attentive! Why, he could not take his eyes off you. He even rented rooms at a hotel in this part of town so he could be near you."

"Oh!" Jane startled at the suggestion. "I do not think he did that on my account."

"You are too modest. I have never seen a man more in love." Lizzy squeezed her sister's hand. "But take care, Jane. Mr. Darcy is reluctant to encourage the match, and Mr. Bingley respects his friend's opinion. Subtle signs may not be enough to persuade them of your affection."

Jane tilted her head, a look of confusion crossing her sweet face. "I hardly see how I could have shown him more notice, without being discourteous to others. What more must I do?"

"Can you not flirt with him?" Lizzy asked, unpinning her hair. "Tap his arm with your fan? Signal with your handkerchief?"

Jane scowled. "I am no coquette. I would not know how to dissemble with a man."

That took Lizzy aback. "I am not suggesting you dissemble. The opposite, in fact. Show your true feelings."

"If I adopt a manner that is not my own, is that not dissembling?" Jane picked up a silver hairbrush and ran it through her long, blonde tresses. "It is not my way to flirt or to flatter. I am honest with him—as honest as I can be. Surely it should be clear to him by now that I prefer his company to any other man's."

Lizzy nodded thoughtfully. Jane was not wrong. Yet Lizzy's

fears were not abated. She worried that more would be required to win Bingley's hand.

Lizzy could not imagine what that *more* might be. But she would have to figure it out. Her sister's happiness was at stake.

Chapter 9

The next morning, a letter arrived for Mrs. Gardiner. As her nieces sat with her, sewing in the parlour, she read it with increasing excitement. Rising to her feet, she said, "Girls, I have wonderful news!"

Happy for an excuse to set aside the stockings she was darning, Lizzy asked, "What is it, aunt?"

"This letter is from my friend Lady Purcell. We attended school together in Lambton. In passing, I had mentioned the difficulties of being so far from Mayfair during the season. She has made us a most generous offer. Her home in Berkeley Square is sitting empty until she comes to town after Easter. She says we may use it in her absence."

"Berkeley Square!" Lizzy cried. "Is not Lady Jersey's home there as well?"

"I believe so. Oh, girls, what fun we shall have!"

Giddy with delight, Lizzy turned to Jane. The eldest Miss Bennet smiled and her eyes glistened. She seemed too overwhelmed to speak.

This was precisely what Jane needed to help secure Bingley. A house in the best part of town would put them in easy distance of the finest parties of London's social scene. The season was not yet in full force. But those staying in Mayfair at this time of year still liked their entertainments.

When Mr. Gardiner heard the news, his response was surprisingly genial. His work would of course prevent his coming with them. However, he wanted his nieces to make the most of the opportunity afforded them by their stay in town. He insisted they buy new gowns in the latest fashion at his expense.

Two days later, when the time came to go, Mrs. Gardiner said a tearful goodbye to her children. She promised to visit often, and admonished them to obey their nurse and their papa.

The servants at the house on Berkeley Square greeted them most graciously. "I am sorry to put you out," Mrs. Gardiner said to the housekeeper. Mrs. Harrison was a kind-looking woman, tall and slim, her dark hair streaked with grey.

"Not at all, ma'am," she said, "we are happy to have a house full of ladies to look after. It gets lonely having nothing to care for but the furniture."

Lizzy looked around, hardly able to believe she would be staying amidst all this grandeur. When she had heard that Lady Purcell was a viscountess, she had not been prepared for such a show of wealth.

In the foyer, the pale oak floors were bordered by dark wood marquetry in a Greek key pattern. A crystal chandelier hung from the tall ceiling. It glittered in the sunlight that streamed in through high windows. Gilded frames held paintings of the Italian countryside. The pastoral images showed vineyards and orange trees and olive groves.

Mrs. Harrison showed the ladies to their rooms. Lizzy's overlooked a beautiful garden. Though dormant, it was lushly green. Low boxwood hedges lined a meandering path. Junipers were trimmed into spiral topiaries.

A longing welled in Lizzy's chest. She could never hope to live in a home so beautiful. It was an extraordinary luxury to be able to stay here for a few weeks.

Unbidden, Darcy came to her mind again, but that was foolishness. Of course his wealth tempted her. But even if she could love the man—which she most assuredly could *not*—he would never deign to propose to a woman like her.

Lizzy refused to let such thoughts dampen her spirits. The day was fine, with sharp sunshine and a cloudless sky. She convinced Jane to walk with her to reinvigorate their bodies and minds.

Berkeley Square was a rural oasis in the midst of the bustling city. The three-acre plot was resplendent with shrubs and plane trees. Lizzy wanted to twirl and skip and revel in the natural beauty.

Unfortunately, propriety demanded restraint. Fine houses constructed of pale grey stone lined the east and west sides. They reminded her she could not roam free here. An iron balustrade enclosed the gently sloping park, keeping it to its proper place.

Lizzy breathed deeply, enjoying the woodsy scents. The air was cold but the ground dry, offering a pleasant stroll along the footpaths. Jane's mood was light, her hope rising at the prospect of spending weeks just a few blocks from Bingley.

"I have been thinking about our trip to the modiste's tomorrow," Jane said. "I went through the trunks of clothes Mama sent from Longbourn—everything is woefully out of date. I could get by on two new ball gowns and a walking dress, if my old clothes were altered."

"I agree. We could bankrupt our uncle trying to outfit two young ladies with new clothes for the season. Kitty must be cursing me—Mama sent me all of *her* prettiest frocks as well."

"And she sent me all of Mary's!" Jane cried. "We are of a size, but our tastes are so different. One might think I was in mourning if I wore all that grey unadorned."

"No doubt the modiste can add some colourful lace or ribbon to give the gowns a more fashionable look."

"Mary will not be pleased if her dresses come back altered."

"All must be sacrificed in the quest to secure Mr. Bingley." Lizzy spoke with a hint of irony in her tone, but she was deadly serious. "Besides, if Mary hopes to find a husband herself, a prettier wardrobe would not go awry."

Jane gave her a smile.

Lizzy turned as two fashionable ladies approached. When they got closer, she recognized Miss Darcy. Georgiana introduced them to her friend.

Lady Cressida Marlowe lived on the square. Sister to the Earl of Greymore, she was a pretty blonde thing who had just made her come-out. With her charm and beauty, she could have no dearth of prospective suitors. Her drawing room must overflow with flowers after every assembly.

"How are you enjoying the season?" Lizzy asked Lady Cressida.

"I have been tasked with making a match as soon as possible," she joked. "That way, my brother will not have to sponsor me again next year. He is a great tease, you see."

Her genteel tone carried a hint of the ennui expected of the upper classes. Heaven forbid girls making their come-out seem excited at the prospect! With Lady Cressida, though, the tone seemed to capture a natural sense of irony. Lizzy found it endearing.

Cressida continued, "These thirty-year-old men who court me leave me quite terrified. I would be happier with a man of twenty-three or four. But they are too busy sowing their wild oats, which of course young ladies of the same age are not allowed to do."

A cool breeze fluttered the ribbons of Lizzy's bonnet. "One might be better off marrying some doddering old fool. Give him an heir, and then live as a merry widow."

Lady Cressida laughed drolly. "I have thought of that, believe me. But the act of getting an heir from such a man…it must be distasteful."

Miss Darcy's face pinked.

"Oh, dear, I have embarrassed poor Georgiana." Lady Cressida touched her young friend's arm. "With as many brothers as I have, a lady sometimes overhears conversations not meant for her. Mr. Darcy would never allow such talk in *his* house, however."

"He is a bit of a stickler," Lizzy concurred. The call of a starling, shrill and demanding, split the air.

"I could not bear the kind of scrutiny poor Georgiana must

endure," Cressida said.

"It is not scrutiny," Miss Darcy objected. Her cheeks pinked and her eyes sparkled with the passion of her response. "He is protecting me, so that I do not come to harm. He is acting out of love."

"I have no doubt of that," Jane said. "He clearly adores you."

"And I him," Georgiana said. "Since we lost Papa, we are all the other has."

The sadness in that statement pierced Lizzy's heart. Her family could be a trial sometimes, but she loved them all the same. She could not imagine being an orphan at Miss Darcy's tender age.

"My dear!" Lady Cressida clutched Georgiana's arm. "You have the entire Fitzwilliam clan."

Lizzy recalled that Fitzwilliam was the family name of the Earl of Matlock, uncle to the Darcys. "How large a clan is it?"

"The earl and countess have four sons and four daughters." Georgiana's bright smile showed that she held her relations in high esteem. "The youngest, Arabella, is a year older than me. Viscount Astridge is the eldest—he must be thirty-five by now."

"His three younger brothers are conveniently unmarried," Lady Cressida said. "Such fine gentlemen—and devoted to you, Georgiana. You must not think of yourself as alone. Any one of them would fight a duel to protect your honour."

"I certainly hope not!" Georgiana cried. "I would hate to see them come to harm. Besides, duelling is illegal." With her wide eyes, she looked impossibly young and innocent. As if she truly believed that men of the aristocracy were obliged to obey the law.

Lizzy herself knew little of such matters. Yet her father had not been scrupulous in insulating her. The vagaries of society amused Mr. Bennet. His daughter had gleaned more from him than might be expected of a gently bred young lady.

Just as Cressida had from her brothers.

With a lilt of hope in her breast, Lizzy wondered if Cressida might be something of a kindred spirit. Despite her youth, she had a refreshing practicality about her, almost a world-weariness. She was not a woman to be led by fancy.

Together, the foursome made a circuit around the park. As Georgiana fell in step with Jane, Lizzy walked ahead with Cressida. Lizzy appreciated the gentleheartedness that both Jane and Georgiana displayed. Lady Cressida, though, made Lizzy feel understood. Not since her friend Charlotte had moved to Kent had Lizzy enjoyed such an easy conversation.

They reached the gate nearest Greymore House. Its silvery stone façade gleamed in the sunlight. As the four parted ways, Lizzy and Jane smiled and waved. Their friends disappeared inside the stately home.

Lizzy let out a little sigh. This relocation to the fashionable part of town might prove to be fortuitous indeed.

∞∞∞

At dinner that evening, Darcy congratulated himself on his display of equanimity. He wanted to leap from his chair when he learnt from his sister that the Miss Bennets were staying in Mayfair. Though whether he was overjoyed or dismayed, he could not say. Possibly both.

It appeared, though, that this information was not news to Bingley.

As the trout almandine was served, Giana asked her brother, "Might I invite the Miss Bennets and their aunt to tea? Mr. Bingley is pleased with the idea."

No doubt he was.

Darcy, however, was conflicted. He believed the Bennet sisters would be a good influence on Georgiana. At the same time, he did not wish to distinguish them in any way. The *ton* thrived on rumours.

He said gently to his sister, "I recall how upset you were when we visited them in Cheapside. I am surprised you wish to pursue this friendship."

Giana's lips parted. "But that was not Miss Elizabeth's fault! She knew nothing of my history with the man in question. She was most kind when she saw my distress."

Darcy considered a moment. He did not object to a friendship between Giana and the eldest Bennet sisters. They lacked the affected airs of society ladies. But how might such a friendship continue, once the season ended?

He did not relish the idea of Georgiana socializing with them in Hertfordshire. Not when it meant being exposed to their relations. Moreover, she was younger than they, and not yet out. "Would you not rather spend time with girls your own age?"

"But I do!" she objected. "I visit Arabelle every day. I called on Lady Cressida just this morning. And while you were away, Miss Peabody spent the afternoon here. She brought me the latest novel by Mrs. Wheedlesuch."

Darcy set his jaw. "You know I do not like you filling your head with such nonsense."

"Right now, my head is filled with the history of the Ottoman Empire. Mrs. Annesley quizzes me on it every day. I like to read for pleasure, too, Darcy. I am not silly enough to think such stories bear any resemblance to real life."

"Do not be a stick in the mud, Darcy," Bingley said, attacking the trout with a fish knife. "Let the girl have some harmless fun."

"I shall thank you to keep your opinions about my sister's upbringing to yourself." Darcy spoke with mock annoyance.

Bingley grinned back at him. The man was right, of course. The last thing Darcy wanted was to be so strict that he drove Giana away. Yet he could not escape his worries about finding the right balance. Her future depended on his decisions.

Georgiana buttered a roll. "You may not admit it, but you like Elizabeth Bennet."

Darcy coloured, fighting the smile that broke over his face, and failing utterly. "Are you playing matchmaker?"

"No!" She broke off, then clarified, "Not exactly." She flopped back in her chair, a childish gesture. He would have to speak to her companion about eradicating it.

"Darcy House feels empty," Giana said at last. "At Pemberley, the situation is even worse. With Mama and Papa gone, and you unmarried..." She sighed. "I suppose I should like to have a sister—that is all. And some nieces and nephews, too. If you will not let me come out for another two or three years...well, it is a rather lonely existence."

Darcy eyed her in surprise. She had never expressed such a sentiment before. In truth, he was in no hurry to marry. He would do so when he found the right woman.

He could not deny that he was attracted to Elizabeth. And in fact, he liked her very much. From everything he knew of her so far, he had no reason to believe she would not suit.

Except for her background. And that obstacle seemed insurmountable.

He had rather thought he would marry a daughter of the aristocracy. Unfortunately, that pool was small. He had not encountered a woman who excited his intellect or his blood the way Elizabeth did.

Was he being too fastidious?

Bingley would say he was. Darcy could seek out his cousin Richard's advice. He had met Mrs. Bennet and her youngest daughters. If the colonel approved of Elizabeth anyway, Darcy would rest easier.

"You may invite Mrs. Gardiner and her nieces to tea," he said to Giana. "You could play the harp for them. Miss Elizabeth expressed an interest in hearing you."

Giana beamed at him. "Thank you, brother." She rose and kissed his cheek. "What fun we will have!"

She and Bingley shared a look. Clearly, the two of them were in league. It was a good thing Darcy trusted Bingley's character implicitly. Otherwise, he could not permit the man to live in the same house with Darcy's young and vulnerable sister.

But Georgiana's companion, Mrs. Annesley, was a reliable

chaperone. Whatever was going on between Giana and Bingley was not unseemly. So Darcy left them to it.

Chapter 10

Lizzy and Jane followed their aunt into Darcy House, the butler leading them down the hallway. "Oh, my!" Mrs. Gardiner exclaimed. "How lovely the crown moulding is. And the paintings—I do love Boucher and Fragonard. What do you think, girls?"

Jane gave a pat reply, but Lizzy felt too much. She had been so mortified the last time she had entered this house, so overwhelmed, she had barely noticed the décor. But now, she could not help but be awed by how lovely it was. The walls were a soft yellow, the furniture neoclassical in style. The fixtures were richly appointed, but without ostentation.

Her aunt was right—the Rococo artwork was delightful. Its pastoral vistas and flirtatious scenes showed the leisure class at play. The paintings did not look like anything Darcy would have chosen. Lizzy suspected his mother's influence.

As they approached the drawing room, the sound of a familiar female voice met them. Lizzy's cheeks went cold and her stomach tightened. She caught Jane's eye, and her sister seemed to share her dismay. Caroline Bingley!

No mention had been made about Caroline attending the tea. But as Bingley was living in the house, Lizzy should not be surprised if his sisters were there. And just as they had last fall, Lizzy expected Caroline and Louisa to seek to undermine Jane.

Let them do their worst. Lizzy was prepared this time. Jane would not have to go into battle alone.

Lizzy straightened her spine and held her head high. Jane

mirrored her posture. Their aunt at their side, they stepped into the drawing room.

As the servant announced them, Caroline turned and blanched. Louisa looked down her nose at them, her face colouring. Mr. Bingley, however, appeared as welcoming and amiable as ever.

Did Lizzy imagine a sardonic smile breaking over his face as he eyed his sisters?

Miss Darcy looked sedate and lovely as she greeted them. The Queen Anne couch on which she sat was upholstered in a cream damask. Her brother was nowhere to be seen, which must have disappointed Caroline.

Sitting beside Georgiana was a young woman—barely more than a girl, really—whom Lizzy had never seen before. The lady was dressed even more richly than their hostess, in silk of pale blue. The soft colour and modest styling complemented Georgiana's own petal pink gown.

Before introductions could be made, Bingley approached the new guests. "Miss Bennet, how lovely to see you." He kissed Jane's hand, then bowed towards her companions. "Mrs. Gardiner, I thank you for the pleasant evening I spent in your home recently. I cannot remember when I enjoyed the music or the company more."

Caroline's face turned red, and her jaw hardened.

Mrs. Gardiner gave Bingley a courteous nod. "I was happy you could join us on such late notice."

He smiled genially. Offering Jane his arm, he led her to a wooden settee with striped upholstery. Together, they sat.

"Why Jane," Caroline said as Lizzy and Mrs. Gardiner took seats near Miss Darcy, "I did not know you were in town."

"How odd," Jane replied, "that *both* my letters to you should have been misdirected."

"Mrs. Gardiner," Georgiana said calmly, "allow me to present you to my cousin." She introduced her companion as Lady Arabella Fitzwilliam. Her hair and eyes were dark, her complexion more olive-hued than was fashionable. Lizzy wondered if the girl might have some Spanish or Italian blood in her ancestry.

Darcy entered with another man at his side, of his own age or a bit older. He was not quite as tall or handsome as Darcy, but he was broad-shouldered and had an amiable appearance.

Darcy introduced him as Colonel Richard Fitzwilliam, brother to Lady Arabelle. The two siblings resembled each other in their colouring and facial features. And they both seemed more outgoing than their Darcy cousins.

Georgiana managed to keep the conversation from faltering. It was no small feat, given the coldness of Miss Bingley and Mrs. Hurst. Darcy was silent as he stood ramrod straight by the window.

Amused by his demeanour, Lizzy rose and walked to him. She noticed from the corner of her eye how Miss Bingley's head spun towards them. Lizzy paid her no mind. Instead, she said to him, "If I did not know better, sir, I might think you a deaf-mute."

He gave her a wry smile. "Forgive me." He leaned down to her and continued in low tones, his mouth so near she could feel his breath on her ear. "My sister asked me if she could invite you and your companions to tea. I did not realize she also planned to invite Miss Bingley and Mrs. Hurst. I suspect Bingley encouraged the scheme, so I cannot be cross with her about it."

His nearness brought a fluttering to her belly. But Lizzy looked at him archly, pasting a serene smile on her face. "Why Mr. Darcy, I am sure I do not know what you mean."

He gave her a smirk, and she challenged him with her eyes. Strange how they could communicate without words, like old friends. In truth, they barely knew each other. Yet her chest rose at the thought of getting to know him better.

His expression turned more serious. "Much has changed since the last time I had the satisfaction of seeing you in my home. I hope your displeasure has abated, and we never have to quarrel on that subject again."

Lizzy recalled their argument over Jane and Bingley. Her cheeks flamed. The uncharacteristic humility in his tone disconcerted her.

"I..." Her mouth went dry. She searched for a witty rejoinder but found none. "I am satisfied, sir."

"I intended no slight towards your sister. My friend's happiness is my only consideration."

"Of course," she allowed. She opened her fan and fluttered it a moment, then closed it again.

"I confess, your anger pained me." He spoke as if weighing each word. "Upon further reflection, I realized the fault was mine. From the night we met, I have not treated you with the courtesy I ought. For that, I apologize."

Lizzy stiffened. What was the man about? Why apologize after all this time?

Civility demanded she accept, so she did. Neither of them seemed able to meet the other's gaze. She wanted to say something that would rival his sentiments, but he had left her speechless.

She looked out the window at the small but immaculate garden. At this time of year, it was a tableau of brick and trimmed evergreens.

The formality of it reminded her of its owner—stark and unyielding. Yet underneath the surface, a riot of life might lay dormant.

Oh, how she had misjudged him! She felt it painfully now. He might be a man she could like, yet she had wasted every opportunity of getting to know him.

She would not do so again. Regaining her composure, Lizzy looked up at him. "How was your trip to Hertfordshire?"

He coloured, then gazed at her softly. "Humiliating. Your father in particular did not hide his irritation. He was not pleased that I allowed Wickham to associate with the people of Meryton as if he were a gentleman."

A little of her old resentment rose up her spine. "Mr. Wickham did *not* present himself as a gentleman. He said freely that his father was a steward."

"I do not refer to his parentage." Darcy's tone gentled. "His father may have worked for a living, but he was a gentleman through and through. The son, unfortunately, has become dissolute. I hope you no longer have any illusions on that score."

She squared her shoulders, poised to spar. Then, her chest deflated. She must rid herself of her prejudices where the two gentlemen were concerned. Darcy was not the enemy.

She forced a sense of calm she did not feel. "Your sister's reaction to the mere mention of his name has cured me of my misapprehensions." She met his eyes. "That was a terrible faux pas on my part, upsetting Miss Darcy as I did. My deepest apologies. I am relieved she does not hold it against me."

"Of course not. You did not act maliciously." He spoke matter-of-factly, almost sternly, but warmth shone in his eyes.

"Not maliciously, no. But I confess, I was motivated in part by the desire to see *your* reaction. Until that point, I believed you had behaved shamefully towards him. That you unfairly denied him the living your father had promised."

His lips pressed into a thin line. Sardonically, he said, "Did the man not mention his refusal to take orders?"

Her eyes widened. She could not help staring. It took a moment to regain her wits. "On the contrary, he claimed to wish for a career in the church."

Darcy scoffed. "Then I suppose he also concealed the fact that I gave him a lump sum payment to fulfil my father's wishes. One that might have kept him comfortable for the rest of his life, had he behaved wisely."

"Good heavens!" Could it be so? Lizzy's mind whirred as the new information altered the landscape of her imagination. Wickham had viciously wrought the truth to make it sound as if right was on his side, and Darcy was the villain.

"What an absolute bounder," she declared. "And I believed every one of his lies."

She spoke with more fervour than she had intended. A few

eyes turned in her direction. She opened her fan to partially hide her face. She could not let Wickham's deceit discompose her this way.

"I am sorry he misused you," Darcy soothed. "I can produce evidence to satisfy your mind, if you like. My cousin the colonel knows the truth, as does my steward and my man of business."

His solicitude surprised her. It showed more respect than she deserved, given how she had treated him. His kindness was unnerving.

"Thank you," she said, "but that will not be necessary. Mr. Wickham is nothing to me."

A smile played on Darcy's lips before he turned serious again. "Forgive me, Miss Bennet. I should have been more open from the beginning, instead of allowing him to impose on you." He pressed her ungloved hand.

A strange warmth rushed over her. She remembered when she had first caught sight of him the night they met. She had thought him the handsomest man she had ever seen.

That impression had not changed, even now. His brown hair was smooth and even, with the studied insouciance currently in fashion. His square jaw and cleft chin communicated strength and decisiveness. Dark, assessing eyes contained depths she could lose herself in.

Swallowing down a surge of emotion, she released his hand. "I shall forgive you, if you forgive me for trying to embarrass you. I should not have done so in front of your sister."

"I would prefer that you did not do so at all." The playfulness of his tone surprised her.

She waved her fan. "Would you deny me the fun of reducing you to the status of mere mortal?"

He scowled. "I do not know what you mean."

The confusion in his eyes surprised her. Did he not realize how his stiff manner affected people? "You are so scrupulous. You keep your emotions well under wraps." She closed her fan and tapped it to his chest. "I want to see the man behind the marble façade."

He looked at her so intensely, her skin began to heat again. Her breathing grew laboured.

Something flashed in his eyes, but she could not read him. The two held still in the moment, gazes locked, as if something buried inside each of them longed to break free. An odd intimacy grew and stretched between them, the rest of the world fading into oblivion.

She knew this man so little—even less than she had thought. Too many of her opinions had been based on lies. Standing with him now was like meeting him for the first time, discovering him anew.

The Darcy she saw now was kind and honourable. The pride she had perceived in him... Yes, he was cognizant of his place in the world, and less humble than he might be. But he was not arrogant. If he were not a sophisticated man of the world, she would have called him shy.

How blind she had been! Malicious gossip had solidified her opinion, before the man could even defend himself.

She was more her mother's daughter than she cared to admit.

Lizzy drew back, her cheeks cooling. An uncomfortable brew of emotions roiled inside her, shame mixing with dread. She did not want to like Darcy. If she let herself think well of him, could she possibly resist his charms?

When she was close to him like this—so close she could breathe his scent of wool and clean musk—her skin prickled with awareness of his masculinity. She must take care. She could never aspire to a man like him.

Disconcerted, she withdrew her gaze from him and looked about the room. Miss Bingley was monopolizing the conversation, pressing her syrupy compliments on Georgiana. Her machinations were transparent.

Darcy cleared his throat. "Georgiana, would you favour us with a song? Miss Elizabeth professed a desire to hear you perform on the harp."

The prospect made Lizzy smile. "Indeed, I would be most gratified, if you do not mind."

"Oh dear," Georgiana cried, "I did not expect to perform in front of such a crowd. But I shall do my best."

She went to the harp. Caroline rose to turn the pages of music for her. Lizzy took her seat, and Darcy sat in a chair in the corner away from the others.

Miss Darcy looked sweet and innocent as she sat at the instrument, fingers poised to begin. The harp was as tall as she was, the carved wood painted in gold.

Under her touch, the strings quivered, and the sound resonated through the room. The tune was simple, yet the notes flowed like a brook over smooth pebbles.

The sedate ambiance did not stop a chill from arresting Lizzy as she glanced in Darcy's direction. His gaze met hers. His face was rigid, his jaw set, his eyes darkly forbidding.

Lizzy shrank from that severe expression. Had she done something to displease him? Perhaps her manner had been too familiar—flirtatious, even. And now he was distancing himself.

She told herself it did not matter. She was not in love with the man. She did not even like him. But his attentions had pleased her. For him to withdraw so completely was humiliating.

She would not make that mistake again. Liking Mr. Darcy could only end in heartache. He was the same man who had scorned her at the Meryton assembly. Who could barely find two words to speak to her at the Netherfield ball. Why had she expected something different from him while here in town?

Instead, she turned her attention to Lady Arabella. "Your cousin plays well," Lizzy whispered.

"She has no idea how talented she is," Arabelle said with a smile, her voice as bright and sweet as a lark's. "All she hears are the mistakes, not the beauty."

Lizzy nodded. Her sister Kitty was the same way when it came to the pianoforte. Except that she did not have Miss

Darcy's persistence. Kitty did not seem to understand that with practice, she would improve. Convinced she had no natural talent, she gave up when a piece seemed difficult.

Miss Darcy seemed to play for the sheer love of it, instead of letting discouragement stop her. Her technique was quite good, and her taste exquisite.

When she finished, the room erupted in applause. Miss Darcy rose and curtseyed.

Caroline took her arm and walked her back to the couch. "Oh Georgiana, I declare I have never heard anyone play with such skill. Would you not agree, Mr. Darcy?"

"She plays well for a novice," he replied. "I am proud of the effort she puts into her accomplishments. Within a few years, she may well deserve your praise."

Lizzy bit her lip to keep from laughing at how far Caroline's arrow had strayed from its mark. Of course Mr. Darcy did not like mindless compliments to his sister. She was not a master. She was still in the schoolroom.

In that moment, Lizzy made a decision. She would stand as a bulwark between Miss Darcy and Caroline's machinations. Georgiana could use a true friend—not one who was scheming to secure Darcy's hand. Lizzy wanted the shy, self-conscious girl to know that she was a budding young woman worthy of admiration. She was not a mere pawn in someone's scheme.

And if that meant Lizzy would be exposing herself to Darcy and his scorn, then so be it. That was a sacrifice she was willing to make.

∞ ∞ ∞

At dinner that evening, Bingley and Georgiana were in high spirits. Darcy said to his sister, "That was quite a joke you played on Louisa and Caroline." He speared a potato slice.

Pressing her hand to her chest, Giana said in a tone of complete innocence, "Joke? Why, I simply invited them here to take tea with some friends they had made in Hertfordshire."

Bingley grinned unashamedly.

"I ought to scold you for it," Darcy said to his sister, "but I will not, since Bingley was complicit. It is the responsibility of a hostess to make sure her guests are at ease. Not to intentionally cause them distress."

"That sounds rather like a scold, brother," she teased. "But Caroline took her revenge, heaping her false praise on me. If she insists on flirting with you, I wish she would keep me out of it."

"Caroline got a first in flirting at Mrs. Buttercup's school," Bingley quipped.

"You are angry at your sisters," Darcy observed.

"Should I not be?" Bingley's fork clanked against the plate. "Seeing Jane again—that is, Miss Bennet," he said, colouring —"has made me realize how much I nearly lost when they separated me from her."

"I do not wish to dissuade you," Darcy said carefully, not wanting to overset his friend further. "The Bennet sisters are here for the marriage mart. There is no shame in it. But make no mistake, Miss Bennet has set her cap for you—"

"If anyone's cap has been set," Bingley thundered, red-faced, "it is mine for her. I have pursued her since the night we met —or were you too full of your own indignation that evening to notice? She is an angel, the sweetest creature I have ever known, and by Jove, I intend to marry her. No matter what my sisters or friends have to say about it."

Darcy sat in silence, feeling the justice in Bingley's diatribe. Yet an offer of marriage at this point would be hasty.

Earlier in the day, Darcy had observed Bingley and Jane. Bingley had spoken intently while the lady nodded and smiled. She did not hang on his words to the exclusion of everything else. Nor did she demand his undivided attention. In short, she seemed pleased by his notice but lacked any sort of possessiveness.

There had been a quiet adoration in her features. Not

the fierce devotion Darcy associated with true love. She seemed easily pleased by everyone and everything. Was her admiration of Bingley so different?

In truth, it was not Darcy's place to say. Bingley was capable of his own decisions. He did not need Darcy's interference.

"Miss Bennet is lovely," Darcy said at last, "and would be a credit to you as your wife. But how well do you know her?"

"Well enough." Bingley set his jaw. "She is no fortune hunter."

"Perhaps not at heart." Darcy cut into his roast beef and swirled it in the shallot gravy. "She needs a husband to keep her in the style of a gentlewoman."

"As do most of the single young women who come to Mayfair for the season," Bingley reminded him.

"Most of them have some marriage portion. Miss Bennet has only her attributes to recommend her. The same is true of her sister. People in desperate circumstances can do desperate things—"

"Darcy!" Georgiana scolded. "Listen to yourself. It is not the Miss Bennets you are describing." She furrowed her brow. "Are you thinking about Wickham? You have been more curmudgeonly than usual since he tried to elope with me last year."

"I am not curmudgeonly—"

"Elope!" Bingley cried. He stared at her in horror. Then, he pushed back his chair, the legs scratching against the floor. Rising, he cried, "By Jove, I'll put a sword through the man." He marched out into the hallway.

Giana giggled. "Bingley, where are you going?"

"*Mr.* Bingley," Darcy warned her. She rolled her eyes.

Bingley stalked back into the dining room. "I'm going to Hertfordshire to demand satisfaction. Darcy, how could you stay silent last fall, when that man came to live amongst us? His friend Denny is a favourite of little Lydia Bennet. If Wickham would try to elope with a *wealthy* girl of fifteen, what would he do with one who was penniless?"

Darcy's face caught fire. "I have warned Mr. Bennet. And I would advise you not to duel with a military man. You may be able to match Wickham at swords, but he can best you at pistols. He would not hesitate to put you in the ground, if only to punish me."

Georgiana gave her brother a prim look. "This is not a civilized dinner conversation for a gently bred young lady."

Bingley sat back down. He glared at Darcy. "You should have told me."

"He was protecting my reputation," Giana said in a merry tone.

Darcy grinned at her. "You are showing scant appreciation for the brother who saved you from ruin."

She reached out and squeezed his hand. Then, tears glistened like diamonds in her eyes. She came and sat in his lap, nestling against his shoulder. He held her tight, chest filling with emotion, loving her more than life.

The three of them sat in silence a while. At last, Giana kissed his cheek and went back to her chair. The scent of roses lingered after her.

Was she right? Had Wickham's betrayal jaded Darcy to the point that he viewed a sweet young woman like Jane Bennet as an adventurer?

Possibly. No, *probably*. He had let himself believe Caroline Bingley on the matter. Even though he knew she had ulterior motives. Her claims jibed with his fears, and that had been enough to sway him.

"I shall grant you, there is no artifice in Miss Bennet," Darcy conceded, cutting into a carrot. "But Miss Elizabeth is not above flirting."

"I say!" Bingley objected. He looked at Darcy with wide eyes, his jaw slack. "When have you ever seen Miss Elizabeth flirt? I have not."

"You have been too wrapped up in her sister to notice," Darcy insisted. "At tea today, she sought me out. She was most charming."

Bingley continued to stare. Georgiana wore a wry smile.

"She was kind to you, Darcy," his sister said. "I know you are unaccustomed to that. But kindness alone cannot be called flirting."

He narrowed his eyes. He did not approve of her teasing her elders in this manner.

In truth, he had been flattered by Elizabeth's attention. Their conversation had been diverting. They were becoming easier with one another. Which meant he was in greater danger than ever of falling for her allure.

"She approached me while I was standing alone," he said. "While we spoke, she fluttered her fan—"

"Dear heavens, her fan?" Bingley cried in mock horror. "What will the lady patronesses of Almack's say?"

Darcy silently cursed himself, embarrassed at voicing such a weak argument.

"Are you certain you did not flirt first?" Bingley asked. "I have seen you flirt with her before. At least, what passes for flirting when you do it."

Giana tittered. It would have been a guffaw, if she had not caught herself in time. "You are in love with her, Darcy. Why can you not admit it?"

"In love?" he protested. "Georgiana, you must put that thought out of your mind. I shall not have her misled into thinking I have intentions towards her. I confess I admire her, but that is all."

Giana smiled and eyed Bingley, who smiled back at her. Darcy resented the carelessness that his sister and his friend showed. It was not a careless thing to him.

He and Elizabeth were learning to trust each other. An emotion gathered in his chest. Something like hope.

He had not mistaken her playfulness that afternoon. When her eyes had met his, he was certain he saw interest there.

Those eyes—deep and glittering with heat, like dark coals. He ached to give in to her teasing, to meet her every parry with a riposte. But did he dare?

If she thought him in her power, she would be a fool not to take advantage. He hated to view her that way—and to view *himself* that way, as if he were nothing more than a bank account.

His attraction made him vulnerable. If he was not careful, he could lose his head to the chit. Darcy had spent a lifetime controlling his emotions. He would not let an innocent country beauty unman him.

A chill shot down his spine. If Bingley married Jane, Darcy would be even more tempted by Elizabeth. Standing next to her that day, inhaling her sweet violet scent, he had felt as if she had been made for him.

Surely that was a passing fancy. He must steel himself against it.

All he need do was find another pretty girl with a lively mind, one of his own station. When the season was in full swing, he would find one to make him forget Elizabeth Bennet.

Bingley's next words, however, seemed to thwart him.

"Would it not be jolly fun," Bingley said, "if the two of us married the Bennet sisters? We could all settle in Derbyshire together. It is a pretty part of the country. I could be content buying a property there."

"Oh, do!" Georgiana encouraged. "Darcy, when it is time for me to marry, you must find me a husband whose estate is in Derbyshire. I could not bear to leave all of you behind."

Darcy did not voice the oaths that ran through his mind. "I hope the duty of matchmaking will fall to my wife rather than to me."

She grinned at him again. "But brother, you do not have a wife," she reminded him in a teasing tone.

"You will not be in a position to marry for some years yet," Darcy said, tiring of the subject. He set his silverware down on his plate and added, "By that time, I expect to be settled. Given her mother's talents, I have no doubt Elizabeth will be adept at finding you a husband—"

Darcy broke off, shocked by how his words had betrayed

his innermost thoughts. Thoughts buried so deeply, he had not realized he had them. His mind and heart had settled on Elizabeth Bennet. There was no denying it any longer.

Bingley and Giana said nothing, only looked at him wearing satisfied smiles. For his part, he could not speak. Marrying her was out of the question.

The resolution filled him with misery. Once he was back at Pemberley, though, life would return to normal.

He would master this attraction. He *would* forget her.

Chapter 11

The next day, after their customary morning walk, Lizzy and Jane joined their aunt in the drawing room. It was their at-home day, though they did not expect many visitors. They had few acquaintances in Mayfair.

Lizzy did not mind the prospect of a quiet day at home. Tomorrow they had theatre tickets, and their uncle would come to take them out for the evening. A break between social events offered a chance to contemplate what was next for her.

Jane's courtship was progressing nicely. What about Lizzy and her future?

She hated the idea of entering the marriage mart. Yet another opportunity like this might never present itself. She must take advantage of it while she could. She wanted to fall in love in her own time, when she met a respectable man who could make her happy. Yet her circle of acquaintance in Meryton was small, and it might be years before someone new came her way.

Her wisest choice was to enter the fray.

With a sigh, she walked over to pick up her embroidery. Then, she noticed the tall stack of mail on the escritoire, where her aunt had sat down. Lizzy was about to ask about it when a footman stepped into the doorway. He announced the Countess of Greymore and her daughter, Lady Cressida Marlowe.

Lizzy turned and pressed a hand to her chest. She and Jane had of course chanced upon Lady Cressida in Berkeley Square a few days earlier. But for the countess herself to call was a compliment indeed.

Cressida greeted Lizzy and Jane by clasping their hands warmly. She wore a gown of hyacinth-blue silk that glimmered with a lovely sheen in the firelight. Though breathtaking, it seemed impractical as a winter walking dress. Lizzy imagined the ensemble must also include a matching pelisse lined with ermine.

With boredom in her tone but an imp in her eyes, Lady Cressida introduced her mother. A woman of about fifty, the countess was just shy of plumpness. Greying blonde curls peeked out artfully from her turban. Dressed in champagne-coloured silk, she expressed her raptures at meeting them. Her high-pitched voice and excitable demeanour contrasted with her daughter's unflappability.

"I understand you are a dear friend of Lady Purcell," the countess said to Mrs. Gardiner as they all sat.

"Yes, we went to school together in Derbyshire."

"Indeed!" the countess cried, fluttering her handkerchief. "Our country estate is in Derbyshire. In which town was the school located?"

"Lambton."

"Oh yes, I know it well. It is not far from Pemberley." The countess sipped her tea. "Did you know the Darcys while you were there?"

"I was not so fortunate, ma'am." Mrs. Gardiner offered a plate of biscuits. "Mr. and Miss Darcy have been most kind to my nieces, however, since they arrived in London."

Lady Greymore accepted a square of shortbread. "Yes, I understood Mr. Darcy met them in Hertfordshire last autumn." The countess turned her smiling gaze to Lizzy and Jane.

Lizzy was not sure what to make of this. How did the Countess of Greymore know so much about her and her sister? Seeking answers, she asked benignly, "Are you close friends with the Darcys, ma'am?"

"Oh yes, Lady Anne was one of my dearest friends. Such a terrible loss, and Georgiana was but six years old when she passed." A distant sadness clouded her eyes. "Young Darcy and my eldest son have been friends since before they left for Eton together. A steady young man, he is. I keep telling Cressida she could do worse."

Lizzy tensed against the wave of jealousy that rushed over her. The mix of anger and dread tightening her chest and pooling in her stomach could be called by no other name. It was preposterous, of course. She did not like Darcy, nor he her.

Lady Cressida tittered. "Mama, I have told you. I admire Mr. Darcy, but he is not the one for me." Gazing sideways at Jane, Cressida gave a little sigh and said dreamily, "Mr. Bingley is the sort of man I prefer. But I understand he has eyes for no one but Miss Bennet."

Jane's lips parted, and a blush rose in her cheeks. She turned her face away.

"Goodness!" Lizzy exclaimed. "Is that rumour circulating? I had no idea anyone knew of us."

"You are entirely unknown," Lady Cressida said, "which makes you a great mystery. Everyone is talking of Miss Bennet's beauty, even though no one has seen her." She sipped her tea. "It is the way of the *ton*. But I daresay they will not be disappointed—except for those who are rivals for Mr. Bingley's affections."

"That is kind of you to say," Jane interjected. "But I cannot see how my sister and I could have excited such notice. We have lived all our lives in the country, and we come to town but rarely."

"Hertfordshire is such a rural outback," Cressida teased. "You may as well be in Australia."

"I did not mean it was as bad as that," Jane added with a smile. Meryton was, after all, just a few hours' ride from London. It was not as if they lived in York or Cornwall.

"Do not underestimate yourselves," Cressida chided. "Miss Bennet, you are kind and attentive. Anyone speaking to you feels like the only person in the room."

"You are right about that," Lizzy said, warmth filling her heart as she turned to her sister.

"As for you, Miss Elizabeth," Cressida said, fluttering her ivory fan, "you are lively and clever. Your wit makes you a true original. The *ton* loves an original."

Lizzy smiled slyly. "I have never considered my impudence a virtue before."

Lady Cressida looked at her askance. "I predict you will be a great success."

"At least until the novelty wears off," Lizzy countered, knowing all too well that Jane was right. The manners of the *ton* were too rarefied for the Bennet sisters to emulate. The best they could hope for was refined but unsophisticated.

And in truth, Lizzy did not care about London's elite. Once Jane was safely engaged, Lizzy would go back to the country. Until then, she would relentlessly seek invitations to the best *ton* events. She and Jane would pursue Bingley at every ball, rout, and Venetian breakfast.

∞∞∞

When the guests had gone, the butler entered. He handed Mrs. Gardiner a silver salver bearing an assortment of calling cards. The cards had been sent by their neighbours that morning, welcoming the family to the square.

"This is a surprise!" aunt Gardiner said to her nieces. Jane was working on a watercolour while Lizzy sat in the window seat with a book in hand. "Suddenly the Berkeley Square families are taking notice of us. And look at all the invitations that arrived in the post this morning! What could have prompted it?"

Lizzy pondered that but was interrupted before she could answer. The butler returned to announce Lady Arabella and Lady Nerissa Fitzwilliam.

Arabelle looked pretty and vivacious in rose-coloured satin. Her glossy dark hair was styled in an elaborate knot high on her head. Nerissa, who appeared to be about Lizzy's age, wore sage-green velvet. She was fairer than her sister, brown-haired with hazel eyes that sparkled impishly. Her demeanour was more placid and in fact reminded Lizzy of Darcy.

"When Nerissa heard I had met you," Lady Arabella said, "she insisted we call at once. How wonderful to have friends of Georgiana's as our neighbours."

"Neighbours for now," Lizzy said, serving the pound cake while Jane poured the tea. Mrs. Gardiner sat at the escritoire, leaving the young ladies to their conversation. Lizzy continued, "A friend of our aunt's is letting us use her house until Easter."

"How splendid!" Arabella cried. "Mr. Bingley must come to the point by then."

Lizzy was startled by her bluntness. From the corner of her eye, she caught sight of Jane blushing deeply.

"Mr. Bingley is darling," Nerissa said jovially. "But he is unlikely to make a decision of any consequence unless someone tells him to do it."

"I daresay that is true." Arabella looked at Jane sideways, wearing a grin. "If Darcy told him to propose, Miss Bennet would be an engaged lady by this evening."

The Fitzwilliam sisters tittered. Lizzy smiled consciously, not wishing to offend their guests. But she felt embarrassed for Jane's sake. In a light-hearted voice, Lizzy said, "Mr. Darcy *is* the key."

Jane, however, showed no hint of mirth. In a firm but gentle voice, she said, "I *do* believe Mr. Bingley capable of making his own decisions."

"Oh, of course!" Arabelle said, patting Jane's arm. "Forgive us. We have known Mr. Bingley since we were girls, and we love to tease him. Truly, from the looks of him at my cousin's house yesterday, he has already made the decision."

Jane's expression softened, and she appeared gratified.

Nerissa looked at Jane pointedly. "If he does not act on that decision soon, he will have rivals aplenty once you are known. I predict that within a month, Miss Bennet will be hailed amongst the *ton* as a diamond of the first water."

Lizzy thought that a tired, meaningless phrase, one that brought colour to Jane's cheeks again. Why would anyone notice the Bennet sisters of Hertfordshire? They had neither title nor fortune to recommend them.

Arabella, however, nodded vigorously, showing her agreement with her sister's statement. "You will be a great success, now that you are established in Mayfair. Georgiana is most pleased. She had been fretting about the distance to your uncle's home."

"I am fond of Miss Darcy," Lizzy said, "and gratified by the friendship she has shown us."

"She appreciates women of intelligence and wit." Arabella's eyes twinkled. "Especially when they can put Darcy in his place. Most young women are either terrified of him, or act like sycophants. The way you stand up to him, Miss Elizabeth, is rather terrifying. I hope you never have cause to turn you wit on *me*."

"Oh!" Lizzy's cheeks burned. She had not thought her treatment of Darcy to be so obvious. "I never meant...that is to say..."

"Darcy *is* particularly bad." Nerissa brushed back a curl that had fallen over her forehead. "With family he is fine, but in company—sometimes, he positively glowers. He has long been in need of a good set-down."

That assessment alarmed Lizzy. "I would not suggest that Mr. Darcy is anything other than a gentleman of high principles."

"Of course," Nerissa said. "His principles are not in question. You will admit that he could be more sociable."

Lizzy's anxiety eased. "I admit, I have sometimes thought so."

Nerissa smiled. "Then we are of one mind on the subject."

Arabelle sank her fork into a slice of pound cake, then turned to Jane. "Miss Bennet, I hope you will not stand on ceremony with Miss Darcy. You and your sister may call on her freely. Even though she is not yet out, Darcy approves of her socializing with the right sort of young ladies."

"'Tis a pity," Nerissa said. "We had expected she would make her come-out at the same time as Arabelle, or right after. But now she prefers to wait. She is such a shy thing."

Arabella's expression turned stormy. "Her shyness could be got over, if it were not for that rogue—" She broke off, colouring deeply, her eyes darting to her sister's.

In a low tone, Lizzy finished for her. "George Wickham."

The Fitzwilliam sisters stared at her, mouths gaping. "You know about that?" Nerissa asked.

Lizzy spoke carefully. "My sister and I had the misfortune to meet Mr. Wickham in Meryton, where his regiment is stationed for the winter. Mr. Darcy was loath to expose him for the blackguard he is, for obvious reasons, but events made it necessary."

Jane added, "Lizzy and I have kept the information confidential, of course. For Miss Darcy's protection."

Nerissa's eyes flitted from Lizzy to Jane and back again. Arabelle smiled sadly and pressed a hand to Jane's forearm. "It is a terrible business when a man one trusted from childhood turns out to be a villain. I would hate to be in Georgiana's shoes."

Nerissa turned to her sister wearing a grim expression. "Take care, then, Arabelle. You have danced with Rolf Peabody at more than one assembly. Even though my brother Richard has warned us against him."

"Oh, pish," Arabelle said with a wave of her hand. "Mr. Peabody is a rogue, but he is not a villain. He has never been anything but kind to me."

"Just as Mr. Wickham had never been anything but kind to Georgiana."

Arabella rolled her eyes. "You need not worry about that,

sister. I shall not run off to Greta Green with Mr. Peabody."

"I take it Mr. Peabody is a family friend?" Lizzy asked carefully. She hoped to sound as if she were making conversation, not expressing a gauche curiosity.

Nerissa replied without hesitation. "His father, the late Viscount Wayne, was friends with my father. They served in the Lords together for many years."

"Our families were always in company while I was growing up," Arabella said. She gestured with her hands animatedly, as was her habit. "Priscilla Peabody and I were inseparable."

"But Rolf turned out quite wild." Nerissa's teacup clinked as she set it into its saucer. "He was sent down from Oxford after his first year. Since then, he and his cronies have been roaming the countryside like a pack of wolves."

"That is nonsense," Arabella quipped. "There are no wolves in England." Despite the joking tone of her voice, she lifted her chin and set her jaw in an expression of pure defiance.

Nerissa shook her head at her sister's poor attempt at a joke. "I would not mind so much, if he were to confine his debaucheries to the streets of St. Giles. But he insists on coming to society functions with his brother, the new viscount. Lord and Lady Wayne are well liked. One can hardly exclude them."

"I have never known him to behave as less than a gentleman when in good company," Arabelle insisted.

"Of course," Nerissa said. "At *ton* events, he is on his best behaviour." She leaned forward and spoke in low tones. "He must be in the market for a rich wife to support his gambling, even though he is but one-and-twenty."

"Goodness!" Jane declared.

"Forgive me," Nerissa said, "I am too frank. But I do wish to warn you, in case you encounter him. One would not guess to look at him that he is so bad. He has the face of an angel."

"A Viking, more like," Arabella said merrily. "He is blond haired and blue eyed and broad shouldered..." The wistful sound in her voice did not suggest brotherly affection.

"Stay away from him, Arabelle," Nerissa warned. "Must I speak to my mother about this?"

"I promise I shall be good." She pressed a hand to her chest. "Whenever I visit Priscilla, I shall take a sturdy footman along to guard my honour. Would that satisfy you?"

Nerissa arched her brows. "It would not be a bad idea."

Lizzy let out a little laugh at that. "Now I am quite afraid of him. Are there any other gentlemen of the *ton* we should be wary of?"

"All of them," Nerissa said dryly.

"Are you such a cynic, Lady Nerissa?" Lizzy asked with a cheerful laugh.

Nerissa spoke in a voice that was almost dreamy. "When I first came out, I was prepared to like every man I saw. I soon learnt, though, that when men admire a pretty woman, even the most rational can lose their heads."

The clock on the mantel chimed the hour, drawing Nerissa's gaze. She and her sister exchanged some parting pleasantries before taking their leave.

Once they were gone, Lizzy pondered the conversation. The information about Mr. Peabody was worrisome. What disconcerted her more, however, was how easy the sisters had been with them. The aristocracy did not casually embrace the country gentry to their bosom.

How had they learnt about the *tendre* between Jane and Bingley? She could not imagine that Darcy had confided in them. Might Bingley himself have done so? He and the Fitzwilliams seemed on close terms.

Regardless, the ladies seemed to think an engagement a settled thing. That was encouraging. Then again, what did they really know?

Lizzy would put no stock in gossip. She would not rest easy until the betrothal—indeed, the marriage—was an established fact.

Chapter 12

The night of the play, Mr. Gardiner arrived at the house in Berkeley Square in time for an early dinner. Then, he took his wife and nieces to the Covent Garden Theatre. He had secured a private box for the performance of Shakespeare's *Richard II*. The ladies wore low-cut silk gowns and long gloves reaching almost to the elbows.

Lizzy vibrated with excitement as they walked the corridor to the private boxes. Chandeliers and fireplaces lit the way. She looked forward to the play. But attending the theatre was about more than the entertainment. Deals were brokered and matches made wherever members of the *ton* gathered.

Against the walls stood statues in the Greek style. They flanked wide benches upholstered in crimson velvet. A few patrons sat drinking lemonade, but at this early hour the crowd was thin. So far Lizzy had not spotted anyone she knew.

Amidst the murmur of conversation, she could not help but wonder at the opulence of the place. Newly built after the fire of 1808, the theatre was grander than anything she could have imagined. She had learnt to school her features, however. With an effort, she showed the placidity expected of the upper classes. She and Jane could not afford to look provincial, at least not until Bingley came up to scratch.

They found their box and stepped inside. The grey walls were painted with gilded wreaths of honeysuckle. The seats were arranged in two rows of three. Upholstered in light blue, they appeared surprisingly comfortable.

Lizzy's eyes scanned the hall, which was encircled by three tiers of boxes. Massive chandeliers hung above the more economical seats on the ground floor. One hoped the candlewicks had been trimmed to the proper length. Otherwise, hot wax might drip down into the pit.

Lizzy was grateful for her position amongst the gentry and the aristocracy.

Mr. and Mrs. Gardiner let their nieces sit in the front row, so they could see and be seen by the assembled patrons. "I wonder if Mr. Bingley's party has arrived," Jane whispered to Lizzy.

"I would be surprised if Miss Bingley and Mrs. Hurst were not fashionably late," Lizzy said.

"But do not forget, Mr. Darcy is bringing his sister. This is to be an educational evening for her."

The words were barely out of her mouth before Darcy entered a box across from them. Georgiana was on his arm, with Mrs. Annesley on her other side.

The sight of him arrested Lizzy's gaze. Tall and broad-shouldered, he surpassed most men with his physical presence alone. And the pure male beauty of his high cheekbones and strong jaw was enough to stop her breath. Amidst this crowd of London's elite, Darcy stood out.

Her body tingled at the vision of him, even from this distance. She warned herself to set aside this fruitless attraction. His glares the last time they had been in company had warned her to expect nothing from him.

She did not realize she was staring until his eyes met hers. He surprised her by nodding in her direction. She smiled and returned the gesture. The rate of her heartbeats quickened from a canter to a gallop.

He was not glowering at her now. From Darcy, she could only take that as a compliment.

Behind him, Bingley stepped into the box along with his sisters. He caught sight of Jane and gave her a bow. She responded with a flutter of her fan.

While the rest of his group took their seats, Bingley stepped out. He appeared at the Gardiner's box a few minutes later. Jane blushed as he chatted amiably with her aunt and uncle before taking the empty chair by her side.

"Good evening, Miss Bennet, Miss Elizabeth. How lovely you look."

The same might be said of him, decked out in his evening kit. Dark coat and breeches, gold waistcoat, white linen. He was the picture of the fashionable gentleman.

"I have heard wonderful things about this production," he continued. "Have either of you seen the play before?"

Lizzy smiled. "Not unless you count the scenes some neighbourhood boys acted one year for Guy Fawkes Day."

Jane laughed at that, then gazed sideways at Bingley. "It was all very serious."

He smiled brightly. "I daresay the quality this evening will be an improvement."

"Mrs. Gardiner," said a musical voice behind them. Lizzy turned to see Lady Cressida Marlowe with a tall, blond gentleman standing next to her. "How happy I am to see you here tonight," she said. "We are but two boxes down. May I present you to my brother, the Earl of Greymore?"

Lizzy's eyes widened. She had come to think of earls as middle-aged men with paunches and thinning hair. Greymore was as fit and handsome a specimen of manhood as she had met in quite a while. And that was saying something. After all, a regiment of military men was stationed in her little village for the winter. Yet the last man she had met who could rival Greymore was—

Her cheeks burned at the thought. *Darcy.* The man devilled her even when he was not in her presence.

Lizzy stood and curtseyed as Lady Cressida introduced them. Lord Greymore leaned over and set a kiss on Lizzy's gloved hand. "It is an honour, ma'am. All London is abuzz with talk of the beauty of Miss Bennet," he said with a nod towards Jane. "But word has not yet spread that she is rivalled by her sister. That will soon be put to rights, I am sure."

"You are all compliments, my lord," Lizzy said.

Lady Cressida tapped his arm with her opera glasses. "You will not win points with Miss Elizabeth that way. Beauty is common enough. You may discover that her wit, however, is unmatched." She turned to Lizzy. "Intelligence in women is not valued as it ought to be."

Lizzy gave her a sly smile. "Perhaps the average man's eyes are better than his mind."

Greymore chuckled. "Brava, Miss Elizabeth! I daresay you are right about that."

Lizzy felt a tickle of pleasure in her chest. Lord Greymore seemed an amiable man on top of the merits of his person. But having been so recently deceived by Wickham, she would defer forming an opinion. She would wait until she had a thorough knowledge of the man's reputation.

Besides, she could not aspire to an earl, no matter how kind he was.

That would not keep her from enjoying his company. They chatted jovially a few more minutes. Then, Darcy appeared.

His sister and her companion were with him, but Lizzy's vision narrowed to only encompass him. Dark wool, white linen, and a ruby-red silk waistcoat that stood out in a crowd. Heavens, why was he affecting her so?

Since learning the truth about Mr. Wickham, she no longer had a reason to distrust Darcy's character. She could admire him all she liked. But was that wise?

From the first night they met, he made it clear that rank mattered to him. She would not set herself up for disappointment.

To make more room for the newcomers, Mr. and Mrs. Gardiner rose and went for refreshments. Lizzy clasped her hands together to avoid fidgeting. She wondered at Darcy's showing up at the box. At their last encounter, he had spurned her flirtation. He would not want her to get the wrong idea now. His sister must have been the one who had wished to come by.

Georgiana's next words seemed to confirm as much. "Miss Elizabeth, I am pleased to see you here tonight. After you mentioned you had tickets, I quite begged my brother to let me come."

"I am glad he allowed it." Lizzy looked on her affectionately. The girl was eager to please, and every bit as sweet as Jane. "Will he let you stay for the pantomime afterward?"

"Certainly not," Darcy said. He did not elaborate.

Lizzy bit back a smile. He was a man of few words, which provided his sister no opportunity to argue. Lydia would have wheedled until her parents gave in just to silence her. But Miss Darcy seemed content with her brother's judgement of the situation.

"Mrs. Annesley will accompany me home," Georgiana said. And, Lizzy suspected, a strong footman besides.

Georgiana greeted Jane cordially. Then, she said, "Miss Bennet, I hope you will pay your respects to Miss Bingley before the curtain rises. I am sure she longs to see her dear friend from her days in Hertfordshire. She has been telling everyone in the *ton* what an angel you are."

Lizzy scowled, wondering how that could be. Bingley, however, seemed to consider it his cue.

"Splendid idea!" he said, offering Jane his arm. Lizzy watched them in confusion. This all felt planned somehow, as if everyone was in on the scheme except herself. Jane and Bingley said a few words to Lord Greymore and Lady Cressida before departing.

Wearing a sly smile, Lady Cressida whispered in Lizzy's ear. "I see the rumours about Mr. Bingley and your sister are not exaggerated."

"Men can be fickle," Lizzy warned.

"Then we must make sure he is not," Cressida insisted.

Turning to Georgiana, who stood on her other side, Cressida said gaily, "I am sorry you must leave after the drama. I would not allow *my* brother to keep me from staying for the pantomime." She squeezed Georgiana's hand. "Call on me tomorrow afternoon, and I shall tell you about it."

Greymore looked at Darcy. "I have no control over her, I am afraid. My mother spoils her terribly."

"My mother understands what is proper for a young lady," Lady Cressida said crisply, "and what is not. I am safe with her. Brothers are far too restrictive. I hope, Mr. Darcy, you will marry before Georgiana comes out. Your wife may temper your more draconian inclinations."

Darcy looked like a feather might topple him. The next moment, though, he regained his composure. "Can you recommend a potential bride?"

"Oh, I have one in mind, I assure you," Cressida replied. "She is far too good for you, but she might take pity on you. I shall not embarrass her, however, by mentioning her name while she is in earshot. Come, brother, we had best get back to our box before my mother sends a footman after us."

They departed, and the Gardiners returned, retaking their seats in the back row. Georgiana grabbed Lizzy by the arm and said in her ear, "Sit with me, I beg you, and do not get up. Miss Bingley has left her box, and I daresay is headed this way."

Too shocked to object, Lizzy complied as Georgiana took the seat on the far end of the front row. Mrs. Annesley sat behind her, alongside the Gardiners. With Lizzy in the middle, Darcy sat in the last empty chair, on Lizzy's other side.

She felt the awkwardness of being situated between him and his sister. Georgiana, however, clutched her arm. She seemed intent on keeping Lizzy from moving to a different place. More than ever, Lizzy felt like an unknowing participant in a game of musical chairs. One orchestrated by Bingley and Georgiana.

Darcy stood again when Caroline and Louisa joined them. "Why Mr. Darcy," Caroline said, "this is where you have gone off to. Miss Elizabeth, what a pleasure to see you. I did not realize you were acquainted with Lady Cressida Marlowe."

"Miss Darcy introduced us," Lizzy said. "She is a lady of such intelligence and grace, one can hardly believe she is in her first season."

"She is the youngest of seven children," Caroline said. "It gives her a worldliness one might not expect in a girl of her age."

"But not unpleasantly so," Darcy interjected.

"Not at all. She is a lovely girl." Caroline did not sound convinced. She turned to Miss Darcy. "Georgiana, are you familiar with this play?"

"Yes," the girl said brightly. "I read it again after Darcy said I could attend."

"Well," said Louisa, "how ambitious of you. Mr. Darcy, I always say that Miss Georgiana Darcy is one of the cleverest ladies of the ton. When she comes out—"

"It may be two or three years before Georgiana comes out," Darcy interrupted. His face was impassive but his tone stern. "Neither of us is in a hurry for it. She is but sixteen, after all. I have brought her to the theatre tonight to further her education, not to make an impression on the *ton*."

"Of course," Louisa said, and Lizzy bit her lip to avoid laughing. There were moments when she did not find Mr. Darcy altogether disagreeable.

Lizzy's mind wandered back to the days she had spent at Netherfield nursing Jane to health. Darcy had remained on the periphery during the evening pursuits. He had not joined in the card games the Hursts had preferred as a pastime. Lizzy had not thought much about it. But perhaps he had long considered Louisa tedious, and had now had his fill of her.

That, along with her presumptions about his sister, might explain his curtness.

Caroline was not deterred by Darcy's mood. She asked Georgiana, "Do you favour the history plays?"

"Not terribly much. *Richard II* is my favourite of Shakespeare's histories, though."

"Mine as well," Lizzy said. "*Richard III* presents a clear case of good versus evil, but *Richard II* is more nuanced."

"Yes, precisely," Georgiana said. "I shall never forget the first time I read the passage about the death of kings. It is so powerful and poignant."

"Oh, yes," Caroline said, "that is a fine speech indeed. It shows your good taste that you recognize it as such."

"That is not a sign of taste," Darcy said, a hint of annoyance breaking through his composure. "It is a sign of an eager mind. Georgiana is not here to put her intellect on display. She is here to learn."

"Oh, Darcy, how you do go on," Caroline said with a titter.

The muscles in Darcy's jaw worked. Despite his otherwise placid demeanour, he appeared to Lizzy as if he might explode.

"It is nearly half past," Lizzy said. "The curtain will rise at any moment."

Darcy gestured towards his chair. "Miss Bingley, Mrs. Hurst, may I offer one of you my seat?"

The sisters looked at one another. Caroline said, "I thank you, no, we had better go join Charles."

With that, having little choice in the matter, they took their leave.

Darcy sat heavily beside Elizabeth. "Well done," she said.

Georgiana let out a little giggle. Lizzy thought she saw a look pass between Miss Darcy and Mr. Bingley, who was sitting in the box across the way. His chair was so near Jane's, she would have been in his lap if they had been any closer. His two sisters made their way into the box moments before the curtain began to rise.

"They talk about my sister as if she were a trained monkey," Darcy said. His voice was so low, Lizzy was not sure whether he spoke to himself or to her.

"That reflects on them," Lizzy said, "not on Miss Darcy."

He turned to her, his eyes incisive. He did not speak, however, but turned back towards the stage as the play began.

Lizzy whispered to Georgiana, "Would you not prefer to sit in the middle, next to your brother?"

"Thank you, but I prefer to be on the end in case I need to step out to the retiring room."

Lizzy nodded, though she did not believe that excuse for a

moment.

Miss Darcy was matchmaking. Bingley seemed to be in on it. But why? How could anyone think Lizzy and Darcy would suit? As for Darcy himself, he seemed ignorant of the efforts being made on their behalf.

Yet here he was, sitting next to her instead of in his own box. Instead of next to Caroline. Had that been his reason for staying? Was Lizzy the lesser of two evils?

Surely that must be the answer. At intermission, he would likely go off and sit with Lord Greymore or some other of his set.

Throughout the performance, Georgiana was a delightful companion. Her pleasure in the acting and the spectacle was contagious. Lizzy could not help being carried away by her enthusiasm. The two of them joked together as if they were old friends.

For his part, Darcy seemed to relax as the play progressed. His rigid posture softened as he focused on the action. The tight set of his features eased. At one point, he even smiled, and Lizzy felt a strange tugging in her chest. He truly was the most handsome man of her acquaintance, as much as she hated to admit it.

At intermission, he and Mr. Gardiner went to get lemonade for the ladies. Miss Darcy grabbed Lizzy's hand and said in low tones, "Whatever you do, do not stand up."

Lizzy leaned towards her. "Not unless the Queen appears, or the Prince of Wales."

Georgiana smiled gaily and continued holding her hand. "What fun this is! I hope you do not mind Darcy and me invading your box."

"Not at all. I am pleased you could join us."

Georgiana's expression turned suddenly teary. "I have always wanted a sister, but for a while, I feared I might get stuck with someone like Miss Bingley. She is beautiful and sophisticated and full of compliments, but she is not kind. I desperately want a sister who is kind."

Lizzy turned to her and held both Georgiana's hands. "Your brother loves you. When he chooses a wife, he will keep your interest at the top of his mind. I have no doubt of that."

"It is difficult for him," Miss Darcy said. "He is not at ease with women he does not know well. For that matter, he has known Lady Cressida her whole life, yet you see how stiff he is with her."

Lizzy nodded, some part of her feeling sympathy for Darcy's discomfort. She opened her mouth to say more on the subject. However, the gentlemen returned, putting a quick stop to the conversation.

To Lizzy's surprise, Darcy stayed in the Gardiners' box. Two of his cousins stopped by to greet them. Male cousins. Handsome, young, and single cousins. Well-dressed, well-mannered sons of an earl.

Oh, my. Lizzy's belly fluttered at so much male beauty.

Dr. Peter Fitzwilliam, unlike his siblings, was fair-haired and blue-eyed. Though tall and slim, he showed no hint of gauntness. His expression was intense and serious, as if a smile might break it. His aloof demeanour reminded her of Darcy's.

By contrast, the reverend Mr. Joshua Fitzwilliam had a face full of mirth. His complexion was golden, as if he were sunburnt despite the dreary weather. His eyes were almost black. His hair had a slight curl to it, and his manner seemed equally insouciant.

"Miss Elizabeth Bennet," Joshua said with a bow, "it is a pleasure to meet you. My cousin has been singing your praises since Christmas, and now you are the talk of the town."

Lizzy had no idea how to respond to that nonsense, so she simply said, "You are too kind, sir."

"I expect my mother has sent round her card," Joshua continued, "to welcome you to the neighbourhood. But I warn you, it is a very serious business, joining the circle of the Countess of Matlock."

"Is it?" Lizzy asked, feigning astonishment.

"Miss Elizabeth," Peter said, "is Miss Bennet with you this evening? I had hoped to meet her."

"She is in Mr. Bingley's box, with his sisters." Lizzy nodded in that direction.

In fact, Bingley's sisters could not have sat any *further* from Jane. Not in the confined space of the box. She was decidedly *with* Bingley, and not his sisters. But it would not have been proper to say so.

Peter looked in the direction Lizzy indicated. "I should have guessed as much. Good heavens," he said as his gaze landed on Jane, "she is as beautiful as they say."

"No more so than Miss Elizabeth," Joshua said jovially.

"I concur," Darcy said. "Beauty is a matter of taste. But you will find that both the Bennet sisters have more than their looks to recommend them."

Lizzy stared. What rubbish was he speaking? If Darcy wanted to discourage her from flirting with him, this was not the way to do it. If she did not know his opinion of her so well, she would almost have found his words encouraging.

Thankfully, she was not foolish enough to be misled. Mr. Darcy had no serious interest in her. But given the praise of men like Lord Greymore and Mr. Fitzwilliam, the season might hold promise for her yet.

Chapter 13

Darcy was a man who valued family above all things. The Matlock estate in Derbyshire was just ten miles from Pemberley. He had grown up with his Fitzwilliam cousins as his companions. In age he fell between Richard and Peter. Some days it felt as if there were five boys in the Fitzwilliam clan rather than four.

But at that moment, Josh was fawning over Elizabeth as if she were a prize mare he wanted to saddle. Darcy wished his cousins gone.

He looked about the theatre with sudden awareness of how the situation must seem. To Darcy's mind, he had accompanied his sister to chat with a friend. They ended up sitting with her during the first half of the play. To observers, though, Darcy had singled out Miss Elizabeth Bennet. Now, he was introducing her to his family.

Good heavens.

In a sense, he ought to be pleased. Such a compliment from his family would raise her standing. Especially if the countess called on the Bennet sisters, as it seemed she might. Miss Elizabeth would find more success in the marriage mart, securing her future.

Josh would, in fact, be a fine candidate. Despite his calling to the church, he was a jovial fellow, and likely to be made a bishop. The role of a clergyman's wife would suit Miss Elizabeth. So why did hot anger burn in Darcy's chest at the thought of it?

Expressing a desire to be introduced to the elder Miss Bennet, Josh and Peter took their leave. Darcy realized he ought to go, too. He had accidentally distinguished Elizabeth. He should sit with another lady during the rest of the play.

Lady Cressida, for instance. She was of his station. The gossips would consider her a proper match for him, and have nothing to say on the subject.

He did not want to generate speculation about himself and Elizabeth. Her hopes might be raised. He could not abide the thought of causing her pain, if he did not make her an offer.

Did that make him an arrogant fool? Thinking she would wish for his attentions? If she was husband hunting, perhaps she would prefer Greymore and his title.

The Earl of Greymore was a friend of his, a man of excellent character and cheerful disposition. Earlier, the man had surveyed Miss Elizabeth's person appreciatively. The look had not been exactly lewd, but Darcy had been tempted to plant him a facer.

Not that Darcy could fault Greymore for admiring her. Elizabeth looked particularly lovely that evening. A gown of pale pink showed her figure to good effect. Her dark, thick curls were piled high on her head and woven with silk roses. And when she chatted about the play, true pleasure brightened her eyes and her smile. She outshone the theatre's glittering chandeliers.

How the devil had he ended up sitting next to her? And Jane was across the way, seated with Bingley.

Darcy looked sideways at his sister. This had not happened by accident. He was not pleased that Giana and Bingley had adopted the habit of scheming together. Especially when that scheme involved his being in company with Elizabeth Bennet.

He ought to bow and take his leave. There might be room in his cousins' box.

But his cousins were settling into Bingley's box. Peter was in front next to Miss Bennet, and Josh behind next to Miss Bingley. The sight of it pleased him.

Peter was not a romantic sort. Miss Bennet might make a good match for him. He would not mind an indifferent wife as long as she possessed beauty, grace, and a placid nature.

And if Josh were to take Miss Bingley off Darcy's hands, he would be most grateful.

Not that he thought Josh had any real interest in her. His flirtatious nature won him the admiration of many women. But he was five-and-twenty, and unlikely to marry soon. Caroline did not need to know that, however.

When had Darcy grown so weary of her? At one time, he had thought her a kindred spirit. Now, Caroline's false friendship towards Giana had begun to appear more sinister.

Giana had already been deeply hurt by one who had pretended to care for her. She did not need to go through that a second time. Fortunately, she had seen Caroline's overtures for what they were.

And what of Elizabeth? Could she be trusted with Giana's friendship? Elizabeth had flirted with him at tea earlier in the week. But this evening, all her attention had been showered on his sister. He almost felt as if he did not exist, sitting here at the edge of their conversation. Caroline would have tried to involve him every other minute. Elizabeth seemed content to ignore him.

He was not sure how he felt about that. He must seem immensely stupid to her, sitting here in silence. She did not like it when he was reticent in company. She had suggested that it made him seem as if he thought he was above them.

Was that true? Ought he to be more attentive to the comfort of others? Bingley did it naturally. He was not bothered by Mrs. Bennet as Darcy was, because Bingley enjoyed people in all their variety. Darcy was too easily put off by those outside his station or those unknown to him. But it was not misanthropy. He did not understand what strangers expected of him.

Giana and Mrs. Annesley went to the ladies' retiring room. Elizabeth turned her attention to Darcy. "How are you enjoying the play?"

He was happy to have her bright eyes on him. "It is well done."

She nodded and looked at him a moment, then said, "You are a man of few words, Mr. Darcy."

He could not tell whether her tone was flirtatious or disapproving. "You consider that a deficiency in my character."

She gave a little titter, a pleasing, musical sound. "Not at all. I have lived enough amongst those who err in the opposite direction to appreciate the value of silence."

He could not help smiling at that. "There are those who have the gift of making themselves amiable to strangers. It is not one I possess."

She motioned toward the stage. "I imagine the actors performing tonight were not always as skilled as they are now. I assume they have reached this level of proficiency through practice. A man of your education cannot be ignorant of suitable topics to discuss. Besides, you and I cannot be called strangers. We once lived three days together under the same roof."

The memories brought a lightness to his chest. "And you were a delightful addition to the company at Netherfield."

"Was I?"

He frowned. It was not like Elizabeth to fish for compliments. Yet it seemed odd to him that her question might be sincere. "Do you doubt it?"

"You did not seem to think so at the time," she said

Her words sent a cold dread through him. "On the contrary, I was grateful for it," he said. Had she been ignorant of how her presence in the house affected him? He had thought himself utterly transparent. Too much so. "I grant that I did not flatter you as Bingley did—"

"I have not known Mr. Bingley to flatter. He speaks with the simple joy in his heart."

Darcy bristled, but then thought a moment. His shoulders eased. "I would agree with that."

"And you, Mr. Darcy, prefer to remain a mystery."

His eyes searched her face. Was that how he appeared to her? "I would say that I am private. I do not wish to be mysterious. I would rather not be noticed at all."

She fluttered her fan. "Because you find most people tedious."

He had nothing to say to that, so he remained silent.

She raised her fan, hiding her mouth. Was she laughing at him?

"I cannot help but wonder," she said, "what kind of boy you were. You must have been an excellent and well-behaved student. And yet you were not taught to overcome your reserved nature. A gentleman is expected to put himself forward. You struggle to carry on a conversation with anyone not of your circle."

He eyed her with shock at her effrontery. "I am perfectly capable of carrying on conversations with farmers and tradesmen—"

"Of course, if you are discussing practical matters. But when it comes to small talk..." She flicked her fan closed.

Her words prickled at him, and his stomach tightened. He said, "Small talk serves no purpose."

"It helps people find common ground. Without it, the social order would break down."

He eyed her quizzically, thinking she must be joking. But her expression was deadly serious.

"Come, Mr. Darcy, we must not quarrel. I have grown fond of your sister. I shall therefore make allowances for your idiosyncrasies."

"And I for your impertinence."

She touched her fan to his arm as she had done once before, and the action had the same effect. A shiver ran through him as if she had placed her hand on his bare skin, branding him.

He looked at her deeply. "Are you still trying to make out my character?"

"I am even more confused about it than I was at the Netherfield ball. Your old friend Mr. Wickham had done me the service of confirming every negative impression I had of you. Now, I have no idea what is real, what is imagined, and what is an outright lie."

"May I be so bold as to ask, what sort of negative impressions?"

"He assured me you were proud. But then, he said the same about Miss Darcy, and that was a lie."

Ire rose in Darcy's chest. "Georgiana has not a bit of worldly pride about her. As for myself...I confess that my mother taught me to take pride in my lineage. I hope I do not set myself above others on that basis."

She gazed at him pensively. "Your friendship with Bingley suggests an egalitarianism that I find refreshing. Others of your station might refuse to associate with one whose fortune came from trade."

"I hope I am not so scrupulous as to pass judgement based on such criteria."

Her eyes grew pensive. "You seem to care less about breeding than manners."

"I believe that is true."

"And that is why you consider my sister Jane to be unsuitable for Mr. Bingley. My family's place in the gentry dates back to Henry VIII. Mr. Bingley's dates back to his matriculation at Eton. Yet my mother sometimes shows a lack of tact, and that is unpardonable. In truth, I believe Mr. Bingley's mother would have shared more in common with *my* mother than with yours."

Her words silenced him. She was right, of course. Why had he not thought of it before? Bingley had likely grown up in a home no more cultured than the Bennets', and possibly less so. Of course Mrs. Bennet did not shock him as she did Darcy.

But Elizabeth's barbed comments were shockingly frank. Neither of them ought to acknowledge the *tendre* between Bingley and Jane.

Yet it was not the first time they had done so. It would be the height of hypocrisy to pretend otherwise.

Darcy's thoughts swam. He struggled to find his voice. He knew he must speak. The moment was critical. If he did not concede the fairness of her assessment, she would forever see him as an arrogant, unfeeling man. One worthy of the scorn that Wickham's lies had inspired in her, even if for different reasons.

"I beg your pardon," he began, his speech halting. "I have been unfair to you and your sister. I hope you see that by allowing my sister's friendship with you, I do not regard my family as above yours."

She eyed him pensively. "You make a good point," she acknowledged with a smile.

In that moment, she looked far too beautiful for him to keep his countenance. He had never admired a woman so much. His heart lurched at the thought.

Could he trust his feelings? Elizabeth Bennet *needed* to marry. What if everything Darcy had seen of her had been some machination designed to lure him in?

Yet he could not believe that. Her devotion to her sister during Jane's illness at Netherfield had not been feigned. Elizabeth had shown no attempt at ingratiating herself to the residents. She had spent most of her time in the sick room, or else alone while Jane was resting. Even in the evenings, while the rest of the party had played at cards, she had mostly read in a secluded corner.

Which had given him many opportunities to observe her unnoticed. To watch her animated expression as it showed the changing emotions inspired by the book. She was lovely when the liveliness of her mind played across her features. Breathtaking, even. Which explained why, at that moment, he found it difficult to breathe.

He realized he was staring. Her brows arched at him. He ought to say something, but what?

Words of love sat on his lips, aching to be spoken. But it was far too soon for anything like that. The two of them had spent little time in company during the five months of their acquaintance. They were still getting to know each other. He had no idea what was in her heart.

Fortunately, Giana and Mrs. Annesley returned. They settled into their chairs, distracting Elizabeth's attention. The play resumed a minute later.

Through the second half, Elizabeth seemed to take pity on him. She involved him more in the witty remarks she shared with Georgiana. She did not distract from the drama, but rather enhanced it with her observations. Poor Giana fought to stifle her laughter.

All too soon, the play ended to rousing applause. With a pout, Giana rose to depart, Mrs. Annesley by her side. Mr. Gardiner offered to take them in his carriage, as Mrs. Gardiner had grown tired. He asked if Darcy and Bingley could escort the Miss Bennets home.

Darcy could see two ulterior motives for this offer. First, Gardiner wished to be alone with his wife. Second, he wanted Jane to have more time in Bingley's company. Darcy could not begrudge the man on either point.

He felt secure in answering for Bingley, saying the arrangement was amenable. The comfort of Caroline and Louisa would prove no impediment. They had come in Hurst's carriage, and so would take the same conveyance home to Grosvenor Street.

The Gardiners went to say their goodbyes to Jane. They sent her and Bingley to join Darcy and Elizabeth, in order to preserve the proprieties. Darcy was glad. He had no wish to go back to his box and sit near Caroline. Thankfully, his cousins seemed content to remain with Bingley's sisters.

Darcy ought to have found the entire situation untoward. He did not. The pantomime was most diverting, and laughter lowered his defences.

More than once, his eyes met Elizabeth's. They shared a smile in their mutual enjoyment of the performance. She was —heaven help him—quite the most beautiful creature he had ever seen when she laughed. There was nothing for it. Every moment, his attraction to her grew. Every moment, he felt himself falling more in love with her.

He was, he was certain, a complete fool. He had been in love with her since before leaving Netherfield. Probably since her stay there while Jane was ill. He had witnessed sisterly affection before, and selfless devotion. But he had not seen those qualities mixed with the wit and animation Elizabeth possessed.

Her virtue was not cold. She was not an angel, as the Bingleys were so fond of calling Jane. No, Elizabeth was a flesh-and-blood woman. Pert and sometimes irreverent, she possessed as much true goodness as anyone he had met.

If he let her go, he would not encounter another woman like her.

∞∞∞

During the ride home, Elizabeth was weary. She was not yet accustomed to town hours. It would have been easy to close her eyes, to rest her head on Darcy's shoulder, but she did not dare.

Jane and Bingley, on the opposite bench, spoke in low tones. Jane's wrapper hid their hands, which Lizzy was sure were entwined beneath it. She was not so missish as to see anything improper in it, so she made no comment.

Lost in thought, she startled when Darcy said to her, "You enjoyed yourself this evening."

Regaining her composure, she smiled at him. "I did, though it may not be fashionable to admit it. I should say something about how the actor who played Bolingbroke was past his prime. Or how King Richard's gestures were too exaggerated for my tastes. But I thought the entire evening was splendid. Which must confirm your opinion that I am horribly provincial."

He gave a little chuckle, and her heart lifted at the sound.

"I would not characterize you as such," he countered. "I would call you delightfully refreshing."

"Why, Mr. Darcy, you must not say so. You will turn my head."

"On the contrary. I expect you see me with perfect clarity."

She narrowed her brow. "I appreciate the compliment, sir, but it is misplaced." In truth, she still could not read him.

He gazed at her a long moment. "I wonder. I believe I am more likely to deceive myself than I am to deceive you."

She tilted her head, unsure what to make of that remark. A man as diffident as Darcy might well be distanced from his own emotions. But he was a puzzle to her.

"You give me too much credit," she said gently. "All my impulses about you have been in error so far. While I can see where I have been wrong in the past, I cannot say I have got the right of you in the present."

"Then we are even, at least."

She gathered her pink and cream shawl closer about her. "Why, Mr. Darcy, are you trying to make out *my* character?"

"I believe I am well acquainted with it. You are devoted to family and friends. You accept the absurdity of life with good humour. You do not take yourself or anyone else too seriously."

She pondered his words, surprised at how complimentary they were. Yet she did not care to be thought frivolous. "I take matters seriously when they *are* serious. Often, though, we give weight to situations that will be forgot a day or a week later. Do you not agree?"

"True. I can be too serious, too deliberative. Sometimes one choice is as good as another, and inaction the worst choice of all."

She nodded slowly. "Precision is important in some cases. When it comes to relations with our neighbours, kindness is often what counts most."

He grew pensive a moment. "It is difficult for me to approach matters lightly. I hate to look a fool."

"You give people too much credit, sir. Even while in

conversation, they are thinking about what to say next, rather than listening to you."

Darcy feigned horror. "You mean I am wasting my time, delivering my words with the éclat of a proverb?"

Lizzy let out a laugh, then covered her mouth. She had made that accusation during the ball at Netherfield. "Nay, you are too naughty, teasing me with my own words."

Their eyes met, and they smiled. His dark, intense gaze glittered in the lamplight and pierced the wall around her heart. He was not the uncaring man she once thought him.

The carriage rocked, sliding her against him. He was solid and warm. Her body wanted nothing more than to curve into him, to inhale his unique scent of wool and spice.

This man was so much more complex than she had given him credit for in Hertfordshire. He fascinated her. She wanted to know everything about him.

She considered how devoted he was to his sister. How wrecked he must have been when Wickham had nearly kidnapped the girl for the sake of her dowry. She eyed Darcy softly. "May I ask you a question about Mr. Wickham?"

His expression grew wary. "If you like."

"Were you close as boys?"

He was silent a moment. Some deep emotion passed over his face. She could not read it in the dim light, but she suspected it was sorrow. "We were inseparable," he said. "Wickham was the nearest thing I had to a brother."

She nodded, letting that sink in. She imagined how it might feel if she was betrayed by her best girlhood friend. Charlotte Lucas, now Mrs. Collins, was married to Mr. Bennet's heir. What if she ordered Lizzy's family out of Longbourn immediately upon Mr. Bennet's death? What if she left them homeless and nearly destitute?

Lizzy could not picture it. Charlotte could not be so cruel. And yet, Darcy must have once thought the same of Wickham.

"His treachery must have been devastating."

Darcy's eyes widened. "I thought only of my sister."

"You may well believe that. I do not. He wounded you, Mr. Darcy, and I am sorry for it. I cannot believe you could have deserved such duplicity."

"My sister certainly did not."

She allowed him his pride. "You said it might be two or three years before she makes her come-out. Do you really think it necessary to wait that long?"

His jaw hardened. "I am determined she shall not come out before her eighteenth birthday. Beyond that, it will be her choice."

Lizzy nodded, pleased with the answer. "I realize my opinion holds no weight with you, especially given how young Lydia was when she came out—"

"Did you have aught to do with that?" he asked with an ironic smile.

"I begged my parents not to permit it. Unfortunately, I hold no sway with my mother. As for my father, he seemed to believe that it was better to keep peace in the household. If Lydia made a fool of herself, she would learn sooner how to behave. As you must have noticed, however, Meryton society does not always keep to the proprieties."

Darcy gazed at her with those acute eyes that seemed to penetrate her soul. "Lydia is very young. Her character is not fully formed."

"She has always been a charming child. If her mind was put to good use..." Lizzy let her voice trail off. There was no point in finishing that sentence.

"You are not to blame for the failings of others. I have not found your judgement lacking. Especially when it comes to the improvement of young women. Your opinions about my sister are welcome."

She looked at him gratefully. His words were kinder than she deserved. "I worry that the longer your sister waits before coming out, the more fearful she might become. She has been hurt by Mr. Wickham, but she also learnt from that mistake. I believe the experience has taught her caution. But she is shy by nature. Making her curtsey to the queen and coming out into society…the prospect must intimidate her. The sooner she puts the initial experience behind her, the happier she will be. If she spends years dreading it, the situation will loom larger than necessary."

Darcy nodded slowly. "I see your point. If she does make her come-out, I do not wish her to enter the marriage mart before the age of one-and-twenty."

Her lips parted at that. She eyed him a moment, then gave him a wry smile. "I am not yet one-and-twenty. Do you consider me too young to marry?"

He startled, appearing disconcerted, and did not reply.

The carriage pulled up in front of the house on Berkeley Square. The footman helped the ladies out, and the gentlemen walked them to the door. "Thank you for a lovely evening," Darcy said, raising Lizzy's gloved hand to his lips. "Your kindness to my sister is most appreciated."

"You need not thank me for that," Lizzy said. "She is a sweet girl. I am happy to call her friend."

Darcy said no more but pressed her hand before departing. She watched him head back to the carriage, giving him a wave before turning to enter the house. Though her body was weary, her mind could not stop turning over the events of the evening. Something had changed between her and Darcy that night, and she had no idea where it would lead.

Chapter 14

Darcy rode his mare in Hyde Park the next morning whilst most of the fashionable set was still abed. The sun hung low in the eastern sky, and frost clung to the grass. The rhythm of hoof beats soothed his mind.

He could not stop thinking about Miss Elizabeth Bennet. The pleasure of her company at the play had turned into an agony of longing as he had lain alone in bed. He had lost his sanity—that was the only explanation for it. How else could he consider making the woman his wife, when he knew her so little?

Her presence in a house just steps away from his uncle's had made his predicament even more difficult. They would be thrown together constantly. Could he resist making a fool of himself?

If he wanted to marry, the countess could introduce him to the most eligible daughters of the peerage. Elizabeth had nothing to offer but herself. That alone, he had to admit, enticed him more than a favourable connection or a vast fortune.

In the weeks after he had left Hertfordshire, he had felt an absence in his life. And when he had spotted her a few weeks ago, huddled against the rain, that emptiness had been filled again.

Would he allow this infatuation to override all other inducements? Could he endure a life without her?

Women of the *ton* did not scold him for his reticence, nor

puzzle out his character. They gave him bland smiles and talked on harmless subjects. They did not leave him with the disturbing sensation they were laughing at him.

No. They allowed him to keep his equanimity. To spend an evening without being swamped by a tumult of emotion.

Elizabeth was beautiful, and he wanted her physically. He admired her brilliant mind and her kind heart. But the feelings she brought out in him were chaotic.

Was that what he wanted in a wife? And could this woman, so aware of his every fault, give him the love he desired?

He considered his options and concluded there were three. First, marry her; second, forget her; and third, find another.

Marrying her was out of the question, at least until he knew her well enough to trust her motives. Forgetting her was impossible. That left the third option.

He galloped along the tan and gravel path of Rotten Row. As he rode, empty stretches of grass and copses of trees flowed past in the distance. He took a mental inventory of the eligible young ladies of his acquaintance.

Darcy's choices were not as plentiful now as they would be after Easter. Lady Cressida was a clever girl, as well as beautiful and kind. But she was little more than a child. Miss Peabody he instantly rejected. He saw no harm in her, but she was insipid and lacked any sort of intellectual curiosity.

Lady Carson's two daughters, Ursula and Eugenia, were perfectly eligible. Ursula, the elder, was blonde and classically pretty. However, she had an aloofness he did not like. She would not be the caring sister Georgiana wished for.

Her sister Eugenia was arresting with her chestnut hair and green eyes. She was also more personable. Her conventionality bored him, though. He had never heard her speak an original thought.

And then there was Lady Belinda Fellows, daughter of the Earl of Featherstone. She was a dark-haired beauty, blue-eyed and wasp-waisted. But the few times he had conversed with her, he found her haughty and ill tempered. Whether she was spiteful by nature or merely peevish, he did not wish to further the acquaintance.

He might as well accept the fact. He would find an objection to every woman he considered. His heart had already made its choice.

When he had seen Elizabeth standing under that awning in the pouring rain, he could have ridden on. But no, he had immediately signalled for his driver to stop, and swept her into his carriage—and back into his life.

Because that was where he wanted her. In his life, in his bed, in his home forever. Did anything else matter?

Yet courting her openly was out of the question. Not until he was committed to making an offer. Given her circumstances, he could not risk creating expectations.

In the meantime, he must preserve Elizabeth's reputation. After their familiarity the night before, gossip would be spreading through the *ton*.

But how?

Perhaps a diversion.

He thought back to something Lady Cressida had said the night before. He had not given much thought to her pronouncement at the time. She had tossed it about as one of those meaningless things ladies say when speaking of love.

Yet in retrospect, it had been full of meaning. She had said she had a wife in mind for him. A woman who was in hearing distance.

The only women in hearing distance had been herself, Giana, Mrs. Annesley...and Miss Elizabeth Bennet.

Blast! Was the entire *ton* scheming to bind them together?

Clearly, Lady Cressida was not attached to Darcy. She had so many suitors, she would hardly notice one more. It could do no harm if he seemed to court her, to distract attention away from Elizabeth.

He hated dissembling, but he needed to put distance between himself and Elizabeth in the *ton*'s eyes. Given her lack of fortune, the vultures would not be kind.

He slowed his pace to a cantor. By the time he returned to Darcy House, his mind was more at ease. With a light heart and a casual air, he spoke to the butler. He ordered flowers sent to Lady Cressida Marlowe with Darcy's regards.

He changed out of his riding clothes and went to the breakfast room. Georgiana joined him as he sat at the table to a meal of kippers, eggs, and toast.

Bingley had not yet come downstairs. After a late evening, it was his habit to stay in his rooms, where his valet would take him a tray.

Bingley's absence was just as well. It allowed Giana to speak uninterrupted about the fun she had had the previous evening. In an animated voice, she asked, "Was not Miss Elizabeth Bennet the most charming company?"

"She was indeed," Darcy answered honestly, adding cream to his coffee.

"I have not met anyone," Giana continued, "whom I would so wish to have as a sister."

Darcy looked at her a long while. *Et tu, Brute?* "It is too soon to discuss anything of that sort."

Giana arched her brows. "You are enamoured of her. It will do you no good to deny it. I can see it in the way you look at her, and hear it in the way you speak."

He tapped a soft-boiled egg to break the shell. "I admit to liking her, but do not get carried away. I do not wish to see you disappointed."

"You think less of her because she has no fortune."

Anger rose in his chest. He wanted to chastise her. Yet he realized Giana was not at fault for his strong reaction. Her words had hit too close to home.

He took a deep breath to calm himself before saying, "I do not think less of her. I am more cautious. I underestimated Wickham's determination to marry a rich wife, and it nearly cost you your future. I shall not make that mistake again."

Giana scowled at him, her lips pinched together crossly. "What if I fell in love with a man of her station? Would you forbid me to marry him? Would you call him an adventurer?"

"It depends on the man."

She narrowed her eyes. "Does something else trouble you about Miss Elizabeth, other than her rank?"

An ache formed at his temples. Elizabeth's rank did not concern him. But Giana still showed incredible naïveté when it came to the threat of fortune hunters. Even after Wickham's duplicity.

In consternation, he dropped his fork onto his plate with a clatter. "Giana, our grandfather was an earl. Do you not understand what that means?"

"Mama and Lady Catherine always thought it meant a great deal. For myself, it seems a way for one person to lord themselves over another—something I have no interest in."

Darcy straightened. He did not care for her answer, but he could hardly scold her for it.

Lady Catherine de Bourgh was their mother's sister, and even prouder of her noble blood than their mama had been. Darcy bristled at the comparison between his behaviour and Lady Catherine's. He did not want Giana to think he regarded Elizabeth as his inferior in any way.

How could he explain it to her? Mrs. Bennet was a conniving woman. She and some others in Meryton had behaved with a strange mix of pride and vulgarity. It had aroused a sort of disgust in him.

Yet neither Miss Elizabeth nor her elder sister had shown a hint of vulgarity. They carried themselves with a graceful sort of propriety. One that showed not only an understanding of what the rules were but *why* they were. There was no conceit in them nor rebellion. They were sensible, upright young ladies.

None of that, however, brought him closer to answering Giana's question.

He looked about, making sure Mrs. Annesley was not in hearing range. Then, he spoke to his sister in low tones. "If a man does not have an independent income, he can join the military or enter one of the professions. A respectable woman in the same circumstances can only become a governess or a companion. That means going into service, which means a loss in status. If the Miss Bennets do not marry well, that will be their fate. Under such conditions, a man must be wary of their motives."

Georgiana gazed at him with frank astonishment written on her features. Her eyes were wide, and her lips moved without making a sound. Finally, she said, "I have never heard anything so ridiculous in my life."

Now it was Darcy's turn to be astonished. His sweet, shy little sister had never spoken to him in such a manner. "If this is how you act after spending an evening in the company of Miss Elizabeth Bennet—"

"This is how I act when my brother, who has always been sensible before, starts spouting nonsense. The Miss Bennets are two of the most genuine people I know."

"Georgiana, I shall not countenance this from you."

She narrowed her eyes and crossed her arms. "I would think, given Miss Elizabeth's circumstances, that you would be eager to raise her up. To save her from a life of genteel poverty."

"Of course. But not at the cost of my own happiness. I have no wish to enter into a loveless marriage. I must be certain of her true esteem before I make her an offer."

Giana perked up. A broad smile broke over her face. "Then you are considering it?"

"I have not ruled it out."

"Oh, Darcy!" she jumped from her chair and threw her arms around him.

"This is no cause for celebration." He released her from the hug. "Sit down and eat your breakfast."

Darcy went back to his kippers, but the next moment a giggle escaped his sister's lips. He glared, and she covered her mouth with her hand, composing herself. But in the time it took him to butter a slice of toast, she was laughing again.

∞∞∞

After finishing his meal, Darcy went to his study to read his correspondence. At the top of the stack was an invitation to Lady Greymore's ball. He lifted his brows at this turn of luck. The event gave him an excuse to call on Lady Cressida and further his plan.

As it was nearly eleven, he made haste and found the ladies at home. "Lady Greymore, delightful to see you again," he said as the servant showed him into the drawing room. "Lady Cressida." He bowed over her hand.

"Mr. Darcy," the young woman said, "thank you for the lilies."

Darcy murmured some pleasantries, satisfied with his butler's choice of flowers.

Lady Greymore gestured for him to sit. As he did so, he said to her, "I was delighted to receive the invitation to your upcoming ball." He turned to the daughter. "Are you free for the first set?"

Lady Cressida blinked a few times, then said, "I am not yet engaged for those dances."

"Then I hope you will do me the honour."

"I would be happy to." The smile she gave him was all civility, but no pleasure shone in her eyes.

A hint of unease swept through him. Perhaps it was unkind to deny her the pleasure of opening the ball with another. A man who sought her heart.

He concluded, however, that it was for a good cause. She was already involved with Georgiana's scheme to unite him with Elizabeth. Diverting the attention of the *ton* was part of that plot.

Even if no one would know it but him.

As it turned out, he had made his request of Cressida just in time. No sooner had Lady Greymore poured the tea than another gentleman caller arrived. Having secured his purpose, Darcy finished his beverage and took his leave. A mere quarter-hour had elapsed since he had arrived. He was gratified that the business had been handled efficiently.

The only delay came when he passed by Lord Greymore on the way out. They greeted each other on the stone steps beneath the sprawling branches of a plane tree. Darcy explained the purpose of his visit.

Greymore frowned. "I had expected you to dance the first set with Miss Elizabeth Bennet."

Darcy stiffened. As expected, the speculation had begun already. "I admit, she has become a dear friend of my sister. That is the extent of the relationship I can claim between our two families."

Greymore nodded slowly. "I am glad to know it."

Darcy did not like that look. Still, he did not question it. He would seem too eager. Instead, he tipped his hat, and was on his way.

He arrived home a little before noon. Bingley had not yet come downstairs but likely soon would. Perhaps they would head to their club.

Darcy was dreading the gossip about himself and Elizabeth that might be circulating. Beguiled by her presence, he had not been as circumspect as he should have been the night before. He had better take action to stop the rumours before they got out of hand.

If a bit of pretence would protect her, then that was a price he was willing to pay.

While waiting for Bingley, he went back to his study to finish his correspondence. He was reading a letter from his steward when the butler announced the Countess of Matlock. At the mere sound of her name, Darcy knew the morning's gossip must have been every bit as bad as he feared.

She stepped in looking regal, dressed for an afternoon of visiting. With two unmarried daughters, she was still very much a fixture in the London social scene.

Darcy kissed her cheek, and she got to the point at once, not bothering to waste her breath on pleasantries. "According to the latest *on-dit*," she said, "I will soon have cause to wish you joy."

He kept his features as still as marble. "If you refer to Miss Elizabeth Bennet—"

"I cannot say I am surprised by this latest news. You were a lovesick puppy at Christmas. You sighed and brought up her name at every opportunity, even though none of us knew her from Eve."

Darcy stared at her in surprise. "I do not deny that I admired her, but I was certainly not lovesick."

She waved her hand, as if his denial was inconsequential. "And what about now?"

His face heated. "I am not courting Miss Elizabeth."

"Then you will not mind if Josh courts her."

Anger flooded his chest. Was this why she had come? She was not one to meddle, but somehow that made her interference even more irritating to him. "Josh?"

"He says the much-praised beauty of the elder Miss Bennet is nothing to her sister's."

Darcy gazed at her, dumbfounded. This must be a joke. Josh could not truly have intentions towards Elizabeth. He had just met the chit. "Does he realize she is nearly penniless?"

His aunt levelled a look at him, eyes narrow, lips pinched. "Indeed, I received a letter to that effect this morning from Lady Catherine. She had heard that the Bennet sisters were in town and sought to warn me about them. Their cousin—their father's heir—is rector in Lady Catherine's parish, you know."

Darcy knew. He remembered the fool well.

Lady Matlock pulled a sheet of paper from her beaded reticule and lifted her quizzing glass. "Let me find the passage…ah, yes, here it is. 'The ladies can expect no more than their share of their mother's five thousand pounds at its four per cents.' The accounting of the Bennet fortune is quite detailed."

Darcy surveyed her as she put away the letter. The countess's intellect was infinitely superior to that of his other aunt. Where Lady Matlock was perceptive, Lady Catherine was imperious. Where Lady Matlock was curious, Lady Catherine was opinionated. At the moment, Lady Matlock seemed unaffected by her sister-in-law's concerns.

"Certainly Josh wants a wife with more promising prospects," Darcy suggested.

"Why should he? He will have the Matlock living as soon as the old rector retires. And I daresay he shall have a bishopric five or ten years hence. Lord Matlock has his eye on one of the more lucrative ones."

Darcy paced, struggling to understand what he was hearing. Was his own cousin truly a rival? "You would approve a match between Josh and Miss Elizabeth Bennet?"

"That is impossible to say. I have not met the girl. You must hold a high opinion of her, if you let Georgiana spend time with her."

"Georgiana is not going to marry her."

She took out her kid gloves, signalling her intention to be on her way. "Is the lady respectable?"

"Certainly."

"Then I have no objection to Josh courting her, if he so chooses." She watched Darcy a moment, then said with a wry smile, "Do you?"

His chest tightened. He would call out his cousin before he saw him wed Elizabeth Bennet. But he did not want to tip his hand too soon. "Of course not."

"Then it is settled." His aunt took her leave, sweeping out of the room with aplomb, head held high. Her features bore no hint of mischief.

Chapter 15

A surprise greeted the Bennet sisters the morning after the play. Bouquets of hothouse flowers crowded their drawing room. The roses from Mr. Bingley brought a delighted cry from Jane. When tulips from Lord Greymore arrived for Lizzy, she was rendered speechless. He had said some pretty things to her the night before, but nothing she would have described as flirting. Such a gallant gesture from him was unexpected.

Good heavens, if her mother knew Lizzy had received flowers from an earl—! The poor woman would have an apoplexy.

Lizzy, however, would not plan her wedding just yet. It amused her to think Greymore might send flowers to half a dozen young ladies after every assembly. As she understood it, he was fantastically wealthy and could afford such extravagance.

She took up her embroidery and strove to think no more about it. Then, a second wave of flowers arrived. Peter Fitzwilliam sent Jane white amaryllis, while Joshua sent Lizzy red amaryllis. Apparently the brothers had acted in concert, making the whole thing more bewildering.

Perhaps they had arrived home in their cups after a late night at their club. On a lark, they asked the footman to send the flowers the next morning. The more she thought about it, the more likely that explanation sounded.

Lizzy understood the charms she and Jane held for the

opposite sex. They had been much admired in Meryton since making their come-outs. But for men from aristocratic families to notice them in this way...

It seemed unreal. Lizzy thought back to the night before. To her feeling that Georgiana had brought Lizzy and Darcy together. Could she have enlisted her cousins to help with her scheme? And to what end?

A few weeks ago, Darcy had thought Jane unsuitable for Bingley. *Bingley*, who had no family connections at all. Now, Darcy's most illustrious relatives were distinguishing Jane and Lizzy. It made no sense.

She was pondering the situation when Lord Greymore himself arrived. The servant showed him into the front parlour. Lizzy could not help admiring how well he looked in buckskin breeches and a hunter green coat. His blond hair and moustache were immaculately groomed.

He bowed to the ladies and handed an envelope to Mrs. Gardiner. "My mother is sending out invitations to a ball," he explained. "I offered to bring this one personally. Miss Elizabeth, might I have the pleasure of dancing the first set with you?" He met Lizzy's eyes wearing a smile that made him even more striking.

She did her best to hide her astonishment. She could not pretend he was not distinguishing her with *this* gesture. Of all the ladies in London, he would be opening his family's ball with *her*.

An earl. A wealthy one. And handsome besides.

Her heart fluttered, and warmth suffused her skin. The offer was almost unbearably exciting. When she had first made her come-out, she had dreamed of such things. Never had she expected her girlish fantasy would come true.

Aunt Gardiner opened the starched envelope and perused the contents. "We are free that evening, I am pleased to say. I quite look forward to it. I am sure the girls do as well." She looked at Lizzy with a placid smile, but her eyes sparkled.

Lizzy forced herself to speak, though her throat was tight

and her voice thin. "In that case, I would be honoured to stand up with you, your lordship."

"Splendid!" he cried.

Mrs. Gardiner rang for refreshments. Pots of coffee and tea arrived, along with a platter stacked with pound cake and buttered muffins. Accepting a cup of tea and a muffin, the earl stayed for half an hour. After he had gone, Jane and aunt Gardiner turned and looked at Lizzy with bright smiles and arched brows.

"I am no less surprised than you are," she assured them. They laughed together, trying to keep their heads. Mrs. Bennet would faint dead away if she knew an earl had asked Lizzy to open a ball with him. If the flowers had not already killed her.

Her mind awhirl, Lizzy went upstairs and looked through her closet. The blue silk might be a good choice for a ball gown. The neckline was lower than she would normally have chosen, but not scandalous for London. Was she a fool to think Greymore might have some serious interest in her?

A nagging, foolish part of her worried that it was some jest. That he had chosen her for the sole purpose of exposing her country manners. She pushed those silly thoughts aside. She could not afford to lose the chance to make herself agreeable to one of the most eligible men in England.

If she became a countess, it would elevate her family's prospects significantly.

She had promised herself she would never marry solely for the sake of money or position. But so far, she liked Greymore. He was handsome and athletic, with a good sense of humour. From what she knew, he seemed kind.

Of course, Wickham had seemed kind, and what a blackguard *he* had turned out to be.

The doorbell rang, and Lizzy stepped into the hallway. Though she kept out of sight, the strains of female voices reached her ears. One belonged to Lady Arabella Fitzwilliam, and another sounded like Lady Nerissa. Lizzy smoothed her dress, a white sprigged muslin threaded with violets. Then, she headed down the stairs.

"Oh, there you are," her aunt said as Lizzy hovered in the doorway to the front parlour. "I was just about to send Sally to fetch you. Lady Matlock, Lady Jersey, may I present my niece, Miss Elizabeth Bennet."

Lizzy caught her breath, thinking she might faint dead away. She had half expected the Countess of Matlock to call...but Lady Jersey! Lizzy could only marvel.

Lady Matlock appeared to be somewhere between fifty and sixty. Her unweathered face was still attractive. With her high cheekbones and serene smile, her expression was confident but kind. A purple walking dress of sturdy wool was beautifully tailored. The drape flattered her matronly figure. Tendrils of brown curls streaked with grey peeked out from beneath her turban.

Lady Jersey was a little past thirty, dressed fashionably in red. Her bright eyes, aristocratic nose, and kind smile lent her an uncommon prettiness. Dark curls piled high on her head were wrapped in a velvet bandeau.

Lizzy stepped into the room and curtseyed to them. "It is a great honour to meet you."

Lady Matlock moved forward and clutched Lizzy's hands. "I have heard so much about you, my dear, I feel as if I already know you."

"Nothing too frightful, I hope."

"I have been warned about your wit," Lady Matlock said. "Have I cause for concern?"

"Not at all, ma'am. A woman as celebrated for her intelligence and taste as you are has nothing to fear from me. And I am certain I cannot hold a candle to Lady Jersey."

Sarah Villiers, Countess of Jersey, was one of the lady patronesses of Almack's. She was renowned for her cleverness and courtesy. It took much to intimidate Lizzy, but she knew better than to try to match the great lady.

Lizzy nodded to Lady Matlock's two youngest daughters. They expressed pleasure at seeing her. As they all took their seats, Mrs. Gardiner called for tea.

Arabella sat on the couch with Lizzy, while Nerissa took a chair next to Jane. Lizzy was flattered by their attention. And until Jane was engaged, Lizzy would make the most of every available connection.

"I have heard many reports of you," Lady Jersey said, "primarily from people who have never met you." Mirth danced in her eyes. Lizzy wondered how one night at the theatre could have attracted such notice. The interest was gratifying, but it did not feel precisely safe. It increased the pressure on them to meet social expectations.

Lady Jersey continued, "Some say Miss Bennet is a brilliant watercolourist. Others claim she studied oils under a Florentine master. And Miss Elizabeth, some allege you play Beethoven sonatas like a professional. Others say you prefer the harp. I am quite mad to know the truth of it."

Jane's complexion turned a bright red and all power of speech seemed to leave her. It fell to Lizzy to say, "I am sorry to disillusion your ladyship. Jane *does* have a talent for watercolours, and I play the pianoforte tolerably well. But we cannot claim any greater skill than most ladies of the *ton*."

"What a relief that is!" Lady Jersey sipped her tea. "I was quite prepared to be jealous, and now we can be friends instead." She set her porcelain cup back on its saucer with a clink.

She asked about their family, their home in Hertfordshire, and any beaux they left behind. When she learnt that they had no brothers and their father's estate was entailed, she gazed at them with wide eyes.

"I hope you will forgive my saying so," Lady Jersey declared, "but I do not approve of daughters being passed over. I am fortunate that my grandfather had no compunction about girls inheriting." According to rumour, Lady Jersey's grandfather had left her his banking fortune. That made her one of the wealthiest women in England in her own right.

"I understand that your father's heir," Lady Matlock said to the Bennet sisters, "is rector at Hunsford." She turned to Lady Jersey. "That is my sister Catherine's parish."

Lady Jersey offered a wry smile. "I trust she has given you her opinion of him."

"I have never known Catherine to withhold her opinion," Lady Matlock said flatly.

Nerissa, who had been sipping her tea, gave a little cough.

Lady Matlock eyed her daughter pointedly before continuing. "Catherine says he is a respectable sort of man. He is all that propriety demands of him."

Lizzy wondered what sort of woman Lady Catherine was, to describe the fawning Mr. Collins that way.

Lady Jersey cocked her head. "That is high praise. Lady Catherine de Bourgh is quite the stickler. How unfortunate that she rarely travels to London."

"Unfortunate indeed," Lady Matlock said.

Arabella let out a choked laugh, then covered her mouth with her hand. Her mother arched her eyebrows at her. Arabella composed herself and sat up very straight.

Lady Jersey turned to the Bennet sisters again. "Is the waltz danced in your little town in Hertfordshire?"

"Not often enough for my tastes," Lizzy said. "There are some who still consider it scandalous."

"And what do you think, Miss Bennet?" Lady Jersey asked Jane. "Do you approve of the waltz?"

"I would not like to see my youngest sister waltz," Jane said, "as she is still quite impressionable. But I see no reason to object if the lady comports herself in a mature manner."

"I quite agree," Lady Jersey said. "I hope, Miss Bennet, that I shall have the opportunity to see you and your sister waltz at the Greymore ball."

"Thank you, your ladyship. I hope we may oblige you," Jane said.

A thrill of delight passed through Lizzy. On such a brief meeting, Lady Jersey had given them permission to waltz! It seemed a silly convention, granting the lady patronesses of

Almack's that power. But then, as Jane had said, it would be indecorous for naive girls like Lydia to waltz. They could be too easily taken advantage of.

The ladies chatted a few minutes more. Then Lady Jersey made her excuses and took her leave. Lady Matlock and her daughters remained, however.

Lizzy felt the strength of the compliment the Fitzwilliams were paying them. She could not account for it. It must have to do with Darcy's friendship with Bingley, and Bingley's attachment to Jane.

Surely Lady Matlock would not involve herself in Georgiana's scheme to unite Darcy and Lizzy. No, that could not be it at all.

Mrs. Gardiner replenished everyone's tea. Lady Matlock took a sip, then asked Lizzy, "Are you enjoying London?"

"The entertainments are more varied than in our little town of Meryton," Lizzy said, "and the company as well. You must have heard of Miss Darcy's kindness to my sister and me."

Lady Matlock nodded. "Darcy does his best with her, but what does a young gentleman know of the needs of an adolescent girl? It seems you are a blessing to her."

"And she to us." Jane passed a plate of apricot scones. "She and I have much the same taste in books. We quite lose track of time when we talk about them."

"She is trying to teach me Italian," Lizzy said, "but I am impossible at it. I hope we can remain friends with her after the season ends."

"That would be delightful," the countess said. "Hertfordshire is an easy distance from London. I am certain Georgiana would be happy to visit you there, and meet your younger sisters."

Lizzy stiffened. Horror washed over her at the thought of Georgiana being exposed to Lydia and her wild ways.

"My youngest sister is of an age with Miss Darcy," Lizzy said, "but Lydia is a high-spirited girl. I doubt Mr. Darcy would approve—that is to say, I believe he would be cautious..." She looked at her aunt pleadingly.

"Miss Lydia Bennet has just turned sixteen," aunt Gardiner said. "She has not yet attained the maturity one might expect of a young lady in London society."

Lady Matlock nodded slowly at Mrs. Gardiner, then turned to Lizzy quizzically. "But I understood that all your sisters were out."

"Yes, ma'am. Lydia came out at fifteen. Jane and I protested, but my mother was deaf to our pleas. My mother cannot bear to say no to her youngest child."

"Yes, I quite understand," the countess said kindly.

Arabella spoke up forcefully. "I am the youngest of my family, and no one thinks twice of saying no to *me*. Besides two parents telling me what to do, I have four brothers and three sisters as well."

Lady Matlock eyed Arabella fondly, then turned to Mrs. Gardiner. "I have been blessed in all my children. Arabella is a good girl, but the most fearless child I ever saw."

"I am hardly a child," Lady Arabella said with a scowl.

"You are barely an adult," her mother countered.

"You must have a dozen suitors lining up outside your door every morning," Jane said.

Arabella looked at her sister. "Between Nerissa and me, we have three or four. Nerissa might be persuaded to marry this year, but I am in no hurry."

"Nor I for you," the countess said. "I was twenty when I married, and that is quite young enough. Of course, I was mad for Lord Matlock, and determined to have him."

"It was the same with my husband and me," Mrs. Gardiner said. "Though he is twelve years my senior, I knew the moment I met him that I would marry him."

"I had not your certainty," the countess said. "My father was an Italian count, and that was not a mark in my favour. I did not have the peaches-and-cream complexion so desirable in an English lady. Thankfully, white face paint was fashionable at the time."

"Pay no attention to her," Nerissa said. "You should see my parents' wedding portrait. She was a beautiful bride."

"Flattery will not win you any points," the countess warned her daughter with a smile. "Beauty is not the only consideration when it comes to the marriage mart. A woman with a cultivated mind will always be sought after."

"I understand that Miss Elizabeth is a great reader," Lady Nerissa said.

Lizzy stirred her tea, the porcelain cup glazed with a pink rose pattern. "I wonder how I have gotten *that* reputation."

"I believe Miss Bingley said so," Arabella replied.

"Caroline Bingley?" Fury burned in Lizzy's chest, but she soon composed herself. "Miss Bingley seems to be sharing her compliments of Jane and me quite liberally."

"I understand she was intimate with the two of you while in Hertfordshire," Lady Matlock said.

Lizzy shot a quick look at her sister, then spoke with as much politeness as she could manage. "Miss Bingley did indeed seek out a friendship with Jane. As for myself, I would say she tolerated me with equanimity."

"She would have tolerated you better," Jane said, "if Mr. Darcy had not tolerated you so well."

Lizzy flushed, taken aback. The Fitzwilliams seemed to share knowing looks, but Lizzy stared at her sister. Whatever was Jane about? Surely she was giving their visitors a mistaken impression.

Lizzy intervened quickly. "The closest Mr. Darcy ever came to singling me out was asking me to dance at the Netherfield ball. And that was after snubbing me in a rather dramatic fashion at a previous assembly. All in all, I feel safe in saying that Mr. Darcy showed no great regard for my company."

"Yet last night," said Arabella, "he sat with you during the entire play. According to Josh and Peter, at least."

"That was his sister's doing," Lizzy insisted. "I have no doubt Mr. Darcy would have preferred to sit with anyone but me."

"If that were true," Lady Matlock said, "then he would have

done so."

Lizzy let those words sink in. She knew Darcy too well to think he would have sat with her out of politeness. The countess was correct on that point.

More alarming, Lady Matlock suggested she *approved* of Darcy's attention to Lizzy. Had she called this morning to pay her respects to the woman she thought her nephew to be courting? Surely not! Her sons had sent Jane and Lizzy flowers, after all.

"You honour me, your ladyship," Lizzy said to the countess. "I would not contradict you for the world. But I promise you, if rumours are circulating about your nephew and me, they are idle speculation. Mr. Darcy has been kind and solicitous, but he has shown me no particular regard."

"Miss Elizabeth," Arabella said, "you must be unfamiliar with my cousin's disposition. His reserved nature may conceal his ardour. I have never seen him look upon a woman with such admiration as he does you. When we took tea with Georgiana at Darcy House, the man could not take his eyes off you."

Lizzy gave her a wry smile. "If Mr. Darcy looks at me, I can only assume his purpose is to find fault."

"Never say so!" Nerissa protested. "Darcy would not be so uncouth. Besides, he does not suffer those he dislikes. If he found fault in you, he would ignore you."

Lizzy's neck and shoulders tightened, and her head began to ache. Could it be that Darcy admired her? Yet if he did, what did it signify? He was not pursuing her. Nor did she wish him to.

Did she?

How fortunate that she had not entered the London marriage mart when she first made her come-out! At seventeen, her head would have been spinning from the attentions now being paid to her by men of quality. At twenty, she was better able to restrain her hopes.

She wondered whether to put any stock in the interest of Lord Greymore or Mr. Joshua Fitzwilliam. She had often imagined she would marry a clergyman, and one who was an earl's son would be most eligible. To marry an actual earl...that seemed out of reach.

And so did Darcy.

"You must forgive my sister," Jane said. "The first impressions she and Mr. Darcy made on each other were not favourable. She may be loath to concede that his opinion might have changed."

Lizzy's cheeks heated. Could that be true? Her feelings towards him had softened over the previous weeks. But she did not consider herself and Darcy to be on friendly terms. Their interactions continued to be stiff and awkward.

He chafed at the inequality between them. In Hertfordshire, he had made that clear. Mr. Darcy of Pemberley was a man of consequence. He could not take notice of the residents of a backward little town like Meryton.

But then why had he sat in her box at the theatre the previous evening? Had that been for Bingley's benefit, so that he could spend the evening with Jane? If so, did that mean he now condoned Bingley's courtship?

Lizzy's thoughts swirled. She hoped, of course, that Darcy now approved of Jane. And yet, Lizzy wanted more. When she considered that Darcy might be indifferent to herself, her gut clenched.

She had awoken that morning with a sense of well-being, of hope and excitement. Some part of her liked Darcy. Some part of her *longed* for him. But that was not sensible. Apart from his physical attractions, the man was cold, aloof.

Yet he had shown kindness when he rescued her from the rain. Plus, he helped reunite Bingley with Jane.

Even worse, Lizzy was growing excessively fond of Georgiana. The girl was everything Lizzy wished she had in a younger sister. Lady Matlock and her daughters did their best to look after Miss Darcy. Still, she seemed desperate for the companionship and guidance of an older sister.

Lizzy would have to take care. She could not allow her

feelings for the sister to affect her feelings for the man. Not given his dismissiveness of Lizzy the night they met. If he considered himself above her—that did not bode well for the kind of husband he might be.

Now she was thinking nonsense. A man who considered himself above her would not make her an offer.

And she did not want him to make an offer. For if he did, how would she ever refuse him?

Chapter 16

Darcy strolled into his club that afternoon, a low murmur of voices humming through the halls. He spotted Colonel Fitzwilliam talking with the Earl of Greymore and Viscount Wayne. Darcy joined them, settling into an armchair. The cognac leather was soft from wear but the cushions still firm. The aroma of cheroot smoke hung in the air.

They discussed politics and farming practices and the state of the war for nigh on an hour. The four men had been friends since childhood, and Darcy knew he could call on them no matter what befell.

They would have helped him dispense with Wickham, if it had come to that. Fortunately, the man had not meddled with Georgiana in an irreparable manner. Thank heaven she had been spared that.

Greymore and Wayne stood to go to the card room. Before they could head in that direction, a slim young man took a shaky step toward them. "What ho!" Greymore said, clasping the man's shoulders to steady him. "Foxed already, Olimand? It's not even five."

Nigel Fellows, Viscount Olimand, was heir to the Earl of Featherstone. Dressed in the finest clothes London tailors could offer, he was an empty-headed dandy. Heaven help the nation if the wastrel ever took his place in the House of Lords.

Olimand looked at Greymore gloomily. "There's nothing for it. Rickers has bested me at piquet again, and now he's calling in his vowels." He brightened a moment. "Say, you wouldn't lend me a hundred guineas, would you? You're always flush."

"That's because I don't lend money to men who habitually lose at piquet."

"Ha!" Olimand declared. "That's a good one." He laughed as if Greymore had said something uproariously funny.

Then, Olimand's eyes focused, and he seemed to notice Viscount Wayne for the first time. "Wayne!" he cried. "Good to see you, old boy. That reminds me, I must get my wager in the betting books. It's six to one that your brother will ruin an innocent by the end of the season. Ha! Excuse me, gentlemen." He gave an exaggerated bow and wandered off with a veering gait.

Wayne's face paled, and the set of his jaw hardened. Greymore placed a hand on his arm. "Pay no attention to him and his set. They are the most foolish puppies I ever saw."

"Worse than we were?" Richard asked with a wry grin.

"We had Darcy to prevent us having *too* much fun," Greymore said.

Richard chuckled, but Wayne maintained his grim expression. Darcy, for his part, did his best to remain stoic. He was accustomed to the jibes, and they no longer stung. Much.

Wayne and Greymore sauntered off. Darcy said to Richard in a low voice, "Can anything be done about Rolf Peabody?"

His cousin's expression turned serious. "Wayne wants to buy him a commission, but Rolf refuses. His father ought to have forced his hand when he left Oxford. That man always was too lenient with him. Fell for his charm, like so many others."

"It must be difficult to admit your own child is a scoundrel."

"The army would be the best thing for him." Richard spoke with the confidence of a man who has known his place in the world since birth. "And it is his duty. He is the second son."

"I am not certain the word *duty* is part of Rolf's vocabulary."

"I worry about Arabelle. She does not seem to understand that he is no longer the boy she knew from childhood."

Darcy nodded thoughtfully. "She is well chaperoned. And she is aware of Giana's misfortune. She will not allow herself to be alone with the man."

"How is Giana? She seems recovered."

"I believe she is. The shock of Wickham's engagement to Miss King cured her of any remaining illusions about the man. Having Bingley in the house has done her good as well. In him, she sees how a true gentleman treats a lady."

"You do not fear her forming an attachment there?"

"Not at all. She mocks Caroline's hopes in that direction. Giana says Bingley is like a brother to her."

"Glad to hear it."

They lapsed into silence a moment. Darcy sipped his port, then broached a topic he had been putting off. "Your mother tells me Josh is thinking of courting Miss Elizabeth Bennet."

Richard let out a low chuckle. "He is not just thinking about it, my friend. He has sent a shot across the bow."

Heat prickled Darcy's skin. "What do you think of the prospect—your family aligned with the Bennets?"

Richard swirled his brandy before taking a sip. "The family has their idiosyncrasies, to be sure. But Miss Elizabeth and Miss Bennet seem quite lovely."

Darcy nodded thoughtfully. The night before, the ladies had acquitted themselves with as much elegance as any woman of the *ton*. Darcy thought about the vexations of the recent trip to Longbourn, however. "Enough to make up for the embarrassment of their relations?"

Setting down his brandy snifter, Richard sat back in his chair. "I imagine the Bennets are no worse than many others of the country gentry."

"Josh hopes to be a bishop one day. Should he not aspire to a woman from a noble family? It would increase his chances."

"Josh is not the one I am concerned about." Richard dismissed the idea with a wave of his hand. "Josh must always be courting *someone*. It is in his nature to chase after pretty women. He chooses the virtuous ones to make sure he does not catch them. No, Josh is in no hurry to marry. Peter, however..."

Darcy startled. "What about Peter?"

"He is smitten with the eldest Miss Bennet. He seems quite in earnest."

Darcy pondered that a moment. "Peter is always in earnest."

"True. He means to give Bingley a good challenge, though."

Darcy scowled. "Peter just met the chit last night."

Richard shrugged. "He decided to become a physician on the basis of one lecture. We all thought he would change his mind, but he did not."

Giving a quick nod, Darcy considered this latest revelation. He was not altogether unhappy about it. The night before, Miss Bennet had seemed devoted to Bingley. Would she remain constant if courted by an earl's son? He expected she would, but he would be happy to see proof of it.

The thought stayed with him the rest of the day. That evening, he mentioned the news to Bingley, who did not seem perturbed by it. As they sat drinking their port after dinner, Bingley swirled his glass. "After last night, I cannot doubt Jane's affection."

"Then why not propose?" Darcy asked.

"If I propose, we will be expected to marry as soon as the banns are read. And if we marry, where will we live? Here with you? With the Hursts? At Netherfield?" Bingley sipped the rich burgundy liquid. "Jane has not had a season until now. She is in no hurry to go back to the country."

Darcy accepted that argument. "And you are not concerned about rivals?"

Bingley scoffed. "I welcome the challenge. Let Peter Fitzwilliam do his worst."

Darcy wished he had Bingley's confidence when it came to Elizabeth. Was Josh a true rival? He was an amiable man in company, a trait she liked. But Darcy did not think Josh in earnest. Darcy would have to keep an eye on the situation. He would not risk losing his chance.

∞∞∞

A few days later, Bingley dined with his sisters. Darcy enjoyed having Georgiana to himself for the evening. Only Mrs. Annesley joined them in the drawing room after the meal.

Darcy took a seat next to his sister on the couch. "Are you content with your life here in London?" he asked. "Is there anything you wish for?"

She set down her embroidery and looked off into space. "Nothing comes to mind. Thank you for asking. The house does seem lonely, though, sometimes. I *do* wish you would marry."

His face warmed. "You know where I stand on that subject. I shall not be rushed, Georgiana. The decision is too important."

She gave an annoyed sigh and went back to her sewing.

"You could invite Lady Cressida for tea sometime," he suggested. "She is precisely the sort of young lady you ought to socialize with."

"I *do* like Lady Cressida. But now that she and Arabelle and their other friends are out in society, they spend most of their time at *ton* events."

He gave that some thought. "I confess, there is not much here to keep you occupied." An idea formed, which he did not much like, but which might be to Georgiana's benefit. "I can ask my aunt Matlock if you can stay with her during the season—"

"No!" Tears sprang to Giana's eyes. "That is not what I meant at all. You are my family, Darcy. My place is here." She bit her lip a moment, looking uncertain. "That is, unless you and Mr. Bingley would prefer—"

"Heavens, no." He clutched her hand affectionately. "But you are lonely. Short of marrying, I am uncertain how to remedy that." He furrowed his brow. "A young lady in your situation might attend certain afternoon entertainments. Musicales and so forth."

A smile brightened Giana's face, and eagerness danced in her eyes. "You know I love music."

His chest swelled with affection for her, the sensation so sharp it was almost painful. "I have been remiss," he said. "Such excursions should have been arranged for you from the time you came to London last year. Mrs. Annesley and I shall put that to rights. She can look through our invitations for some suitable events."

He met Mrs. Annesley's eyes. She gave him a smile and a nod. "It will be my pleasure," she said. "I would not wish to take her out of the schoolroom every day, but twice a week would do her good. Especially if the outing is educational."

Giana looked from her companion back to Darcy again. She threw her arms around his neck and hugged him. "Thank you, brother."

The affectionate gesture caught him by surprise. He drew her closer. He loved her more than anything. There was nothing he would not do for her.

He sat back, not wishing to make a spectacle of himself in front of Mrs. Annesley. This decision would open more doors for Georgiana, and that pleased him. He kissed his sister's forehead and left her to her needlework.

The following day, he visited his aunt. He wished to consult her about what events Georgiana could properly attend.

Giana was hovering at that in-between age. She was no longer a girl but not yet a woman. Darcy had no idea how to navigate it. A wife would make it easier—Giana had been right about that.

But winning Elizabeth's heart would be no simple matter. And he would not make her an offer until he was certain of her affection.

As he approached Matlock House, his heart leapt. The Miss Bennets were being shown inside. As much as he wanted to see Elizabeth, it would give the gossips more fuel. Should he join them, or delay his visit with his aunt?

On one hand, he valued Elizabeth's advice about his sister.

On the other, he wished to avoid the temptation of her company. He had been overly familiar the night of the play.

In truth, he had stayed away too long. The play had been days ago. If he wished to court her without *seeming* to court her, he would have to be in company with her from time to time.

When he stepped into the drawing room, she was on the sofa with Josh. She laughed and touched her fan to Josh's arm, as she had done a few times to Darcy. He nearly growled at the sight.

When Darcy was announced, Elizabeth's eyes turned his way. He saw surprise in her face, and perhaps pleasure. Or did he flatter himself?

The ladies of the house were there—the countess, Arabelle, and Nerissa. Peter, too, sitting with Miss Bennet. Mrs. Gardiner was not present.

Darcy extended a general greeting to the room. Then, he sat in a chair near Elizabeth. "Where is your aunt today?" he asked.

Elizabeth smiled cordially. "She went to Cheapside to see her husband and children."

Darcy nodded. "The separation must be difficult for her."

"It is," Elizabeth said, "but she is enjoying the entertainments in Mayfair. As Jane and I are. It is difficult to be homesick when we are kept so busy."

Elizabeth turned to Josh, then back to Darcy. "I was just telling your cousin," she said, "about the church in Meryton. I think the stained glass there quite fine for so small a town. What think you, Mr. Darcy?"

He sat silent a moment. He had not been to that church above a dozen times. What had he thought when he first entered it? Had he noticed the stained glass? He rather thought it *was* particularly good. "I must agree with you, Miss Bennet."

"I should like to see it," Josh replied. He offered Elizabeth a plate of macaroons. She declined with a shake of her head, her dark curls bouncing with the movement. Darcy wanted to thread his fingers through them, then caress his way down the nape of her neck…

Elizabeth spoke to Josh. "Perhaps when you are traveling from London to Derbyshire, you could call on us at Longbourn. My father would be happy to show you the church."

"I would enjoy that," Josh said, pressing her hand, "especially if you would accompany us."

Darcy set his jaw. He considered the ways his cousin might pay for that liberty the next time they sparred at Gentleman Jack's.

"So I will," Elizabeth said, "if I am at home." She turned and gave Darcy a smile and arch look, before returning her attention to Josh.

What did that look mean? Did she expect to leave home? Did she expect that Darcy would take her away from it? His heart lurched at the thought. Or perhaps she had only looked in his direction to keep him involved in the conversation.

Elizabeth continued in a cheerful tone. "My neighbour, Sir William Lucas, started a committee to restore the stained glass a few years ago. I believe, Mr. Darcy, that Sir William was impressed with you when you stayed at Netherfield."

Darcy lifted his chin. "Was he?"

"I remember he once asked if you ever danced at St. James."

"Good heavens," Josh cried, "why would anyone want to do that? The balls mainly consist of standing about watching the royal family dance. And the women must all wear court dress with those huge hoops. That makes the crush of the crowd even more unbearable. No one would go to a ball at St. James if they could avoid it."

Darcy, being untitled, had thankfully never had to make an appearance at such an event. He did not much like, though, to hear Elizabeth speaking of that assembly at Sir William's home. Darcy had asked her to dance, and she had refused. Playful as she had been at the time, he now realized she had actually disliked him.

Elizabeth said, "Sir William was presented at court. I daresay he thinks the balls there must be grand. I would hate to disappoint him. His eldest daughter Charlotte is my particular friend, you see. In fact, Mr. Fitzwilliam, you may meet her the next time you visit Rosings Park. Her husband, Mr. Collins, is rector at Hunsford."

"Collins, you say?" Josh drew his brow and seemed to consider a moment. He gave her a crooked smile. "I believe I have met him. The man is—"

"Miss Bennet's cousin," Darcy said, in time to prevent Josh from making a fool of himself.

"My father's heir, in fact," she added.

Josh looked at her in wide-eyed horror for only a moment before recovering himself. "How fortuitous for your friend."

"To all appearances, it seems an excellent match for her," Darcy said.

Elizabeth eyed him as if she wanted to bludgeon him, but instead gave him a sweet smile.

"Joshua," called the countess from across the room, "do come settle a dispute for us."

He turned to his mother, lifting his brows.

"It is of great doctrinal importance," she insisted.

With reluctance, it seemed, Josh bowed to Elizabeth and did as he was bid.

Grateful for the reprieve, Darcy said to Elizabeth, "The day is unseasonably warm. Would you care to take a turn in the square?"

Darcy held his breath a moment. The question had been pure impulse. He did not want to share Elizabeth with Josh or anyone else. But how would she respond?

Her wide eyes showed surprise, but she quickly recovered. With an enigmatic smile, she said, "That sounds lovely."

His heart gave a little squeeze. If he had thought through the request, he likely would have come up with a reason against it. Instead, he had followed his heart, and been rewarded. Now, he would have Elizabeth to himself.

∞∞∞

Outside, they stepped through the gate and onto the green of the Berkeley Square garden. The sun was bright and the air filled with birdsong. "This *is* a pleasant spot," Darcy said, offering Elizabeth his arm. "One could almost forget we are in town."

"Do you miss Derbyshire?" she asked. She tucked her gloved hand into the crook of his elbow, warming him. The feel of her so close wove his stomach into a cat's cradle.

"I am used to spending the season in town," he said. "London feels almost as much like home to me as Pemberley does. The retirement of the countryside might grow tedious if I were there all the time."

"I do not find that to be the case," she said. "But then, Longbourn is an easy distance from London."

They walked along at a slow gait, enjoying the fine weather. "Have you been to the north?" he asked her.

"Never. My aunt Gardiner is talking of traveling to the Lake District this summer. She knows I have always wished to go."

"If you make the trip, you must stop at Pemberley on the way. Georgiana would love to see you."

"Georgiana would?" she asked with an arch look.

His cheeks heated. He stopped and turned to her. "I would be happy to show you around the property."

"Does the house have many rooms?"

"About a hundred. Most of them are closed up." He raised her gloved hand to his lips and kissed it. "We could spend hours there alone, and no one would notice."

She tittered and pulled her hand away. "How scandalous!"

He looked into her eyes, aching to kiss her. She did not shrink from his gaze. He must take care. The temptation—

"Miss Elizabeth!" a feminine voice called from the pavement. "Mr. Darcy!"

He turned to see Lady Jersey standing beyond the waist-high iron balustrade. His heart fell. This was why he should not have invited Elizabeth to walk with him. He had been familiar with her, *again*, and they had been seen.

Elizabeth raised her brows at him. She gave an almost imperceptible nod in the countess's direction. He liked Lady Jersey, but felt no particular warmth toward her as they ambled in her direction. "What brings you out on this fine day?" Lady Jersey asked.

"We were both visiting my aunt," Darcy said, "and her drawing room grew crowded."

"I imagine it did. And now you are having a tête-à-tête under this beautiful sunny sky. That is much more the thing."

"It is far too lovely a day to waste indoors," Elizabeth said.

"I agree. I am off to Bond Street. Do give your families my regards."

As she walked off, he and Elizabeth headed back to the path. "Devil take it," he murmured under his breath.

"I beg your pardon," Elizabeth scolded.

"My apologies," he said, though he did not believe she was such a stickler as to mind a mild oath.

"You are not fond of Lady Jersey?"

"I have nothing against her. I do not wish for you to become the subject of gossip."

"We are doing nothing improper." She looked over to where her maid stood by the shrubbery, out of hearing distance.

"No," he said as they walked on. "But you must have heard about the talk inspired by our night at the theatre."

She grinned. "I pay little attention to such things. Besides, Caroline Bingley probably twisted the rumours, to deny any *tendre* between us."

"Thank heavens for Caroline Bingley, then." He placed his hand on top of hers where it rested on his arm, brushing his thumb over her gloved fingers. "You and I are entirely unsuitable, would you not agree?"

"Oh, entirely," she teased back. "We have nothing in

common."

"Except for our appreciation for the theatre," he suggested.

She nodded. "And music."

They passed through the broken shade of a plane tree. "And books."

"Long walks out of doors."

He turned and smiled as they continued to stroll along the path. "Country estates."

She bumped her shoulder against his. "Lemon pound cake."

"Chocolate ices."

She stopped and looked at him. "How did you know I like chocolate ices?"

"Wild guess." As they were in sight of Gunter's, he asked, "May I buy you one?"

She scowled and looked back toward Matlock House. "We shouldn't."

"I believe we should." He leaned in that direction, and with a sly smile, she followed.

She removed her hand from his arm and opened her reticule. "I shall get one for Sally, too."

"It is my treat. You cannot think I would begrudge a few pennies for your maid?"

"I would not wish to impose," she said, but put her reticule away.

For practicality's sake, they bought Sally her favourite sweetmeat instead of an ice. Then, they sent her to let Jane know where they were. At Gunter's, a single young lady could take refreshment with a man without a chaperone. It was the one spot in London that could make such a boast.

They sat at a table eating chocolate delights moulded into the shape of swans. Darcy let a spoonful of the sweet cream melt on his tongue. Eyes fixed on Elizabeth, he swallowed. "Mrs. Annesley and I have decided to allow Georgiana to attend afternoon entertainments. That is the reason I called on my aunt. To discuss it with her."

"That is a wonderful idea. And yet, here you are enjoying

this confection with me." She sucked on her spoon, and the sight of it did wicked things to him.

"I could not resist. You are as sweet as any confection."

She raised her brows, seeming to disapprove. "Jane is the sweet one."

"Why can you not both be sweet? In your separate ways, of course."

"My wit is too sharp, I think."

That took him aback. Her wit was not sharp. She was delightful. "You are never unkind. When you were at Netherfield while your sister was ill, you were utterly devoted to her."

"Jane is the soul of goodness. What could be more fulfilling than tending to her?"

He considered a moment. "Reading a letter over my shoulder as I write to my sister, perhaps? Or reading volume two of the book I am reading, when you have not yet read volume one."

She coloured and let out a little laugh. "You are unkind! Miss Bingley did attend to Jane during daylight hours. It was only in the evening that she hung on your every action."

"Whereas you did not care a whit about what I did."

She did not deny it. "Should I have?"

"Not at all. I prefer a woman of independent mind."

Playfully, she pressed her fingers to her chest. "Should I be flattered?"

"I did not mean to flatter. Merely stating a fact. What sort of man would want a wife so frivolous that she is fascinated by the most mundane words that he speaks?"

She startled a moment, staring at him. Then, recovering herself, she replied, "A man equally frivolous."

He gave her a wry smile. "And do you think me so?"

Her spoon clinked as she laid it on the plate. "Not at all. You are the least frivolous man I know."

He furrowed his brow. He was not sure how to take her words. "Is the opposite extreme just as ridiculous?"

"Do you think you are ridiculous?" she challenged.

He looked at her deeply and said with perfect honesty, "I never did until I met you."

She laughed, then stopped when she saw he did not join in her mirth. She laid her ungloved fingers on his. "You are not ridiculous. You are reliable and kind. Perhaps a bit stubborn."

His whole body was on fire from her touch. He forced his mind to focus on the conversation. "And proud?" he asked.

"I was mistaken about that." She pulled her hand away, leaving him bereft. "You know your place in the world, yet you are not vain. You seek to improve yourself where you can."

He could not take his eyes off her. "I hope so. I would do well to be instructed by you."

"By me! Why, Mr. Darcy, what could a simple country maid like me have to teach a man of the world like you?"

"You are the farthest thing from simple. And as much as you do not wish to believe it, you are no more countrified than I am. As for your status as a maid, I would not dare speculate," he teased.

She pressed her hand to her mouth to stifle a laugh. "How wicked you are! Who shall I call upon to defend my honour? My father? Or perhaps my cousin, Mr. Collins. He will next be head of my family."

"Good heavens." Darcy had met Collins but once. Although *met* was too strong a word. Without a care for propriety, the man had introduced himself as rector of Lady Catherine's parish. He was fawning and supercilious and could not be a man of great intellect. Darcy wanted Elizabeth as far from that man's sphere of influence as possible.

"You need a husband," Darcy said plainly.

She eyed him intently a moment. "I am afraid I do. I would like to argue in favour of women's economic independence. Yet I am not so principled as to seek a post as a governess just yet."

He waved his hand. "It shall not come to that. If you ever find yourself in desperate straits, Lady Matlock will find you a match."

"Will she?"

He continued in a light tone, hoping he was not too transparent, "She likes you. The morning after the play, she came to Darcy House and was scheming on your behalf."

"Matchmaking, you mean? Did she have a particular gentleman in mind?"

"I believe she had more than one," Darcy recalled.

"Would any of them suit, do you think?"

"That is difficult to say. I know not what sort of husband you have in mind." He knitted his brows. "I can hardly imagine a man who would not find you delightful—who would not be a better person with you by his side. But what sort of man could be worthy of Miss Elizabeth Bennet?"

She pressed a finger to the side of her chin. "He would have to have fifteen thousand a year, and be a marquess at least."

He pretended to consider that. "Elwood would suit, then. He is a widower, nearing ninety. Due to his health, he never leaves Cornwall."

She gazed at him, her eyes wide and merry. "Why then, to Cornwall I must go."

"Be forewarned. His nephew guards him vigorously against the prospect of siring any heirs male."

"Perhaps I could be obliging and provide him with a daughter. That would secure my place as dowager, would it not?"

"Indeed." He looked at her assessingly, turning serious. "I shall not be easy until you are well settled. It is not my place, I know. Remarkably rude, in fact. You are vulnerable. It should not be so."

She watched him for what seemed a long time, as if trying to make out his character again. "That is a strange sentiment."

"Is it? Are you so unused to a man wishing to protect you?"

She blinked a few times, her eyes glistening. She seemed to withdraw inside herself. "Oh, dear," she said suddenly, "we are keeping Sally waiting. She has been back from Matlock House for some time."

He turned to see the maid standing on the sidewalk outside the shop. "May I walk you home, then?" he asked Elizabeth.

"I...yes, thank you."

He stood and offered his outstretched hand. She seemed rather dazed a moment before taking it and rising to her feet. She held his arm as he manoeuvred her through the crowd. It felt right somehow to have her at his side, under his protection.

That was where he wanted her. And for the first time, with the way she held on to him, she hinted that she felt the same.

Chapter 17

Lizzy stood in Gunter's amidst the sweet scents and the hum of conversation. She had never felt so strange in her life. Her head was light and her heart beat wildly. Thankfully she had Darcy's arm to hold onto as they walked to the door and stepped outside.

Sally, waiting for them, curtseyed. She followed behind as they strolled along the pavement. Lizzy could hardly attend to the maid, her mind was so muddled. Was Darcy courting her? Or was his concern more brotherly in nature? His demeanour had swerved from one direction to the other. She could not keep up.

Did she want him to court her? It was a stupid question. Of course she did. As much as he infuriated her, she liked him unaccountably well. She especially liked how it felt when he held her hand protectively against his arm, as if she were his.

His. That was what she wanted to be. Was it so wrong to wish for the care of a man who could save her from poverty? Who could remove her forever from Mr. Collins' influence? What a little tyrant he might be, if he thought it was his job to marry off her and her sisters!

The square was crowded due to the fine weather, and they greeted friends along the way. Darcy seemed rather grim about it. What had he said about Lady Jersey? That he did not want Lizzy to become the subject of gossip?

There was some protectiveness in that, too. Was he troubled about speculation of a *tendre* between them? That seemed to suggest a brotherly interest, then.

The thought hurt her heart. Why did not Darcy allow himself to be read, like every other person in the world? No, he must maintain his dignity at all costs. Even when it meant putting a barrier between them.

When they reached her house, she said, "Thank you. That was lovely."

"The pleasure was all mine." He bowed over her hand and placed a kiss atop her glove. It was all quite gallant. But what did it mean?

She watched him walk away, then entered the house. Jane rushed up to her. "You must tell me everything."

For privacy, they went upstairs to Lizzy's room and sat together on the bed. Lizzy glanced out into the garden. The first signs of spring were starting to appear.

"I have never known Mr. Darcy to be so attentive or kind," she said at last. "At times I thought he was flirting, but at others..."

She swallowed down the thickness in her throat. "He said he would not be easy until I was well settled. If I fell into circumstances where I needed to make a match, I should consult Lady Matlock." Lizzy shook her head. "Those do not sound like the words of a suitor."

Jane drew her brow, confusion showing in her brilliant blue eyes. "Why would he ask you out to walk, to discuss such a topic?"

"We did not start on that topic. Our conversation was light most of the time. But when I mentioned that Mr. Collins would be the head of our family one day—"

Jane let out a little gasp. "Surely not. We would fall under the care of my uncle Gardiner, not Mr. Collins."

Lizzy pursed her lips. "I do not know enough about the law to say." If Mr. Collins wished to pursue his familial rights, who knew what the outcome might be? Might he have the right to demand their obedience? To beat them if they failed in their obligations? She did not think him a violent man, but she could not say for certain what he was capable of.

Nor did she wish to find out.

Mr. Darcy had said she was vulnerable. Perhaps that was what he had meant. She would trust him a thousand times over before she would trust Mr. Collins. The simpering fool might not be clever enough to realize a woman had the sense to govern herself.

Jane grabbed Lizzy's hand. "But you also said you thought Mr. Darcy might have been flirting with you."

Lizzy nodded, her eyes unfocused. "It was the oddest thing. He said he liked my independent spirit. That he could not understand why any man would want to marry fawning woman like Miss Bingley. Something about the way he said it made it sound like he wanted to marry *me*. But that might have been my imagination."

Jane smiled, and was practically bouncing. "But that is a good start. That is, if you think you could like him. He said you are the sort of woman he admires."

"I already like him, Jane. But I am not convinced he likes me —not in *that* way. Although he was terribly familiar with me. Scandalously so, in fact." Her cheeks warmed at the memory of his words.

Jane's eyes widened. "What did he do?"

"I called myself a simple country maid. He said I was neither simple nor countrified, but he would not speculate as to whether I was a maid."

"Lizzy!" Jane cried, pressing her hand to the base of her throat. "You must have misunderstood."

"I understood perfectly."

Jane narrowed her gaze. "Then he must be planning to make you an offer. No gentleman would take such liberties in speaking to a lady otherwise."

Lizzy smoothed the skirt of her soft muslin walking dress. "Not unless he wished to insult, which he clearly did not. When Mr. Darcy is relaxed, he has a wonderful sense of humour. I did not know that about him before today."

Jane sighed. "How wonderful it would be, if you married Mr. Darcy, and then Mr. Bingley bought a country house in Derbyshire..."

"You are getting ahead of yourself," Lizzy warned, a grin breaking out over her face. "Mr. Darcy is one of the wealthiest men in England. Why would he marry a penniless woman like me?"

"Because of your independent spirit, which he admires. Because you are nothing like Caroline, whom he does not. Lizzy, you know your worth. Do not pretend otherwise."

"Ever since I came to London," Lizzy said, "it feels as if I have been living in a dream. Mr. Darcy swept me up into his coach, as if he were responsible for me. And I liked that feeling. For so much of our lives, we have been on our own."

Jane looked as if she might protest, but Lizzy stopped her.

"Yes," Lizzy conceded, "our parents looked after our physical needs. But our intellectual needs, our emotional needs... I am not certain either of them was equipped for that. I feel as if I could trust Mr. Darcy. As if anything I needed, he could provide. It is a wonderful feeling, but also terrifying. He is not mine." Her gaze fell to the counterpane.

"Not yet," Jane encouraged. "But if you want him, do not let him slip away. Do not make the same mistake I did, because I was too ashamed to pursue Mr. Bingley. If you want Mr. Darcy, then make him yours."

∞ ∞ ∞

Darcy entered Matlock House for the second time that day. Instead of following the butler to the drawing room, Darcy asked to speak with her ladyship alone. He did not wish to be distracted from his task a second time.

She joined him in the library, looking pleased to see him. She approved of his courting Elizabeth, he knew that much. But he had not come to satisfy her curiosity about the walk in the square. Instead, he spoke to her about his plan to take Georgiana to afternoon entertainments.

"I can see no harm in it," she said. "It is not uncommon for girls her age to be in company from time to time as long as they are properly chaperoned."

He nodded, unsure how to put his thoughts into words. "Mrs. Annesley is a fine companion for her, in a motherly sort of way. Georgiana has…she has expressed the desire for a sister. I would suspect her of being enthralled with the idea of matrimony, like any other young lady of the *ton*. But there is sadness in her when she says it. She lost her parents too young. Some days, she seems to consider me the only person she has in the world."

The countess seemed to consider that a moment. "I would not be alarmed about that. A girl of that age is figuring out her place in the world. Melancholy is bound to overtake her from time to time. And with her come-out approaching… For a shy girl like Georgiana, the prospect can be terrifying."

Darcy nodded. He remembered how nervous his cousins had been when they made their curtsey to the queen. They were all more outgoing than his sister.

The countess continued, "Giana wants someone she can rely on for advice. Someone who can give her their undivided attention in a way I cannot. I confess, my hands are full with Arabelle this year. I am not giving Nerissa the attention I ought."

Though he did not say so, Darcy wondered whether Nerissa needed her mother's attention. Nerissa was a self-possessed and mature young woman of nineteen. She seemed to enjoy her independence.

Lady Matlock worried the embroidery on her sleeve. "My focus should be on finding a match for Nerissa. But Arabelle's high spirits distract me. The girl is too trusting. She thinks she is grown up and worldly, when in fact she is hopelessly naive."

Darcy could not argue with that. Most of the time, Arabelle seemed poised and sensible, wise beyond her years. Then she would say something childlike and shockingly innocent. And he would remember she was only seventeen.

"I wish I could do more for Giana," the countess said. "But she is right, Darcy. Given her situation, it would be desirable for you to marry before she comes out."

Darcy gritted his teeth. Even though he knew her words were well intentioned. "I plan to, in my own time."

She folded her hands together at her waist. In an even voice, she said, "Take care, my boy. You have rivals—more than one. Every day you hold back, another man could swoop in. That little trip to Gunter's was a good start, but your courtship should be further along by now."

He hardened his jaw. With a wave of his hand, he said, "I do not wish to mislead her. I have not made up my mind."

Lady Matlock's eyes widened. "What is there to decide? She has no fortune, that is true, but you have fortune enough for both of you. Giana adores her, and you are in love."

The words sent a flush through him. He did not like anyone making such observations about him. Especially when they were so astute.

"I admit," he said, "I admire her. I cannot say whether she feels the same about me. You know her situation. If I made an offer, she might be tempted to accept whether she esteems me or not. I would not wish a loveless marriage on either one of us."

Lady Matlock stiffened. "Clearly she esteems you." Her tone grew more animated. "I hate to see such a kind, clever girl facing the prospect of reduced circumstances. If ever I can do anything for her, I shall. But Darcy, I cannot understand this hesitation. You have known her for months. If you are unsure of her affection for you, it is high time you learnt the truth."

He walked to the window and looked out at the garden. The skeletons of plane trees spread out like a canopy above the dry grass. The multihued bark interrupted the winter greyness.

"I do not wish to make a spectacle of myself."

"I cannot imagine a man less likely to do so."

He turned to face her. "You know how catty the gossips can be. If they think me pursuing her, they will tear her apart."

"Some, yes, like Miss Bingley and her ilk. Not the ladies who matter."

"You think Elizabeth will be accepted into society?"

"It is a *fait accompli*. Lady Jersey has already accepted her. I admit, the *ton* is fickle. Opinion could turn quickly. I would advise you to propose sooner rather than later."

Was she right? He shook his head. Why *was* he hesitating, after all?

His aunt arched her brows. "Josh is courting her outright. He is not holding back."

Anger rushed through him. "Josh is not being circumspect. A man in love should try to behave rationally."

Lady Matlock smiled, then schooled her features. "What makes you think love is rational?"

"Choosing a person to spend one's life with *should* be a rational exercise. I need to proceed carefully. Miss Elizabeth and I have different backgrounds and dispositions."

"That was true of your parents. They fell madly in love and had a fine, happy, marriage."

"They were not as different as Miss Bennet and me."

The countess's tone softened. "Difference is not necessarily a disadvantage. In the best marriages, husbands and wives complement each other. They make up for each other's lacks." She eyed him pointedly. "From that perspective, you and Miss Elizabeth are well matched."

He looked at his aunt in frustration. A wave of unease crashed over him.

Darcy loved Elizabeth. He wanted to marry her and fill Pemberley with the sound of children's laughter.

But he also wanted her to love *him*, as his mother had loved his father. Their relationship had been a source of stability for him. He wanted that for his children. If Elizabeth married for security rather than love, he would feel the pain of it forever.

Chapter 18

The next morning after breakfast, Lizzy entered the drawing room. A bouquet of pink roses sat on the credenza. She walked up to admire them, expecting them to be for Jane from Bingley. Leaning down to breathe their heady scent, she noticed that the envelope was addressed to her.

Excitement pulsed through her. She had not received an arrangement this large or elaborate before. *Please let it be from Darcy.* She tore open the seal. Her stomach tumbled as she saw his signature. In his own neat hand, the card said, "You are the sweetest confection."

Tears prickled her eyes. Her heart beat harder in her chest. How had this happened? A month ago, she had considered him her archenemy. When had she developed this infatuation for him?

She must be more circumspect. She could not allow herself to have these feelings. If she grew attached and it came to nothing, the disappointment would be unbearable.

Elizabeth Darcy. She loved the way that sounded.

Jane and Mrs. Gardiner joined her. Lizzy startled, then put on a placid expression. She tried to make light of the flowers, but could not keep from smiling.

They worked on their embroidery before visiting hours. Jane ordered some willow bark tea. "Are you well, my dear?" Mrs. Gardiner asked.

"Just a headache," Jane said. "A little tea should take care of it."

Indeed, Jane soon looked her usual, cheerful self. Whether this was due to the tea, or the arrival of Mr. Bingley and Mr. Darcy, was impossible to say.

Lizzy struggled to keep her countenance. She wanted to stake her claim on Darcy, but she allowed him the proprieties first.

Her patience was soon rewarded. After paying his respects to Mrs. Gardiner, Darcy sat with Lizzy on the sofa. Her chest expanded as she looked into his dark eyes. "Thank you for the flowers," she said. "They are lovely."

"You like them?"

"Roses are my favourite."

He pressed her ungloved hand. "Then you should have roses every day."

She beamed at him. She wanted him to know his attention was welcome, while still maintaining her modesty. After all, this man had questioned Jane's affection for Bingley—

No, she would not think on that. The past was done with. Best to put that unpleasantness out of her mind.

She forced herself to withdraw her hand from his.

He gazed at her deeply, his expression intense. "I meant what I said yesterday. I care about your well-being. You are protected while your father lives. But if you ever find yourself in need, I wish you to call on me."

"You are all kindness, Mr. Darcy," she said noncommittally, still unsure of his feelings for her.

"At Gunter's, you spoke about becoming a governess. I have not been able to stop thinking of it. I beg you, if you find yourself in such straits, apply to Lady Matlock before seeking a position. She recognizes your worth. She would happily take you as her protégée."

Lady Matlock again. He had sent Lizzy roses, yet now he spoke as if she lacked marriage prospects. "I am but twenty, sir. I have not yet begun to think of myself as on the shelf."

"No, of course not," he said quickly. "That was not my

meaning at all. The future is uncertain for all of us, and yours by no means secure." He scowled and looked away, then turned his attention back to her. "Forgive my forwardness. It pains me to think of you falling upon misfortune."

Resentment stirred in her stomach. What was she to say to that? His words conveyed only the truth. Yet they were not the words of a man who intended to make her an offer. Apply to his aunt? Good heavens!

If Mr. Darcy did not mean to propose marriage, then she had no desire for his pity. His cousin Joshua Fitzwilliam was courting her. Lord Greymore had asked her to open the ball with him the following day. She had suitors enough. She need not consider going into service as a governess or companion just yet.

"I thank you for your solicitude," she said at last.

He looked at her a long moment, his lips pressing into a thin line. "I beg your pardon. I have offended you."

She did not deny it.

He let out what could only be called a low growl. "Let me be frank. I would be shocked, madam, if you did not receive at least one offer of marriage before the season ends." His conciliatory words soothed some of her pique. He continued, "I would not wish you to marry for the sake of security, if you do not care for the man."

Lizzy could only stare at him. His familiarity left her too shocked to speak. Darcy was normally a paragon of reserve, and now his address was downright insolent.

She forced herself to remain calm. The intensity in his eyes said he meant no offence. He was worried, as any true friend might be. She would allow his candour.

"My point is," Darcy said fervently, "you have other options. Please forgive my plainness. I realize it is inexcusable. I can only say in my defence that I value your happiness too much to stay silent."

She nodded. "I appreciate your concern, Mr. Darcy. But it is not your place. Surely you see that."

He was silent a long moment. "Yes, I do see. It is insulting for me to even speculate upon such matters. Propriety calls for us to never acknowledge the situation to each other. Should I care more for propriety than friendship? Should I let you fall into a desperate situation, because to do otherwise would be impolite?"

"My situation is not desperate."

He nodded slowly. "That is true. A month from now, you might be engaged to one of the most eligible men in England. That outcome would not surprise me at all." He pressed her hand again. "It is what I hope for you, and the man would be lucky to have you."

His voice was deep and rough, the sound almost primal. His expression grew pained before he let her hand drop and turned away.

He stood and strode to the window overlooking the garden. Lizzy considered ordering another pot of willow bark tea. Her head ached from trying to understand this man.

She took a few long, deep breaths, then rose and walked up beside him. "Let us not quarrel, Mr. Darcy. I appreciate your concern for my welfare. I do not begrudge your openness."

"I mean only to say, Miss Bennet, that I hope you will not act rashly out of necessity. I hope you will follow your heart."

She could not prevent a smile from curving her lips. Those sounded more like the words of a lover. She tilted her head, and a cascade of curls tickled her neck.

With delicately slippered feet, she stepped closer. "Only the deepest love will persuade me to marry. Even if that means living out my days as aunt to Jane's children. I shall teach them to speak French and play the pianoforte decidedly ill."

"In that case," he said with a grin, "I am satisfied. But you are severe on my sex. Do you think not one amongst us might please you?"

"It is not enough that I am pleased." She fluttered her fan. "The gentleman must also be pleased with me."

"I believe, Miss Bennet, you will find the former condition to be the more challenging. The fashionable men of London are in your thrall."

With an arch look, she said, "In that case, I shall try not to leave a trail of broken hearts in my wake."

After a half hour, the gentlemen took their leave. Bingley voiced his enthusiastic regret that other obligations called him away. He and Jane exchanged smiles. Even Darcy looked somewhat less serious than when he had arrived.

In Lizzy's estimation, it had been a productive morning. She was encouraged, at least. Yet Darcy still puzzled her. She was no more reassured than she had been the day before about his intentions toward her.

∞∞∞

Once the gentlemen had gone, the Miss Bennets and Mrs. Gardiner donned their pelisses. They walked across the square and called at Greymore House. They were returning the ladies' most recent visit. The earl was not at home, which Lizzy bore with surprising equanimity. She would see him at the ball the following night, after all.

Lady Greymore was her usual, cheerful, talkative self. Lizzy had come to value her immensely. Lady Greymore was not astute, but she was kind and appreciative of the smallest details.

"You must try the apple biscuits," she said to her guests as Lady Cressida poured the coffee. "They have just the right amount of cinnamon, and enough butter to melt in your mouth. Our cook is a treasure. She has been with the family for thirty years. She keeps threatening to move into a seaside cottage with her sister. So Greymore keeps upping her wages to convince her to stay. She is a sly thing, but worth every penny."

"She spoiled him atrociously when he was a boy," Cressida exclaimed. She draped an embroidered blue shawl over her white muslin gown. "My sister says he was always sneaking sweets at the first whiff of baking coming from the kitchen. I remember him on his trips home from Eton. He would devour a full meal in the kitchen before dinner, and then another in the dining room with the family."

"Growing boys, Cressida," her mother said. "You shall find out for yourself when you have your own brood."

Mrs. Gardiner smiled. "Mine are not quite at that age yet. My eldest boy is twelve."

"Nearly there, then," Lady Greymore said with a merry smile. "Every age comes with its own trials but its own joys. I have been blessed in my children. Not a bad egg in the bunch." She pressed her lips together as if wanting to say more, then shook her head.

"I wonder if Miss Peabody will call this morning," Cressida said, as if changing the subject. "I saw her and Mr. Peabody enter Matlock House about twenty minutes ago."

"Oh," said Lizzy, "I must see if I can catch her. I have finished the two books she lent me."

"Which were they?" Cressida asked.

Lizzy thought a moment, trying to recall their sensationalistic titles. "*The Mischievous Marquess* and *The Lascivious Lord*."

"Heavens!" Mrs. Gardiner cried.

"Ah, that Mrs. Wheedlesuch," Lady Greymore said. "She *does* know how to get attention. But truly, I cannot see any harm in her novels."

"Nor I, Mama," Cressida said. "They divert Priscilla from her troubles, which I regard as a blessing." She leaned toward Lizzy. "What about you? Did you enjoy them?"

"Very much," Lizzy said. "They were quite fanciful. Mr. Darcy would not approve. We must make sure to keep him from looking into them before Miss Darcy has a chance to read them."

"They are not as scandalous as they sound," Jane protested.

Lizzy said in a low-pitched voice, "They are not the sort of thing that should grace the shelves of Pemberley."

Cressida laughed. "Oh, you sound just like Mr. Darcy. I would not dare tease him, but that was perfect!"

As the laughter subsided, Cressida rose and looked out the window. "We could walk about the square. We might catch Priscilla before she leaves."

Lizzy thought that a fine idea. The weather continued unseasonably warm. Jane, however, felt her headache coming back. She and Mrs. Gardiner returned to the house. Sally stayed behind with Lizzy.

Lady Cressida chatted with Lizzy in low tones, leading her and their maids out of the drawing room. Lizzy stopped to smell a bouquet of lilies. "How wonderful," Lizzy said. "Nothing is as sweet as the fragrance of lilies."

"They are lovely," Cressida said with a wave of her hand. "But I have grown so accustomed to the scent, I hardly notice it anymore. Surely Mr. Darcy sends *you* lilies, too? The *ton* cannot stop talking about your visit to Gunter's yesterday."

"Mr. Darcy?" Lizzy's glance fell to the card, and she saw his name. Her stomach hollowed out. He had sent Lizzy flowers only once. Yet he apparently sent them to Cressida often enough that they were a commonplace thing.

Lizzy struggled to find her voice. "He...he has sent me roses."

Cressida must have seen from Lizzy's expression that she had said the wrong thing. "Oh, but roses are much more romantic! Mr. Darcy has known me all my life—I am like a sister to him. He makes sure I have flowers from a gentleman in my drawing room on my at-home days. It is not even his signature on the card—probably his valet's or his butler's."

Lizzy looked at the card again, and realized Cressida was right. Lizzy knew Darcy's hand from the letters she had seen him write during her time at Netherfield. This looping scrawl did not match the neat, careful signature on the card he had sent her.

"Of course," Lizzy said, but the tightness in her chest persisted.

She was more baffled than ever about Mr. Darcy's feelings

for her. Were they nothing but a brotherly sort of concern? Perhaps she was not special to him at all.

In a daze, she put on her wrap and walked with Cressida to the park, their maids just behind.

"La, my lady," Sally declared as they got underway. "I have never had so much exercise since coming into service as I do with Miss Elizabeth. She is a prodigious walker."

Cressida turned and looked at her from beneath raised brows. "Is that so?"

Cressida's maid pulled Sally aside, seeming to speak rather pointedly in low tones. Sally blanched at the scolding.

In a downcast voice, she said, "Apologies, my lady. I should not have been so forward."

"Think nothing of it," Cressida said. "Miss Elizabeth has told me how fond she is of you. I would not wish to see you distressed in any way."

Sally gave a curtsey, but she did not meet Cressida's eyes.

Cressida walked over and took Sally's hands. "I shall not tolerate dull spirits in you. Miss Elizabeth says you lift her mood every day. Now, chin up."

Sally looked at her, and they exchanged smiles.

Lizzy was struck once again by what a lovely young woman Lady Cressida was. The perfect match for Darcy, in fact. Was Lizzy reading too much into that bouquet of lilies?

The uncertainty was torment. The only thing to do was put him out of her mind. After all, she was opening the ball the next day with Lord Greymore as her partner. A man she liked very much. A man who could make her a countess.

If Mr. Darcy did not want her, she was not, after all, without options. As he himself had so courteously reminded her.

Insufferable man! And yet he was exasperatingly handsome. And unaccountably kind.

Lizzy gritted her teeth, determined to set aside her distressing thoughts.

From across the green, a threesome approached, with a footman in Matlock livery by their side. Lizzy recognized the two ladies as Miss Peabody and Lady Arabella. The gentlemen —could that be Rolf Peabody?

Arabella had called him a Viking, and that was not far off. He was tall and broad and blond, with chiselled cheekbones and a strong jaw. Though not handsomer than Darcy or Lord Greymore, he was appealing.

Lizzy reminded herself of Lady Nerissa's warnings about him. The presence of the footman, as opposed to Arabella's maid, seemed a confirmation. The countess was concerned about the girl's safety. The footman was not as broad as Rolf, but he was taller and sturdy looking.

Introductions were made, and Lizzy curtseyed to Mr. Peabody. He was a friendly sort—perhaps too friendly—and Arabella persisted in holding on to his arm. She did not appear besotted, but enamoured certainly. One could hardly blame her, though. He had been a friend of the family her whole life. And he had grown into a mountain of a man whose smile could liquefy a lady's knees.

"Miss Peabody," Lizzy said, "if we walk to my house, I can return the books you lent me."

"Oh, yes," Miss Peabody said, "let us all head in that direction. Lady Eugenia has been asking to borrow them." She and Cressida led the way.

Rolf offered Lizzy his other arm, and she took it. "How are Lord and Lady Wayne?" she asked him. "I understand you live with them."

"My brother is kind to spare me the expense of bachelor quarters," Rolf replied. Was there a hint of resentment in his tone? "He and the viscountess are well, I thank you."

"I would think a man in your situation would be happy to be on his own," Lizzy suggested. "Might your brother buy you a commission? We have a militia regiment stationed near my home in Hertfordshire. My sisters would be quite giddy to see a man of your attributes in a red coat."

He chuckled. "The militia might well suit me. Thank you for the suggestion."

"Oh," cried Arabella, "that is a fine idea. I live in fear that my brother Richard will be sent to the Continent again. But the militia—we could all go to Brighton for the summer for some sea-bathing and watch Mr. Peabody parade." She looked up at Rolf. "You might be Captain Peabody before too long."

"Would you like that?" he asked, all smiles as he turned to meet Arabelle's eyes.

"Very much."

"Then I shall consider it, if for no other reason than to please your ladyship."

Lizzy was not sure what to make of his gallantry. Despite his words to Arabella, he had all the hallmarks of a worthless young man. But Lady Arabella seemed to take his sentiments to heart.

The group entered the house. Mrs. Gardiner rang for tea while Lizzy got the books. She returned to find that Jane was looking better. She sat on the sofa with Lady Cressida while Lizzy joined the others around the coffee table.

"I am pleased to meet you at last," Rolf said to her. "The *ton* is awash in gossip about the Miss Bennets. There is a bet on the books in my club about when Mr. Bingley will finally offer for Miss Bennet—"

"Mr. Peabody!" Lizzy cried. This was not at all an appropriate conversation for a young gentleman to have with a young lady, and he well knew it.

"Forgive me," he said. "It is scandalous, I know. I would not engage in such an activity myself. But I must warn you, there is also a wager about you and a certain gentleman from Derbyshire—"

"Please, Mr. Peabody," Lizzy said in a sharper tone, "I must beg you to say no more."

"I beg your pardon." His brow furrowed in apparent contrition. "You are right, of course. I meant you no insult. If it were me, I would wish to know what was being said about me. But of course, a lady of your character would not allow her curiosity to sway her from the proprieties."

She refilled his coffee, and her own. "I confess to having little curiosity about the idle chatter that goes on at gentlemen's clubs."

"You are wiser than me, Miss Bennet. I shall endeavour to follow your example, and thereby improve myself."

She knew he was mocking her, but she did not care. Lady Nerissa was right to warn her sister away from this man.

The guests soon rose to depart. Lizzy sent along a footmen to join the Matlock's man in seeing Lady Arabella home. She did not trust Rolf Peabody one bit.

∞∞∞

On the day of the Greymore ball, Darcy met his cousins at Angelo's Fencing Academy around noon. A small crowd milled about, many still in their coats and tall hats, watching the matches. Some sat on a long bench, while others stood around the periphery.

The space might once have been a fashionable drawing room. Wainscoting and crown moulding decorated the walls. A few landscape paintings were hung near the ceiling.

Yet the room contained almost no furniture, aside from a writing table with paper and ink. It sat near the door in case a gentleman needed to send a servant out with a note. But the most prominent feature was the row of hooks that held foils, epees, masks, and boxing gloves.

Darcy donned a fencing kit and faced off against Richard. He was barely able to get in a touch against the colonel. He redeemed himself, though, by soundly defeating Peter and Josh. In a jolly mood and invigorated by the exercise, the four headed to their club for a light repast.

Entering the building, they strolled down the hallway and past the morning rooms. They headed up the staircase with its curving bannister to the coffee-room. The word *room* did not do it justice, as it spanned the entire width of the building.

The arched ceiling was two stories high. An enormous crystal chandelier hung from the central panel.

They sat near the windows overlooking the street. After a brief discussion, they ordered a large platter of meat, bread and cheese.

Richard complained jovially of his mother's efforts to find him a suitable heiress. Listening to the colonel, Darcy missed most of Josh and Peter's conversation. But his younger cousins drew his attention when Josh barked, "The devil? You do not mean to steal Miss Bennet away from Bingley! That is not very sporting of you."

"To my knowledge," Peter said, "Miss Bennet is not Bingley's property. Therefore, she cannot be stolen. If he wished to make an offer, he has had ample time to do so."

Josh turned to his cousin with a pensive look. "What think you, Darcy? Is Miss Bennet's heart not spoken for?"

Darcy drew his brow. "I have no intimate knowledge of Miss Bennet's heart. If her affections can be won away from Bingley, then it is best done quickly. Before he marries the chit."

"Is that his intention?" Josh asked.

"I cannot say." For though Bingley had told Darcy his plans, it had surely been said in confidence.

Josh frowned, seeming ill at ease with his brother's proposition.

"Miss Bennet would make me an excellent wife," Peter said. "Unlike most ladies of the *ton*, she is not fastidious about my place as a physician. My income is comparable to her father's. She is intelligent and kind, and unlikely to be squeamish. Her calm nature will cause me no embarrassment. And her lack of fortune is more than reprieved by her exceptional beauty."

Darcy noticed that tender feelings did not factor into Peter's assessment. Yet he seemed to consider himself a serious rival of Bingley's.

It would not be a bad thing if Jane had other options. The depth of her attachment to Bingley would be easier to gauge. Though Peter's income was lower, his social position was higher. He might be able to tempt her away from Bingley if her heart was not fixed.

Darcy eyed Josh narrowly. "It would be better for Bingley to lose Miss Bennet and find another, if her affections are not involved. He would not wish to be forever bound to a woman who chose him solely for his wealth."

"You insult her," Josh said with some heat, his face reddening. "From what I have seen, there is nothing mercenary in her, nor in Miss Elizabeth. Despite their lack of fortune."

"You must concede," Richard said, "that Darcy knows the ladies better than you."

"I would not describe them as mercenary," Darcy said, "though their mother certainly is. Mrs. Bennet would have married her eldest daughter to Bingley sight unseen."

Josh eyed him acutely. "Your opinion of the mother may have coloured your opinion of the daughters."

Darcy nodded slowly. "It is possible."

Mentally, he conceded it was *probable*. Darcy's mother had admonished him about those who might seek to benefit from his wealth and position. Wickham had proven the justness of that warning. Better to lose a friend owing to too *much* caution than too little.

But he would no longer let such fears get in the way of his happiness. Elizabeth Bennet had charmed him so thoroughly, he no longer doubted her motives. It was time to court her openly.

He excused himself and headed for the retiring room. He stopped short when Viscount Olimand nearly crashed into him. The miserable pup was in his cups again.

"I say, Olimand, have a care." He did not disguise the disapproval in his voice.

The young viscount looked up with unfocused eyes. Then, recognition seemed to dawn on him. "Darcy!" he cried, patting his back. "The man of the hour. I've laid down five guineas on you."

Darcy stiffened. "On me? What nonsense are you speaking?"

"That sweet country chit. She *is* a tasty morsel. Rickers saw you with her at Gunter's. He wagers you'll set her up in an establishment within the month. Odds are running two to one."

Blind with rage, Darcy balled his hands into fists. It took all his self-possession to keep from pummelling the smaller man into a bloody heap. Instead, he loomed over Olimand so he could not miss the menace in Darcy's eyes.

"Miss Elizabeth Bennet," he said, "is a gentlewoman. If I hear you cast aspersions on her character, I shall call you out. Do we understand each other?"

"Darcy, old boy," Olimand said with a conciliatory smile, "I meant no insult. Besides, I am not the one who entered the bet into the book." The next moment, his eyes widened, and he turned a sickly grey. He rushed into the retiring room.

Darcy stared into the space where Olimand's pathetic figure had stood. What the devil? Surely Darcy's behaviour towards Elizabeth had not been *that* familiar. Rumours now circulated that he intended to make her his *mistress*?

He closed his eyes a moment and took a long breath to calm himself. Blast, what would he do now?

He spotted Greymore across the room. Nodding to the man, Darcy formed a plan. At the ball that night, he would divert the gossip by focusing his attention on Greymore's sister. In a few days, the nonsense would be forgotten. Then, he could begin in earnest with his plans to court Elizabeth.

Chapter 19

That evening, Lizzy sat at her vanity, bright candlelight reflecting off the mirrors. She had never been this excited before an assembly. Her first *ton* ball! Tonight could change her life.

The tedium of getting ready was almost unbearable. She gritted her teeth but held her head still as Sally's hands deftly worked the hairpins and curling iron. The faint scent of violet perfume rose from Lizzy's wrists and throat.

Seed pearls woven through her coiffure complemented the strand at her neck. The silk of her pale blue gown shimmered in the light. A tinge of rouge and lip salve enhanced her natural glow.

"You will do Lord Greymore proud," Sally said when she had finished. "La, ma'am, I never thought I'd be so lucky as to dress such beautiful ladies as you and Miss Bennet. And you are to open the dance with the earl himself! What a fine thing it would be, if you became a countess! Although I must say, I am partial to Mr. Darcy. He was prodigious kind to us that day in the rain, and I have never seen a man more handsome."

Butterflies somersaulted in Lizzy's belly. Her thoughts of Greymore were pure anticipation. She did not know him well enough to have formed an opinion. But Darcy? Her emotions were in such turmoil where he was concerned, she could not put them into words. She was filled with an indecipherable sense of unease.

Where did she stand with him? His last visit had only

confused her more. She was in such a state over the man—that must signify something. She at least wished for his esteem. And that was a terrifying prospect, given how sparing Darcy was with his good opinion.

"You do not think Mr. Darcy proud, Sally?" Lizzy no longer did, but she wondered about her maid's impression of the man.

"No, ma'am," the girl said, her eyes wide. "I saw no pride in him. No more than in any other of that set. His uncle is the Earl of Matlock, is he not? The earl is a great man, with his work in the House of Lords. They say he made a fine speech about reforming the vote. He is a friend of the common man, and I like Mr. Darcy the more for it."

Lizzy nodded absently. "I wonder whether Mr. Darcy holds his uncle's sentiments."

"That day in the rain, he spoke kindly to me and looked after me as well as if I were a lady. I cannot see how anyone could think him proud."

Lizzy did not push the point. It was strange—all of Meryton had perceived him one way, while Sally perceived him another. In London, Lizzy never heard him called proud.

She recalled his behaviour at the ball where he had first been introduced to Meryton society. Had that night alone sealed his unfavourable reputation?

In London, amongst those of his own station, Darcy was indeed courteous and kind. The fact of it puzzled her. But she did not wish to think about him at that moment. She was exhausted with trying to make him out.

Instead, she wished to think about Lord Greymore. To dream of being a countess, however improbable the dream might be.

Her thoughts continued in that light manner during the short ride to the Greymore home. Then came the tedious wait while the carriages pulled up one at a time in front of the house. Mrs. Gardiner had allowed a full hour, since Lizzy was to be Greymore's partner for the first dance. It would not do to be late. Even so, given the delay, Lizzy worried whether they would arrive in time.

As it was, the footman announced them to the gathered assembly at what seemed the perfect moment. They were neither punctual nor fashionably late. Lady Greymore greeted them with a fluttering welcome; Lord Greymore with a deep bow; and Lady Cressida Marlowe with a conspiratorial whisper.

They had the pleasure of meeting the rest of the Marlowe brothers. Five in total, if Lizzy counted correctly. There was also another daughter, but she was currently in her confinement. Lady Greymore was rapturous at the prospect of her first grandchild.

Jane had barely stepped out of the receiving line before Bingley claimed her. She was to be his partner for the first set, of course. Yet, the music had not started. Lizzy wondered whether they ought to be so obvious about their partiality.

But Lizzy would hardly advise Jane to show less of a preference, and risk Darcy's interference again. Yet somehow, that thought did not inspire the same rancour it had before.

Had he arrived? She looked about the room and spotted him speaking with Lady Arabella and Miss Peabody. Arabella was dressed in white, Miss Peabody in a cerulean blue that seemed showy for a girl who had just come out.

From what Lizzy had heard, Viscount Wayne was eager to see his sister married off in her first season. She was pretty enough, but a bit nondescript in both her appearance and her personality. The colour of her gown was doubtless designed to counteract that effect.

When Darcy leaned down and kissed Miss Peabody's gloved hand, a sudden wave of emotion washed over Lizzy. It was hot and sharp and dreadfully unpleasant, as if something that had belonged to her had been taken away. Was she jealous? Was that possible?

Darcy was not hers. What she was feeling...it was pure possessiveness. He had showered her with attention that night at the theatre, and again at Gunter's. Now, he was with someone else. Her pride was hurt. That was all.

Their eyes met across the ballroom. He gave a little bow, and she a little curtsey. But he did not move towards her. So she turned to greet as many others of the guests as she could before the dancing began.

She was chatting with Lady Nerissa when Greymore came for her. "My mother has instructed the musicians to ready themselves. May I lead you out to open the ball?"

She gave him her hand. They walked to the floor as the first strains of music began. Some stares and whispers accompanied them as they went. Clearly, this was not what the guests had expected of Greymore for the first dance.

She did not let the reaction affect her equanimity. Elizabeth Bennet was the daughter of a gentleman. She had as much right to dance with an earl as any other young woman in England. She gazed at her partner and held her head high, while butterflies waged war in her stomach.

As the couples took their places in the set, Darcy startled. Greymore escorting Elizabeth—what the devil? It was one thing for the man to flatter her at the theatre. It was another for him to distinguish her in this way at a ball thrown by his mother. The dancing had not even started, and already the matrons were whispering.

Darcy turned his attention to Lady Cressida. At the Netherfield ball, Elizabeth had scolded him for his reticence. Tonight, he was determined to play the gallant to his partner.

"Your mother must be pleased with the turnout," he said to Cressida. "I imagine more guests will join us as the evening progresses."

"That is generally the case," she said blandly. "There are not so many couples yet that we might be squeezed. One wonders whether it will continue so for the rest of the evening."

Scintillating conversation it was not. At least Darcy's partner could not accuse him of neglecting her.

As the cotillion got underway, Lady Cressida's pale green gown swirled as she moved through the turns. She looked young and carefree and beautiful.

Darcy had always thought her pretty, but her exuberance as they danced brought a sparkle to her eye. Her movements were so graceful, a sort of transcendent joy stirred in his chest. With Lady Cressida, dance was not just an entertainment. It was an art.

They exchanged partners around the square. She promenaded with Greymore, he with Elizabeth. An altogether different sensation came over him. When his gloved hand pressed to Elizabeth's, he felt it like a brand.

Her eyes were not just bright from activity. Their dark depths invited him to lose himself. The stirring was not only in his heart, but also in his loins. And there was nothing transcendent about it.

He could not disguise the huskiness in his voice as he said, "How good to see you, Miss Bennet."

"And you, sir."

Those were the only words they had time to speak before the dance parted them again.

The rest of the half hour proceeded in much the same way. He was all politeness to Lady Cressida. However, every time he found himself by Elizabeth's side, gazing into her eyes, the rest of the room fell away.

"I saw you speaking with Lady Jersey earlier," he said, searching for a topic of conversation. "Have you secured permission to waltz?"

"Indeed I have."

As she moved back in Greymore's direction, Darcy realized what a blunder he had made. Now she would expect him to ask her to waltz.

He could do no such thing. And not only because of the potential for gossip. He could not trust his body if he were so close to her.

No woman had aroused such uncontrollable desire in him before. Darcy took pride in his mastery over his passions—but all that seemed lost in her presence.

He turned his attention to Lady Cressida. Setting his jaw, he resolved to concentrate on the dance.

How long would it be until he could propose to Elizabeth? A month's courtship should be enough. She must have a hint of his feelings by now, and she had not discouraged him. Given another three weeks for the banns to be read, they could be married by Easter.

Or he could get a license, and they could be married sooner.

His blood stirred as he watched Elizabeth dance. Her pale blue gown showed off her beguiling figure. The sooner, the better, as far as he was concerned. By April, she would be his.

∞∞∞

Lizzy told herself to stop watching Darcy out of the corner of her eye. Seeing him chat so amiably with Lady Cressida when the dance first began had raised Lizzy's anger. She seethed with it. He had never been so courteous to any of the young ladies in Hertfordshire.

But as the dance progressed, he seemed to lose his sociability. He had grown taciturn, and now seemed to be staring daggers at Lizzy. What had she done to offend him?

She suspected tongues were wagging about his choice of partner for the first set. Some of the guests had clearly expected she and Darcy to dance together. Now those rumours had been put to rest. It was plain for all to see that Mr. Darcy was not courting Miss Elizabeth Bennet.

Fortunately, they were both dancing in a place of honour. No one need pity them, or assume one had spurned the other. They were, one might conclude, just friends.

That was exactly what she had most wished from this

dance. The effect was perfect. She could not be more pleased.

But then, how could she explain the sensations that had beset her when Darcy had led Cressida to the dance floor? The heaviness in her chest and the lump in her throat? She had felt it like a slap.

That petite blonde thing, with her forty thousand pounds, would make him the perfect wife. Darcy knew it, and Lizzy knew it. He was parading the girl under Lizzy's nose so she could not misunderstand the situation.

She blinked back the sting in her eyes.

Remembering herself, she looked up at Lord Greymore. He was a graceful partner, his movements smooth and easy. When they came together in the dance, he gazed at her intensely. The look brought a flush to her—one more of embarrassment than excitement. But he was excessively handsome, not to mention tall and well formed. She told herself to enjoy the moment and cast off her self-consciousness.

"How are you enjoying London?" he asked her. "Do you miss the countryside?"

"I do not miss the quiet, but I do miss the landscape. Fortunately, Berkeley Square provides a lovely venue for my morning walks."

The dance separated them. When they came back together, Greymore spoke again. "My mother's great passion is the garden at our country estate. She does what she can here. She has put in several new plantings this year."

"I would love to see them sometime."

"The garden is lit with lanterns tonight, so our guests can take the air. Might I accompany you outside after the dance?"

That seemed a bit forward to Lizzy. But if they stayed close to the house, there could be no impropriety in it.

So when the music ended, Greymore led Lizzy to Mrs. Gardiner. "Might I have your permission, ma'am, to escort Miss Elizabeth out to the terrace? I have been telling her of the plantings my mother installed, and she is eager to see them."

"Of course." Aunt Gardiner handed Lizzy her shawl, and off they went.

Lizzy wondered what Greymore's intentions were. He did not have a reputation as a rake, or even a rogue. Yet, even the most upstanding male might try to sneak a kiss.

Such a liberty would not be welcome. She did not wish him to think her the sort of woman who would allow such intimacy after a single dance. No, she would keep him at arm's length. He seemed gentleman enough to respect that.

The broad terrace shone with the light of a dozen lanterns. The stone beneath their feet was a pale brown, and a few steps led down to the formal garden. Huge urns on either side of the stairs were planted with hollies. Red berries burst from branches covered with glossy green leaves. Winter jasmine grew around the trunks. The slender stems of yellow flowers cascaded over the edge of the pots.

"Very pretty," Lizzy approved. "It is not Longbourn, but the hollies give me a sense of home."

"Their beauty is complemented by your own."

She looked up at him slyly. "If I did not know better, I would think I had conjured you from a novel. A dashing and handsome earl, all kindness and flattery..."

"I assure you I am most real." He lifted her hand and placed a kiss on it.

"But like any romantic hero, you must have some flaw. They do in all the novels. Did you witness a murder as a child, and lock away the memories? Or perhaps it is nothing so dark. Your property is mortgaged, and you must marry a crass, hateful upstart of an heiress to save it."

"Nothing so interesting." He narrowed his brow. "If I had to name my greatest flaw, I would say it is this: I intimidate my fellows with my extraordinary talents at sporting pursuits. Boxing, shooting, fencing, billiards—I surpass them all."

Lizzy looked at him askance. "I agree, your lordship. Your greatest flaw is your lack of humility."

He grinned at her. "And what is yours?"

A cold breeze rustled the trees. She hoped it would not muss her coiffure. She drew her shawl close around her and considered the question a moment. "Sometimes I place more stock in being clever than in being wise."

He nodded slowly. "There is a story there."

"There is. But it is not mine to tell. Suffice it to say that I shall never again trust my first impressions."

He stepped closer. "And what is your *best* quality?"

She drew back. "I learn from my mistakes."

"That is a fine trait indeed. But it is not the one I would choose as your *best*."

"And what would your choice be?"

He looked at her with a gaze so intense it stopped her breath. His pale eyes sparkled in the lamplight, his wry smile dimpling at the corner.

For an anxious moment, she thought he might kiss her. She was relieved when he suddenly pulled away instead. In a dramatic fashion, he stepped up onto a stone bench as if it were a stage. In a rich baritone, he recited,

> *She walks in beauty, like the night*
> *Of cloudless climes and starry skies*
> *And all that's best of dark and bright*
> *Meet in her aspect and her eyes*
> *Thus mellow'd to that tender light*
> *Which heaven to gaudy day denies*

He stepped down and approached her, a soft smile on his face. She watched him appreciatively. He took her gloved hand and kissed it.

"How romantic, your lordship," she said, heart fluttering. "You rival Byron himself." She slipped from his grasp. "But if you believe beauty to be my best quality, that is not a compliment to my character. If you get to know me better, I hope you will discover more laudable ones."

He gazed at her deeply. "Now I know two more things about

you. You are not beguiled by poetry, and you prefer to be admired for your mind."

"How disappointed you must be."

"On the contrary, I am charmed."

She looked up at him, scrutinizing his face. He was ridiculously handsome—stormy eyes, an aristocratic nose, a neat blond moustache. His shoulders were broad, his waist lean, and his legs muscular. His dark breeches showed off the latter to excellent effect.

"With all you have to recommend you," she asked, "why would you open a ball with me?"

"You are an original," he said without hesitation. "Cressida likes you, and she likes hardly anyone. She has an uncanny knack for recognizing when someone is dissembling. She said you might be the most honest person she ever met." He gave Lizzy a wicked grin. "That might have something to do with your *penchant* for being clever rather than wise."

She arched her brows, but voiced no objection to his assessment.

The wind picked up again, and the trees above them creaked. Lizzy hoped it would not storm. The sky looked clear, thankfully.

Greymore's voice interrupted her thoughts. "I noticed that your sister opened the ball with Bingley. Some think there is an understanding between them."

She knitted her brows, troubled by the rumour. Could it be true? Might Jane have entered into an engagement with Bingley and told no one—not even Lizzy?

"I cannot believe that to be the case. Jane would know the impropriety of it, and it is not in her nature to flaunt social expectations. Besides, what would be the advantage of secrecy? He is independent, and she of age."

"One must wonder, then, what is keeping him from coming to the point."

She wondered how much to reveal to him. "There are those, I believe, who sought to prevent the match. They convinced him my sister's affection was more for his fortune than for himself. Now that the two have been reunited, he is perhaps more wary than he would otherwise be."

Greymore's brows drew together in consternation. He said sharply, "Who would impose on him in such a way? From all his sisters say, they adore Miss Bennet."

Lizzy had to give Miss Bingley her due. Even a man of Greymore's discernment believed she held Jane in affection. Caroline was a fine actress indeed.

Lizzy chose her words carefully. She did not wish to seem catty. "Miss Bingley has been most generous in heaping praise on my sister and me. Why, she has convinced the entire *ton* to take notice of us. Jane has acquired so many suitors, one might expect her to turn her attention away from Bingley. Leaving him free to pursue a more advantageous match."

Greymore's expression changed to one of confusion, then surprise, then understanding. "By Jove," he said, "I have always known Miss Bingley to be clever. And her kindness towards you and your sister did seem out of character. But tell me, Miss Elizabeth, is your sister so fickle? Are her affections likely to be swayed?"

Lizzy warmed as thoughts of Jane's generous nature swelled her heart. "Not at all, your lordship. I have never seen anyone so constant. In that aspect, at least, Miss Bingley's plan will fail."

"And what about in your case? She pays as many compliments to you as she does your sister."

"I believe Miss Bingley regards me as a rival for Mr. Darcy's affection. She hopes someone else will sweep me off my feet."

Greymore looked at her significantly, his brows arched. "*Are* you her rival for Darcy's affection?"

Lizzy gave him a coy look. "You would have to ask him that."

He grinned. "Let me put that another way. Should I consider Darcy a rival for *your* affection?"

Her breathing grew shallow as she felt herself caught in his aura. Her heart experienced such palpitations, her impulse was to call for Hill to bring her a tonic. But Hill was back at Longbourn attending to Mrs. Bennet's ills, both real and imagined.

Lizzy contemplated the question. Did she wish for Lord Greymore to court her? Of course she did. She would be a fool not to.

But what of Darcy? Her feelings for him were as muddled as ever. If she were in love—and if she believed him to feel the same—it would be wrong to string Greymore along.

But she did not know her own heart, much less Darcy's. Had the past few weeks been the start of a *grand passion*? Or a fleeting and insignificant interlude? Only time would tell.

So she answered carefully, leaning in to offer encouragement. "My affection has not yet been given. At this time, it is entirely my own."

He hesitated a long moment. "I see the way Darcy looks at you—as if you are the most fascinating creature he has ever beheld—and I wonder why."

His words left her breathless. She took a moment to recover. "I cannot help wondering myself. Sometimes I believe he is assessing my faults."

Greymore chuckled. "I doubt that. I was surprised, though, when he made a point of asking Cressida for the first two dances tonight. Otherwise, I would not have dared to request the same of you. He and I have been friends a long time. If he had a prior claim on you, I would step aside."

"He has no claim."

"Odd, that." He shifted his weight. "I would not have thought him a stickler, any more than I am. I do not seek a wife from a noble family—only one who can make me happy. I would expect Darcy would want the same."

"You and I have different impressions of him. In Hertfordshire, he made it clear that rank mattered."

Greymore nodded thoughtfully. "Yes, I can see how that might be the case. It was not always so, I assure you. When we first started at Cambridge, his closest friend was a man of no rank at all, barely even a gentleman. His father was the steward at Pemberley."

"Ah," Lizzy said. "Mr. Wickham."

"You know of him?"

"I considered him a friend before I learnt of his true nature." Lizzy still felt a pang in her heart over the man. Except it was no longer for the friendship she had lost, or the disillusionment she had felt. Rather, it was for the foolishness of letting him colour her opinion of Darcy. She hated that she had ever thought ill of him.

"Then you understand a little of Darcy's disappointment," Greymore said. "He clung to that friendship our first two years at Cambridge. Meanwhile, Wickham grew ever more dissolute. The break finally came when Darcy let him linger in debtor's prison for a week before paying what was owed. After that, Darcy told the man he would not help him again. He said Wickham would have to apply directly to Darcy's father. Of course Wickham did not do that. He knew on which side his bread was buttered. The old man went to his grave never knowing what Wickham had become."

"Poor Mr. Darcy."

"Poor Darcy indeed. His oldest friend in the world had come to regard him as nothing more than a financier."

Lizzy swallowed the lump in her throat.

"It was shortly after that incident when Darcy met Bingley. Bingley has all of Wickham's amiability but none of his vices. He truly is amongst the best of men, Miss Bennet."

Lizzy beamed at that praise of her sister's sweetheart. "He has shown all evidence of being so. Mr. Bingley has been exceedingly kind to my family from the first we met—to the entire town, in fact. He is much beloved in Meryton."

"I imagine he is beloved wherever he goes. He has that talent for ingratiating himself to everyone he meets. Yet there is no dissembling in him. He genuinely likes people and sees the best in them."

"He and Jane have that in common."

Greymore smiled. "I am glad to hear it."

The trees above them swayed. Was a storm brewing? Perhaps they ought to go back inside. But no, the sky was still full of moonlight. As long as it did not rain, a little wind would not bother her.

She said, "Mr. Darcy does not possess the habit of ingratiating himself to strangers. Yet he seems comfortable here amongst the *ton*."

"He is well regarded, though his circle of close friends is small. By his own choice. He does not trust easily."

"No, he does not."

Greymore nodded, giving her a significant look. "After the disappointment with Wickham, Darcy particularly distrusts those not of his rank."

And that includes me, she thought, though she did not say it. She did not have to. Greymore understood.

Lizzy pulled her shawl close against another gust of wind. A snap rent the air, and Lizzy jumped as a tree bough hit the ground with a crack. It fell just beyond the terrace, not three feet from her.

"Good heavens!" Greymore cried, clasping her shoulders. "Are you well, Miss Bennet?"

She took a calming breath. "Yes, fine. It...startled me more than anything."

He looked up at the canopy of branches above them. "I must have the groundskeeper check that tree tomorrow to make sure it is not rotten. I would never have forgiven myself if you had been injured."

She gave him a smile, her composure returning. "I thank you for your solicitude. I am fine, truly."

He went to inspect the bough. It was a yard long and as thick as her wrist. It would likely not have killed her, but it might have done some harm if it had struck her head. She winced at the thought.

Greymore tossed it behind a shrub, clearing the path. "I would not want anyone tripping over that in the dim light."

"No," she concurred.

He brushed off his hands as he approached her. "I fear you are getting chilled. Let us go back inside."

She nodded and took the arm he offered. She decided she liked the Earl of Greymore very much.

Yet some part of her rebelled at the thought. In her heart, she yearned for Darcy.

Chapter 20

When Darcy saw Greymore lead Elizabeth out onto the terrace after the first set, his blood boiled. It was early in the evening, and the terrace was likely to be deserted. What was Greymore's design in getting her alone?

Darcy warned himself to keep calm. Greymore was a gentleman, one Darcy would trust even with his own sister. He should rejoice that such a man treated Elizabeth as an equal.

Even as he told himself this, the vision returned of his planting the man a facer.

He accompanied Lady Cressida back to her mother. "Your ladyship," he said to the countess, "I must compliment you on the excellent music. This promises to be a festive evening."

"Thank you, Mr. Darcy. You and Cressida made a fine-looking couple on the dance floor. So graceful, both of you. After such vigorous exercise, I am sure my daughter must be thirsty."

"Mama—"

"Of course, ma'am," Darcy said, then turned to Lady Cressida. "May I bring you a lemonade?"

"Thank you. That would be most welcome." Her voice contained that sound of aristocratic ennui that was typical of her. But a sweet smile shone in her eyes.

In the refreshment room, he ran into his cousin Josh. "Lady Cressida?" his cousin teased. "I expected you to open the dance with Miss Elizabeth Bennet."

"Miss Elizabeth Bennet is my dear friend," Darcy said noncommittally.

Josh nodded pensively. "Do you have designs on Lady Cressida?"

The question caught Darcy off guard. Why did the minds of the *ton* jump so effortlessly from dancing to matrimony? "None at all."

"She is, as they say, a diamond of the first water."

Darcy pondered that. Did Josh admire Lady Cressida? Of this year's crop of young ladies making their come-out, she was amongst the most eligible. "How well do you know her?"

"She and Arabelle have been friends forever," Josh said. "I have always been fond of her, but it is odd thinking of her as a woman rather than a girl."

"No dark secrets?" Darcy asked with a wry grin.

"None at all. She is exactly as she seems. Any man would be lucky to have her."

A burst of raucous laughter emerged from the card room. Probably a group of puppies who had sneaked a flask into the party. Darcy should warn a footman to keep an eye on them.

He turned his attention back to Josh. "I noticed you dancing with Miss Peabody."

Josh chuckled. "Read nothing into that. She is a sweet girl, and I want to help make her first season a success."

Darcy nodded. He was not surprised. The Fitzwilliam and Peabody children had been friends since birth. But lately the relationship with Rolf Peabody had become strained.

Darcy said to Josh in low tones, "I did not expect to see Rolf here."

Josh pursed his lips. "Lady Greymore could hardly invite the viscount and viscountess, and exclude him. He lives with them, you know."

"One wonders how Wayne convinced his wife to agree to that arrangement."

Josh looked around and dropped his voice still further. "Wayne cut off Rolf's allowance. Wants him close, to keep an eye on him."

"The man is a menace." Darcy's jaw clenched. "He should not be permitted in polite society."

Josh frowned. Finally, he said. "Without his father to protect him any longer, perhaps he will turn over a new leaf."

Darcy gave his cousin a hard look. "Do you truly believe a man like that can change?"

"I believe in repentance and forgiveness, yes."

Josh had to say that, being a man of the cloth. Darcy took him at his word, but did not view the situation with the same certainty.

"Only if the repentance comes from the heart," Darcy insisted. "If Rolf thinks his brother will throw him out on the street, then his goal will be to avoid getting caught. Not to change his behaviour."

Josh patted Darcy's back. "Come, cousin, this conversation is too serious for a ball. The lovely Miss Peabody awaits this lemonade. I had best get back to her."

Darcy watched him go, then ladled out two cups of lemonade—one for Lady Cressida and one for her mother. He hoped Josh was right, but Darcy's misgivings were strong.

Josh did not know the whole story. He had been out of town establishing himself in his new parish the previous season. That was when the rumours about Rolf Peabody had begun to surface.

Rolf was a thorough villain. Darcy had seen with his own eyes how the man had tried to impose himself on an unwilling housemaid. Reports about tradesmen's daughters soon followed. Darcy did not believe for a moment that the loss of the old viscount's indulgence would change the man.

Darcy looked into the card room and spotted the group of young bachelors. Lord Wayne was standing before them, lecturing them with what must be a confiscated flask in one hand. Darcy grinned at the sight.

Then, his stomach tightened. Wayne was as fine a man as Darcy knew. A pity his brother had turned out wild.

Darcy found Lady Cressida and handed her a cup of lemonade. Her mother was standing some distance away, talking with Viscountess Wayne. Darcy sipped the second cup himself. "Do you know Lady Wayne well?" he asked Cressida in low tones.

"She has long been friends with my sister."

"I understand Lord and Lady Wayne toured Scotland after they married."

Cressida gave him an enigmatic smile. "Yes, and I was terribly jealous. She sent my sister some lovely letters describing the moors with the heather blooming around the lochs."

He said in a more serious tone, "It is a pity the old viscount passed away soon after the newlyweds returned."

She pressed her hand to her heart, and her eyes glittered. "Yes, the dear old man. I was excessively fond of him. He declined quickly during their absence."

"And now Rolf has moved in with the newlyweds. That must be difficult."

Cressida's eyes widened a moment, but then she smiled sweetly. "Every marriage has its challenges, Mr. Darcy."

Her tone made it clear the subject was closed. Yet he suspected she knew more than she let on. Her smile was deceptively light hearted.

Was Josh right? Should Darcy forget about Rolf Peabody and enjoy the ball? He did not wish to see Arabelle, nor any of the other young ladies, suffer at the hands of a rogue as Georgiana had. But he could do little aside from keeping an eye on the man.

The next set began, and Lady Cressida's partner came to claim her. Darcy looked about and saw Miss Peabody without an escort. He asked her to stand up with him and led her to the floor.

Priscilla Peabody was a girl of seventeen—and as naïve upon her come-out as any young lady he had known. Wayne ought to have waited another year before presenting her to society.

Rumour had it, though, that the viscountcy was in distressed circumstances. He seemed eager to marry off his sister to a man of fortune as soon as possible.

Miss Peabody was pretty enough, fresh-faced with that coveted English rose complexion. Her hair was ash brown, her eyes almost black. Her figure was neither particularly slender nor curvaceous. But her gown complemented her to pleasing effect.

Silence ensued while they waited for the dance to start. She was not poised and demure like Lady Cressida had been, but shy and awkward. He supposed it fell upon him to put her at ease.

"How are you enjoying the season?" he asked.

"I feared I would be lost without Mama to guide me through it, but Lady Wayne has been kind in helping me. I am fortunate Wayne married when he did."

"I heard it was a love match."

"Very much so! But Papa's death has put a strain on us all, I am afraid."

He nodded sympathetically, his heart squeezing. "I understand how it feels to lose your parents too soon."

"Yes, you do." She looked at him with sad eyes and touched her fan to his arm. "Georgiana has been a great friend to me through it all."

"She is quite fond of you." He wondered if he should invite Miss Peabody to come to Pemberley in the autumn, if she had not made a match by then. It would do Georgiana good to have a friend with her, and would likely ease some of the strain on Wayne's household.

He said to her, "Wayne and his wife must have many stories of their trip to Scotland."

"Oh, they do!" she cried. "But I get so confused. I cannot keep the cities straight. I keep thinking that Inverness is in Austria or Bavaria—"

"Are you thinking of Innsbruck?"

"Yes!" She looked relieved. "And by the time I realize they're speaking of Scotland, I have missed the whole conversation."

He nodded his understanding. The girl seemed impossibly young. How could Wayne think of letting her marry? Yet the right husband might be better able to care for her than Wayne himself, if the rumours were true.

The country-dance began, giving them little opportunity to speak to one another. Still, he enjoyed the reel. His partner was lively and energetic, and a pretty blush soon touched her cheek.

Afterward, he got her a drink from the refreshment room before returning her to Lady Wayne. The viscountess was young and pretty, about twenty-two. Hazel eyes were set in a heart-shaped face. Her chestnut hair was arranged in a chignon.

"Mr. Darcy, good to see you. How is Georgiana?"

"She is well. I hope you and Miss Peabody will visit her soon."

"We will. She is a lovely girl. Will she come out next year, do you think?"

Darcy contemplated that. It was a prospect he wished he could avoid altogether. "Perhaps the year after. To be honest, I cannot bear the thought of her marrying."

Lady Wayne's expression turned coy, her eyes gleaming. "Ah, but that is because you are still a bachelor. That condition is easily remedied."

He nodded while wearing a tight smile. Time to make his escape. "So my aunt reminds me daily." He bowed and went to find a partner for the next dance.

As the evening wore on, Lizzy could not stifle the hope that Mr. Darcy would ask her for the supper dance. Nothing of the sort happened. He did not speak to her, he did not approach her, he did not meet her eyes across the room. In fact, if she wandered in his direction, however unintentionally, he seemed to walk the other way.

It happened again when she approached Arabella and the Countess of Matlock. As she got close, Mr. Joshua Fitzwilliam stepped aside to reveal Darcy. When Lizzy was twenty feet away, he bowed to his aunt and hied towards the card room. Lizzy could hardly believe he would behave in such a childish manner.

"I can hardly believe my nephew would behave in such a childish manner," she overheard Lady Matlock say.

"I beg your pardon, ma'am?" Lizzy asked.

"Ah, Miss Bennet, how good to see you," the countess replied. "You have had a partner for every dance, I noticed."

"*Some* gentlemen seem happy for my company," she replied.

"Might I escort you for the supper dance?" Joshua asked.

Her heart lifted, then dipped again. She liked Joshua, and so would be happy for his company. But now there would be no chance at all of giving the dance to Darcy.

Why was she letting herself think about the man in such terms? Darcy had made it painfully clear that he did not intend to dance with her that evening. He had only spoken to her during the first set because he had been forced to do so.

Anger burned in her chest. She had been such a fool. She had let herself believe his attentions over the past two weeks had signalled a change in him. When in fact, he had made his attitude plain the night they had met. Elizabeth Bennet was beneath his notice.

She was good enough to be a companion for his sister, but nothing else. He would no more consider Lizzy a potential marriage partner than he would Mrs. Annesley.

Her anger steeling her, she said, "Yes, Mr. Fitzwilliam, I would be happy to join you for the supper dance."

"Excellent! Your sister is engaged to my brother Peter for that dance. Perhaps we can all sit together afterward."

"With Peter!" Arabella cried. "Did not Mr. Bingley ask her?"

Josh gave his sister a wry grin—one he sported much of the time, Lizzy was coming to realize. "Peter approached her when we first arrived, before Bingley had led her out to open the ball. Perhaps Bingley did not think to secure her for a second dance before they had finished the first."

"I hope," Lizzy said, "that your brother's interest in my sister is sincere, and he is not simply trying to best Mr. Bingley."

"Peter would not impose on a young lady in that way," Mr. Fitzwilliam assured her.

"My son Joshua, however..." the countess said, letting her voice trail off.

Her youngest son put his hand to his heart. "Mother, I am desolate," he said dramatically.

They chatted a while longer, then Joshua led her out for the cotillion. When they had met at the theatre, she had quickly discerned him to have an appealing sense of humour. But she was not prepared for the way he left her laughing during the course of the dance. It was all she could do to keep from losing her place in the set.

After the dance, she walked in to supper on Joshua's arm. They joined Jane and Peter, who were seated at a spot with only two chairs left. Lizzy noticed Bingley looking at them from across the room. Jane gave him a coy smile.

The tables were laden with sumptuous dishes. Cold ham, glazed carrots, bread, cheese, fruit, and a variety of pastries were just a few of the offerings. The aromas made Lizzy's mouth water. Her stomach rumbled with hunger after so much dancing. She forced herself to take delicate bites and attend to the conversation.

"Is this the first time you have been to town for the season?" Joshua asked them.

"It is," Jane said. "I did not expect to find it so busy in February. We receive more invitations than we can accept. Will it slow down for Lent, do you expect?"

"There will be no balls during Lent," Peter said, "but the social activities will continue."

"What else has the *ton* to do, after all?" Joshua asked sardonically.

His words made Lizzy realize how idle their own lives had become since removing to Mayfair. With some degree of embarrassment, she said, "There must be charitable work."

"Yes," he replied, "and many ladies of the *ton* provide assistance to various worthy causes."

Lizzy thought a moment. "Can you recommend anything? Jane and I could do some sewing to help the orphanage."

"Oh, yes!" Jane cried. "We have little to keep us occupied, now that we are staying at Lady Purcell's home."

"The hospital always needs linens and bandages," Peter said.

"Yes, thank you, Dr. Fitzwilliam," Lizzy said. "That is an excellent suggestion. I wish we had inquired sooner." Upon her request, the gentlemen instructed the Bennet sisters on how they could help.

Once they had made their plans, Jane turned to Joshua. "I have been wondering—while you are in town, does a rector in your parish fill in for you?"

Joshua swirled a glass of wine. "The curate takes care of Sunday services and other parish business. I am not completely idle, however. I am writing a book of sermons."

"How wonderful!" With a twinkle in her eye, Jane asked, "Will you be the next Mr. Fordyce?"

"Good heavens, I hope not," Joshua said gravely, although a smile curved his lips. "For all his sincerity, the man's view of young womanhood was both idealized and infantilized. Only the most placid of creatures would have benefitted from his ideas. The man obviously never met my sisters."

Lizzy laughed at that. "Nor ours. Though our sister Mary reads his work quite studiously."

Joshua scowled. "I can recommend some books that might be of more benefit," Joshua said. "Fordyce has his place, but young ladies profit from a wide variety of ideas. That way, they can better reach their own conclusions."

"Good heavens, Josh." Peter's fork clanked against his plate. He said in mock horror, "The last thing we want is for ladies to have ideas or reach conclusions."

"They will do so whether we want them to or not," Joshua replied. "Better they receive the benefit of an education to guide them."

"You must have heard the rumours," Jane said, lifting her cup of punch, "that Lizzy is a great reader."

"I have," Joshua said, turning towards her. "Any truth to it?"

Lizzy held up her fan until she could suppress her smile. "I enjoy reading, as I do many things."

"Such as?" Peter asked.

"Country walks, for which Berkeley Square is a serviceable substitute. Playing the pianoforte, at which I am barely proficient."

"Come, now," Joshua said. "Your humility does you credit—but do you not wish to amaze us? Tell us what you excel at."

"She would excel at delivering set-downs," Jane said, "except that she is too polite to say them aloud. Instead she regales me with them after the fact."

"You must give us an example!" Peter demanded.

"It would be unkind," Lizzy said.

"Come, now," Joshua complained. "What would you say of me?"

She thought a moment. "That you will be a bishop before you turn thirty, if your skills at dancing are any indication."

Joshua chuckled. "Do you disapprove of me, Miss Elizabeth?"

She took a sip of champagne. "I must see your sermons before I decide that."

"Then you will. I would value your opinion on them."

She raised her brows, then smiled, pleased at the prospect.

The more Lizzy came to know the Fitzwilliams, the more she liked them. But the family member she most wanted to spend time with was not at the table. She spotted him on the other side of the room, and Darcy's eyes met hers for the briefest moment before he looked away.

All lightness left her. *Stupid, stupid, stupid.* She must stop pining for a man she could not have.

Chapter 21

Darcy looked away from Elizabeth's gaze a moment after it caught his own. Seeing her with Greymore had been a trial. Watching her with his cousins was torture.

At his side, Lady Cressida spoke sweetly. She was a talented and clever conversationalist. Well-versed in art, history, science, and current events, no subject seemed beyond her.

But he could not help noticing she was something of a dilettante, with no real depth of understanding. Which could not be helped, really, as she was only seventeen. In another five or ten years, she would be brilliant.

As much as he enjoyed speaking with Cressida, his gaze kept wandering to Elizabeth. Why had he not asked her for the supper dance? He had let those puppies at the club discourage him. Yet he did not care what they thought. He cared only for her reputation.

Perhaps, in his desire to protect her, he had been overly scrupulous. Surely one dance could not hurt. He had been avoiding her all evening. It was not only rude—it was unkind.

"Mr. Darcy." Lady Cressida recaptured his attention from the pair of fine dark eyes across the room. "I understand your cousin Mr. Joshua Fitzwilliam is writing a book of sermons."

Darcy blinked a moment, regaining his bearings. This lovely girl had a dozen suitors trailing wherever she went. He had engaged her companionship, and now he was neglecting her. He must do better. In answer to her question, he said, "He is."

"Does he subscribe to a particular moral philosophy? That is, beyond the usual teachings of the Church?"

Darcy refilled her wine, and his own. "He believes that the best way to lead a moral life is to find a pursuit that brings happiness and contentment. In that way one can avoid the temptations of idle pleasure."

She picked up her glass and took a delicate sip. "He is not what I would call a studious type."

"No indeed. No one likes to laugh more than Josh."

Cressida's eyes turned from Darcy to Josh, and back to Darcy again. "I see he is keeping Miss Elizabeth Bennet entertained."

Darcy's face heated. Earlier in the evening, he could have warned his cousin away from Elizabeth. Josh had provided the perfect opportunity. Instead, Darcy had called her a dear friend. What a dunce he was!

He thought Cressida's lips curved up slightly before she spoke. "She and your cousin seem compatible. Do you think they are a match in the making?"

"Certainly not," he said, then realized he had spoken more emphatically than he ought. He did not offer an explanation, as he had none, other than his own preference for Miss Bennet. Fortunately, Lady Cressida did not ask.

Instead, she continued, "Mr. Joshua Fitzwilliam is an eligible man. Do you believe him opposed to matrimony at this particular time of life? I would think a clergyman would want to marry as soon as possible, to set an example for his flock."

Darcy looked into her beautiful green eyes. She was not speaking idly. Was she trying to arouse some jealousy in him towards Josh and Elizabeth? Or did she herself have designs on his cousin?

"I believe, ma'am, that he is not particularly inclined to marry at the present moment. But he might be persuaded in that direction by the right woman."

"And what sort of woman would that be?" While her tone conveyed boredom, he suspected her feelings were quite the opposite.

"Obviously, her character must be above reproach." Darcy

set down his fork and gave the subject some thought. "Beyond that, she must be educated and intelligent. Not attached to worldly pursuits. Kind and generous, and eager to do her part to help his parishioners."

"And does that describe Miss Elizabeth Bennet, do you think?"

He considered a moment. "It does. But then, it also describes you."

A blush touched her cheek—the first hint of emotion he had seen from her all night. So that *was* the reason for her interest. She wanted Josh for herself.

If her brother would allow it, it would be an excellent match for Josh. But was his cousin interested? Josh's heart was not engaged elsewhere, not really. It ought to be easy enough to turn his attentions to Lady Cressida.

When the supper party broke, he led her in the direction of his cousin and Elizabeth. Cressida curtseyed to Josh and gave him a coy glance. He did what any red-blooded male would do, and asked her to dance.

Darcy met Elizabeth's eyes and forced himself to speak. "You look well this evening. But then, you always do. I hope you have been enjoying the dancing?"

"I have, I thank you. I noticed that you have exerted yourself, and danced every set."

He hated having this conversation. He should have asked her to dance. Or at least explained why he had not. But how could he tell her what the rumourmongers were suggesting? That she would soon become his *mistress*?

Instead, he said, "It has been a trial, I assure you. But I learnt my lesson during my time in Hertfordshire. I was schooled on the rudeness of leaving ladies unattended." He gave her a teasing smile, which she did not return. Clearly she was upset with him for avoiding her earlier.

He must undo this. He pressed her hand. "Did you receive the roses I sent this morning?"

"I did. White roses. The colour of newly fallen snow."

"The colour of perfection."

She blushed and pulled her hand away. "I am far from perfect, as you well know."

"I know nothing of the sort."

The orchestra began to play. His heart sank in his chest. He wanted to continue this conversation, but it would have to wait. "Excuse me. I am to escort Miss Peabody for the next dance." He bowed and sauntered off.

With every step he took away from her, he cursed himself. *The colour of newly fallen snow.* After his behaviour that evening, she now thought him cold. And why should she not? Everything in his demeanour had sent that message.

It was time to be honest with her. He was hopelessly in love. His uncle's family and the rest of the *ton* had already accepted her. Why was he holding back?

She was a woman who spoke her mind. She hinted at the passion within her, like a vein of lava flowing just beneath the surface. He wanted that ardour—not the placidity of Lady Cressida or Caroline Bingley.

Or worse, the silly prattling of a chit like Miss Peabody.

He approached the girl for their second dance of the evening. He noted again that her face was pleasing enough. Her bright blue gown became her, and the white flowers looked pretty in her hair.

Darcy tried to pay her the attention he ought. She was in her first season, after all. He did not wish to hurt her feelings.

"What a splendid evening this is!" she cried as the dance got underway. "I am desolate that we will have to go *six weeks* without a ball during Lent. Does that make me very wicked, do you think?"

"Not at all. You may regret those words, however. In the height of the season, you will attend parties every night. You may miss the quieter pace leading up to Easter."

"I cannot imagine I would." The dance parted them a moment, but she continued as she returned, "I adore parties! How could anyone want to stay home, when so much is going on?"

"I daresay your brother Wayne would."

"Oh, Wayne is a stodgy old man."

"Old!" Darcy grinned at that assessment. "He is but a couple of years older than me."

"It is not his age so much as his manner. He would rather read a book than watch a play. Can you imagine?"

"I can. I suppose it depends on the book, and on the play." The dance took them in opposite directions, but they soon came back together. "Who is your favourite playwright?"

She knitted her brow. "I cannot remember all their names. Who wrote *The Beggar's Opera*?"

He stared. "You have seen *The Beggar's Opera*?"

"Rolf took me, before Wayne came to town. Wayne would never allow it. But oh, how I laughed! I do enjoy a comedy, do not you?"

Darcy nodded, but his mouth formed a grim line. What was Rolf thinking, taking his seventeen-year-old sister to such a play? She had just come out. A girl that age was impressionable. He would not expose Georgiana to such entertainments until she was at least twenty.

When the dance broke up, he handed his partner over to Lady Wayne. As Miss Peabody's mother was no longer living, her sister-in-law was her chaperone. The young viscountess, however, did not seem to keep a very good eye on her young charge. Darcy made a mental note to speak of the matter to the Countess of Matlock.

A wave of exhaustion rushed over him. He could not do this anymore. He could not prance around making conversation with foolish girls. Or even exert himself to be pleasing to sophisticated young women like Lady Cressida.

He had found the wife he wanted. She was in this very ballroom. Why not propose? He could do it tomorrow.

He could do it tonight.

No, that was not rational. He should sleep on it. It was two in the morning, for heaven's sake. He was not exactly at his best mentally. Doubtless, neither was she.

But Elizabeth *would* accept him, would she not? As much as she liked to spar with him, they were friends. At least he thought they were friends.

In truth, he had not behaved as a friend that night. He had been too concerned about convincing the world he was not in love with Miss Elizabeth Bennet. Under the circumstances, he had to admit, he had not done much to endear himself to her.

But she *must* marry. She must marry a wealthy man. And he was a wealthy man.

As, of course, was nearly every other man in the room.

What a fool he was! His greatest fear was that Elizabeth's only reason for marrying him would be his money. Yet he assumed his money would be the only reason she needed. If he wanted her, he would have to court her. To shower her with attention the way Bingley did Jane.

And that was precisely what he would do. He would ask her for the next set. He would—

But as he spotted Elizabeth, Rolf Peabody stepped towards her. Darcy's blood roiled. In three short steps, he was by her side. "I beg your pardon," Darcy said to Rolf, "but Miss Bennet has promised this dance to me."

Darcy swept her towards the floor before she could object.

He did not meet her eye, just kept walking. The waltz music began before they could take their places. Darcy's skin heated.

He had not realized it was a waltz. Holding Elizabeth so intimately through an entire set would be a grave temptation. But there was no getting around it now.

They got into position, his hand on her waist, hers at his shoulder. This dance had been designed with the intention of torturing a man. He kept a respectful distance despite the raging desire to pull her body to him. To press his lips hard to hers. His body strained against the ache.

Elizabeth's eyes flashed at him as the dance got underway. "I do not recall your engaging me for a waltz this evening, sir."

He met her intense gaze and barely contained a shudder of

longing. "Forgive me. I had to get you away from Rolf Peabody. He is a blackguard and a fortune hunter."

Her brows arched, and a wry smile curved her lips. "If he is a fortune hunter, then I have nothing to fear from him."

The words cut him. He hated the reminder that she had no dowry to speak of, as if that made her less desirable. She was as brilliant a jewel as he had ever seen.

But he could not let that distract him. He must keep this conversation practical, and warn her of the dangers Rolf posed. "He would as happily take a woman's virtue as her money."

She stiffened, and her cheeks flushed. "Do you think my virtue so freely given?"

He swallowed. Clearly she felt insulted, inferring a meaning he had not intended. He explained with a grave tone in his voice, "What is not given, Rolf might take by force."

Her eyes widened as she seemed to comprehend his meaning. "Surely he is not as bad as that. Otherwise he would not be permitted into polite society."

He wished that were true. Her country upbringing did not serve her in this instance. "His father was a viscount," Darcy said, "and got his son out of any number of scrapes. The old man doted on Rolf and never believed the stories about him. But I have seen with my own eyes that he *is* as bad as that."

Elizabeth turned silent. The strains of the music stretched between them. He left her to her thoughts. At last, she said, "Then I shall take you at your word."

"Thank you." The tension in his shoulders eased. He recognized the compliment she offered. It was no small thing to win the trust of Miss Elizabeth Bennet.

The air was heavy for a few beats before she said, "It is I who should thank *you*. I have danced with many fine gentlemen this evening. None, though, are as fastidious as you in selecting partners. Your willingness to dance with me raises my value."

His mouth grew dry. She was teasing him, and he did not much like the way it felt. Especially when her words were justified.

With an overabundance of feeling, he declared, "Any man who cannot see your worth must be a blockhead."

Her lips parted, and some emotion flashed in her eyes, but he could not read it. The next moment, it was gone. "You did not seem to think so when you first came to Hertfordshire."

A fact that testified to what a blockhead *he* had been—though he dared not admit that to her. Not when her violet scent was driving him mad, and his lips ached to kiss her.

"There is a goodly crowd here tonight," Darcy forced himself to say. "But the floor is comfortable enough for dancing. That will likely change after Easter. It will be a great squeeze."

He sounded an absolute dolt. Could his words be any more insipid? He hated nothing so much as small talk. Yet he could not say the things he longed to say, nor do the things he longed to do.

As they danced, she fit perfectly in his arms, and their feet moved in harmony, as if they floated on a cloud. He wanted to feel her softness against him, to trail kisses down her neck.

This was madness. He must have her. He could not endure a month-long courtship, nor waiting for the banns to be read. With a license, they could be married in a matter of days.

Would this infernal waltz never end? He was moments away from throwing her over his shoulder and carrying her off to have his way with her. How was a man to bear this agony?

He could not speak. He could not find words. A confession of love was on his lips, and all other thoughts had flown from his mind.

Elizabeth leaned towards him and said, "Mr. Darcy, I perceive there are eyes upon us." She nodded in Miss Bingley's direction. "Should we pretend to be enjoying ourselves?"

Her words were like cold rain. Was she not enjoying herself? Was he?

No, he was sullen and distracted. He ought to be giving this woman all his attention, and instead his brain was fogged by lust.

What could he say? "I am your humble servant, ma'am. If you wish me to prattle stupidly, I shall be happy to oblige."

She let out a soft laugh that sounded like bells. "I do not believe a man of your intellect could do anything stupidly."

"You might be surprised."

Her eyes danced enticingly. "Why Mr. Darcy, that is the first self-deprecating thing I have heard you say."

"You think me insufferable."

Her hand caressed his shoulder, and he bit back a curse at the wave of desire rushing over him.

She, apparently, had no idea how her touch plagued him. She said, "You set high standards for yourself, and live in fear of not meeting them. But no one likes perfection in another. It makes us feel our own imperfections more acutely. Others might tolerate your foibles better, if you tolerated them better yourself."

Whoever had invented the waltz should be drawn and quartered. He could not escape her penetrating gaze. "You take liberties with your observations."

"I do. Ought I to apologize?"

"No." He lifted his brows. "I should thank you for your wisdom."

"And yet I perceive you do not." Her voice held a laugh.

This time, he was able to smile at her teasing. "Perhaps the wound has hit too close to home, and is too fresh to be appreciated."

The music came to a stop at last. Inwardly, he praised Jove for it. Outwardly, he bowed and smiled and led Elizabeth back to the chaperonage of her aunt. With a few polite words, he left her in that lady's care.

He must get a grip on himself. A ballroom was no place to decide whether to make an offer of marriage. He must wait until the morrow, until his head was clear.

In the meantime, he would remain in torment.

Chapter 22

Lizzy simmered, looking about the ballroom but seeing nothing. Darcy had dismissed her. He had deposited her with her aunt and walked off without a backward glance. As if their intimate conversation had meant nothing to him.

They had spoken frankly to one another. Not in an overly familiar way, but in a manner that signalled a commonality of understanding.

But within a matter of seconds, apparently, all that had been forgotten. Now he was asking his old friend Caroline Bingley to dance, and Lizzy wanted to cry.

Strange as it was to admit, Lizzy had never felt more herself with anyone than she did with Darcy. It was as if they could say anything to each other without being judged. He accepted her gentle chiding and she his seriousness. They did not always agree—but each understood the other's essential integrity.

And now, he was heading out to the dance floor with Miss Bingley.

Miss Bingley—with her twenty thousand pounds and her fashionable education and her sharp-tongued wit. She could never make him happy, but the world would not think him a fool for marrying her.

Lord Greymore approached and asked Lizzy for the next set. She felt a temporary thrill of victory. But it fled once the dance got underway. Darcy experienced no uncomfortable breaks in conversation with Caroline. They chatted like the old friends they were.

Why did Lizzy allow herself to think twice about him? In the grand scheme of their lives, Darcy was no more than a passing acquaintance. A man so conscious of his place in the world, so determined to do the right thing, would never marry a woman of her station.

And why was she thinking of marrying Darcy? She had despised the man since the night they met. Recalling herself, she turned her attention to Lord Greymore, even flirting with him a bit.

Her heart stuttered, though, when she caught sight of Lady Arabella. She was dancing with Peabody. Darcy's words repeated in Lizzy's mind. A cold sense of dread rushed through her, washing away her own petty disappointments.

The two looked comfortable together, perhaps more than they ought. Their demeanour could be forgiven, considering the history of their two families. But did not their connection make it easier for a fortune hunter to prey on an innocent?

With a tight sense of unease growing in her midsection, Lizzy asked Greymore, "What do you know of Mr. Peabody?"

His lips pressed together. He narrowed his brow as if giving the question serious consideration. At last he said. "I respect you too much to give you a vague response, so excuse my bluntness. Rolf Peabody is a reprobate and a scoundrel. My mother did not invite him here tonight—he came with Lord and Lady Wayne. I have had a sturdy footman watching him all evening to keep him from getting any of the young ladies alone."

Lizzy's lips parted and her stomach dropped.

"I apologize," he said. "I have shocked you."

"No," she said. "Mr. Darcy warned me of the same thing. But *his* standards are so high, one does not know how to assess his opinions."

Greymore gave her a pensive smile. "He is exacting but fair. He would not disparage a man without good cause."

She nodded, glad to hear Greymore's opinion on the subject.

She turned her gaze back towards Arabelle and Peabody, assessing them. The girl looked at ease, and not at all alarmed by the familiar way he seemed to address her. Even though the distance between them was too close for mere acquaintances.

He could not accost her in the middle of the ballroom. If he managed to get her alone, however... Was Lizzy's imagination running away with her? It sounded like something out of a novel.

In fact, it sounded exactly like a novel Miss Peabody had lent her. *The Mischievous Marquess*, perhaps? Or was it *The Lascivious Lord*? A man had compromised an heiress so she would have to marry and turn over her fortune to him. If Miss Peabody had told her brother about it, might he not have designs on Arabella?

Instinctively, Lizzy looked in Darcy's direction. His eyes seemed trained on his young cousin dancing with the blackguard. Then, his gaze travelled about the room and met Lizzy's. She gave him a nod of understanding.

When the dance ended, Lizzy was nearer the couple than Darcy. She watched in dismay as Peabody led Arabella out into the garden. She was about to say something to Lord Greymore when a servant came and whispered to him. Lizzy curtseyed and excused herself. Without even getting her shawl, Lizzy followed after Arabella, pulse pounding.

Lizzy stepped outside and scanned the surroundings. If Greymore had had a footman watching Rolf Peabody, should not the man be nearby? But no servant was in sight.

She spotted the couple at a distance. Perhaps she was overreacting. But if Peabody meant no harm, why was he leading Lady Arabella away from the house and onto an unlit pathway?

Lizzy came upon the spot where Greymore had tossed the

fallen tree branch earlier in the evening. After hesitating a moment, she stopped. Better to take precautions and feel foolish, than to regret a lack of preparation.

She reached over the low boxwood and gripped the rough branch. She gave no more than a passing thought to ruining her gloves. Now was not the time to worry about such petty things.

Instead, she rose to her full height and assessed her weapon. The limb was about three feet long and two inches in thickness. It was heavy in her hand, suggesting that the wood was sound rather than rotted.

Looking around, she had lost sight of Peabody and Arabella. Carefully, quietly, she moved in the direction they had gone, keeping to the shadows.

A sharp, feminine voice caught her ear. Lizzy was too far away to make out the words, but she headed towards the sound. A few moments later, a scream pierced the air. Lizzy clutched her skirts and ran forward.

"Unhand me!" Arabella demanded.

Approaching from the side, Lizzy could not see Peabody's face. But with the lamps burning behind her and a full moon overhead, what she *could* see alarmed her. His fingers were wrapped around Arabella's wrist while the fist of her free hand pushed at his chest.

Lizzy did not bother to warn him. She clutched the branch in both hands. With all her force, she brought it down between his shoulder blades.

He lurched forward and fell to his knees. Turning to look behind him, he scrambled to his feet. His eyes met Lizzy's, his expression dark with rage. "Why you little—"

He swore most vilely, looming over her. Breathing hard, she held her weapon poised to strike again.

Heavy footsteps approached from behind. Lizzy dared not turn her attention from Peabody. Eyes glittering with fury, he took a step towards her.

A figure from behind surged forward and felled him with

a single blow. With a groan, Peabody stayed down this time, clutching his jaw.

"Darcy!" Arabella cried. She rushed towards him and he caught her in one arm. Then, he stepped between her and the man on the ground.

Trembling violently, Lizzy gripped the branch harder. A hand covered hers. She jumped, and Darcy gently took the weapon from her. She exhaled, her breath rasping in her chest. She was safe now. Darcy would handle things.

More footsteps came. "What happened?" the colonel's voice asked.

Half gasping, half sobbing, Arabella said, "He dragged me... into the shadows...and tried to...force himself on me."

"I did nothing of the sort," Peabody said. "I did not have to. She was willing."

"Liar!" Lizzy cried. "I saw her struggling. I heard her tell you to let her go."

The sound of a sword unsheathing behind her straightened Lizzy's spine. "Richard, no!" Arabella cried. "You cannot kill him!"

Lizzy's blood roared in her ears. Fear played in Peabody's features as the sharp tip of a metal blade pressed to his throat.

"Don't do this," Peabody cried, his voice shaking. "You'll hang."

"I think not." The colonel's tone was cold as ice. "I am the son of an earl, protecting my maiden sister."

"Richard, steady," Darcy said in a calm tone.

A stream of epithets left the colonel's lips that no gently bred lady ought to hear. "Give me one reason why I should let this blackguard live."

Peabody gasped. "My brother—"

"Would be better off without you," the colonel spat. "You're a drain on his finances, a disgrace to your name."

"This is not a battlefield," Darcy said carefully. "We should settle this like gentlemen."

"I'm amenable to that," said the colonel. "What's your

preferred weapon, Peabody? Swords, pistols, fists? I can best you at any of them." The way he brandished the blade, he seemed to be relishing the cat-and-mouse game.

Darcy said, "Miss Bennet, perhaps you could help Lady Arabella back to the house. And send out her brothers Peter and Joshua."

"I won't go," Lady Arabella cried. "I won't let Richard kill him."

"He won't," Darcy said. "Not unless Peabody tries to escape before the constable arrives."

"Constable!" Peabody said derisively. "You wouldn't ruin the lady's reputation that way."

"There are four of us here," the colonel said, not moving an inch, "who can testify that you are entirely to blame."

"You are all connected to the lady. You would lie to protect her, and everyone knows that."

"I am not connected to the lady," Lizzy said pointedly.

Peabody scoffed. "Please, Miss Bennet. Anyone who saw you dancing with Darcy could recognize the intimacy between you."

"Intimacy! How dare you!" Lizzy stood ramrod straight, her eyes so focused on Peabody she could see nothing else.

"You have set your cap on him," the villain said, voice dripping with malice. "Do not deny it."

A blinding rage pulsed through her. "You are a fool. Mr. Darcy and I are nothing to each other."

A silence followed. At last, Colonel Fitzwilliam said, "I would be obliged, Miss Bennet, if you would take my sister to my mother. Darcy and I will handle this blackguard."

Her mind in a haze, Lizzy stepped backward. Awareness of her surroundings slowly returned: The cool breeze. The rustling leaves. The glimmering torches casting shadows on the ground.

She set her arm around Arabella's waist. As they turned, Lizzy spotted a garden gate a short distance away. Just outside the gate, a carriage sat as if waiting.

As if waiting to drive Mr. Peabody and Lady Arabella away.

∞∞∞

They walked in silence, and Arabella shivered. Lizzy wished she had her wrap. All she could do was pull the girl closer until they reached the warmth of the house.

They stepped onto the lit pathways, the cloak of darkness lifting. "Mr. P-Peabody is my friend," Arabella said in bewilderment, her teeth chattering. "He's always been my f-friend."

"You are not the first young lady to be deceived in a man's friendship."

"How could he do this?" Arabelle asked, the pitch of her voice rising. "If you had not come, he would have...he would have..." A sob escaped her throat.

"You are safe now. We will find your mother—"

"You do not think Richard will hurt him?"

Lizzy's heart beat wildly. She knew little of how the aristocracy handled matters of honour—apart from what she read in novels. Finally, she said, "The colonel will do what is right."

That seemed to calm Arabella. Lizzy, though, had no idea what *right* meant under the circumstances.

Inside, they spotted the countess. Lady Matlock took one look at her daughter and blanched. Abandoning Lady Featherstone midsentence, she rushed towards them and grasped Arabella's hands. "What is wrong?"

"Mr. Peabody, he..." Arabella let out a nervous titter. "He tried to kiss me, but Miss Elizabeth stopped him."

Her voice very cold, the countess said, "Did he touch you?"

"He grabbed my wrist—"

"He what?" Lady Matlock roared. Then, composing herself, she said in a harsh whisper, "When I am through with him—"

"It is fine, Mama. Richard and Darcy are dealing with him."

Lizzy got Arabella's shawl and laid it over the girl's shoulders. Her mind still reeled from what she had seen. Peabody had planned this. Somehow, he had distracted the footman Greymore had watching him, and...

Joshua approached, with Peter just behind him. Lizzy spoke to them in low tones, telling them what had happened. As the expression in their eyes turned from confusion to fury, fear crept into her voice. "Peabody had a coach waiting. He meant to kidnap her."

Joshua paled, and he gripped her hands. "Thank heavens you were there to stop him."

"Darcy was not far behind me. Please, you should join him and your brother in the garden. They may need your help with...the disposition of Mr. Peabody."

Joshua's eyes met his brother's, and Peter nodded.

The gentlemen stole away. The countess told her daughter Nerissa to take Arabella to the ladies' retiring room. The countess would join them presently. The girl would need a few moments to compose herself.

Lizzy stood watching them go, numb, unsure what to do next. The countess snapped her out of her reverie. In a sharp voice, she asked, "What happened?"

Lizzy wondered how much to tell. The countess deserved to know the truth, even if Arabella had been reluctant to reveal it. But Lizzy wondered whether the woman could keep her composure, here in the middle of a ballroom. Even a sturdy woman like Lady Matlock was not immune to shock. Her youngest child had nearly been kidnapped by a villain.

At last, Lizzy spoke in as firm a voice as she could manage. "Mr. Peabody took Lady Arabella out to the garden for some air. Mr. Darcy had warned me that the man was not to be trusted, so I followed them. When I came upon them, he had hold of her and she was pushing him away."

"It was clear she was unwilling? He could not have been mistaken?"

"It was quite clear. Colonel Fitzwilliam said he would see the man at dawn, but I believe cooler heads have prevailed."

The countess looked grave. "No doubt Peabody was trying to ruin her, to get his hands on her fortune."

Lizzy nodded but said nothing.

The countess looked about, brow drawn. Then, she turned her intelligent eyes to Lizzy. "If we keep this between ourselves, it should not have a permanent effect on Arabelle's reputation."

"I agree," Lizzy reassured her. "The poor girl has been hurt enough."

"I shall put it out that the man insulted her. My friends and their daughters will cut him. I hope I may rely on your discretion."

"Of course!" Lizzy gripped the countess's hand. She did not want the woman to have any doubts. With resolution in her tone, Lizzy said, "Lady Arabella did nothing improper. She is not to blame."

Lady Matlock's eyes glistened a moment, but she blinked and shook off the emotion. "Thank you. I trust my sons will mete out the appropriate punishment to Mr. Peabody. His brother the viscount will not protect him the way his father did."

Lizzy nodded weakly.

Lady Matlock squeezed Lizzy's hand. "Thank you, my dear, for your kindness to my daughter. I shall go and check on her now. I hope you will call on her tomorrow. I suspect she will be happy to have someone she can confide in about her ordeal."

The invitation surprised Lizzy. But in fact, it would ease her mind to see Arabella on the morrow—or rather, later that day. "I shall do so, if she wishes for my company."

The countess gave her a grateful smile and nod before heading away.

Lizzy looked about the room, hardly noticing her surroundings. Then, she caught sight of Darcy re-entering the ballroom from outside. He strode towards Viscount Wayne. They spoke briefly. The viscount turned ashen, then headed outside. When Darcy did not follow, Lizzy went to speak to him.

"How is Arabella?" he asked in low tones.

"She is with your aunt and Lady Nerissa. Lady Arabella told her mother Mr. Peabody had tried to force a kiss on her."

"Do you think she believed that?" Darcy asked.

Lizzy's mind blanked a moment. She did not know which *she* he meant. The stress of the previous quarter hour was catching up to her.

Wearily, she said, "The countess seemed to believe it. As for Lady Arabella...no, I do not think she is as innocent as that. The way he held her against her will, he clearly had more than a kiss in mind."

Darcy swore under his breath. Lizzy had never heard him use such language before. She placed a hand on his arm, feeling his turmoil. "Are you needed outside?" she asked.

"Not at the moment. I shall accompany the ladies home. Wayne and my cousins will handle Peabody for now. I must say, I am grateful for the colonel's military training."

"If you had not helped him keep his head," Lizzy countered, "things might have gone worse for Mr. Peabody."

The cold rage in his eyes was so unlike him, she hardly knew what to make of it. She remembered what he had been through with Wickham and Georgiana. This event must have reawakened those feelings.

She forced herself to ask, in a voice that came out as a mere whisper, "Did you see the coach that was waiting?"

Darcy gave a curt nod. "I believe we must involve the earl in administering justice. Peabody is a menace. He must be stopped, or he will do this again."

Lizzy gripped his arm tighter, a lump forming in her throat. He gazed at her a long moment, then laid his hand atop hers. Suddenly remembering they were in a ballroom full of people, however, she pulled away.

"Mr Darcy..." She wanted to apologize. She wanted to say she had been angry and terrified. She had not meant the thoughtless words she had spoken.

He was not *nothing* to her. She was in love with him. She knew beyond a doubt that she could never esteem a man as she did him.

But her emotions were raw and jumbled after everything that had happened that night. Nothing the two of them had spoken could compare to what had nearly happened to Arabella. Peabody had planned to abduct her, and…and…

The thought sent a shiver through Lizzy. She could not speak. There were no words.

"You are overwhelmed," Darcy said. "Let me take you to your aunt."

She nodded and accepted the arm he offered. Mrs. Gardiner greeted her with concern. "Lizzy, how pale you look!"

"I am tired, that is all. Perhaps we could go, when Jane finishes this dance."

"Of course," Mrs. Gardiner said with a kind smile. "Thank you, Mr. Darcy, for looking after my niece."

"My pleasure, ma'am." He bowed and took his leave. Watching him go, Lizzy wondered whether he would ever speak to her again.

Chapter 23

Amidst the chill of the February morning, Darcy entered his carriage. It was still dark in the last hour before dawn, but the lamp inside offered a soft glow. He settled into the supple leather seats and waited for Bingley, a few steps behind him, to say his good-byes. Bingley considered everyone a friend, so it might take some time.

Could the Greymore ball have been more of a disaster? He had offended Elizabeth. Her cold words had cut to his heart. But he could not blame her. The fault was entirely his own.

And then there was the attack on Arabelle. What was to be done about Rolf Peabody? The man could not be left free to roam the streets and assault another young woman. Lord Wayne would not protect him as his father had done.

Darcy would see Bingley home, then head to Matlock House. Ultimately, the earl would decide what must be done about Rolf. Exhausted as Darcy was, it would likely be hours before he could sleep.

Bingley, though, stepped into the carriage looking as if he could keep revelling for hours. "What a splendid evening!"

It had been for him, of course. He had danced two sets with the woman he loved, the woman he would assuredly marry before the season ended. Bingley had always been a lucky fellow. True, he had lost his parents too young, as Darcy had. With that exception, Bingley had the most astonishing good fortune. No wonder the man was cheerful.

Darcy tapped the ceiling, and the carriage got underway.

Bingley frowned at him and asked, "Why do you look so glum?"

"Rolf Peabody insulted my cousin Arabella."

"Good heavens!" Bingley paled, his expression one of concern.

Despite trusting his friend implicitly, Darcy withheld the details. His first responsibility was to protect Arabelle. "My aunt is not taking the situation lightly. I expect Rolf will be persona non grata as far as the *ton* is concerned."

Bingley's face fell. "Is Lady Arabella well?"

"I believe so. She has had a shock, and will likely feel the effects of it for a while. Much as Georgiana did after Wickham's treachery. But Arabelle is surrounded by family. She will be herself again."

His brow narrowing, Bingley pressed, "You seem worried. Is something else amiss?"

Darcy winced. The memory of Elizabeth's words still stung. He considered how much to tell his friend. "I am going to make Miss Elizabeth Bennet an offer of marriage."

A huge grin swept across Bingley's features. "Capital! I knew you would come around. Jane will be delighted. Should not you be happy, now that you have made this decision?"

Hoof beats clomped on the cobbled streets. "I worry that Miss Elizabeth will not have me."

Bingley squinted in confusion. "Why would you say that?"

"This evening, she said with some vehemence that we are nothing to each other."

Pursing his lips, Bingley seemed to contemplate that a moment. "I can see how she might draw that conclusion. You did avoid her all night. If that is how you ply your suit, might I recommend a different tactic?"

Darcy gave him a sardonic smile. "I confess, I began the evening determined to give all my attention to Lady Cressida."

At that, Bingley bridled. "I thought you wanted *me* to marry Lady Cressida."

"Do you wish to marry her?"

"Of course not. I am going to marry Jane. And you may tell your cousin Peter I said so."

Darcy nodded slowly. "Do you fear he might win her away from you?"

"Not at all. I would not wish him to waste his time and look a fool."

Darcy wondered whether the same could be said of himself. Elizabeth's words could not be considered encouraging. But then, to counter Olimand's gossip, Darcy had actively tried to distance himself from her. It appeared he had succeeded.

Now he had to undo it.

With his prospects looking bleak, Darcy could not say why he had confided his plans in Bingley. Yet he was glad he had. Somehow, stating his intention made it more real, more solid.

He leaned back and gazed out the window. The sky was lightening, and the shapes of buildings were coming into view. It had been a long night. He hoped tomorrow would be better.

It could hardly be worse.

"By Zeus, man, why did you not come to me?" The Earl of Matlock stared down Viscount Wayne, who looked deeply chagrined. Darcy felt almost sorry for Wayne, despite his brother's behaviour the night before.

At first light, Colonel Fitzwilliam and two sturdy footmen had taken Peabody to his fate. Matlock's funds purchased him a commission in His Majesty's army. The coachman's testimony would have been enough to send Peabody to Newgate if he had not complied.

Now, the colonel was back. After a sleepless night, he, Darcy, and Wayne were gathered in the earl's library.

The room was familiar to Darcy. He had spent many happy hours there as a child looking through his uncle's books. The varied tomes were stacked high in dark cherry bookcases.

The earl's massive desk faced the door, an assortment of chairs gathered around it in shades of green and gold. Velvet drapes pulled back with tassels framed the floor-to-ceiling windows. Beyond them lay the skeleton of the dormant garden.

Matlock, standing behind the desk, was a formidable man. With eight children, he and the countess had run a tight ship, yet the house had been full of love. Darcy's uncle was generous to his friends but a powerful opponent to those who crossed him.

Peabody had been a fool. If he had succeeded in coercing Arabella into marriage, it would not have been legal. He would not have seen a penny of her dowry. And if, Heaven forbid, he had forced himself on her, he would have hanged.

The shape of Peabody's scheme had emerged through the questioning of servants. Each of them had known only their own part, and had not suspected that Peabody intended to abduct the girl. The valet in particular was distraught over the unwitting role he had played.

Wayne sat slumped in a leather chair, eyes trained on the floor. His hair was dishevelled and his cravat long gone. Bitterness laced his barely audible voice as he said, "I did not imagine he could do anything so desperate. I had hoped the harvest would save us, but 1811 was as bad as 1810. Rolf seemed to think marrying an heiress was the solution. I expected him to offer for Lady Arabella—"

"Good heavens, man," the earl said. "Did you think I would let that reprobate marry my daughter? A rake who would break her heart and use her dowry to pay his gambling debts? He has no income, no prospects. When he asked permission to court Arabelle, I turned him down. Just as any responsible father would."

Not to mention, Darcy mentally added, Rolf's nasty habit of meddling with the housemaids.

"Heiress, indeed," the colonel scoffed. "Rolf needs an occupation. The army will make a man of him. I shall see to it."

The muscles in Wayne's face tightened. He gripped the arms of the chair until his knuckles turned white. Then, he met the earl's eyes. "Thank you for handling this matter privately."

"Your father was my friend for thirty years," Matlock said. His voice rose in intensity. "If I had known he had lost control of his faculties, I would have helped in having him declared incompetent. Why did you not come to me?"

Wayne shook his head wearily. "By the time I returned from my wedding trip, it was too late. The money was gone. The steward had bought the unentailed properties for a pittance. He sold them for an enormous profit. And the secretary had mortgaged the entailed properties. He escaped with the funds to America."

Darcy looked at the viscount in disbelief. Old Wayne had been an intelligent, vigorous man, astute in his business dealings. How could it all have gone wrong so quickly?

"What did you do to recover the funds?" Darcy asked. "Surely the steward can be held accountable."

"I spoke with my solicitor, and he said nothing could be done."

"Nonsense," the earl said gruffly. "Young man, you are a viscount now. You sit in the House of Lords. If the law gives you no recourse, then change it. A viscount treated in such an infamous manner! Every aristocrat in the nation would be horrified to learn of it."

"How could I face them?" Wayne asked. "How could I admit I had failed my family so completely?"

Darcy's chest ached for his old friend. He admired Wayne's sense of responsibility, but in this case it was misplaced. He was not to blame for his father's illness nor his brother's villainy.

Matlock said in a clear, confident voice, "Senility is no shame, sir. It happens in the best of families. Why, the King himself is mad."

A look of pain twisted the viscount's features. "I was a fool. I should not have trusted my brother to look after my father while I was gone. As long as Rolf could treat our ancestral home as a gaming hell, he did not care what the rest of the household did."

Wayne sagged in the chair as if all the fight had gone out of him. "The house was a den of iniquity when I returned. And my father..."

His voice broke, and Richard set a steadying hand on Wayne's shoulder. The viscount continued, "My father had been a bit forgetful when I left, but I thought that was just his age. He was seventy, after all. But when I returned from Scotland six months later, he didn't know who I was." His voice broke. "Surely he would not have declined so rapidly if he had not been neglected. I should not have trusted my brother. But I didn't know. I didn't know."

His face sank into his hands. The grief in his words cast a silence over the room.

"Wayne, I have known you all your life," the earl said. "You are a good man. Your brother is entirely to blame in this matter. A couple of years fighting Boney will force him to reform his ways."

The viscount looked up and nodded absently.

"Tomorrow," the earl said to Wayne, "you and I will meet with my man of business. We will discover what is to be done towards making you solvent again. In the meantime, I shall hire an investigator to chase after your father's old secretary in America. Perhaps some of what he stole can be recovered."

Wayne looked at him in awe, and his Adam's apple dipped. "Thank you, sir. I am sorry your family got mixed up in my troubles."

The earl waved away the words. "You did not bring this hardship on yourself. There is no shame in accepting help to raise you out of it."

"At least my sister's dowry was not affected," Wayne said, exhaustion evident in his voice. "My parents' marriage contract protected it. My mother's portion was put into a trust for herself and her daughters. My father could not touch it, nor can I. Priscilla will gain access to it when she reaches her majority, or when she marries. If we make a match for her this year—"

"Your sister should still be in the schoolroom," Darcy interrupted. His old friend needed to hear this. "Forgive my bluntness, but no sensible man would seek the hand of a fanciful child. Given another year or two to mature, she could make a brilliant match. As it stands now, she will be sought only by fortune hunters and old men in need of an heir."

Wayne jumped to his feet, his animation returning. His cheeks flushed and his eyes glittered with anger. "I say, Darcy. This is no concern of yours—"

"If any woman ever wanted a love match," Darcy insisted, "it is Miss Peabody. She is full of romantic dreams. I understand you wish her to gain access to her dowry. But if you marry her off to escape your current troubles, you will destroy her happiness forever."

Wayne continued to glower. Darcy set a hand on his shoulder. "If Miss Peabody is not married by the end of the season," Darcy said, "I shall invite her to spend the autumn at Pemberley. She and Georgiana would benefit from each other's companionship. And a respite from your sister's care might ease some of your burden."

Wayne narrowed his brow. "I cannot allow it. Not with you unmarried."

"By autumn," Darcy said, giving the man a wry smile, "I do not expect to be unmarried."

Despite the late night, Lizzy rose at nine, unable to sleep any longer. She donned her pelisse and left the house with Sally at her side. Walking the short distance to the Matlock residence, she planned only to leave her card. She would call on Lady Arabella later in the day. To her surprise, however, the butler ushered her inside. It seemed she was expected.

The splendour of Matlock House still awed Lizzy. The foyer opened into an Adam-style grand salon under a domed ceiling. It was ideal for greeting guests before a large assembly. The Prussian blue walls were decorated in white Etruscan bas-relief. Four Corinthian columns defined the centre of the room. They broke the space into more intimate areas perfect for conversation.

While Sally headed to the kitchen, the butler led Lizzy towards the drawing room. Before they reached it, however, a door opened. Lizzy stopped short. Darcy stepped into the hallway.

Her breath stuttered. She had not imagined he might be there. On so little sleep, the sight of him was discomfiting. She did not know which way to look.

Clearly he had been up all night and was a little worse for wear. Or rather, *better*. The less formal look was inviting on him. His ruffled hair begged her to comb her fingers through it.

The thought sparked a rush of warmth through her body. Memories of their waltz the night before tugged at her, and she swallowed. The feel of his arm around her, of their gloved fingers intertwined, of her hand on his shoulder branded by his heat…

How was she still breathing? How did she not dissolve at his nearness? She had insulted him. The embarrassment of it —along with the raw, masculine power radiating from him— ought to have rendered her a puddle on the carpet by now.

"Miss Bennet," he said with a bow. "You are up early."

She curtseyed. "As are you."

"I have not yet been to bed." He coloured and looked away.

Oh, he should not have said it! Now she was envisioning him in a bed with his hair mussed. Something tightened in her belly. A frisson of electricity rushed through her. In her mind, she could feel his lips on hers.

Taking a deep breath, she forced herself to be rational. "You must be exhausted. Pray, do not let me keep you."

"I...yes, of course." He seemed about to take his leave when he grasped her forearm and said, "It was good of you to come. Arabelle can use a friend."

She gave him a nod and a smile, and he quickly departed.

Oh, what a fool she was! She should have apologized for her unkindness the previous evening. But would her words not be sooner forgotten if she acted as if nothing had happened? Perhaps he did not feel insulted at all. Perhaps he agreed with her assessment.

And what could she say? That his coldness at the ball had angered her, after the notice he had paid her before? That was precisely why he had been cold at the ball. To quell any rumours.

She dared not suggest that a close friendship existed between them. Darcy would despise any appearance of social climbing on her part. The fact was, she did not care a jot about Darcy's wealth or position. She had fallen in love with *him*.

Thoughts of Darcy dimmed as she entered the drawing room. Lady Matlock and Arabella sat alone, the girl looking pale and listless. Her eyes were ringed with red. Lizzy's heart lurched at the sight.

The countess rose and greeted Lizzy with a hug. A hug! How had she become intimate with this family so quickly? She liked the Fitzwilliams, and Georgiana, too.

Almost as much as she liked Darcy.

She more than liked him. She was mad for him. She would rather spar with him than have an agreeable conversation with anyone else. Did he feel the same? Had her bitter words destroyed the growing affection between them?

Somehow, she would have to make amends. She could do that, could she not? Some sort of gift, or...well, she knew not what. She would find a way to wipe the slate clean.

"May I make you a cup of tea, Miss Bennet?" the countess asked. "We also have coffee."

"Coffee, if you please."

Lady Matlock turned to her daughter. After a moment, she

prompted, "Arabelle, please do us the honour of serving the coffee."

Arabelle looked up as if her mind had been far away. "Of course." She busied herself with the task. Then, she said, "Miss Bennet, you must help me convince my mother to host a musicale next week. My cousin Darcy has agreed to let Georgiana attend social events in the afternoons. Does that not sound splendid?"

Though surprised Arabelle had raised the subject, Lizzy nodded. "It will please me to see Miss Darcy out in society. The opportunity to mingle more will help build her confidence."

"I agree," the countess said. "I am not opposed to a musicale next week, Arabelle. I must check my calendar, as I said."

Arabella handed Lizzy the coffee with cream in a delicate porcelain cup. The blue rose design was complemented by a cobalt band along the rim and base. "I think," Arabelle said, "I would like to avoid evening activities for a while. Perhaps I should not have come out until Nerissa marries."

The countess's mouth pinched and her eyes glittered, but she remained silent.

Lizzy thought it best to take control of the conversation, to diffuse some of the emotion. "Does Lady Nerissa have a beau?"

"No one in particular," Arabella conceded. "She is looking for a love match. Our sisters made love matches."

"To prominent men, as I understand," Lizzy said with a grin.

"Yes," said the countess. "It is easy to indulge a daughter's romantic inclinations when the man asking for her hand is a duke's heir." She gave Arabella a sideways look. "Do not think we will be so cooperative if he is a St. Giles resurrection man, as in that silly novel by Mrs. Wheedlesuch."

Arabella giggled. "Do not worry, Mama. I am not enamoured of Mrs. Wheedlesuch, as Priscilla Peabody is."

In a moment, the girl's smile disappeared, and her complexion turned ashen. Lizzy grabbed her hand, and Arabelle blinked back tears. Taking out a handkerchief, Arabelle said, "I am sorry to be such a watering pot. I thought I was done crying."

"You have been through an ordeal," Lizzy soothed. "It is natural to be upset. I barely slept last night. I suspect you suffered the same affliction."

"If you had not come when you did," Arabelle said to Lizzy, "I would be locked in a carriage on the way to Gretna Green right now. I cannot get the thought out of my mind."

"But that did not happen," Lizzy said. "You are safe."

"Am I?" the girl asked. "As long as men think they can gain access to a young lady's fortune by stealing her virtue, we are all at risk."

The countess stroked Arabella's hair, and Lizzy sat in silence a moment. She thought about her own younger sisters. They might have been taken in by an unscrupulous officer if they had had any fortune to speak of.

She would not allow such thoughts to reign over her. Danger was a constant in life. Living as if in a prison would be no solution, and would make life intolerable.

"You have not yet developed the instincts," Lizzy said, "to recognize when a man is unscrupulous. I confess that I myself was taken in by Mr. Wickham last fall. I can see now that the hints of his true nature were there, if only I had attended to them."

Arabelle nodded absently. "Richard warned me that Mr. Peabody was a rake, but I did not believe the man was as bad as my brother said." She hung her head and covered her face with her hands.

The countess spoke in a gentle tone. "Sometimes, men try to protect us from hard reality by mollifying their language. They called Peabody a rake, when they meant he was a criminal. If you had known the truth, you would not have gone into the garden with him."

Arabelle looked up at her and shook her head as if trying to clear it. "When Rolf was eight or nine, and I was three or four, I used to ride on his back like he was a pony. We have been friends all our lives, Mama. I knew he had intentions, but I thought they were honourable." The word caught in her throat. She flopped back against the seat cushions. "I shall never trust a man again."

The countess said nothing, but she gave Lizzy a significant look. Lizzy blinked a moment. Then it occurred to her what the countess might want.

Arabelle might be more open to encouragement from someone her own age. The fact that Lady Matlock trusted Lizzy's advice was a great compliment. Tears pricked her eyes, and emotion gathered in her chest.

"Of course you feel that way now," Lizzy said. "How could you not? I admit, I am shaken, too. But some men *can* be trusted. Your brothers, for example. And Mr. Darcy, Mr. Bingley, Lord Greymore…they are all excellent men."

Arabelle's eyes did not soften.

Lizzy considered a moment. "Have you heard men declare that all women are fortune hunters and not to be trusted? And have you felt how unfair it was for them to paint our entire sex that way based on the actions of some? It is the same with men, and treating them all as Lotharios. One must be careful, yes. But most people, I think, are essentially good. If we treated every man as a potential enemy, we would create more harm for ourselves than we would avoid."

Arabelle seemed to consider that. She gave a quick nod. "Perhaps." Then, she sighed and resumed her normal upright posture. "I am tired of that topic. Let us talk of something fun. Like the musicale."

The countess eyed her daughter. "It might be better to hold the assembly at Darcy House. The gathering could be smaller and more intimate there. And Georgiana could play the harp. We do not have a harp here."

Arabella clapped her hands together. "Oh, that is a fine idea! Now I must only get Darcy to agree."

"I believe, my dear," the countess said with a crooked smile, "he would do just about anything you asked of him right now."

The girl's eyes danced. "I had better take advantage of that while it lasts."

Chapter 24

Lizzy returned home to find the drawing room crowded with bouquets and visitors. Bingley ambled amongst the vases of flowers, reading the cards. Each one seemed to increase his consternation. Jane was in a tête-à-tête with Dr. Peter Fitzwilliam. His brother Joshua chatted with Lady Cressida and Lord Greymore. The other gentlemen callers seemed rather bored. They sat with their coffee or walked about the room.

"Lizzy," aunt Gardiner said, "I am pleased you are back. Mr. Witherspoon was about to despair of seeing you before his next appointment."

She curtseyed to him, and he approached. He was about thirty with blond hair and a kind face. His fortune had come from trade, but like Bingley, he had been raised up by the education of a gentleman.

A month ago, she would have thought him an excellent match. Now, however, she had become accustomed to mixing with noble families. Her initial reaction was to dismiss him as a suitor.

She scolded herself inwardly. He was a perfectly nice man as far as she could tell. His blue eyes and pleasing features were complemented by a quick mind. She could not afford to take a cavalier attitude about one so eligible until she was safely engaged.

Her heart gave a little lurch at that. Lately, the thought of marriage brought only one face to her mind. *Darcy*. And now they were at odds with one another.

She should not have let herself voice the pique she had felt towards him the night before. Her feelings had been hurt. She had been hoping for his attentions—expecting them, even. Instead, he had given her every reason to believe he had no romantic interest in her.

Still, she should encourage him, not reproach him. If the man had not yet been won, perhaps he still could be.

She put that thought out of her mind for the moment and listened attentively to Mr. Witherspoon. She decided she liked the man enough to learn more about him. An Oxford graduate, he had an estate in Surrey. He developed new strains of wheat for improved yields in England's damp climate.

Though she could not meet his passion for the subject, she had a passing interest in agriculture. In particular, she admired his dedication to improving the lot of his tenants. However, after only ten minutes, a previous engagement required him to take his leave. She was disappointed.

Her mind quickly returned to its previous occupation. She rose to speak with Bingley. "I saw Mr. Darcy at Matlock House this morning," she began.

"Yes, I believe he was out all night, occupied with a family matter." Bingley's attention was only half turned to her. His eyes kept darting to Jane. "I say, Peter Fitzwilliam has been monopolizing your sister since I arrived. That is not very sporting of him."

"I get the impression he is not a very sporting fellow. He follows his own rules."

"Indeed." Bingley narrowed his brow and said. "Will you excuse me? I wish to speak with your aunt on a particular matter."

She wondered what he was about. He approached Mrs. Gardiner and spoke in a voice loud enough for the entire room to hear. "Ma'am, might I have a word with Miss Bennet alone?"

Lizzy's heart pounded. She met Jane's eyes. Her sister flushed, then beamed, then schooled her features. A thrill went through Lizzy, but she forced herself not to smile.

"Why, yes," Mrs. Gardiner said. "I believe the library is empty. Jane can lead you there. Sally, do go with them and wait outside the door."

Jane rose and Bingley offered his arm. He led her out of the room.

Lizzy's head grew light, and her stomach tensed with apprehension. She warned herself to assume nothing, to maintain a calm demeanour. But really, to ask for a private audience in such a public setting, what other intention could he have?

She looked over and saw the scowl on Peter Fitzwilliam's face. Lizzy took the seat beside him that Jane had vacated, assuming her sister's place by the coffee service.

"You must not take it personally," Lizzy murmured to Peter. "He had a four-month head start on you."

Peter's brow grew heavy. "It is not a foregone conclusion," he replied with a sulk in his tone.

"Perhaps not," she encouraged with feigned brightness. If Bingley was proposing, Jane would say yes.

Then, it occurred to her that Peter's glum demeanour might have more to do with his sister than with Jane. His next words seemed to confirm that suspicion.

"I hope you are well," he asked, "after the shock last night."

Before she could answer, Joshua Fitzwilliam came and sat on Peter's other side. "I understand," Joshua said to her, "that you did my family a great service."

A squeezing sensation gripped Lizzy's solar plexus. In the Greymore's garden the previous evening, everything had happened in a rush of panic. Looking back on it now, some moments were remarkably clear, others a blur.

"I suspect I behaved foolishly," she said. "I have never brandished any sort of weapon before. The man might have overpowered me."

"But he did not." Joshua smiled gravely. "You laid him low, from what I heard."

She gave a nod of acknowledgment, then said, "It was your brother's sword that kept him on the ground."

"Your action delayed the man," Joshua insisted, "while Richard got his sword from the cloak room. You are as much a hero as anyone."

She did not argue further. Instead, she accepted the compliment with grace. Then, she said, "I have just come from Matlock House. Have you seen Lady Arabella this morning?"

"Briefly, at breakfast," Joshua said. "She seemed herself."

"I found her more sensitive than usual," Lizzy said. "As if she fears what thoughts might come if she were alone and silent."

"Perhaps," Peter said, contemplative, his eyes unfocused. "She had a scare. If she suffers any nervous complaints, I can prescribe a draft to help. I hope it will not come to that."

Lizzy nodded. "She is lucky to have older brothers to look out for her welfare."

For not the first time in her life, Lizzy wished she had a brother or two. The events of the previous night reminded her how vulnerable a woman could be.

Lord Greymore and Lady Cressida came and greeted Lizzy. Their kind words cheered her. Greymore cut a fine figure as he always did. His dark coat and buckskin breeches were perfectly tailored to his form. His presence did not knock the breath from her body, however, as seeing Darcy that morning had.

The Fitzwilliam brothers gave up their seats as she served coffee to the newcomers. Dropping two lumps of sugar into Cressida's cup, Lizzy asked them, "Is your mother having a good rest? Such a gracious hostess she was last night."

"That is her speciality," Greymore said. "She loves to entertain. I am sorry I could not avoid telling her about Lady Arabella." A dark look fell across his features.

Lizzy's eyes darted to Cressida, wondering how much she knew.

"Arabelle is my dearest friend," Lady Cressida said. "She told me everything."

Greymore let out a resigned sigh. "And what she did not hear from *her*, she overheard when we questioned the servants."

Lizzy drew in a quick inhale of breath, but then forced a placid look onto her features. Those conversations could not have been appropriate for the ears of a gently bred young lady. But then, Lizzy suspected the lady in question would have been difficult to deter.

"Are you suggesting I was eavesdropping?" Cressida teased her brother.

"Are you denying it?"

Lizzy smiled at the easy banter between them. She liked them more than was fitting upon so short an acquaintance.

Cressida touched her brother's arm. "At any rate, I had no choice but to stand up for poor Martin. As angry as you were, the man worried you would dismiss him without a reference."

Lizzy soon surmised that Martin was the footman watching Peabody. As brother and sister chatted, Lizzy pieced together the events of the night before.

Some extra servants had been hired for the ball. Peabody had sought help from two of them in luring Martin from his post. First, a footman had offered to stand watch for a few minutes so Martin could use the necessary. The dancing was still underway, so Martin could see no harm in it.

But then a maid asked his help in carrying some heavy trays from the kitchen. Though he returned to the ballroom as soon as the music ended, it was already too late.

Lizzy said in low tones, "I understand Mr. Peabody is now an ensign in Colonel Fitzwilliam's regiment."

"A fitting fate, that," Greymore said. "I imagine he will be sent to the Continent once the weather permits."

"No doubt," Cressida said. "I predict a Forlorn Hope in his future."

Lizzy had heard the term before. She understood it as a desperate mission which no one was expected to survive.

Greymore looked at his sister askance. "One must volunteer for a Forlorn Hope."

Cressida fluttered her fan. "So they say."

Lizzy caught the implication. Despite what Peabody had done, she doubted Colonel Fitzwilliam would behave dishonourably.

A murmur rippled through the room as Bingley and Jane re-entered. All other thoughts receded. Jane's expression was radiant, and Bingley was all smiles.

Lizzy's heartbeat sped up. What a relief it would be, if her speculation was correct! Indeed, what else could account for those happy faces?

Though tempted to run to Jane's side, Lizzy kept her composure. Cressida leaned towards her and said in low tones, "So he has come to the point at last."

"One hopes." Lizzy gave her a sly smile.

It was not long until the drawing room emptied. Cressida kissed Lizzy's cheek in parting. The brother and sister were on their way to call on Arabelle, to offer what comfort they could.

When they were gone, Lizzy turned and looked around the near-deserted room. She took a deep breath. Only four of them remained in the drawing room, which was large enough to serve as a ballroom. They looked at each other in anticipation before Bingley approached Mrs. Gardiner. Jane, for her part, came and took her sister's hands.

"Oh, Lizzy!" she cried, but could say no more before emotion overwhelmed her. Tears fell onto her cheeks. Lizzy hugged her, and Jane managed to say, "Surely I must be the happiest of women."

It was all the confirmation Lizzy needed. The relief was so strong, her legs might have given out if Jane had not been there to support her. All the worry for the future was gone. Jane would soon be irrevocably united with the man she loved.

Lizzy stepped back and gazed into her sister's eyes. "If you are the happiest, then I am the second happiest."

"Thank you. Oh, Lizzy!" She hugged her again, then pulled back and said, "Bingley will ride to speak to my father today. When I think of the pleasure and peace of mind this will bring my mother and sisters, I feel so very blessed. Could any woman deserve such joy?"

"If any woman does, it is you, dearest Jane."

Stroking her sister's shoulders, Lizzy felt the satisfaction of a mission completed. This, after all, had been her purpose in coming to London—to see Jane and Bingley engaged. But the hollow in her chest reminded her that she had unfinished business.

She had made a grave misstep the night before. She told herself that it had been the distress of the moment—that Darcy would understand. But could any man understand? Must he not think her pronouncement held some hint of truth? That he meant nothing to her?

Darcy had been all kindness to her since the thoughtless words had left her mouth. Somehow, she had to make amends. What could she do? A simple apology was not enough.

She determined to take Sally and walk to Piccadilly. A walk always cleared Lizzy's head. It was not their at-home day, after all. So before they received more callers, she donned her pelisse and went on her way.

Somehow, she would fix this.

Chapter 25

As the crowd bustled past the storefronts, Lizzy berated herself. Why had she thought this walk through the shopping district a good idea? A single young lady did not buy a gift for a gentleman who was not a family member. She had seen a few items she had thought might appeal to Darcy, but how could she give them to him?

She was about to despair and head home. Then, she and Sally approached the bookstore where they had stopped that fateful day. The day when Darcy had saved them from the rain. In the window was a placard reading "First Edition." She looked closer and noted that the book was by Walter Scott. Had not Darcy been looking for a first edition of a Scott book that day? Which one had it been? She could not recall.

She and Sally stepped inside, and Lizzy asked the proprietor about the book. The price was dear, but she had enough coin with her. She could give the book to Georgiana. She could say, rightly, that it was the sort of book her brother would approve of.

As the proprietor got her change, Sally whispered, "Was that not the book Mr. Darcy was looking for? I remember thinking how romantic it sounded, 'The Lady of the Lake.' Does it not, miss?"

Lizzy could not help smiling at that. "It does."

She wondered whether the poem was as romantic as it sounded. What did that say about Darcy, if it was? He seemed stiff and rational, but perhaps he had a softer side.

"Oh!" Sally cried. "I just remembered. If you do not mind, Cook asked me to get some ginger root from the market if we came this way. It should take but a minute."

"Of course." Lizzy watched her go, the bell on the door ringing in Sally's wake. After a wistful moment, she turned as the owner, an Indian man of about thirty, brought the change.

Whilst she waited for Sally, she ran her hand over the book. The paperboard cover was russet red, the spine gilded with a leather panel for the title. Inside, an engraving showed Scott sitting with a dog in his lap. The sweet image touched her heart.

As she perused the poem, she found it rather more sentimental than she would have expected of Darcy's tastes. She smiled at the thought.

Engrossed in the story, Lizzy did not notice a patron step up beside her until he spoke. "You are a fan of Mr. Scott?" Darcy's voice asked.

She spun to face him. He must have been reading over her shoulder. Her cheeks blazed as if he had caught her in some untoward act. But in fact, he could not know her purpose in coming to the bookstore that day. She had no reason to feel ashamed.

She was about to speak when her careless words from the night before resounded in her head. *Darcy and I are nothing to each other.* How could she have let her guard down so completely, and spoken in such an unkind manner?

Her temper had gotten the better of her. Darcy ought to resent it. Yet here he was, speaking courteously. It was more than she deserved.

She tried to swallow, but her mouth had gone dry. "The last time I was here," she said, "I heard you mention this book to your sister."

She realized her mistake instantly, but it was too late. The look on Darcy's face showed that he perfectly understood her meaning.

"The last time..." He blinked, his mouth pinched. "I do not

recall seeing you here that day."

"No, Sally and I were in the corner, behind a stack of books." Her cheeks grew even hotter, if that was possible. She must be bright red.

Darcy's voice was dull as he said, "And you chose not to make your presence known to me."

She breathed deeply. Things could not get much worse between them, so she spoke honestly. "I believed you might thwart my efforts to find Mr. Bingley and inform him Jane was in town."

He looked at her with wide eyes a moment. Then, the corner of his mouth lifted. "That was why you were in Mayfair that day? You were looking for Bingley?"

"Yes," she confessed, head high, showing a defiance she did not feel. "His sister's letters had convinced Jane of Mr. Bingley's indifference. I did not believe it. You may accuse me of scheming. But it was no worse than your conspiring with his sisters to separate them in the first place."

Oh, heavens! She was making things worse. What a charge to launch at him! Even if it was true, he must resent the insinuation.

Instead, he let out a low chuckle. "You are quite right. I begin to understand your claim last night. You have seen me as your enemy." He leaned in closer and spoke in a low voice, his breath tickling her ear. "But as it turned out, I did not thwart your plan of finding Bingley. In fact, I led you directly to him. So I hope I may be forgiven."

The closeness of him made her shiver. Her chest expanded as her breathing quickened. She held her hands at her sides, squeezing her skirts to avoid the temptation to touch him.

The ball of pain in her gut began to unravel. He displayed no anger—only tenderness and understanding. Where was the stiffness she had seen in him in Hertfordshire? It was all gone now.

"You were most accommodating," she said in reply. Her lips curved into a faint smile. Then, the directness of his gaze sent a flush of embarrassment through her. She could not meet his eyes.

"So you see," he said, lifting her chin with a gloved finger and forcing her to look at him. "Perhaps we are not enemies after all."

His face was so close to hers, she could almost feel the warmth of his lips. They hovered just above hers like a ghost of a kiss. "No. I have been mistaken on that score." Excitement skittered up her spine.

She gazed into the dark depths of his eyes. He was even more handsome than usual, if that was possible.

She pulled back under the weight of his stare. "I am the one who needs forgiveness. Last night in the garden, I was overset. When that vile accusation was launched against me, I lashed out. Unfortunately, the strike hit you rather than my intended victim."

He pressed her hand. The scent of him, bay rum and wool, filled her nostrils. She wanted to bury her face in his shoulder and feel the fabric of his jacket against her cheek.

"Apology accepted," he said. "I wonder, though, how you could think me indifferent. I grant you, my behaviour last night was abominable. But in the past few weeks, I thought we had become friends. If I have offended you in any way, it was not done consciously, I assure you."

She looked away, mortified. Yet she owed him the truth. She thought about the courtesies he had shown her in London. Her previous resentment of him seemed childish now.

"Last night, when you seemed to avoid me, I fear it reminded me of an old offense." Her stomach contracted painfully. "The night we met, you refused to dance with me, despite the urging of Mr. Bingley. I must apologize for having overheard *another* conversation not meant for my ears—"

He clutched her arm, face pale, a look of horror twisting his features. "Good heavens! I do not remember my precise words that evening, but they could not have been complimentary. Bingley was determined to like everything he saw, and I was just as determined to like nothing. I must beg your forgiveness for any distress I caused you."

Tears stung her eyes, and she had to turn away. "Think nothing of it, sir. I did not expect a man of your station to take notice of a nobody like me."

She choked on the words. She tried to blink away her tears, but they fell traitorously onto her cheeks. What a fool she was! Surely she could no longer pretend to be unmoved by this man. He must see through her as if she were made of glass.

He took out a pressed white handkerchief. Instead of placing it into her hand, as she expected, he gently dabbed her face.

"I assure you," he said, his gentle baritone growing deeper with emotion, "you are not *nobody*. It was ungentlemanly of me to treat you so at the time. You are a woman of taste, beauty, and intelligence. The man I was in September was a great blockhead for not asking you to dance that night. I should have done so. I wish I had."

She could not speak. She could barely breathe. He spoke those courtly words with such fervour, they seemed sincere. But dared she believe him? Did he truly think her beautiful?

She grew more aware of his proximity. Heat radiated from him. She wanted to lean in, to be enveloped by the sensations of him. To feel his lips on hers.

Oh, she should not have come! If she had any sense, she would never leave the house again. Mr. Darcy, of all the men on earth, could surely see that she pined for him. If she allowed herself the luxury of these feelings now, she would never know another moment's peace.

"I must go," she said in a rush. "Sally is next door at the market. Cook will be waiting for us."

"Allow me to escort you, then."

She really could not refuse. In Hertfordshire, she could wander the woods alone for hours. In London she could not walk unchaperoned to the shop next door without risking a scandal.

He offered his arm, and she took it. As they headed to the

door, he said, "Did you wish to buy the book?"

She looked down, remembering herself. "I already did." She held it out to him. "It is a gift for Georgiana."

"Oh," he said in surprise. Then, his features softened and his eyes grew in intensity as the truth seemed to dawn on him. In a deeper tone, voice barely above a whisper, he said, "Oh." He took the book from her and looked at it in wonder. "I—that is, I am sure she will cherish it. Thank you."

She tipped her face up to him and smiled. "You are welcome."

The look he gave her was one of true friendship, and a sense of absolution washed over her. However humiliating this encounter had been, she had made amends. Now there need be no ill feelings on either side. They could be friends at last.

Except now, it might be too late. Unless he made her an offer of marriage, she would have to avoid him after she left London. The love in her heart was too strong. She must forget him.

∞ ∞ ∞

Darcy walked home fairly skipping as he went. Good heavens, he had not been tempted to skip since he was eight years old. When was the last time his heart had felt so light? Was he mad to let Elizabeth affect him this way?

The book was a peace offering. That did not mean she was in love with him. He must not get ahead of himself.

In fact, the engagement between Jane and Bingley had hurt his chances. A week ago, Elizabeth might have felt compelled to accept an offer from Darcy. Now, the women of her family were at least saved from poverty. She no longer *had* to marry. She could afford to be choosy.

When he arrived home, he followed the sound of the pianoforte to the drawing room. Georgiana rose from the bench and walked over to greet him. He gave her the book, explaining it was a gift from Elizabeth.

Giana cocked her head as if perplexed. She turned the book over in her hand, then paged through it. "But she knows *you* are the one who likes Scott. We have spoken of it." She gasped and stared at him with wide, blue eyes. "The book is for you!" she cried, her voice full of youthful jubilation. "It is the first edition you wanted."

Darcy spoke blandly. "Do not be absurd. A single young lady cannot offer a gift to a gentleman." He tried and failed to suppress a smile.

Giana set down the book and paced about the room, practically jumping up and down. "Are you going to propose to her?"

He furrowed his brow and considered a moment. "Not today, at least. Her sister has just gotten engaged—"

Giana ploughed into him, wrapping him in her arms and squeezing. "Oh, Darcy, this is wonderful news!"

He brushed her wispy blonde hair away from her face. "It is not news yet. I have barely started courting her. And after a sleepless night, I forgot to send flowers this morning. Josh said that when he called on her, the drawing room was overflowing with bouquets."

Giana planted her fists on her hips. "Why is Josh paying her more attention than you?"

"Because I am a dunce."

Giana smiled slyly and rotated from side to side. "I like her very much."

"I do, too." It felt good to say the words, as if some tension in his body had opened and released.

Giana picked up the book again and hugged it to her chest. "Are you in love with her?"

"I *have* been these four months, I suspect. I was loathe to admit it to myself."

"Because you are a dunce."

"Indeed." He shot his sister a warning glance. With a gentle smile, she left him to his thoughts.

Bingley would likely return from Longbourn the next day.

Darcy had never seen his friend so eager in his life. As far as Darcy knew, Bingley had not left the house that morning intending to propose. The drawing room full of flowers and gentleman callers might have driven him to the point.

Josh had said Peter was taking it rather hard. Which was ridiculous, since he barely knew Jane. Perhaps Darcy and Josh should take Peter to the club that evening to get foxed. Probably the best thing for him.

Darcy would not ask Josh to stop his attentions towards Elizabeth. But he would tell his cousin they were rivals. Josh would likely back off amiably and find another.

Lady Cressida, for instance. The two of them would make a fine pair. She would be an excellent bishop's wife.

Darcy went to Matlock House. The butler greeted him and said the countess was in the drawing room. Darcy showed himself back.

As he drew closer, the sound of sobs reached his ear. Rushing forward, he found Arabella crying on her mother's shoulder. The sight of her was a punch to the gut. He had let his own happiness distract him from her troubles.

He sat beside her and took her into his arms, drawing her onto his lap. The countess silently rose, patted his shoulder, and left them alone together. Arabelle wrapped her arms around his neck and said, "I am such a fool."

"No." He stroked her dark brown hair, the smooth tresses hanging loose about her shoulders. "You trusted your friend."

"Richard warned me about him. Nerissa warned me about him. I could not believe he had turned out so bad. He has always been kind to me. Now I understand why. It was my dowry he wanted."

Darcy suspected that Peabody had wanted her for more than her dowry. In his own twisted way, perhaps he had even loved her. But telling Arabella so would be no consolation. Peabody had demonstrated a selfish possessiveness. He had been willing to hurt her in order to win her.

"You will not have to worry about the man again,"

Darcy reassured her. "Six months from now, he will be on the Continent fighting Bonaparte, under your brother's command."

She nodded absently.

"Has Georgiana been to see you?" Darcy asked.

Arabelle shook her head. Her mouth tightened, giving her a forlorn expression.

"Send her a note," he suggested, "asking her to come. She will be a comfort to you. She has been through something similar."

"Wickham did not try to kidnap her."

He hugged Arabelle closer. "I wish you had not learnt about that part."

Her voice rose, and fire burned in her cheeks. "I saw the carriage. I knew at once what he intended. What a villain he is!"

Darcy was glad to see her angry rather than sad. He did not like her blaming herself. He hated to think this experience might calm her exuberance, but perhaps that was for the best. She had let down her guard, and a man had taken advantage.

The thought chilled his blood. His jaw tightened. When Georgiana came out into society, Darcy would not let her out of his sight for an instant. Elizabeth would be just as vigilant. Her quick action the night before had gained them valuable seconds. Time that might have protected Arabelle from ruin.

That was the sort of woman he wanted for his wife. Last night, she had looked like a warrior. Standing over Peabody's prone figure, a club in her hand ready to pummel him if he tried to rise... He had known then that he *must* have her.

He had felt her hand shaking with terror when he took the club from her. But she had fought like a tigress protecting her cubs.

She was magnificent.

Richard stepped in. "Is all well here?"

Arabelle rose and wrapped her arms around his shoulders. "My hero."

"As long as there is breath in my body," Richard said, returning her embrace, "I shall make sure you are taken care of."

She kissed his cheek, then sauntered off, saying something about finding her mother. The two men watched after her for a moment.

Standing next to his cousin, Darcy said in a low voice, "She seems to be holding up."

Richard looked at him sadly.

"Come now," Darcy said with forced joviality, "she is a spirited girl. She will be over this in a month."

"A week, more like." Richard gave him a thin smile. "What brings you here?"

"I was about to look for Peter and Josh." He listened a moment, the snick of billiard balls reaching his ears from a few doors away. "I thought we could take Peter to the club to cheer him."

Richard nodded his approval. "I wish I could join you. Unfortunately, I have to be at the war office in the morning." He looked Darcy over, and the corner of his mouth rose. "Something is different about you. You look oddly relaxed."

Darcy squared his shoulders. He *felt* more relaxed. Joy bloomed in his chest. "I have made a decision that has been weighing on me."

Richard raised his brows expectantly.

Darcy hesitated a moment, then said, "I am going to marry Elizabeth Bennet."

Richard laughed, hand at his belly. "She threw down the challenge last night. Are you rising to the bait?"

"I have stopped resisting the one thing that will secure my happiness."

"My mother will be pleased. If you manage to win the chit, that is."

"Do you doubt me?" Darcy asked with feigned offense.

"She knocked Peabody onto the ground. Are you sure she will not do the same to you if your advances are unwelcome?"

"She might." He grinned like a naughty schoolboy. "I shall be cautious."

"Then I wish you good luck, my friend."

They shook hands, and Darcy went to find his other cousins.

∞∞∞

Darcy was awakened from sleep the following day by the sound of a door rushing open. Bingley's voice cried, "I have ridden all the way from Hertfordshire this morning, and you are still abed?"

Darcy sat up and ran his fingers through his hair, smoothing out the knots. He looked at the clock. It was not quite noon. Bingley must have left at dawn to be here so soon.

"It is your fault," Darcy said. "I was up half the night convincing my cousin Peter that Jane Bennet is not the loveliest creature in the world."

"I shall call out anyone who says so," Bingley countered merrily, sitting on the side of the bed. "At any rate, Peter is the reason I had to propose. He was talking to her about blood transfusions." Bingley shuddered. "Can you imagine anything more ghastly? I had no choice but to save her from that discussion."

Darcy could not keep the smirk from his lips. Peter was impassioned about advancing the field of medicine. His latest obsession was blood transfusions. They had been tested on dogs with some success. If the procedure was adapted for humans, Peter said, it might save countless lives.

The subject did not make for scintillating drawing room conversation. Poor Jane must have nodded politely, too kind to let him know she was horrified. Darcy wondered what Elizabeth would have said in the same situation. The thought almost made him laugh aloud.

He lounged back against the pillows. Changing the subject, he asked Bingley, "How were you received at Longbourn?"

"Not as enthusiastically as you might expect," his friend answered. He was still grinning like...well, like a man in love. "Mrs. Bennet did not know what to make of me. Whether to be angry at me for deserting Jane, or to be encouraging in case hope was not lost."

"And Mr. Bennet?" Darcy asked, brows raised.

Bingley scowled. "He was so stern in his lecture on inconstancy, I began to think he would refuse my suit. Not that we need his permission—Jane is of age—but I would not like to marry against her family's wishes. In the end, though, Bennet patted my back and welcomed me to the family."

Darcy gave him an impish grin. "I imagine I shall receive an even more reluctant reception when I ask for Miss Elizabeth's hand."

Bingley's brows rose. "Have you made her an offer?"

"No, but I want to secure her before the season is in full swing. Otherwise, she might throw me over for someone she actually likes."

Bingley frowned, concern written in his eyes, but Darcy could only smile.

"I have been a complete blockhead," Darcy said. "Meanwhile, Greymore has been charming and kind. And he is titled." He scowled a moment. "She would be a fool to choose me over him. But I *shall* persuade her."

"Jane will be delighted!" Bingley stood, his eyes sparkling with mirth. "I shall buy a property as near to Pemberley as I can find."

Darcy nodded. "The sisters will both be pleased at that prospect. It might be enough to tip the scales in my favour," he added drily.

Darcy's valet cleared his throat, standing in the doorway with shaving supplies on the tray in his hands. Bingley made his excuses and took his leave.

While Darcy went through his morning rituals, he considered his chances with Elizabeth. Her warmth at the bookstore had said he already had a tenuous hold on her heart.

He would use that to his advantage.

As for his rivals, they could go to the devil.

Chapter 26

The next morning, Lizzy went downstairs and joined her aunt and sister in the breakfast room. The sideboard was set out with a variety of delights. Toasted muffins, raspberry jam, boiled eggs, and plum cake were amongst the offerings. She poured herself a cup of chocolate, the sweet aroma wakening her appetite.

It was their at-home day, so they took their morning meal a little earlier than usual. With Jane engaged to Bingley, they would have fewer gentlemen callers. But the ladies of the *ton* would come to offer their best wishes.

They moved into the drawing room to await their visitors. Jane exclaimed at the new bouquets. Lizzy enjoyed their beauty, but had otherwise become inured to them.

The *ton* had declared Lizzy an original. Some men, it seemed, were attracted to that appellation. Their butlers sent her flowers of a morning, and they danced attendance on her for a quarter hour out of their day. It was sheer gallantry, without any substance to it. She did not expect an offer from any of them.

A vase of red roses, however, drew her eye. The colour was unexpectedly rich, almost black at the edges. The texture had the look of velvet.

She expected that the flowers were for Jane from Bingley, but she checked the card anyway. Her lips parted when she saw it was addressed to her.

Thank you for the book of poetry. Georgiana cannot put it

down.

Yours &c.

Darcy

Lizzy stared at the message, written in a clear, firm hand. She did not mind his terseness. It was what she expected of him. Still, she did not know what to make of the gesture. Had he truly sent this bouquet to thank her for a kindness towards his sister?

Did he not realize the book had been meant for him? Or was this a way of communicating something more? Something a single gentleman could not say directly to a single lady?

Her pulse quickened. The bouquet itself was not extravagant, but...red roses. She leaned in and breathed their sweet scent. Did Darcy understand what they signified? Lightning shot up her spine at the thought of it.

Despite appearances, she warned herself not to read too much into it. She would not contemplate the possibility that Darcy was in love with her. She paced to distract herself, to burn up the excitement pulsing through her muscles.

Her musings were interrupted by the arrival of Greymore, Cressida, and their mother. Greymore was attentive as usual, but she felt no spark with him. The only man on her mind was Darcy.

Lizzy turned her attention to their female visitors. "Lady Greymore, I must compliment your cook. The supper at your ball was the best I have had since coming to London."

"Thank you, my dear," she said fretfully. "We put so much planning into that evening. Everything went well, I thought, until poor Arabella..."

She broke off at that, her eyes glistening and her lips trembling. "Greymore tried to protect me from the worst of it, but—oh! I wish I had never thrown that ball. Every time I think of it, I get such flutterings in my heart. Thank heavens, dear Miss Elizabeth, you saved her from that scoundrel. Otherwise, I would be confined to my bed with the horror of it."

Lizzy bit back a smile, regarding the older woman with

surprising fondness. Lady Greymore seemed like a more cultured version of her own mother. Mrs. Bennet had been weighed down by five daughters and an entailed property. Without those worries, she might have been a different person.

Now that Jane's engagement had lessened that burden, would her mother's anxiety ease? Would she grow more graceful over time? It must be exhausting, seeking husbands for her girls. Constantly inserting herself into the concerns of others. She would likely appreciate a respite.

After the requisite half hour, the Greymore family took their leave. They were soon followed by the arrival of the Countess of Matlock. With her were two noblewomen, each between forty and fifty, whom Lizzy had not yet met. They were the picture of fashion. Their perfectly tailored walking dresses were decorated with ruffles and bows.

Lizzy felt small and insignificant by comparison. Yet she forced herself to hold her head high. Lady Carson and Lady Featherstone seemed happy to meet the Bennet sisters. Lizzy suspected their attitude resulted from their respect for Lady Matlock.

Were the other women close friends of hers? Or were they simply influential women the Bennets ought to meet? Lady Matlock was a master of diplomacy, a seasoned political wife. She understood the value of connections, even where no personal attachment existed.

The visitors had been there about ten minutes when a commotion was heard in the hallway. "My trunks are in the carriage," a familiar female voice said. "Have the housekeeper ready a room for me. I am staying indefinitely. Now where are my dear Jane and Lizzy?"

The Bennet sisters' eyes met. Jane appeared as surprised as Lizzy, who then turned to her aunt. Mrs. Gardiner sat frozen a moment, then rose to her feet.

"I beg your pardon, Lady Matlock, Lady Carson, Lady Featherstone. My sister Mrs. Bennett has arrived...earlier than anticipated." Before she reached the door, however, the unexpected guest glided into the room.

"Oh, sister!" Mrs. Bennet greeted. She was wearing her best day dress, a striped silk of coral and brown. "I have come to relieve you from chaperoning my daughters. What a lovely house this is! Your friend Lady Purcell must have a pretty penny. A pretty penny! And there is my dear Jane. Come and give your mama a kiss."

Jane rose obediently and kissed her mother's cheek. Lizzy, gathering her wits, followed suit. Her mother's rosewater fragrance transported Lizzy back to Longbourn. To the comfortable feeling of home. But that sensation was all wrong now, in this place where a single false step could wreck her future.

Mrs. Gardiner made the introductions whilst Lizzy held her breath. She prayed her mother would not say anything foolish. To her surprise, her mother was all graciousness, without being obsequious.

"What a pleasure to meet you all," Mrs. Bennet said. "Lady Featherstone, I quite admire that gown. I have heard that longer sleeves are the fashion now in London."

"The modistes must make their money somehow," Lady Featherstone quipped. "If they did not lengthen or shorten the sleeves or hemlines, we could wear last years' fashions. No one would be the wiser."

"Heavens, Amelia," Lady Carson objected. "I have known you twenty years, and have not seen you wear the same gown twice."

"I admit," her friend said, "clothes are my vice. Featherstone scolds me to no end on that score."

Behind a plastered smile, Lizzy gritted her teeth. She wished the small talk would end. The longer the conversation lasted, the greater the chance her mother would make a faux pas. "Mama," she said gently, "you must be tired after your journey. I am sure our guests would understand if you wished to rest—"

"Not at all," Mrs. Bennet said, looking darkly at her. "I would not dream of abandoning our guests."

Our guests, she said, Lizzy noted, as if her mother was now lady of the house.

"Did you have a long journey?" Lady Carson asked.

Mrs. Bennet waved her hand. "It is an easy distance, just one change of horses. I travelled with my friend Mrs. Long, who has come to see her nieces. They are staying with her cousin, Baroness Manley. You know the baroness, of course. Everyone who is anyone does."

Lizzy cringed at her mother's airs. The room grew silent. Judging from their guests' faces, they did *not* know the lady in question. Lizzy had not heard the name mentioned at a *ton* event. She might live mostly in the country, and had come to town only to sponsor her young cousins.

The crack in her mother's thin veneer of gentility soon spread. Lizzy felt as if she were sinking into a cold lake, a layer of ice freezing over her. What had her mother been thinking, arriving unannounced? All hope of making a good impression on Lady Matlock's friends was now lost. Lizzy could imagine the gossip.

Thank goodness Bingley had already made an offer and could not back out now. Not that he *would*. He had never been put off by their mother as Darcy had.

At the thought, Lizzy's chest tightened. Things had been improving between her and Darcy, but now...

Could anything more than friendship exist between them? Perhaps she was a fool to think so. If he did not share her feelings, how could she hope to get over him?

Once Jane and Bingley were married, Lizzy and Darcy might frequently be in each other's company. He had hinted that he would marry soon, for Georgiana's sake. And it was right to do so. Georgiana would show more confidence at her come-out if she had a sister guiding her.

The prospect cut like a rapier into Lizzy's chest. She had not realized until that moment how much she had wanted that role. Darcy's wife, Georgiana's sister—that was who she longed to be. Seeing her mother again might drive any amorous intentions out of Darcy's heart.

She pushed the disloyal thought from her mind. If Darcy could not endure Mrs. Bennet, then he was not a husband worth having. She could not live with a man who made her feel ashamed of her family.

Pushing aside her musings, she forced herself to keep her wits about her. Aunt Gardiner would need help steering the conversation. Jane was too distracted since her engagement to be of much use—in this or any other capacity.

It spoke well of Lady Matlock and her friends that they did their best to put Mrs. Bennet at ease. "Do you have any other daughters at home?" Lady Carson asked. Pleasantly plump and dressed in yellow, she looked like a grapefruit. But as her husband was a crony of the Duke of Devonshire, she might be one of the most powerful women in England.

"I have five daughters," Mrs. Bennet said. "The youngest three are at home in Hertfordshire. Jane is the first betrothed, as she ought to be, since she is the eldest. Now that we have made this alliance with Mr. Bingley, my other daughters will be thrown into the way of other rich men. I expect Lizzy will be next. Though I confess she would have been married by now, if only she did not think herself too high for her cousin. Mr. Collins is rector at Hunsford. Lady Catherine de Bourgh is his patroness. But now he is married to our neighbour, Miss Charlotte Lucas that was. More's the pity."

"Charlotte tells me," Lizzy cut in, "that she is comfortably settled into her role as a rector's wife. I could not be more pleased for her." The lie rolled off her tongue so easily it surprised even herself. Such was testimony to her desperation. "She makes Mr. Collins happier than I ever could." That much, at least, was true.

"Well, Mrs. Bennet," Lady Featherstone said, a kind smile on her face. "I daresay Miss Elizabeth will make a fine match soon. You will forget about her rector cousin."

"Are you aware, Mama," Jane said, "that Lady Matlock is sister by marriage to Lady Catherine de Bourgh?"

"Is that so, ma'am," Mrs. Bennet remarked, turning to the countess. "I have heard wonderful things about her grand manor house at Rosings Park. Is it true that the fireplace alone cost eight hundred pounds?"

Lady Matlock blinked twice and said in a matter-of-fact tone, "I confess I cannot say."

Lizzy wanted to sink through the red-cherry floorboards. After that horrifying exchange, she could not relax for a moment. It was nerve-wracking enough to be entertaining two countesses and a marchioness. How could she carry on an intelligent conversation? She would be preoccupied with guarding against her mother's missteps.

The visitors took their leave so Mrs. Bennet could settle in. Lizzy took Jane aside. "We must convince Mama to return to Longbourn."

Jane looked at her in confusion. "But Lizzy, think what a relief this must be to aunt Gardiner. If Lady Purcell does not object, aunt Gardiner can return home to her family, while we stay on with Mama."

Lizzy's spirits sank. She could not argue with Jane's point. Of course Mrs. Gardiner longed to be home with her husband and children again.

What was left of Lizzy's hopes fell into despair. She had been so enjoying the season with their aunt as chaperone. Now, she half wished she could hide in the country until Jane's wedding.

But of course that would not do. At a minimum, the wedding clothes would need to be purchased. They would have to remain in town at least another week, possibly two. But Jane might wish to stay longer. Indeed, why should she not?

The thought struck Lizzy that there was no reason for *her* to stay, however. Her father would be eager to have her home, now that he was alone with her youngest sisters. Poor Papa!

She had entertained the hope of finding a husband from amongst the *ton*. But with her mother as chaperone, she would soon become a laughing stock. She could not endure that. Better to leave at the height of her popularity than to stay and watch it plummet.

Lent was approaching. The balls would stop then, until after Easter. Parliament would go into recess, and many families would return to their country estates.

Amidst the noise of her mother's demands to the servants, Lizzy secreted herself in her room. Silently, she contemplated her next steps. Standing at the window, she watched the grey, sooty clouds amass above the city.

Sadness washed over her. She could picture the scorn in Darcy's eyes when he saw her mother again. Leaving London was not what Lizzy wanted, but the humiliation of staying would be worse.

∞∞∞

Lizzy sat in the modiste's shop jumping out of her skin. After four hours of looking at fabrics and patterns, she had reached her limit. Jane's patience seemed to have no end, but Lizzy lacked her sister's gentle nature.

"Mama," Jane said, "I believe we have ordered enough night rails. And this fabric is so sheer—"

"My dear, I have been married to your father for twenty-five years. I know better than you do what a man prefers in his wife's night rails."

Lizzy's stomach rolled. The image conjured by her mother's words made her want to wash out her eyes with lye. Jane seemed shocked into silence.

"Mama," Lizzy spoke up, "would my father approve of all these purchases?"

"Jane is marrying a wealthy man. We cannot skimp on her wedding clothes."

Lizzy took a deep breath and blew out a thin stream of air. Her mother's extravagance was beyond anything Lizzy had seen. For all her mother's faults, she knew how to economize. She must be using up the clothing budget for all her daughters for the next year.

While the modiste showed Jane the selection of bridal bonnets, Lizzy spoke to her mother in low tones. "I know Jane's wedding is an important event for our family. I do not begrudge her the expense. But have you tallied up the cost of all this? London modistes are more expensive than the shops in Hertfordshire. Are you quite certain my father can afford this?"

Her mother did not turn to her. She looked straight ahead, watching Jane. "It matters not whether your father can afford it. It matters only that Bingley can afford it."

Lizzy furrowed her brows. "But Bingley is not the one who will be paying—"

A gasp escaped her, cutting off her words. Surely her mother did not mean...even she was not capable of...

"Mama, please tell me you are not expecting Mr. Bingley to pay for Jane's wedding clothes!"

"I do not see why not. They will be married by summer. If we economize, he will only have to buy her more clothes later."

Lizzy's head spun. Her mother's logic was not wrong, but it simply was not done. A man did not pay for the clothes of a woman who was not a family member, unless she was his mistress. Expecting Bingley to pay was unseemly.

"Has he agreed to this?"

"It is not the sort of subject for a lady to discuss with a gentleman."

"Then has Papa discussed it with him?" As if that would be better!

"I see no reason for your father to be involved. When Mr. Bingley receives the bill, he will gladly pay."

Lizzy clutched her reticule, running her fingers over the blue beadwork. How could she make her mother understand how improper this was? "You are having the bill sent to him without warning?"

Her mother turned, her features pinched. "I have had enough of this inquisition, Miss Lizzy. I shall not have my judgement challenged by a girl who knows nothing of the world."

Lizzy said no more. It would be pointless, anyway. Should she tell Jane? Her sister would be horrified. Neither of them could warn Bingley, after all. Lizzy considered writing to her father. But by the time any correspondence was received from him on the matter, it would be too late.

Oh, how Lizzy missed her aunt! Lady Purcell had given her blessing for Mrs. Gardiner to return home to Cheapside. Mrs. Bennet and her daughters could stay on in the Berkeley Square house. Without aunt Gardiner to act as a buffer, Mrs. Bennet had free rein. Her daughters had no choice but to go along with her dictates, however foolish they might be.

Chapter 27

On the day of the Darcy musicale, the Bennet sisters dressed in satin pastels. Lizzy chose a pale lilac, Jane a butter yellow. The colours seemed a harbinger of spring, like a bouquet of hyacinths and daffodils.

When they and their mother arrived at Darcy House, they were shown into the drawing room. Georgiana and Bingley greeted them. The only other guests present were Caroline and Louisa.

Their brother took his fiancée to a quiet corner while Georgiana poured the tea. Lizzy attempted small talk with Bingley's sisters. She had hoped the engagement would force a détente between the Bennets and Bingleys. The opposite seemed to have occurred. Caroline and Louisa seemed even more haughty and aloof.

When her mother joined the conversation, Lizzy excused herself. There was little point in smoothing over Mrs. Bennet's faux pas. Their families were soon to be united. Either they would learn to tolerate one another, or they would not. It was not Lizzy's role to make them behave.

Taking a seat next to Georgiana, Lizzy was about to ask after her brother when the man himself entered. On his arm was Lady Matlock, with Arabelle and Nerissa following.

He looked stunningly handsome. His dark jacket was offset by a gold waistcoat and buff breeches. Lizzy felt his sudden appearance like a shock to the system. Her whole body began to hum.

He had taken to calling each morning along with Bingley. A few times they had talked of riding in Hyde Park, but the weather had not cooperated. Naturally the sun had chosen this day to shine, while they had indoor plans.

Georgiana rose to greet the newcomers, and Lizzy followed. After a brief exchange of pleasantries, Lady Matlock took Lizzy aside. Walking her to the window, the countess said, "I hope you plan to play something for us today, Miss Elizabeth."

"Yes, a Beethoven sonata."

"Splendid." Lady Matlock's features shone with delight. "Darcy has told me how much he enjoys hearing you perform on the pianoforte. And you know he does not give compliments easily."

Lizzy hardly knew what to make of that remark. She had played a few times in Darcy's company, but only with passing skill. She did not feel equal to the praise. Nor could she fathom how she had impressed Darcy.

Hope shimmered in her breast. His kind words implied affection. Or was it only her fanciful heart that made her think so? Darcy's attentions to herself had been noticeable while Bingley visited Jane. Was that in response to the engagement, or was there more to it?

Darcy's diffident manner confused her. It held no particular warmth. Expressions of feeling were not in his nature. His increased sociability might be nothing more than courtesy.

Instinctively, she looked in his direction. Their eyes met. He gave her a soft smile, which she returned.

Anxiety twisted with elation in Lizzy's stomach. To the countess, she said in a light tone she did not feel, "I hope Mr. Darcy has not misled you. I am far from expert. Music is one of my great loves, but I am not as disciplined in practicing as I ought to be."

The countess touched Lizzy's arm. "Sometimes love for the piece brings more joy than technical precision does."

"I shall do my best," Lizzy said with a coy grin. Then her eyes fell on her mother, still speaking animatedly with Caroline and

Louisa. The sisters attended her with polite composure while contempt shot from their eyes.

The usual mix of outrage and embarrassment rushed over Lizzy. Her mother was a trial, to be sure. But should Bingley's sisters not bear it with more grace? The marriage had not been their wish, but what was to be gained from their continued ill humour?

Collecting herself, she lowered her voice as she spoke to Lady Matlock. "I want to thank you, ma'am, for your graciousness towards my mother the day you met. We were all quite surprised by her arrival."

Lady Matlock clasped Lizzy's hand, her palms warm. "You must not thank me. Your mother seems a friendly sort of person. I know of your country roots, my dear. They are of no consequence. You and Miss Bennet will be well regarded wherever you go."

Lizzy swallowed the pebble in her throat. Recalling the Fitzwilliams' recent trouble, she asked, "How is Lady Arabella faring?"

The countess's lips pursed into a thin line. "She has attended but one evening event since the unfortunate incident. We are hoping the ball at Matlock House will restore some of her confidence."

"I hope so as well. I am quite looking forward to it. I shall be happy to do my part to help Lady Arabella, whatever that might be. Whether encouraging her to dance, or sitting out a few sets with her."

The countess shook her head. "That is kind of you, but I would not have you miss out on opportunities to dance. A London season is an expensive enterprise. Do not waste it, my dear."

Lizzy's chest felt as if it were weighed down by a sack of stones. Unless Darcy gave her a reason to stay, the Matlock ball would be Lizzy's last event of the season. She could not let other men court her when her heart belonged to him alone. She would remain in town for the Ash Wednesday services, then return to Longbourn the next day.

She turned to Darcy again, and found this time that his gaze was fixed on Mrs. Bennet. His brow was furrowed and his lips pursed.

That was all the sign she needed. Sorrow gathered in her throat, and tears pricked her eyes. No reprieve would come for her.

For three days, Darcy had grown increasingly restless as he sat in a drawing room with Mrs. Bennet. The rain prevented the relief of an outdoor excursion. Mrs. Bennet's nonsensical remarks elicited incredulous looks and sullen silences from him. He seemed to school his features better now than he had in Hertfordshire. But Lizzy did not think him any less appalled by her mother's behaviour.

If any chance had existed of Darcy proposing, Mrs. Bennet had driven it away. He was not so unkind as to drop the acquaintance. But his manner was stiff again, as it had been in Hertfordshire. Could she blame him? Mrs. Bennet vexed her own family, who loved her. How much more wearisome must she be to a stranger?

Lizzy had to be realistic. Marriage to one of the most eligible men in the kingdom had always been an unlikely outcome. More the fool her, for pinning her hopes—and her heart—on a man who had disliked her family from the beginning.

Darcy pulled himself from his musings. He had been studying Mrs. Bennet's face for hints of Elizabeth. The daughter strongly favoured her father. Barely any evidence of her mother showed in her features. The high cheekbones, perhaps. The upturned nose that on Elizabeth looked like defiance.

He dared a look at Elizabeth, and her fierce beauty lanced him. What a fool he had been to ever think her relations should be an impediment to a match between them!

He had begun, over the past few days, to feel a sort of compassion for Mrs. Bennet. An entailed property and five daughters to marry off. What mother would not turn into a ridiculous husband-hunter?

Her impudence had become a sort of amusement to him. He could not condone a lack of propriety. But a cleverness in getting one's way by skirting the rules held a certain appeal for him.

After all, the rules had robbed Mrs. Bennet's children of their inheritance. She was not idle in seeking a remedy—the only remedy available to gently bred young ladies. He could see no fault in that.

True, she was crass and provincial. Stunningly so sometimes. It was all the more astonishing that Elizabeth and Jane were so cultured. Crediting their natural intelligence and sensibility, he admired them the more for it.

His eyes wandered again to Elizabeth, watching for an opening so he could speak with her. At last the countess took a seat with Georgiana, and he made his way to Elizabeth. He pressed her hand in greeting. "How lovely you look, Miss Elizabeth. Purple becomes you."

She smiled. "Thank you. You look rather stunning yourself."

"Oh," he said stupidly, taken aback. His thoughts became muddled as a powerful longing gripped him. Finally, he remembered to speak. "Thank you."

A coy smile curved her lips. "Jane and I were happy to be invited today, even though we will have to sing for our supper, so to speak. I am always pleased to see Miss Darcy and your Fitzwilliam relations."

"The feeling is mutual, I assure you." He realized he was still holding her hand. She had not let it drop, nor had he released it. But he must, he realized. People would be looking at them, speculating.

He patted Elizabeth's hand and reluctantly let it go. The break in contact seeped into him like icy water. He had the strongest impulse to reach for her again, to feel her warmth.

Instead, he crossed his wrists behind his back. "I am eager to hear you play."

She gave him a wry grin. "I hope that once I have begun, you are not eager to hear me finish."

"Nonsense, you play beautifully. I cannot explain why one musician's performance is stiff, while another's flows. Perhaps you focus on the music as a whole and not just on the individual notes, so it has a more coherent feel."

Her brows arched. "I have not heard it put that way before."

"When one focuses on the notes," he said more earnestly, "one is aware of every imperfection. But little imperfections do not always harm the music. They may even enhance it. They give it humanity."

Her eyes locked with his so intently he could scarcely breathe. She was a revelation to him. If he had been asked to describe the perfect woman, he would not have described Elizabeth. And yet, as she stood in front of him, in flesh and bone, she *was* perfect—or at least, perfect for him.

After a long moment, she said in a sultry tone, "I have not known you to speak so poetically, Mr. Darcy."

"I credit the company. You have warned me more than once to worry less about perfection and more about enjoying life."

She smiled, her lips slightly curved but her eyes shining brightly. "And have you come to my way of seeing things?"

He considered a moment. "I have. Something happened yesterday, and...well, a few months ago, I would have been put out by it. Instead, I was amused." He contracted his brows. He might have made an error in bringing the subject to Elizabeth's attention. He kept his tone light, however, as he said, "Although I am not certain you would be as entertained by it as I was."

"I should be the judge of that," she replied teasingly. "You have piqued my interest, sir. You cannot back out now."

He lifted his chin. "Only if you promise you will not distress yourself over it."

Her face fell. His gut tightened at the sight of her expression.

He had distressed her.

The only thing for it now was to tell all. Pressing her hand again, he said in a gentle tone, "I received a bill from a modiste's shop."

Lizzy gasped and tried to pull her hand away. Darcy clung more firmly. He would not let her shrink in embarrassment. He would ease her discomfort, soothe and reassure her. He did not wish her to ever feel embarrassed—not with him.

She turned away, but he lifted her chin and looked into her eyes. With a smile, he said, "You can imagine my confusion. I confronted Mrs. Annesley about allowing Georgiana to make such extravagant purchases."

Lizzy groaned.

He caressed her cheek with his thumb. She was exquisitely soft. "You promised me, Miss Elizabeth, that you would not distress yourself."

Her features eased somewhat. "As I recall, I made no such promise."

He smiled at her taunt. Hoping to soothe her, he let his hand drop from her face to her shoulder and down her arm. With the thumb of his other hand, he massaged her palm. Flame rushed across his skin, and her cheeks pinked as well.

Continuing the story, he explained, "I went to the shop to inquire about the error. We sorted the confusion to everyone's satisfaction."

"I begged my mother not to be so bold," Elizabeth said in a rush. "Jane knows nothing of it."

He smiled warmly. "I am glad of that, at least. I would not wish her to be embarrassed."

"Yet you do not mind embarrassing me," Elizabeth teased, then looked away.

He clasped her other hand in his. "Have I told you how much I admire you and your sister? Your manners are impeccable, for which the two of you deserve all the credit. Your sister will make Bingley a brilliant wife. As for yourself..." He had to swallow down the knot in his throat before he could continue,

"I have never been so impressed by anyone."

Her eyes widened, giving her a look of astonishment. Neither of them spoke. He longed to take her into his arms and kiss her. The moment seemed to demand it.

But of course, that was impossible. Nor could they continue standing there in that pose. They had been holding hands through nearly the entire conversation. They both seemed to need the contact.

What a sight they must be! Her mother likely already had the wedding planned in her head. But what of it? Marrying Elizabeth was what he wanted.

If he kissed her now, what would happen? It would seal the matter, certainly. But he did not wish to force her. If—when she became his wife, it would be of her own volition.

And so he let her go, though his chest ached at the absence. Every part of him wanted to know every part of her. With a license, they could be married in a matter of days. Was it madness to think so?

They would need her father's permission, since she was not of age. If Elizabeth consented, her father would be a fool to stand in their way. No, Darcy had no fear where Bennet was concerned. The only question was Elizabeth. Words of love were on his lips, but was she ready to hear them?

Regardless, a drawing room in front of witnesses was no place to propose. He would wait for a better time, a time when he could be more certain of her answer. As comfortable as she seemed with him, she was not yet his.

Chapter 28

That evening, Lizzy arrived at the Featherstone ball in a state of restless anticipation. Darcy's attentions to her at the musicale had been too marked to be denied. More than once, he had looked on the verge of kissing her. She had wanted nothing more than to melt into his arms.

As she had dressed that evening in a gown of violet silk, all thoughts of caution had fled her mind. Tonight, she was determined to secure him. He must intend to make her an offer after such an obvious display. Otherwise, she would never believe in the honour of gentlemen again.

The interactions between them had not gone unnoticed by Mrs. Bennet. In the carriage, she was pointed in her remarks on the subject. She advised Lizzy in myriad ways how to wheedle a marriage proposal out of a wealthy man.

As her mother pointed out, *that* was a subject on which she herself had some expertise. She had been on the fringes of the gentry as the daughter of a solicitor. Yet she had married the richest man in the environs of Meryton.

Her mother's efforts on Lizzy's behalf were less tiresome than they might have been. Lizzy was hoping for a proposal from Mr. Darcy. Unlike the match her mother had tried to arrange between Lizzy and Mr. Collins.

Lizzy would not stoop to her mother's machinations, but she was not without her own ideas on how to spark a man's interest. She had taken great pains with her dress and her coiffure that evening. If Darcy was indeed thinking of proposing, she was not above giving him a nudge.

Mrs. Bennet had insisted on being fashionably late to the ball, which had tried Lizzy's patience. She could see the wisdom in making a man wait. But she did not wish for other young ladies to have their turn with him. Not before she tantalized him with what was to come.

He had promised her a waltz. She wanted him to spend the evening imagining how it would feel to hold her in his arms again.

Yet when they finally arrived at the ball, Darcy was nowhere to be seen. Lizzy looked about, spotting the Bingleys and the Fitzwilliams, but no Darcy.

His absence filled her with sudden dread. Had he had second thoughts after their encounter earlier in the day? Perhaps he realized he had been too familiar, and now sought to avoid her.

These thoughts ran through her head as Bingley came to greet them. She listened anxiously to his explanation that Darcy was home with a migraine. Lizzy's stomach dropped, disappointment filling her.

Her fingers ached to soothe the poor man. If they were married, he could lie with his head in her lap while she massaged his scalp. She wanted that intimacy with him, to care for his every need.

Tears burned her eyes. It was ridiculous to feel bereft at the loss of his company that evening. She had seen the man just hours before. He would almost certainly call the next day if he was feeling better.

The thought did little to cheer her. She had been looking forward to waltzing with him. To feeling his arms around her. To moving with him to the pulse of the music.

His touch brought out the most delicious shivery sensations in her. She could not get enough of it.

Was he truly ill? Worry crept beneath her skin that he wanted to elude her, that he was feeling trapped. Yet that was unkind. She would not allow herself to think him capable of such petty deception, not without proof.

To escape her musings, she scanned the ballroom, looking for a distraction. Glimpsing Arabella with her brothers, Lizzy set aside her dismay.

She went to wish them a good evening. It pleased her to see Arabella out in society. Clearly she had overcome some of her fear of attending evening assemblies. It did not hurt, Lizzy was sure, that the lady had three stalwart brothers nearby for her protection.

Colonel Fitzwilliam asked Lizzy for the first waltz. She was happy to oblige him. He was tall and sturdy, the largest in stature of his brothers. Though not precisely handsome, his features were pleasing and his movements graceful. His manners, of course, were impeccable.

"I was sorry to hear that Mr. Darcy was too unwell to attend this evening," she said. She hoped to prompt the colonel to share some news, if he had any.

"He would not have missed it unless he were truly miserable. When I spoke to him today, he was looking forward to the dance you had promised him. Unfortunately, he has been plagued by these headaches since he was a boy."

The colonel's words softened her worries that Darcy was avoiding her. Yet now she was more concerned for him than ever. "Is there no remedy for the pain?"

"Resting in a dark, quiet room seems the best treatment."

"I hope he will feel better on the morrow," she said, feeling helpless, her heart aching.

"Do not overset yourself, ma'am. He would not wish you to worry. He will be himself again soon."

"I believe it would be impossible for me *not* to worry." She pictured Darcy lying in his room, alone and in pain, while the rest of the *ton* danced. How she wished she could offer him solace!

The colonel's eyes scrutinized her face. "Miss Bennet, I shall be frank. Your kindness to Darcy has not gone unnoticed. I hope your regard for him is genuine."

His words created a jumble of feelings in her breast, from

embarrassment to deepest joy. She would not shrink from his directness. Surely the colonel had Darcy's ear.

She replied, "I admire your cousin above any man I know. Does that put your fears to rest?"

"It does, ma'am. And your father—does he hold Darcy in esteem? My cousin says he did not endear himself to the Hertfordshire gentry last autumn."

She could not help a soft laugh. "My mother and Jane and I —we have all seen your cousin in a different light during our time in London. I believe the three of us together can convince my father of Mr. Darcy's worth."

"Splendid! I hope I may be forgiven for speaking with the bluntness of a soldier. I thank you for enduring my candour with good grace."

"Your affection for your cousin becomes you."

He returned her to her mother at the end of the dance. Lizzy could not stop running the conversation over in her mind. Was the colonel conjecturing about his cousin's feelings? Or had Darcy confided in him? If Darcy did not propose soon, Lizzy might develop one of her mother's nervous complaints.

In the carriage on the way home, Mrs. Bennet offered advice. It only exacerbated her daughter's state of unease. "Now Lizzy," her mother said, "it is unfortunate that Mr. Darcy was not at the ball this evening. But you must not give up hope. The attentions he showed you at the musicale today could mean only one thing. And if he does not come to the point, I shall write your father. He will come to town to fight Darcy and *make* him marry you."

Lizzy's jaw fell open. She eyed Jane a moment, then stared at her mother. "Mama, you cannot mean for Papa to do anything so rash. Mr. Darcy is an athletic man twenty years my father's junior. And besides, I do not wish Darcy to be *forced* to marry me—"

"He took liberties with you my dear, in front of the Countess of Matlock. Of course he must marry you, by force if necessary."

Her spine tingled with alarm. "Mama, if you have any regard for my happiness—"

Lizzy broke off, chagrined. Of course her mother had no regard for Lizzy's happiness. At least not in the terms Lizzy meant. Her mother wanted her daughters to live a comfortable life as gentlewomen. That had been her own goal in marrying. Surely love had not entered into the equation. No two people could be less suited than her parents, by both affection and temperament.

Jane stepped in. "Papa cannot come to London. Mary, Kitty, and Lydia would be left without a chaperone."

"They can come, too," Mrs. Bennet said. "Perhaps we can find husbands for them as well."

Now Lizzy truly began to panic. "Lady Purcell did not give permission for our entire family to take up residence in her home. If we take advantage of her hospitality in that way, it could cost aunt Gardiner her friendship. And who knows when we might want to make use of that connection again?"

Lizzy hated to resort to such a callous argument. But an appeal to her mother's better nature...that would assume her mother *had* a better nature.

"Lizzy is right," Jane offered. "Besides, as you say, we must not despair of Darcy coming to the point on his own. Mr. Darcy was not making excuses—Bingley said he truly did have a terrific headache. Mr. Darcy was sorry to disappoint Lizzy after promising her a waltz."

"We shall see," Mrs. Bennet said tightly. "We shall see."

∞∞∞

Darcy woke the next morning in a dark room, the curtains drawn. The memory of the migraine came back to him. The pain had been so intense, he had taken to his bed and forgone the evening's activities. Thankfully, a good night's sleep had driven off the worst of it.

He sat up and assessed the situation. Yes, he was much better. Sliding on his dressing gown, he walked to the windows and cast the curtains aside.

Street traffic was light this time of day. The sky was overcast but did not appear as if it might storm. Darcy rang for his valet, thinking he should call on Elizabeth. Greymore certainly would.

He had to admit to himself—Greymore was a serious rival. Darcy could not afford to let his guard down. He must make an offer before Greymore did.

The earl's feelings for Elizabeth could not equal his own. The man had a new favourite every month or two. Darcy had never felt this way about a woman. Elizabeth deserved a man who loved her with the same intensity as she gave love. Greymore might admire her, but he could not cherish her as Darcy did.

He went down to breakfast to find Bingley filling his plate with baked eggs and toast. Darcy's stomach growled at the aroma. He had barely eaten the night before.

"You look a hundred times better," Bingley said.

"I am, thank you." Darcy filled his own plate. "How was the ball?"

Bingley snickered. "Shall I regale you with how lovely Jane looked in her gown? How heavenly it was to dance with her? I suspect you have something else in mind."

Darcy gave him a level look.

"Let me see," Bingley said. "Where might your curiosity lie? Ah, yes. Elizabeth. I fear she was upset by your absence. I have never seen her so out of sorts. Without exaggeration, I could describe her as *stricken*."

Darcy's heart lurched. "Truly?"

Bingley waved his hand. "You know her temperament. Usually, she casts off any bad feelings by making a joke. Last night, nothing seemed to cheer her."

Darcy contemplated that, wondering what it meant. He hated to think he had ruined her evening. At the same time, her lack of spirits showed a welcome attachment to himself.

They sat at the table, and Darcy sipped his coffee. Rather than soothing his hunger pangs, the sweet-nutty flavour intensified them. "Did Miss Elizabeth dance with Greymore?"

Bingley stirred his tea. He replied wearing a cheerful expression that was surely meant to taunt his friend. "Twice, including the supper waltz."

Darcy set his jaw. The very dance he himself had promised her. The situation was intolerable. He must see her at once.

"I assume you are calling at Berkeley Square this morning," Darcy asked.

"Of course. Directly after breakfast."

"Good. I shall be ready to join you without delay."

Lizzy could not think. She had never found Lord Greymore's company so tedious. When he spoke, she could not attend to more than half a sentence at a time. Images of Darcy kept floating through her mind. Her fevered thoughts made it impossible to carry on a conversation.

Red roses. Darcy had sent another bouquet that morning. Did he know that red roses meant love?

Her stomach tightened. She jumped to her feet, thinking she might cast up her accounts. Why had no one warned her that falling in love felt like a dreadful illness?

Greymore stood up beside her. "Miss Bennet, are you well?"

"Pardon me. I was queasy for a moment, but the feeling has passed."

He looked at her with concern in his eyes. "Can I get you anything? A cup of tea?"

She gave him a soft smile. "That would be most welcome."

He bowed and stepped over to the sitting area where Mrs. Bennet was serving the guests. Lizzy was grateful for a moment alone so she could collect her thoughts. Perhaps she ought to pay attention, to make sure her mother did not say anything to offend the earl. But at the moment, Lizzy could not force herself to care about that.

She liked Greymore immensely. She hoped they would remain friends. But he was not the man she loved. Her other suitors felt like an encumbrance to her.

It was getting close to the time Bingley generally called. Would Darcy come with him? If so, what would she say?

Surely farming families did not go through these intrigues when it came to courtship. No, that was a special torment saved for the gentry. Her father's tenants seemed to fall in love and marry with little fuss.

But men and women of her class could not simply *say* what they felt. Oh, no. Because marriage was not just a man and woman coming together to join their lives and raise a family. It was an alliance. There were dynastic considerations.

And one of those considerations was handing Greymore a cup of tea. Did Lizzy have any hope of winning Darcy, with her mother here to remind him of how provincial she was?

Greymore brought Lizzy the beverage, sitting next to her as she lifted it to her lips. It was prepared with milk, exactly as she liked. A memory floated back to her of a time when she was about six years old and came down with influenza. Her mother had cooed to her, feeding her tea and toast, placing cool compresses on her head.

Lizzy swallowed down the lump in her throat. If Darcy could not accept her family, then she did not want him. Though it pained her to think it, he must accept her for who she was.

"Miss Bennet, you are unwell," Greymore said with a sudden urgency in his voice.

"No, I assure you, I am fine." Then she realized tears were streaming down her cheeks. She set down her cup and took the handkerchief he offered. "It is the oddest thing. Ever since my sister's engagement, I have been growing emotional without warning. One expects that of a bride, but not the bride's sister." She handed the handkerchief back to him.

He smiled at her as he slid it back into his pocket. "I imagine you will be a bride yourself, soon enough."

"If I am so fortunate," she said absently. Then, her eyes went wide, and she looked away from him.

He let out a little chuckle. "Never fear, Miss Bennet. This is not the first time I have found myself in the company of a woman in love with a man who was not me. I bear you no ill will, I promise."

She clasped his hand. "Forgive me. I have not been very good company today."

"You are always good company. I hope we shall remain friends."

"Oh yes, I was thinking the same thing. I hold you in the highest esteem."

Before he could respond, the butler announced Mr. Bingley and Mr. Darcy. She looked up. She felt as if she were underwater, trying to rise to the surface to breathe while heavy clothing pulled her down. But when Darcy's eyes met hers, everything inside her bloomed. She turned into a feather, lighter than air. The rest of the room fell away, and Darcy gave her a smile.

∞∞∞

Greymore. Darcy should have known. The man was stuck to Elizabeth like a clod of clay to her shoe.

To Darcy's surprise, however, Greymore rose and bowed to her. As he walked past on the way out, he patted Darcy's back and said in low tones, "She is all yours, my friend. Do right by her, or you shall answer to me."

Greymore met Darcy's look of astonishment with a wide grin. Then, he donned his hat and headed out the front door.

Before his mind could process this change in circumstances, Elizabeth was by his side. She looked up at him so earnestly, his mouth went dry and his eyes could see only her. Without bothering to offer a formal greeting, she said, "You must be feeling better."

"Much, thank you. I am sorry I missed our waltz last night."

Her eyes glistened, and she looked away. "I shall not insult you by laughing and pretending it was nothing. I worried about you dreadfully, probably more than I should have. Colonel Fitzwilliam assured me your condition would pass."

"Such headaches always do, although they are deuced unpleasant while they last." Blood drained from his face. "Pardon my language, Miss Bennet."

She smiled warmly. "I am not such a stickler as to deny a man the use of a mild oath. We are friends enough that we can dispense with such strict social niceties."

"Friends indeed," he said, and squeezed her hands. The feel of her skin was soft and inviting, but he did not allow himself to linger. She was too much of a temptation.

Jane poured him a coffee, then he and Elizabeth sat on the window seat. It was set away from the others and big enough for only two. Lizzy greeted new guests as they arrived, but always returned to Darcy.

All his misgivings were removed. Even the most objective onlooker would believe her to be encouraging him. If she did not mean to have him, he could not be called a fool for thinking she did.

He pondered when the right moment might be to make his proposals. He could do it now and announce the engagement at the Matlock ball that evening. But what if she *did* refuse him? He could not endure his aunt's ball under those circumstances. Lady Matlock would be displeased if he cried off.

He would wait until the morrow. After all, what difference could a day make?

Chapter 29

The skies brightened that afternoon. With the weather finally cooperating, Darcy and Bingley took Lizzy and Jane for a ride in Hyde Park. Darcy's barouche was perhaps the most impressive vehicle Lizzy had ever ridden in.

While his coach had been designed for comfort, the barouche had extra details for show. Red leather, dark cherry wood, gleaming brass fittings. As Darcy handed Lizzy up, she felt like a princess. At the feel of his touch, tingles pulsed from her fingers to her spine.

Jane and Bingley sat together, which gave Lizzy the chance to share a seat with Darcy. He helped her arrange the rug around her for warmth. With him so close, her heart fluttered and her breathing grew shallow.

Their eyes met as she thanked him, and he gave her a smile. She thought she would melt on the spot. Had a handsomer man ever lived? Surely not.

"Are you comfortable?" He sounded as if he spoke out of true concern, rather than politeness.

"Quite," she said. "I have never been in a more pleasant conveyance."

Her words seemed to gratify him, for his smile deepened and a hint of colour showed in his cheeks. Of course, that might have been the weather. Still, a hope rose in her breast that she had evoked some pleasurable emotion in him.

They clopped through the street beneath a wide, blue sky. Some of the early-leafing trees were showing a hint of green, bearing the promise of spring.

"I hope you do not mind riding backwards," Darcy asked.

"Not at all. It provides a more varied view than the hindquarters of the horses."

"You are a good sport, Miss Elizabeth."

She considered that a moment. "I suppose I am."

"You endured my insufferable behaviour in Hertfordshire, and yet show no resentment."

"And you endure my teasing. I would say we are even."

"I confess, I hope you never stop teasing me. I enjoy the way your mind works."

Her stomach thrilled at his words "And I admire your intelligence. I confess, now that Jane and Bingley are engaged, I hope to have the opportunity of observing more of it."

His Adam's apple bobbed. "I imagine we will frequently be in company together. It is a prospect I find most satisfactory." His speech was somewhat halting, and he seemed to force himself to continue. "Georgiana is also happy with this circumstance. She is fond of you and your sister, and hopes the friendship can continue beyond the season."

Lizzy pressed his hand. "Jane and I adore Miss Darcy."

He clasped her hand between both of his. "I am pleased to hear it. I think…she would like to be on a first name basis with you, but may be too shy to ask."

"Then I shall certainly do so."

He looked at her intently. She ought to pull her hand away but felt no desire to. Nor did he seem inclined to let it go.

And so they sat, in full view of passers-by, hands intertwined as they chatted. But in truth, Lizzy lost all awareness except for Darcy.

Somehow they got onto the topic of the artwork at Darcy House. "My mother was something of a connoisseur," he explained. "She was a talented water colourist. My father encouraged her to try oils, but she never did. She preferred the softness of watercolours. Her eye for art was first rate."

"Did she select the Fragonards and Bouchers?"

"She did. Fragonard was her favourite artist. I think, in her own way, it was a sort of rebellion against the Terror." His tone grew serious as he said, "She had cousins who were murdered by Robespierre."

Lizzy's breath stopped. "That must have been horrifying."

"I still remember her weeping for what seemed like days. She had not been close to them, but they were family, and their deaths were senseless and brutal. Even the babes were killed —two little girls of four and six. I was about six myself at the time, so you can imagine my mother's feelings."

Lizzy swallowed, but the knot in her throat did not subside. "I cannot fathom it." Her voice was barely more than a whisper.

"Nor can I. But believe me, my uncle has not forgotten, and it affects the way he votes in the House of Lords. It is a tightrope, navigating between reform and revolution. In this age, only a fool would think wealth and privilege are a birthright. They are a responsibility to be wielded with great care."

She brushed her thumb across the leather of his gloves. "I want to know everything about your family," she said impulsively. Her cheeks flushed at her forwardness.

Darcy responded with a soft smile. "And I about yours."

She grinned at that. "I suspect you already know more than you would like."

He spoke intently. "While I was at Netherfield, I did not spend enough time getting to know the people of the neighbourhood. You have taught me to pay better attention."

"I suspect Meryton is a very ordinary town."

"You are not ordinary. You are anything but."

"That is quite a compliment, coming from you."

He was silent a moment before he spoke. "If so, that shows how little I have sought to make myself agreeable to strangers. It was never your responsibility, nor anyone else's, to prove themselves worthy of my notice. I should have been more gracious."

She pressed her free hand to her heart. For a moment, she was too overwhelmed to speak. Then, before she could say anything, they passed through the gate into Hyde Park.

As they did so, Lady Carson hailed them. She and her daughters were in their own barouche, headed out of the park.

"We are well met," cried Eugenia, the younger daughter. "I would have hated to miss you. Mr. Darcy, I am looking forward to your uncle's ball tonight."

They chatted a while before traffic forced them to move on. Lizzy could not help thinking perhaps Lady Eugenia had her sights set on Darcy. It must have irked her, the daughter of a marquess, to see Darcy sitting at Lizzy's side.

The driver made his way to the serpentine. Lizzy loved the sight of it. The lake stretched almost the entire length of the park and into Kensington Gardens. A pair of swans glided across its glassy surface.

The carriage stopped, and the four passengers alighted. Jane took Bingley's arm, and Lizzy took Darcy's. The water sparkled in the bright sunlight as they walked along the footpath. Birds flitted amongst the tree branches. The robins and larks raised their cheerful songs.

The foursome had not gone far when they met up with Lady Cressida walking arm-in-arm with Miss Peabody.

"Why, Priscilla," Cressida said to her companion, "if it is not the happy couple. Miss Bennet, how good to see you. Although I should be peeved at you for taking Mr. Bingley off the market."

"Yes," Lizzy agreed. "The number of your potential suitors has dropped from forty-two to forty-one. And the season has not yet begun in earnest."

"If you are not careful," Jane said to Cressida, "you will be declared a diamond of the first water. And I know how you would hate that."

Lady Cressida looked at them placidly. "I hope anyone who wants to pay me a compliment will be more clever than to resort to that tired cliché."

"Shall he compare your eyes to emeralds?" Darcy suggested with a grin. "Your lips to rubies, your hair to spun gold?"

Cressida tittered. "Even worse."

Bingley took up the mantle of finding compliments worthy of Lady Cressida. Lizzy eyed Darcy sideways. "You are lavish in your praise, sir."

"Pretty words are easy enough to devise," he said in low tones, "when one's heart is not involved."

"You are not amongst the lady's many admirers?"

"Only in the way of friendship. I confess, my heart is engaged elsewhere."

Heat suffused Lizzy's body. She took a moment to recover her wits. Finally, she asked, "Is the lady aware of her good fortune?"

Darcy gave a low chuckle. "I am such a dunce at courtship, it is possible she is not. And under the circumstances, she might not consider herself fortunate."

"In that case, *she* must be the dunce." Lizzy tried to keep her tone light, but in fact, she had never been in such a state of grave apprehension. Either he was in love with her, or he was in love with someone else. Either she had won him, or he was lost to her forever.

He patted her forearm where it was linked with his. "I can offer her Pemberley, at least."

"Surely offering yourself would be a greater inducement."

"You have not seen Pemberley."

She laughed at that, and the tension between them dissipated.

Seeing Miss Peabody standing alone, Lizzy walked up to her and asked, "Is the viscountess here with you?"

"Always," she said with a mirthless smile. "She has not let me out of her sight since my brother Rolf took up his commission."

Lizzy's heart clenched. The sound of Rolf Peabody's name inspired a sort of horror in her. Still, Priscilla was not responsible for her brother's actions. The girl must be suffering some pain at the separation, and fear for his safety.

Gently, Lizzy asked, "Are you close to your brother?"

Priscilla swallowed. "He has always watched over me. Wayne is older, you see, more like a father than a brother. But Rolf has been my confidant and friend."

Lizzy wondered how much Priscilla knew about her brother's reasons for joining the army. It was best, of course, to say nothing about it.

Darcy, hovering nearby, stepped over. "Miss Peabody," he said, offering that young lady his arm. "I regret that I was deprived of the pleasure of dancing with you last night. If you will, please tell me what I missed at the assembly."

They took the walkway along the serpentine. Jane and Bingley were some distance ahead of them. Lizzy and Cressida walked behind Darcy and Miss Peabody.

Lizzy was happy to see him pay some notice to the girl. The sort of guidance she received from the viscountess did not seem to be having the desired effect. Darcy's intelligent conversation might steer her in a better direction.

"You must tell me," Cressida said conspiratorially. She leaned towards Lizzy. "Are you and Mr. Darcy engaged?"

Lizzy stopped short and looked at her in astonishment. "Good heavens! Why would you ask such a question?"

Cressida arched her brows. "Why would you avoid answering it?"

Lizzy covered her mouth to suppress a startled laugh. "There is no understanding between Mr. Darcy and myself," she said calmly. "At least, not yet," she added impulsively, then bit her lip. She should not have spoken so indiscreetly.

Cressida just laughed. Lizzy relaxed. Though she had only known the girl a few weeks, Lizzy believed she could trust her.

"Surely a proposal must be coming soon," Cressida insisted. "Arabelle told me he held your hand at the musicale yesterday before I arrived."

"Fortunately, only our families were witness to that indiscretion. If the Bingleys can be called family."

"I think they must. Though I can only imagine what Caroline's reaction must have been."

Lizzy stopped short again. "Goodness! I was so distracted, I did not even notice Miss Bingley."

"Of course not. You only had eyes for Mr. Darcy."

Lizzy instinctively looked towards him, and realized she and Cressida were falling behind. They picked up their pace.

"'Tis a pity," Cressida said, "that Caroline has turned bitter. She used to be friends with my sister. But ever since she set her sights on Mr. Darcy, she has changed. There is a desperation about her that was not there before. It is needless, of course. She is a wealthy, beautiful, accomplished woman. She had even caught Greymore's eye at one time. Now he wants nothing to do with her."

They walked along in silence a moment. "I hope you know," Lizzy said at last, "how much I like your brother."

"Oh, pish, you must not think about that. Greymore is not a sore loser. To be honest, I believe he has yet to fall in love completely. He likes women, and likes courting them. But I promise, you have not broken his heart."

"I am glad to hear it." Lizzy furrowed her brow. "I think."

Cressida tittered. "A union between you and Mr. Darcy will be to everyone's benefit. Even Caroline's. The sooner she gives up hoping for a man who will never love her, the better off she will be."

Darcy walked at Miss Peabody's side, wondering how so much nonsense could fit inside the head of one young woman. It seemed the only books she had read were novels, and only the most lurid ones would do. She was the silliest, most ill-informed creature he had ever met.

Had she always been thus? He had known her all her life, although he supposed he had never paid much attention to the state of her education. She had been a talkative child, prattling on as girls do. At some point, should she not have outgrown that state?

Perhaps after her mother had passed away, her father had neglected her education. She had the accomplishments expected of young ladies. Beyond that, she seemed alarmingly ignorant. Darcy wondered if she had the mathematics skills to oversee the household accounts.

He forced himself to listen as she spoke in an excited tone. "My favourite book is *Camilla Cartwright's Conundrum*. It is the best Mrs. Wheedlesuch has produced so far."

"I prefer Walter Scott myself."

Her shoulders slumped. "I find Scott dreadfully boring." Colour rose in her cheeks. "Oh dear, not that I find you boring, Mr. Darcy! I suppose each of us must like different things."

"Tell me, Miss Peabody, what else do you like? Besides novels, that is. For instance, do you paint?

"I haven't any talent with a brush. But with a needle, I have some skill. I can embroider a very pretty screen. I knit and crochet as well."

"Those are useful accomplishments for a young lady. As I recall, you are also a fine pianist."

"Thank you. I enjoy singing also. The viscountess and I have been practicing some French folk songs." She gave a little sigh. "I am hopeless with the pronunciation, though."

"You do not speak French?"

"My mother wanted me to learn, but my father refused because of Napoleon."

Darcy frowned at that but did not remark upon it. "Did you learn another language instead? German or Italian, perhaps?"

"I am afraid not. My governess used to say a patriotic Englishwoman should speak only English."

Darcy cringed. Her *governess* said that? What other excuses did the woman come up with for failing to do her job?

What would become of this girl if she had no one to look after her? Viscountess Wayne seemed ill equipped to oversee her young sister-in-law. Especially while running a household on the brink of ruin.

If he invited Miss Peabody to Pemberley, could Elizabeth manage her? Truly, the girl needed the guidance of a sensible woman. And a secure environment, where the spectre of bankruptcy was not hanging over her.

As things now stood, the viscountess would marry her off to the first doddering fool who offered for her. A man looking for a filly to provide him with an heir. Miss Peabody of all people would find such a fate insupportable.

Darcy thought about the eligible young men in the environs of Pemberley. The rector was single. About Darcy's age, he was kind, sensible, and pleasant looking. Not dashing like the hero of a novel to be sure. But dependable, and with an income sizeable enough to support a family comfortably.

"Miss Peabody," Darcy asked, "would you like to visit Pemberley in the autumn? Spend a few weeks with Georgiana? I imagine Bingley and his bride will be there as well, perhaps a few others."

"Oh, Mr. Darcy, that sounds divine!"

"Splendid. I shall arrange it with your brother."

They made their way back to Viscountess Wayne and Lady Greymore. Darcy helped Lizzy into the barouche. Bingley and Jane sat on the bench across from them, and they made the requisite drive along Rotten Row.

Elizabeth said to him jovially, "You seem to have turned Miss Peabody's head. She was beaming at you."

"I invited her to spend the autumn at Pemberley with Georgiana."

Elizabeth's eyes widened. "Goodness! I did not realize the two of them were close."

"They are not close, precisely, but are old friends." Darcy could not speak of the Waynes' financial situation without breaking a confidence. He decided to go a different direction.

"She has been lonely, I think, since her brother joined the army. And to be honest, I find her education to be somewhat lacking. I hope that spending time with Georgiana, under Mrs. Annesley's guidance, will help with that."

"That is most kind of you." She did not sound entirely at ease, however.

"Miss Elizabeth, are you jealous?" he teased. "Were you hoping I would invite *you* to Pemberley? To spend the autumn with Georgiana under Mrs. Annesley's care?"

Elizabeth gave him an arch look. Then, her expression softened. She said in a voice both quiet and full of emotion, "I confess, I would like to see Pemberley."

"Then you shall. Before the autumn, I hope."

Her intake of breath twisted his insides into an ache of apprehension and longing. He adjusted the rug covering her lap and slid his hand into hers. "I have it on good authority that the third dance this evening, and the supper dance, are waltzes. I hope you will promise them both to me."

She squeezed his hand, and a look of subdued pleasure spread over her features. Her lips curved into a smile, and her eyes sparkled. "Might that not cause tongues to wag?"

"I do not mind a little gossip. Do you?"

"We will raise expectations," she warned.

"Then let them be raised."

Her eyes glistened. He did not let go of her hand for the entirety of the ride through Hyde Park nor back to Berkeley Square.

Chapter 30

Lizzy's heart fluttered as her party entered the ballroom at Matlock House. A hum of conversation greeted them. Bouquets of hothouse flowers scented the air. The watered silk wallpaper shone in the candlelight.

Predictably, Darcy was already there—whether of his own desire, or at his aunt's urging. Perhaps a little of both.

Remaining calm, at least outwardly, Lizzy approached the receiving line. Greeting a family the size of the Fitzwilliam clan took some time. When she reached the end, she pressed Arabella's hand. "How are you faring this evening?" she asked in low tones.

"Nervous," Arabella replied, "but better than I expected. I was terrified at the Featherstone ball, but tonight it is not as bad."

Lizzy met her eyes meaningfully. "If you need anything, do not hesitate to find me."

"Thank you. You are so kind. With anyone else, I would feel ashamed. But you have helped me understand I am not to blame..." Her eyes glistened, but she blinked the tears away.

"Indeed you are not," Lizzy said earnestly.

Arabella nodded, her confidence seeming to rise, and Lizzy gave her a parting smile.

Lizzy looked around to find Jane standing with Bingley and Darcy. Lizzy's thoughts ceased a moment as she took in the stunning sight of the man she loved. Darcy was dressed in black and white, his silver waistcoat shimmering.

Their eyes met, and a flush of desire ran through her. She did not try to fight it. She recognized the carnal longing for what it was. She imagined his lips running along the curve of her neck. That need could not be satisfied until they exchanged wedding vows. But she would not wish away the craving. Nothing else had made her feel so alive.

Taking a deep breath to cool the urgency in her blood and the apprehension in her belly, Lizzy joined them. The gentlemen bowed deeply, and she gave them a matching curtsey. She stepped closer to Darcy, wanting to inhale his scent and feel his heat.

Surreptitiously, she raked her gaze over him, wishing she could do the same with her hands. She wanted to feel the soft wool and linen. Her eyes stopped at his cravat, the knot so complex she could not imagine unravelling it.

Then, suddenly, she *was* imagining herself unravelling it. Baring his skin, pressing her lips to the pulse of his throat...

"Miss Elizabeth," Darcy said, waking her from her reverie, "you look flushed. Might I get you a lemonade or some other refreshment?"

"I thank you, sir, but I shall wait until after the dancing begins."

"As you wish." They looked at one another awkwardly. The public nature of the ballroom thwarted a more affectionate greeting.

How she ached to touch him! His hand on hers during the ride through Hyde Park had been heaven. She had allowed him to take a liberty with her, but surely it was the right sort of liberty to encourage a man to propose.

If Darcy did not propose now, he was not the honourable gentleman she believed him to be. His hints had been too pointed. Of course, a man could plan to make an offer, then something happen to change his mind. If her mother...but no, Lizzy had to put that worry aside. If her mother had not scared him off by now, he must be immune to her.

Darcy said, "Bingley and your sister have been discussing

where to hold the wedding. He would like to have it here at St. George's, and she would rather marry in Hertfordshire. What say you?"

She arched her brows. "That will not do, Mr. Darcy. I shall not be drawn into their disagreement."

"Then let us treat it as a general question. Is it preferable to be married in town during the season, or to return to one's country parish for the ceremony?"

Lizzy considered that a moment. "It would depend on the couple. For myself, I would rather marry in the country. That is where my friends of long-standing are. Some of them would find it a hardship to travel to London. But the fashionable set would see no difficulty in a journey to Hertfordshire."

"It is an easy distance, to be sure," Darcy said. "If I asked my friends to trek to Derbyshire, the situation might be different. I might find myself in the church alone with the vicar and my unfortunate bride."

Lizzy tilted her head quizzically. "Why unfortunate?"

"Would not most women rather be surrounded by a church full of people?"

Lizzy pictured the scene. She and Darcy standing at the altar with no one else but the vicar and two witnesses. She could not find the image wanting.

"There is something terribly romantic," she said, "about the private ceremony you describe. A woman lucky enough to win the hand of the man she loves could hardly wish for more."

"But if he loves her, ought he not sacrifice his own comfort to give her the wedding she desires?"

"I would hope that no sacrifice would be required on either side. That they could find a solution agreeable to both."

She turned to Jane and Bingley, who had been listening with interest. "What say the two of you?"

"I would not mind marrying at the church in Meryton," Bingley said. "Louisa says Hurst has been complaining about the trip to Hertfordshire. He may not go to the wedding if it is held there."

"Is that an argument for or against?" Lizzy asked. The rest of the party tittered, but Lizzy did not crack a smile. "If he cannot travel thirty miles for your wedding, then why give a moment's thought to his preference? You owe him no more loyalty than he shows you."

"I have been telling him the same thing," Darcy said.

"But should not family come first?" Jane asked. "As much as I would prefer to marry in Meryton, that is only for the sake of our neighbours. Those who wish to attend could travel here."

"At great trouble and expense, they could," Lizzy pointed out. "Whereas Bingley has a comfortable coach and his family can stay at Netherfield. A property he has let for a full year, and has so far stayed in for all of two months."

"You seem to have strong opinions," Darcy noted, "for one who did not wish to get involved."

She turned and eyed him disapprovingly, stung by his teasing. "I suppose so," she said, adopting a sly smile. "I do have opinions about those who put their own comfort first. Ahead of others whose circumstances make travel more difficult."

Heat ran up her neck. She struggled to contain herself. Her opinions were not wrong, nor her anger misplaced—but she should not express them so freely.

She took a deep breath, then straightened her spine. "Bingley, please forgive me. As Mr. Darcy has been kind enough to remind me, this is not my concern." She gave them a curtsey and walked off.

Darcy followed. "Miss Bennet, please. I did not mean to sound as if I were scolding you."

She turned to face him. "No, you were teasing me, as I am in the habit of doing to you. You are quite right. As it turns out, however, my feelings on this subject are stronger than I realized."

"You are distressed." He drew closer. "Is there something I might do for you?"

A wave of heat rushed over her. There were a thousand things he might do for her, but none of them involved a ballroom. If they could find somewhere private—

But no. Nothing good could come of that. Something wonderful, perhaps, but nothing good.

So she met his eyes and gave him a wan smile. "Thank you for the offer, but no, that is not necessary. Your kindness itself gives me ease."

$$\infty\infty\infty$$

Darcy's chest swelled at the words. He wanted to claim her as his own that very moment. It would be more than an hour until the waltz. The country-dances until then would be torture.

She looked a vision in pink satin, her hair swept up and adorned with silk flowers. But there was sadness in her eyes, and he did not understand it. "Pray tell me what is troubling you. It is not merely Hurst, to be sure."

She shook her head. "When I first met you, I did not imagine that your mother had grown up in a house like this. I would have been too awed to tease you if I had."

He briefly pressed her gloved fingers. "Then I am glad you did not. I have always enjoyed your teasing, even when it cut to the quick."

A rosy blush touched her cheeks. "You are more patient with me than I deserve."

He said in a husky voice, "I cannot help but think you have been the patient one."

For long moment, she gazed at him. Then, her eyes scanned the ballroom. She seemed to deflate. "I am out of my depth here."

He wished he could take her in his arms and soothe her sadness. "I felt out of my depth at the ball in the Meryton assembly rooms. As my abominable behaviour there can attest."

Her eyes danced merrily. The sight eased the heaviness in

his chest. He was glad she could smile about it now.

He massaged the heel of his hand with his opposite thumb. "With time and experience, you will gain your footing. One day you will feel at home here, just as I do."

The nod she gave him was almost imperceptible. Not an agreement, per se, but more an acknowledgment of his sentiments. Did she understand what he meant? Did she share his feelings?

Tomorrow. Tomorrow he would propose, and put all these uncertainties aside.

∞∞∞

Peter Fitzwilliam claimed Lizzy for the first dance, as Joshua did for the second. She would not allow herself to examine what that might mean. It was difficult to imagine, however, that they were *not* distinguishing her in some way.

Did they have knowledge of some intentions on Darcy's part?

She must not think about it, she told herself as Joshua led her to the dance floor. All this rumination would ruin her peace of mind. Instead, she looked about the room—gilded mirrors, carved crown moulding, glittering chandeliers...

One day you will feel at home here. She pondered those words, holding them in her heart. Might this ballroom come to feel as familiar as her beloved Longbourn? Might *her* daughters be introduced into society here?

Her stomach wrenched. She wanted so badly to be Darcy's wife that the prospect of losing him made her physically ill. Had she not done enough to encourage him? The ball this evening would be the perfect opportunity to announce an engagement. Why was he hesitating?

The music started, and the dance got underway. The steps of the cotillion were complex. She might lose her place if she let her imagination wander. To make conversation, she said to

Joshua, "How does your book of sermons progress?"

He grinned sheepishly. "I find I am a better orator than a writer. When I put the words to paper, they feel flat."

She arched her brows. "Perhaps you could enlist your cousin Mr. Darcy to assist you. I understand he is most studious in his correspondence."

"Indeed. His letters are quite precise."

"Not the effect you are looking for?"

The dance separated them, but when they came back together, he said, "My sermons need animation. Passion, if I may use the word, yet without becoming overwrought."

"Perhaps a woman's touch would help."

He grinned. "Are you offering?"

For a moment, she contemplated his suggestion. Yes, she might enjoy reading his sermons, and even give some helpful hints. But at that moment, she had no idea what the future held.

"That depends. I am not sure how much longer I shall be in London. I was thinking of returning to Hertfordshire after Ash Wednesday. Certainly my family can stay no longer than Easter. Lady Purcell will come to London, and will want the use of her home again."

Joshua looked at her with wide eyes. "Then you must stay here at Matlock House for the remainder of the season. My mother will insist upon it, I am sure."

She stared at him. "Good heavens. That is a generous offer, but I could not intrude."

"It would be no intrusion at all. Arabelle and Georgiana are attached to you, and would be sad to see you go. I shall speak to my mother as soon as the dance ends."

"Oh, but Mr. Fitzwilliam, you must not! I would not wish to put her out."

He furrowed his brows. "Do you not wish to stay in London for the season?"

Her eyes burned. She blinked a few times to stop her tears. Before speaking, she swallowed the knot in her throat.

"Little could appeal to me more than enjoying your mother's hospitality for the London season. But you must not offer on her behalf. Pray, do not let her know you have spoken to me already. I would not wish her to feel obligated."

"As you wish, ma'am. But only to ensure your own peace of mind. I have no doubt of what her reaction will be."

She nodded and gave him a grateful smile. In her state of confusion and overwhelm at this new prospect, she forgot to be anxious about the next dance. Until the first chords of the waltz played, and Darcy came to claim her.

When he appeared at her side, offering his hand to lead her to the dance, she could think of nothing else. Looking at her with those intense dark eyes, he became her whole world. The man was achingly handsome. When he set a hand on her waist, she turned lightheaded a moment until she remembered to breathe.

She tried to speak, but words escaped her. Her brain kept echoing *Darcy, Darcy, Darcy*. Yet when the waltz got underway, her body knew exactly what to say.

They glided around the floor in time to the music, their gazes locked, and words were unnecessary. His hands were strong, his movements graceful, his expression open and happy. He was not smiling exactly—he hardly ever smiled. But his chiselled jaw had an easy set to it, and the corners of his mouth were upturned.

Now she was staring at his lips, thinking of all the wonderful things he could do to her with them. If the novels were to be believed, a man's lips could drive a woman mad with desire. No, she must not think about that. If she let him kiss her, Heaven knew where it might lead.

A woman's virtue was theoretical until put to the test. Lizzy was wildly, madly in love with this man. She vibrated with pure pleasure at the feel of his hands on her body in this most genteel of poses. If he took her into his arms, if he kissed her, could she resist whatever desires he pressed on her?

But the moment the thought came to her, she knew that the

answer was moot. Darcy would not press his advances. He was a gentleman. It would not fall on her alone to resist.

She must put these thoughts out of her head, and now. She grabbed the first idea that came to her as if it were a lifeline. "Earlier you spoke as if this house were a second home."

"It is," he conceded.

"Will Miss Darcy make her come-out here, do you think? Rather than at Darcy House?"

He seemed to consider that a moment. "That depends on whether she wants an intimate gathering, or to make her debut in front of the entire *ton*. Knowing Georgiana, she would prefer the former."

"You are right, of course. Perhaps your daughters might one day make their come-out here."

A sly smile curved his lips. "Perhaps."

As she realized what she had implied, her face heated. What was she thinking—her daughters making their debut in the home of an earl?

She was struck again by how little she belonged in this place. Should she not flee to Hertfordshire for Lent, as she had originally planned?

No, she must not think such nonsense. She loved this man. She would not give him up over a bout of insecurity.

Lizzy Bennet was made of sterner stuff.

∞∞∞

The dance ended all too soon. Darcy's arms felt empty without Elizabeth in them. When he accompanied her to her mother's side, he said, "Mrs. Bennet, Miss Elizabeth appears flushed. Might I take her onto the terrace for some air?"

"Of course!" Mrs. Bennet said with a smile on her face and a gleam in her eye. She handed Elizabeth her wrap, an Indian shawl woven of cream and pink that matched her gown. Darcy led her outside.

A few couples stood talking on the broad flagstone terrace, which was well lit by torches. He escorted her out into the garden, where they could talk more privately.

Chinese lanterns edged the path, illuminating boxwood topiaries and urns of winter-flowering heather. Lenten roses blooming in pure white dotted the flowerbeds. The sweet scent from unseen shrubs of daphne wafted into the air.

"It is like something out of a fairy tale," Elizabeth said as they ambled along the brick walkway. Yet she did not sound happy. "This night...I feel like Cinderella, an imposter at a ball. And the clock is about to strike."

"You are no imposter."

She stopped and looked up at him, blinking back tears. "Mr. Darcy, the truth is, Jane and I do not belong here. Our father is a gentleman, that is true, but we have led a retired country life. Life in Mayfair has been a revelation. I have seen how extraordinary wealth is taken for granted by those who possess it. Mr. Hurst cannot comprehend the difficulty of a London wedding for our friends in Meryton."

"Hang the man." Anger rose in Darcy's chest. "He is not worth the unhappiness he has caused you."

"It is not just him." She hesitated a moment, her throat working. Her next words escaped in a tight whisper. "Jane and Bingley are well-matched. He would never look down on her for her lack of fortune, nor she on him for his heritage. But I..."

He took her hand, but she withdrew it.

She moved further down the path. "Lord Greymore has called on me nearly every morning since we met. But Lizzy Bennet of Longbourn is no match for an earl." She stopped in the encroaching darkness and gestured towards the house. "Nor the son of an earl, nor the nephew of one. This is the grandest home I have ever been in, and to you it is only your uncle's house in Mayfair. I cannot imagine what his country estate must be like. Or yours. I am no more than the ragged girl who tends the fire. I do not belong with the handsome prince."

He stared at her dazedly. Then, he gave her a handkerchief

and watched in silence as she dried her eyes. They stood out of the reach of the lanterns now. The heady scent of daphne was stronger in this corner of the garden.

Struggling to find words to comfort her, he said, "You are every inch a lady—and the most enchanting woman I ever met."

"You are unutterably kind," she said, her voice choked. She folded the handkerchief and handed it back to him.

He slid it into his pocket and grasped her hands. "What if the nephew of an earl called on you every morning, until he convinced you that you *do* belong here? What if he did not care about your lack of fortune, or your country upbringing?" He raised a trembling hand to her cheek. "What if he loved you for you?"

Her eyes glittered in the moonlight as they locked with his own. He brushed the pad of his thumb over her lips. Through his gloves, he could not detect the softness there. So he leaned closer, needing to know the feel of them, the taste.

"Mr. Darcy." Her voice was a mere whisper. Was it a warning or a plea? He gave her a moment to pull back, to resist. He was not the sort of scoundrel who forced unwanted advances on a woman. If she wished to stop him, she could.

He laid his other hand on her waist, and a faint gasp escaped her. She made no effort to break away. He leaned in closer. "Dearest Lizzy," he groaned. Closing the distance between them, he placed his lips on hers.

Chapter 31

For a moment, Lizzy could not think. It had happened so quickly. Then, the brush of his lips, light but firm, set her body aflame. This was what it felt like to be kissed. To have a man so near that she was enveloped in his scent, his heat. It was all Lizzy could do to keep her knees from buckling at the intensity of it.

He cupped her face, and his mouth grew more insistent. She did not know what to do with her hands, so she simply surrendered to him. Opened to him. Allowed his tongue to part her lips and plunder her.

He tasted of lemonade and something deliciously male. She pressed her palms to the silk of his waistcoat. His chest was hard and masculine beneath her hands.

Some part of her brain told her she should not allow this intimacy, but sensation crowded out the thought. The smell of his bay rum soap exploded through her senses. His teeth nipped at the corner of her mouth, and sparks of pleasure blinded her.

One of his hands grasped the small of her back, dragging her closer. Her gloved fingers explored the superfine wool that covered the broad planes of his back. A soft, involuntary moan escaped her throat. She wanted to discover more of him, but she did not dare.

His kisses slowed, and she whimpered. The next moment, he pulled away and gazed at her with heavy-lidded eyes. He did not speak nor step away. He just watched her as she continued to stand within the range of his body heat.

Bereft and panting, she gazed back at him. Before her conscious mind awoke to her intention, she gripped his nape and hauled him back to her.

This time, he held nothing back. His tongue explored every crevice of her mouth. He drew her hard against him, chest pressing against her bosom. Her hands mauled him, roaming over the taut muscles of his back.

Her breath came in gasps now, as if she could not get enough air. Did she need air, when she had Darcy? Would his kisses not be enough to sustain her?

A groan caught in her throat. She did not *have* Darcy. This was not a wedding vow. It was nothing but desire.

What if she had been mistaken? What if he wanted her not as a wife, but as a mistress? By allowing his kisses, was she not placing her virtue in doubt?

She forced herself to step away. She hugged herself, now chilled without his warmth to protect her from the night air. "I am sorry," she said, her voice strangled.

"Miss Bennet, I—"

"You need not say it. I expect nothing of you. Please understand, I am not the sort of woman who—"

"No, of course not. I am not the sort of man who—"

"I have never done anything like that before. I do not know what came over me."

But of course, she knew exactly what had come over her. Desire. Passion. Lust. In the few minutes of that kiss, she had lost her innocence.

She was still a virgin, of course. She had not been utterly compromised. But now she understood how a woman could risk her reputation, her future for a man's touch. How wholly she could be swept away. How she could do things that five minutes earlier would have seemed impossible.

Her hands felt branded by the sensation of his body beneath them. She had never wanted anything so much. His eyes were still on her, still filled with longing. Was more there? Dared she hope for love?

Tears welled in her eyes, and he clutched her in his arms. "Dearest Lizzy, you must not cry. I have you, my love. I shall never let you go."

They were foolish words, born of passion. But his lips were soon on her ear, whispering between tantalizing kisses, "I love you. I shall always love you."

Fool that she was, she allowed herself to believe him.

Darcy did not know what madness had seized him when he first kissed her, but now he was lost in it. She tasted like heaven and felt like sin. Finally his Lizzy was in his arms, precisely where she belonged.

She was everything he had dreamed of in a wife. Beautiful, intelligent, witty, and passionate. The way her body had yielded to his kiss—the way she gripped him even now, as she rested pliant in his arms—this woman would be an eager bedmate. Not one who gave herself to him only for the purpose of bearing children.

He had no need of a dowry from her. Pemberley provided an ample living, and he had healthy investments besides. He could provide for her and a dozen children, if it came to that.

He loved her. He had been born to love her. This was destiny. And at last, she would be his.

A noise caught his attention. He pulled back and put a finger to her lips. Looking towards the terrace, he found it now empty but for two men emerging from the house.

Darcy drew Lizzy deeper into the shadows. It had been foolish to lead her into the darkest recesses of the garden like this. If they were seen, her reputation would be ruined—a stain even marriage would not entirely erase.

He must herd the gentlemen back into the ballroom so she could come out of hiding. He hated to leave her alone, but it could not be helped. He said in her ear, "I shall take care of them. Once we're inside, wait a few minutes, then come back in."

She nodded her understanding.

He looked her over. "You have only your wrapper. Will you be warm enough?"

"I shall not freeze to death," she said in low tones, her voice teasing.

He wanted to kiss her but did not dare. He squeezed her hand and walked reluctantly towards the house.

∞∞∞

Lizzy hugged herself again, rubbing her hands along her arms in a futile attempt to keep warm. She watched, still and silent, as Darcy greeted the two men. Through the darkness, she could see the red tips of their cheroots.

How in Heaven's name had she allowed this to happen? She should have been careful to remain within the light of the lanterns. She should not have stayed out with Darcy for more than the few minutes it took to cool down. If the two men— she knew not who they were—caught sight of her, they would know exactly what she and Darcy had been doing.

He would have to marry her. And knowing Darcy, he would.

But she did not want him to act out of a sense of honour. She wanted him to love her, not to feel trapped.

Darcy was everything to her. But if he did not feel the same, what torture would it be to live in his home, to lie in his bed, knowing he regretted it? Regretted her? She would not subject herself to that humiliation every day for the rest of her life.

She shivered. She was truly cold now. Nothing less than the threat of ruin could have kept her in that spot much longer. After what seemed like an hour, but was probably five minutes, the men finally went inside.

She would have to wait a bit before entering, at least if she used the door leading back to the ballroom. Was there another option? She followed the path in a different direction and came upon a side door, barely visible in the darkness.

Slowly, silently, she turned the knob. Then, she pushed the door open a crack. In the dim light beyond was an empty corridor. She slipped inside. Soundlessly, she faced the door and pressed it closed.

Letting out a sigh of relief, she turned. Her heart lurched. At the end of the hall stood a young woman, a maid, peering at her. "May I help you, ma'am?" she asked in a broad accent.

Lizzy's mind went blank a moment. "Forgive me. I stepped outside to get some air..." Her mind worked. She was not an accomplished liar, but her reputation was at stake. "I thought I might look for the necessary, but I got turned around."

"Good heavens, you're shivering! Let's go to the cloak room so you can stand by the fire. There's a water closet there, too."

"That is most kind of you."

Ten minutes later, warm and comfortable, Lizzy re-entered the ballroom. She caught Darcy's eye to make sure he saw her. She did not wish him to worry for her safety. He gazed at her tenderly and gave her a quick smile before turning away again, looking nonchalant.

Her heart rose in her chest. His outward coolness did not trouble her. It was as if the two of them shared a secret—which of course they did—and she liked that.

Her sense of normalcy restored, some of Lizzy's earlier fears receded. Above all else, Darcy was a man of honour. He would not have kissed her recklessly, without a thought of consequences. His passion had not been wild and unruly, but measured and gentle. She had no doubt he would be an exuberant bed partner—good heavens, what a thought! On this night, however, he had shown restraint.

His kisses had been intentional. They had been designed to comfort and reassure. *What if the nephew of an earl did not care about your lack of fortune, but loved you for you?* That held the sound of a promise. And Lizzy allowed herself to believe as she never had before.

∞ ∞ ∞

Darcy let out a long sigh of relief even while keeping his expression safely masked. The past quarter hour had been one of the longest of his life. Lizzy must have been freezing in that thin ball gown, with nothing but a cotton shawl to protect her.

But her reputation had been at stake, and he had not dared expose her. He had hurried Wayne and Greymore into the house as quickly as he could.

Making his way towards Lizzy, he did not approach close enough to speak. But he could see that she did not shiver, and her skin was a healthy pink. She must have found a way to warm herself before coming back to the ballroom.

Drat him for getting carried away like that! He had placed her in danger, and that was unforgivable. Tomorrow, he would ask for her hand and spend the rest of his life making it up to her.

An unbidden smile crossed his face at the thought of it. He schooled it instantly. In the corner of his eye, Lizzy was looking in his direction. He gave her a quick glance and a nod, but did not let his eyes linger. He did not wish her to think he was leering at her.

What a bungled mess this had become! The memory of her in his arms...that taste had not been nearly enough. Elizabeth Bennet was not the cold jewel that the young ladies of the *ton* strove to be. She was warm with an animal passion. He wanted her beneath him with her limbs wrapped around him, his body encompassed by her heat.

He could not speak to her now without raising suspicion. He had already danced with her once, with the supper waltz promised later in the evening. He did not wish to draw attention, in case anyone had noticed them leaving the ballroom together. If they remained discreet the rest of the evening, the gossips might forget that lapse.

No, tonight called for nonchalance, but that would soon change. His mind worked through the next steps. Tomorrow, propose. The next day, ride to Longbourn for her father's permission. Spend the night at Netherfield and ride back to London the next day.

How long would it take to get a license? They would marry in Meryton, as Lizzy wished, surrounded by her friends. Those from London who wanted to travel there could do so. Netherfield would be large enough to house the Fitzwilliams for a night or two.

He ought to stop this train of thought. She had not yet accepted an offer from him. But she had accepted his kisses. That was the same thing for a young woman of her background. She would not have kissed him with such abandon if she had not been expecting a proposal.

And why should she not? He had been doing his best to convey his intentions for two weeks now. A woman of her intelligence could not be blind to his advances.

Perhaps they should all remove to Hertfordshire at once. Nothing was keeping the Bennet ladies in London now. As Lizzy had said, Lady Purcell would soon want her house back.

Lizzy's wedding clothes were a consideration, of course. But then, if Mrs. Bennet were involved, he would be getting the bill for those anyway. Lizzy might as well wait to order them until after they were married.

He, Bingley, and Georgiana could stay at Netherfield until the wedding. The Fitzwilliams could come for the ceremony itself. He would of course invite his aunt, Lady Catherine de Bourgh. But she was unlikely to come, given the weakened state of her daughter Anne's health.

Yes, it could be accomplished in a week, he was sure. Soon, very soon, and in every sense of the word, Lizzy would be his.

He would let nothing stand in his way.

Chapter 32

Darcy checked in with Arabelle, who warned him to stop fretting over her. Her eyes sparkled when Greymore came to claim her for the next dance. Seeing her so animated, he was happy to leave her to her fortunate partner.

Stepping away, Darcy scanned the ballroom. His plans for tomorrow were life altering, but he still had tonight to get through. He would dance and be gallant, as he knew Lizzy wished him to be.

He noticed Miss Peabody standing alone nearby, and asked her for the next set. As it got underway, they made polite conversation. At length she said, "I have just started reading *Pamela Pepperington's Predicament*. It is the latest by Mrs. Wheedlesuch, and it is divine. I shall lend it to Georgiana when I have finished."

He shuddered. He had read nothing by that author. But Georgiana had pronounced the books to be sensationalistic frivolities. It would do Miss Peabody no good to continue with her passion for such literature. Not to the exclusion of everything else.

"Have you read *Sense and Sensibility*?" he asked. "Georgiana has a copy she might lend you."

Miss Peabody eyed him assessingly. "Does anyone get compromised in it? I like a book where the heroine gets compromised."

Darcy blinked. He ought not have such a conversation with an impressionable young lady. "As I recall, the heroine's sister narrowly avoids being compromised."

"I suppose that is nearly as good," his companion replied.

As the Scottish reel progressed, Darcy stole glances at Lizzy when he could. However, he made a point of focusing his attention on Miss Peabody. He wanted to learn more about her, to determine how best he could help her.

Perhaps part of him hoped to atone for his lapse with Georgiana by attending to her friend. He had placed too much trust in Mrs. Younge, Georgiana's former companion. He had learnt the hard way—adolescent girls required guidance and strict vigilance. Just as adolescent boys did, now that he thought on it.

When the dance ended, Miss Peabody exclaimed in an exuberant voice. "That was vigorous indeed! I declare, I am quite parched after all that exertion."

"Of course." He went to the refreshment room and fetched two glasses of lemonade.

When he returned to the ballroom, he stopped, his brow drawn. For a moment, he could not find Miss Peabody again. Then, he spotted her, standing off to the side, some way from whence they had parted. He approached, and she took the cup from him.

"It is a bit quieter here, is it not?" She sipped the drink. "Oh dear, I have had better punch at Almack's."

He grinned, knowing that Almack's was renowned for the poor quality of their punch. He himself never went.

She hummed and swayed, making a few steps as if still in the reel. "There is nothing I adore more than dancing. I hate that no balls will be held during Lent."

"Never fear. I daresay some of the dinner parties will include impromptu dancing. They often do." He looked around. They had stepped into a little hallway outside the ballroom proper. He offered his arm. "Come, we should return."

"Return?"

"Yes, we have strayed from the company. The viscountess will be looking for you."

Miss Peabody rolled her eyes. "She is always looking for me. She never lets me have any fun." Still dancing to her imagined music, she giggled.

He took another step towards the ballroom. "Come, Miss Peabody, I must insist."

"What a killjoy you are," she scolded with a coquettish grin. Moving in his direction with a sway in her hips, she tripped. The glass of lemonade spilled down the front of her gown. "Oh!"

Her bodice was completely drenched. Looking away to protect her modesty, he removed a handkerchief from his coat and held it out to her. Instead of taking it, she dabbed her chest with it. As he waited patiently, a voice behind him cried, "Mr. Darcy!"

He turned. His confusion quickly gave way to an unsettling feeling. Unwittingly, he had stumbled into the starring role in a comic opera.

Viscountess Wayne stared at him. She squeaked, "How dare you touch an innocent like Miss Peabody in such an intimate way!"

Darcy was too shocked to speak. The accusation was so ridiculous, he could hardly summon the energy to deny it.

I like a book where the heroine gets compromised. Good heavens, how could he not have seen this coming?

Whether the viscountess was in league with Miss Peabody, or saw what the girl wanted her to see, he could not tell. Either way, he would not allow himself to be manipulated. He would counter Lady Wayne's claim and be done with this nonsense. No one else had witnessed the incident, after all—

Until Lizzy walked up behind the viscountess, and the blood drained from Darcy's face.

∞∞∞

While dancing the reel with Mr. Witherspoon, Lizzy had been

unable to escape an awareness of Darcy. The grace of his movements. The confidence of his bearing. The kindness of his expression as he spoke to his naïve young partner.

After the dance had finished, however, a sinking feeling came over Lizzy. Darcy returned from the refreshment room with two drinks in hand. Miss Peabody seemed to lure him into a dark corner.

As one who had recently been in a dark corner with Darcy herself, she knew it could be a compromising position. And had not Miss Peabody been pleased by Darcy's attentions to her earlier in the day?

An oath crossed Lizzy's mind that she dared not say aloud. This would *not* happen. Darcy belonged to her now, and a foolish girl like Priscilla Peabody would not get her talons into him.

Lizzy crossed the room as quickly as she could do so gracefully. Lady Wayne—Miss Peabody's strict but easily distracted chaperone—looked around in confusion. She seemed to spot the couple a moment after Lizzy had. The viscountess got to them first.

Lizzy had not been near enough to see what had happened. But she heard Darcy beg the girl to return to the ballroom. There had been no lapse in propriety on his part. Once Lizzy caught up and saw the spectacle of the ruined gown, she hardly knew whether to laugh or cry.

The idea that he had spilled lemonade on Miss Peabody so that he could put his hands on her bosom was preposterous. After all, if his intent had been to touch a woman in that manner, he might have done so to Lizzy while he was kissing her.

However, she could not exactly use that as testimony in his favour.

"Good heavens, Miss Peabody, do take my wrap." Lizzy's pink shawl did not complement Miss Peabody's green gown, but it would have to do. The wet fabric showed more of her than was proper.

"Darcy," the viscountess said shrilly, "I must insist that you marry Miss Peabody."

Oh, good heavens. Did Viscountess Wayne really think this would work? That a man of Darcy's intellect and character could be trapped into marriage by a splash of lemonade?

By now some other guests had come into view, no doubt drawn by the sound of raised voices. Wayne was amongst them. Colonel Fitzwilliam, at his side, looked stern and wore his commanding officer face.

"I assure you," Darcy said, "I did not harm Miss Peabody in any way. She spilled some lemonade, and I gave her a handkerchief. I did not touch her."

"It did not appear that way to me, Mr. Darcy," the viscountess protested, her face turning red.

Wayne stepped over and laid his hand on the small of his wife's back. "I am sure we can resolve this civilly. Darcy is no blackguard."

"Lady Wayne," Lizzy said, "you must be mistaken. I applaud your desire to protect your sister. But I overheard Mr. Darcy imploring her to step back into the ballroom. He was not trying to lure her into something untoward."

"Miss Peabody," the colonel said in a cool tone, "I have known you all your life. You are a good girl. I am not sure you understand the seriousness of the accusation being made here. Tell us the truth, as your sainted mother would wish you to. What happened?"

"I spilled some lemonade...that is, *he* spilled the lemonade... that is, the lemonade spilled. He took out a handkerchief and touched it to my..." She coloured and said no more.

"For heaven's sake, Lady Wayne," the colonel said. "Whether Darcy touched her or not, it is clear he was only trying to dab up the lemonade. Not to make lascivious advances on Miss Peabody."

"Whatever his intentions," the viscountess said, "he has ruined her reputation."

Wayne spoke between gritted teeth. "Perhaps her reputation

would not be ruined, if you could manage to keep your voice down."

The crowd tittered, breaking some of the tension in the atmosphere. Lady Wayne looked around. Her face turned a deeper shade of red as she seemed to realize the moment had turned from drama into farce.

The viscountess stamped her foot. "If you are any kind of gentleman, Mr. Darcy, you will marry her."

"I am afraid I cannot," Darcy said, rising to his full height, his spine straight.

"Why not?" Lady Wayne demanded.

Darcy's eyes strayed to Lizzy wearing a beseeching look. Then he turned back to Lady Wayne, his stern countenance defying anyone to contradict him. "Because I am engaged to Miss Elizabeth Bennet."

Lizzy let out a gasp as all eyes turned to her. She stared at Darcy in disbelief. His pleading expression returned. He held out his hand to her.

Happiness rolled over her like an ocean wave. She wanted to laugh aloud, to take him in her arms, to claim him as her own. But all she could do was wear a smile that conveyed the joy in her heart.

She was not fool enough to hold him to the facts. Composing herself, she moved towards him. "He made his proposals this evening, and I accepted." She took his offered hand.

But Darcy apparently was not content with that show of commitment. He drew her into his arms and placed his lips on hers.

His brazenness startled her, but even more unexpected was his ardour as he deepened the kiss. He gripped her nape and his mouth plundered hers. She wrapped her arms around his neck and held on for support as her knees buckled. With a hand at the small of her back, he arched her into him.

Lizzy gradually became aware that a hush had fallen over the group. Scattered applause followed, and a few hoots. Pulling away, she looked into the shocked faces. She ought to school her features into something missish. But she could not. She did not feel missish. She felt...triumphant.

Not because of Darcy's ten thousand pounds nor his estate in Derbyshire. Not because he was the handsomest, cleverest man she had ever met. But because she loved him. With him at her side, she could fly.

The colonel stepped forward to shake Darcy's hand. "Congratulations, my friend. How did this happen?"

"We went out into the garden for air after the waltz," Lizzy said quickly. To save Darcy, she would do whatever was needed. Including compromising herself even more thoroughly than Miss Peabody had been. "We were surprised to find ourselves the only ones there. He proposed then."

"I did not see you," Wayne said in some surprise. "Greymore and I spotted Darcy when we stepped out with our cheroots..."

"Oh, dear," Lizzy said, eyeing the floor in a show of embarrassment she did not feel. "I am afraid we feared it might lead to gossip if anyone found us there together. I slipped in through another door. One of the maids—Jenny, I believe her name is—led me to the cloak room so I could warm by the fire." She looked up at the colonel with wide eyes. "But it was not so very wicked for us to be alone together, was it, since we are engaged?"

Mrs. Bennet pushed through to the front of the crowd. "Not at all, my dear. Darcy asked for my blessing earlier today. I wrote to your father to secure his permission, and to my brother Philips to begin the contracts."

Lizzy stared at her mother a moment, then turned to Darcy. His wide eyes bore the same look of astonishment that hers must. Surely her mother was speaking nonsense. But on this occasion, for once, the nonsense worked in Lizzy's favour.

Darcy seemed to be of the same mind. "Quite right," he said, and pulled Lizzy closer.

∞∞∞

A half-hour later, Darcy was sequestered in his uncle's study. Along with him were the Earl and Countess of Matlock, and Lord and Lady Wayne. Two large candelabras lit the seating area by the desk. The sounds of the orchestra playing a jig could be heard muffled through the door.

"Felicia, really," Lady Matlock said to the viscountess in a pitying tone, "I know this year has been a trying one for you. But when a chit of a girl makes a ploy for an upstanding gentleman like Darcy..." The countess shook her head. "The role of her chaperone is to chastise her for it, not to encourage her."

"I know what I saw," Lady Wayne insisted. Darcy gritted his teeth but said nothing.

"My dear," Wayne said to his wife, "you saw what Priscilla wanted you to see. And perhaps *you* wanted to see it as well. I understand the strain you have been under. Chaperoning a girl of Priscilla's temperament is no easy task. Marrying her off would be a relief to you—"

"I shall sponsor Priscilla for the rest of the season," Lady Matlock said. "She will live in this house and obey my rules. In return, Felicia, you will put a stop to this gossip. You will say that the accusations tonight were a misunderstanding. Priscilla spilled some lemonade on the front of her dress. Darcy handed her a handkerchief. You were confused by what you saw, but now realize your mistake."

Lady Wayne still glared, but some of the tension was gone from her expression.

Darcy spoke up. "To compensate for any loss of reputation, I will add one thousand pounds to her dowry. I do this for the sake of the late viscountess, who was kind to me when I was a boy. If she were alive, none of this could have happened."

Wayne shook his head. "My mother would have been ashamed to see her children end up in such a state."

"All is not lost," the countess said. "Priscilla needs guidance, and she shall have it. Starting with correcting her reading habits. Mrs. Wheedlesuch has her place. But such titillating fare is not appropriate for a girl of Priscilla's maturity level." Lady Matlock turned to Darcy. "I hope Miss Elizabeth will stay in town for the rest of the season. She might serve as a companion to Arabelle. Between her and Priscilla, I shall need all the help I can get."

"I cannot speak for her, but I believe she would be happy with that arrangement." A sense of pride welled up in Darcy's chest. Lady Matlock's high regard for Lizzy boded well for his family's future.

"Splendid!" the earl proclaimed, a smile lighting his face, his tone brooking no argument. "I am glad that is cleared up."

Lady Wayne opened her mouth as if to protest, but wisely closed it again.

The earl said to Darcy, "I understand Miss Peabody is to go to Pemberley to visit Georgiana in the autumn. Is that plan still in place?"

Darcy eyed him in surprise. He had not given the subject any thought since the incident in the ballroom. "Unless anyone objects," he said after some consideration. "It would help put any rumours to rest, if my new bride invited Miss Peabody to our home."

"Yes, it is a good scheme," Lady Matlock said. The earl and viscount both nodded. Lady Wayne pressed her lips tight but made no argument.

Darcy wondered how Lizzy would react. She would tease him mercilessly he was sure. In the end, though, he believed she would consent. She was not the sort to hold a grudge, and she understood the silliness of adolescence as well as anyone. Her three younger sisters rarely let her forget it.

With a relieved sigh, Darcy went back to claim the supper waltz with his betrothed.

Chapter 33

Lizzy was dancing a cotillion with Colonel Fitzwilliam when Darcy re-entered the ballroom. He looked grave but not the worse for whatever he had encountered in his uncle's study. She caught his eye, and he gave her a reassuring smile.

"What do you think, Colonel?" Lizzy asked. "Has my reputation been utterly ruined?"

"Do you mean your reputation as the most bewitching woman in London? On the contrary, Darcy has sealed it. The man is besotted."

She grinned. "You are too kind."

"Not at all. I daresay Darcy is the envy of half the men here tonight."

Lizzy let the subject drop. Only time would tell what the fallout would be of the night's events. If anyone could manage a potential scandal, it was Lady Matlock.

Lizzy would not mind for herself. She would happily retire to the country and leave the *ton* behind. She worried for Georgiana. If this evening's foolishness hurt the girl's prospects... Ah well, there was no point wondering about that now. They would have to wait and see.

After the dance, Lady Cressida came and kissed Lizzy's cheek. She looked radiant in a gown of yellow silk, with white flowers in her hair. "My dear, I am so happy for you. You and Mr. Darcy will be deliriously happy."

Lizzy tilted her head as a smile crept over her lips. "I believe we shall."

"You and I will be neighbours, you know," Cressida said. "Greymore Park is not an hour's ride from Pemberley. I shall convince Mama to hold a house party in October. The men can go shooting, and the ladies... We can decide what our husbands and brothers will work on when Parliament reconvenes."

Lizzy chuckled. "That sounds delightful."

Cressida stepped closer. "We must be serious a moment, though. Priscilla is one of my dearest friends, but a complete ninny. You must have deduced that by now."

Lizzy nodded. "She reminds me of one of my sisters. Kitty is too easily influenced and exposes her mind to all sorts of foolishness."

"Then you understand. Priscilla has a kind heart but not a bit of sense. I know you will not hold that against her. As for Lady Wayne, however..."

Lizzy stiffened. Cressida had touched a nerve. Viscountess Wayne was somehow more difficult to forgive. She had leapt on the opportunity to rid herself of an unwanted charge. And to saddle Darcy with a bride who would have made him miserable for the rest of his days. That kind of selfishness seemed unpardonable.

"Lady Wayne has had a difficult time since she married," Cressida explained. "Lord Wayne was then heir to a title and a vast fortune. He was precisely the sort of man she had been raised for. From what I have heard, it was a love match. But one cannot live on love alone."

Cressida hinted at the challenges the Waynes had sustained. Unscrupulous business associates had preyed on the old earl during his final illness. Lizzy pressed her hand to her chest in shock. "How awful! Lord Wayne is such a kind man—at least he has always been so to me. I am sorry for the trouble that has befallen his family."

"I am afraid the viscountess was unprepared for the change in her circumstances." Cressida spoke gravely. "She was raised for a life that revolved around parties and fashion. Her current situation is nothing like what she thought she was marrying into."

Lizzy shook her head, a sudden sorrow welling in her chest. "It must be a dreadfully difficult adjustment."

Cressida nodded. "Perhaps you can understand why, when she saw a chance for Priscilla to marry well, she grabbed it. It would have been a disastrous match, to be sure, but Priscilla would have been provided for."

"Yes...yes, I see." Lizzy swallowed hard. With her background, she could appreciate the viscountess's desperation. The need to see a charge well married could drive a woman to all sorts of ridiculous machinations.

Lizzy thanked Cressida for the information. If the viscountess would let the matter drop, Lizzy was inclined to do so as well.

When the time came for the supper waltz, Darcy claimed her without ceremony. They got into position on the dance floor as they waited for the set to begin. Placing a hand at Lizzy's waist, Darcy leaned towards her and said in her ear, "You are mine, Lizzy."

"Goodness," she teased, breathing his scent of wool and bay rum, now so familiar to her. "Is that a promise or a threat?"

He looked at her with wide eyes, as if taken aback. "A promise, I assure you. You are mine, just as I am yours."

She regarded him, losing herself in a wave of bliss. With her palm resting on his shoulder, she stroked her thumb over the wool of his jacket. Gently, she murmured, "I like the sound of that."

He growled, and his gaze fell to her lips.

"Behave," she warned.

"If I must." His eyes grew dark. "But I hope I shall not have to behave for long."

Her chest rose with a quick intake of breath. She looked up at him in a panic. She had heard of engaged couples taking liberties before exchanging their vows. But she had no intention of—

"I ride to Hertfordshire tomorrow," he explained, "to ask your father's permission. I can secure a license, and we can be married within the week."

Unable to speak, she stood frozen. When the music began, she followed the steps mechanically. A week! She had not conceived of marrying so soon. If she had thought of it at all, she had imagined a double ceremony with Jane and Bingley after Easter.

"I expected we would wait for the banns to be read," she said at last.

He said lightly, "A license is but a few pounds, and then the banns can be dispensed with."

"Yes, of course," she replied. To a man of Darcy's means, a few pounds was nothing.

"You would rather wait?" he asked, eyeing her, his brows drawn.

"Not necessarily. This is happening so fast, I can hardly think."

He nodded, hesitating a beat. "Forgive me. I should not have assumed—"

"Please, sir, you have me at a disadvantage." She swallowed and collected her thoughts before continuing. "A man may make plans, where a woman may only wait and hope. I had given no thought to a wedding until tonight. I am open to your suggestion, but I may need some hours to adapt."

He looked away, his expression downcast. "I was foolish to think you would wish to marry so soon."

The disappointment in his face touched her heart. "Not at all," she insisted. "I simply need time to think through our options. In the meantime, pray do not be discouraged. Your wish to marry quickly is most endearing." She gave him a smile.

Darcy's lips quirked up at that. "I am glad you see it that way. I would not wish to pressure you."

"I must warn you, sir, you shall not find me so docile as to relinquish my every wish to your command."

"That is a relief."

She laughed, a sense of pure joy rushing through her. No man could be more perfect for her than Darcy. But a week! Could they truly be married in a week? Her head spun at the possibility.

∞ ∞ ∞

Darcy led Lizzy into the supper room, feeling conspicuous. What had he been thinking, kissing her in front of the assembly? He and his betrothed would be the subject of gossip for the next fortnight.

Somehow, the prospect did not bother him in the least.

Lady Matlock insisted they sit at her table. They would need to put up a united front, she said. Arabelle and Greymore joined them.

"How are you enjoying the ball, Lady Arabella?" Lizzy asked. "I see you have had a partner for every dance."

"Oh yes, it has been a splendid evening! And you must call me Arabelle, now that you are to be family."

"Thank you. And please call me Lizzy."

Greymore inserted, "You are a lucky dog, Darcy."

"I am," Darcy said with a quick nod, giving him a grin. He remembered what Greymore had said in the house at Berkeley Square, when he gave up his suit. Lizzy might have been a countess if she had pursued the man. She had chosen Darcy.

His heart swelled with the joy of it. He had been the worst possible suitor, and yet their hearts had recognized the truth. The two of them fit together effortlessly.

As the meal wound down, Darcy leaned towards Lizzy. "You recall this afternoon, I said I had invited Miss Peabody to Pemberley?"

"Heavens!" Lizzy said. "I had forgotten about that."

"Lady Matlock suggested that you extend the invitation to

Miss Peabody as well. An olive branch, so to speak, but also to show that you do not consider her a rival."

Lizzy suppressed a laugh, her cheeks pinking from the effort. "Indeed I do not. Should I speak to the Waynes now, do you think, or wait until some of the discomfort has subsided?"

"The sooner the better, I would say."

She arched her brows and said in his ear, "Wish me luck."

∞ ∞ ∞

When Lizzy spotted the Waynes, Miss Peabody was sitting with them. She looked forlorn, wearing a gown Lizzy recognized as Arabelle's. The Fitzwilliams had made sure Priscilla was supplied with dance partners. But the poor thing must be feeling chastised after the way the night had turned out.

Lizzy took the empty seat next to Lord Wayne. "I understand Darcy invited Miss Peabody to visit Georgiana at Pemberley this autumn."

"The subject has been discussed, yes." The viscount gave her a wary smile, with no enthusiasm in his eyes.

Lizzy turned to Miss Peabody and met her eyes. "I certainly hope she will be able to come, if the viscountess can spare her. Georgiana's companion, Mrs. Annesley, and I shall arrange a variety of activities for the girls. Perhaps we can start a reading circle, as Miss Peabody is fond of books."

"Acting as mistress of Pemberley already," the viscountess said with a saccharine smile.

"Darcy and I hope to be married within the week," Lizzy replied, surprising herself. Well, why not? If that kiss had been any hint of what marriage held for them, they might as well get on with it.

"By Jove," Wayne exclaimed, "that Darcy wastes no time."

Lizzy tittered. "One might say that." Or, she thought, one might say it took him an inordinate amount of time to propose, given their history. She recalled the days she had spent at Netherfield while Jane was ill. Darcy's eyes had followed her whenever they were together. She had thought him looking to disapprove, but had he loved her even then?

It occurred to her that in truth, Darcy had *not* proposed. He had kissed her. He had said he loved her. He had told the assembly they were engaged. But he had not, in fact, asked for her hand.

For some reason, that troubled her. Would he have proposed, if circumstances had not forced his hand? When faced with the prospect of marrying Miss Peabody, had Lizzy been the lesser of two evils?

Her blood chilled at the idea. She ended the conversation with the Waynes on a cordial note. Then, she went back to Darcy just in time for him to escort her into the ballroom for the final dances of the evening.

Distressed as she was, she hardly attended to her partners. She would rather die a spinster than spend her life with a man who did not want her with his whole heart. She could not let him make that sacrifice, no matter what it cost her.

Part of her berated herself for doubting him. In truth, she was not thinking clearly. It was late, and she was exhausted. She would speak with him on the morrow.

Chapter 34

Darcy called on Lizzy the next morning directly after breakfast. It was not yet the visiting hour. But he wanted to speak with her before travelling to Hertfordshire to ask her father for her hand.

The truth was, Darcy had not in fact made her a formal marriage proposal. Everything had happened in a muddle the night before. He wanted to make sure they were both clear on where things stood between them.

He waited in the front parlour, considering what he would say. First, he would assure her of his deep and abiding love. Second, he would thank her for getting him out of a scrape the night before. Third, he would make sure she did not feel trapped into the engagement.

At the sound of slippered feet, he turned. Lizzy stood before him in a plain white morning dress, her hair in a simple chignon. To him, she had never looked lovelier.

All his practiced words fled his mind as he strode forward and took her hands. "By Heaven, you are beautiful," he cried, then raised her hands to his lips. Her skin was unspeakably soft.

Lizzy pulled away with a shy smile. She glanced towards her maid, then back at Darcy. "Would you care for some tea?" Lizzy asked him.

"Yes, thank you," he replied, hoping to get rid of the maid long enough to give Lizzy a proper kiss.

Lizzy turned to Sally. "A pot of tea and some lemon tarts."

Sally curtseyed and withdrew.

Once the maid's footsteps faded, Darcy wasted no time. He closed the door and took Lizzy in his arms.

Her body yielded to his as he met her lips in a gentle kiss. She smelled of violets and strawberries, the scent light but intoxicating. He pulled her closer and deepened the kiss, knowing he must stop, but resisting. Finally, he pulled back and said, "Are you happy, love?"

"Nothing could make me happier than marrying you."

His heart filled with a joy unlike anything he had known before. He could imagine her walking through the halls of Pemberley. Giving instructions to the servants as they planned a house party or a ball. That life, which had been just a dream to him the day before, was now his future. It did not seem real.

She eyed the closed door, then opened it. "I would not wish Sally to encounter a closed door while carrying a heavy tray," she said.

"Of course." He admired how Lizzy cared for the staff, just as his mother always had.

Lizzy came and took his hands. "We must speak seriously a moment. Last night, things happened quickly. I do not wish to go through the rest of my life wondering whether you acted under duress. If you have any doubts about this engagement —"

"None at all. I resolved to offer for you weeks ago. Bingley can vouch for that, and so can Colonel Fitzwilliam."

Her hand went to her throat, and her eyes glistened. "I confess, I am relieved. I barely slept last night. I worried you claimed an engagement between us to escape the situation with Miss Peabody."

"Oh, my love," he murmured, kissing her temple. "Forgive me. Perhaps I should have acted sooner. I wanted only to be certain of your regard for me."

She flashed him a coquettish grin. "And you found the assurance you were looking for in the garden last night?"

He growled and hooked his arm around her waist. "Do not

tempt me, minx. You have no idea of the things I would like to do to you right now."

"I believe I could take a few guesses."

He kissed her cheek. "I want to do this right." He got down on one knee. "Miss Elizabeth Bennet, you must allow me to tell you how ardently I admire and love you. Will you do me the honour of becoming my wife?"

She pressed her palms together as if she were praying, then touched her fingers to her lips. "Yes, Mr. Darcy. The honour would be mine."

∞∞∞

Tears pricked Lizzy's eyes as Darcy rose and stepped towards her. He took her hand, and the feel of his flesh on hers sent a shiver through her. Raising her hand, he pressed a kiss to it, then another. Her gaze swept up and locked with his. He brushed his lips against each of her fingertips, one by one, and desire flamed inside her.

How could such a simple touch turn her into something wanton? She knew she should stop him, but had not the strength. Sally would return at any moment—they could not continue like this. But instead of pulling her hand away, she wished he would take her in his arms again. She wished he would lay her on the sofa and...and...she knew not what. Give her something more than this ache, this longing. Give her some sort of satisfaction.

Yet that was exactly what he must *not* do. She had sense enough to know that much. Growing up in the country, she had seen the rams with the ewes. She was not entirely ignorant.

At the sound of footsteps, she jumped back. A moment later, her mother entered. "Why, Mr. Darcy! I did not know you were here."

He bowed. "Forgive me. I should have asked for you. I only

just arrived."

"Sally went to get refreshments," Lizzy quickly explained, then remembered who she was talking to.

Mrs. Bennet motioned towards the seating area. "Let us sit down, then." She and Lizzy took their places on the couch, and Darcy on a chair perpendicular to them. "Mr. Darcy," she said, "where is Mr. Bingley this morning?"

"He is...that is, he had not come downstairs yet when I left. I realize it is early for me to call, but I am heading to Longbourn today to speak with Mr. Bennet. I wanted to talk with Lizzy before I left."

"Yes, Mr. Darcy, it is most proper of you to call on her father. Perhaps I could send a note along with you, assuring him that Lizzy and I are of one mind."

"I agree, Mama," Lizzy said in a rush, remembering Mr. Collins' proposal. On that, she and her mother had had decidedly different opinions. "I would like to send a note along as well."

∞∞∞

Darcy's stomach twisted as Hill the housekeeper led him into Bennet's study. This might be one of the most momentous occasions of his life. He did not believe Bennet would refuse his suit. And if he did, Lizzy was nearly of age. They had only to wait a few months, and they could marry without permission if necessary.

But surely it would not be necessary—would it? Lizzy would be unhappy to act without her father's blessing. The two were close. If Bennet disapproved, would Lizzy go forward with the wedding?

Darcy forced those thoughts from his mind as Bennet stood. The man received him with the shake of a hand and a sardonic grin. "This is a surprise. Surely you are not here to warn me about another worthless young man of Colonel Forster's regiment."

"No indeed." Darcy's mouth grew dry as the weight of what he was about to say gripped him. "I have come to beg for your daughter's hand in marriage."

Bennet startled, eyeing him curiously for a moment. Then his shoulders relaxed as he said, "I have four daughters yet unspoken for. Was there one in particular you had in mind?"

Darcy's face warmed. Did this man truly intend to taunt him? "Miss Elizabeth, sir."

Bennet nodded thoughtfully. "Excellent choice. She is a jewel amongst women. In fact, I am rather loath to part with her. Are you sure I cannot interest you in Mary? She has as many arms and legs as the other. I would be willing to add in Kitty as a bonus."

Darcy stared at the man as if he were mad, bartering his daughters like horseflesh. Then, he saw the gleam in Bennet's eye. Darcy did not much care for the man's joking at his daughters' expense. But if Bennet was to be his father-in-law, he supposed he had better get used to it.

"The last I heard, polygamy was illegal in this kingdom. And I confess I am rather attached to Miss Elizabeth."

"Well, then, Lizzy it will be, if she will have you. But I assume you have already spoken with her, or you would not have ridden all the way here."

"Yes, sir. I have spoken to Miss Elizabeth and to Mrs. Bennet. They have sent letters with me to assure you of their consent." Darcy handed the envelope to Mr. Bennet.

The man took the missive but made no motion to open it. "Did you think I would need their persuasion before granting your suit?"

"The ladies seemed to think you would welcome their opinions on the matter."

Bennet took out a letter opener and sliced through the seam. He read a moment, then took off his spectacles and tossed them onto his desk. "Is this true? You ruined Lizzy at a ball last night?"

Ah, Mrs. Bennet, making sure that Darcy could not slip through her claws. He explained the incident with Miss Peabody. Partway through, he realized he was getting in deeper than he intended. His behaviour with Lizzy had not been all it should have been, if looked at in a certain light. Her father might take exception.

Leaving Lizzy shivering in the garden, after kissing her half senseless... It had not been his finest moment. And yet, the memory of the kiss could not but make him smile.

Bennet's frown only deepened, however. "You ruined *two* young ladies last night?"

Darcy sat forward. "No sir, I did not touch Miss Peabody. I swear it on my father's grave."

"So it was just Lizzy, then." Bennet's tone was icy.

The man confounded him. Bennet had had a quarter century to set aside dowries for the daughters he was blessed with. He had not saved a penny. And here was Darcy, one of the wealthiest men in England, offering to provide for one of those daughters. Yes, Darcy had kissed Lizzy before proposing, but the intervening time had not been above an hour. Who, pray tell, was the less responsible man?

Despite the anger simmering in his breast, Darcy said, "I confess that I was more ardent than I ought to have been. But my behaviour was not dishonourable. A gentleman does not kiss a gently bred young lady without intending to marry her."

A wry smile curved Bennet's lips. "I appreciate the sentiment, however idealistic it might be."

Fighting to keep the exasperation out of his voice, Darcy said, "I am in love with your daughter, sir. I am in a position to care for her in a manner befitting a woman of her sensibilities. Do you mean to refuse my suit?"

"Heavens, no. My wife would kill me in my sleep. You understand that with the entail on the property, I cannot offer you a dowry. Lizzy is entitled only to her share of her mother's five thousand pounds at its four percents, upon my wife's demise."

"Miss Elizabeth's lack of fortune is nothing to me. I want her for herself, and consider myself lucky to have found her favour."

"In that case, you will be a happy man, Mr. Darcy." Bennet rose and extended his hand.

Darcy stood and took it. "I shall indeed. I am honoured that you entrust your daughter's future to me."

"Take good care of her, young man. She may not have brothers, but she has uncles and cousins who will see to her welfare after I am gone. If you harm her in any way—"

"I would not think of it." Darcy stared at him, aghast. Did Bennet think him such a rogue? "She is in every way precious to me. I desire only her happiness."

The man nodded, looking grey and weary. Darcy had expected joy. Instead, he realized, Bennet was mourning the loss of his daughter. Darcy would take her away to Derbyshire, a distance of more than a hundred miles. They would stop in Hertfordshire a few times a year, on their way to and from London. But Lizzy would never again be a daily presence in her father's life.

Darcy felt somewhat guilty about that. If Jane and Bingley also move to Derbyshire, Bennet would be twice bereft. But the man had a wife and three other daughters to comfort him. If he found their company wanting, well, he had no one to blame for that but himself.

∞ ∞ ∞

Later that week, Georgiana called at the house on Berkeley Square. Jane and Mrs. Bennet had gone shopping for soaps, perfumes, and potions to take back to Longbourn. Lizzy was in her room deciding what to wear for the wedding. She bounded down the stairs, took Giana's hand, and led her to the bedroom.

"Miss Darcy!" Sally greeted. She was dressed in the sage green frock Giana had given her on the day they got caught in the rain. "We could use your help. Which gown is your favourite?"

Lizzy had hired Sally as her lady's maid. Mrs. Gardiner was sorry to lose her, but glad the girl would have the opportunity to work in a great house.

Sally continued, "The pink and violet gowns flatter Miss Elizabeth the best. They bring out the colour in her cheeks. But she prefers the blue as better suited for a wedding."

Giana examined the frocks that hung about the room. The three ball gowns were all in pale pastels suited to an unmarried lady. The pink was Lizzy's favourite from Longbourn. It was in a simple style with updated sleeves and a new white ribbon about the waist.

The other two had been purchased in London for the season. The violet was a shimmery satin with puffed sleeves and a delicate lace overskirt. The blue silk was the colour of a summer sky, the skirt dotted with white rosettes.

"We will need to add a fichu," Lizzy said to Giana, "to make the neckline more appropriate for morning wear. Otherwise, I think any one of the gowns would do very well. What do you think?"

Giana smoothed her hand over the fabrics, rubbed the flounces between her fingers. "They are all so lovely, it is hard to decide. Have you thought about jewellery? If you choose the blue, I can lend you a sapphire set that belonged to my mother."

Lizzy pressed her hand to her heart, touched by the offer. "Oh, that would be splendid!"

Sally gave a little pout. "The violet is the prettiest, I think. It has such a lovely sheen, and all that lace. But I suppose it *is* better suited to a ballroom than a church."

"Shall we go with the blue, then?" Lizzy asked, bubbling with excitement.

"Darcy will love it," Giana urged.

The mention of his name brought a flutter to Lizzy's stomach. The idea of him waiting at the altar while she walked down the aisle on her father's arm... It was thrilling, and hardly seemed real. But in a few short days, she would indeed become his wife.

"I have an appointment with the modiste this afternoon to make the alterations," Lizzy said. "She has assured me she can finish before we leave for Hertfordshire." With a sly grin, she added, "I find tradespeople are far more accommodating when you tell them to spare no expense."

Giana smiled brightly. "My father raised us never to be wasteful, but this occasion is an exception. Do you mind if I accompany you to the dress shop?"

Lizzy squeezed her hands. "Nothing would please me more than having my newest sister with me."

Giana's eyes teared. "A sister at last! I cannot tell you how happy that makes me. I shall not be nearly so frightened making my come-out with you by my side."

"We will have such fun." Lizzy looked into Giana's pretty face, fresh with the glow of youth. She was still innocent despite the tragedies that had befallen her. She had lost her parents too young. Experienced the betrayal of that blackguard Wickham. Yet her eyes still beamed with hope.

Georgiana was resilient like her brother, and like Lizzy, too. They had persevered through hardship, and now had found this happiness as a new family. With luck, their joy would be increased by the addition of children. Lizzy's heart raced with exhilaration as she anticipated the adventure before them.

Chapter 35

Two days later, the Darcys and Bingleys descended on Netherfield. The Bennet ladies returned to Longbourn. The younger sisters greeted the elder ones excitedly. Mary and Kitty were happy to have their best gowns returned to them. Kitty fussed over the new flounces and ribbons that updated them to the latest style. Lydia cooed over the bonnets her mother brought her, as the ones in the Meryton shops were too ugly to be endured.

With the gifts distributed, the drawing room conversation turned to the betrothals. "What did Bingley say when he proposed?" Kitty asked. "Was it terribly romantic?"

"I cannot remember the exact words he used," Jane said, "only the sentiments. It *was* terribly romantic, because I had loved him for so long, and he was mine at last."

When talk of Bingley waned, the room descended into silence. At last, Mary said to Lizzy, "In your last letter, you told us Darcy is not the proud man we thought him to be."

"He has no improper pride," Lizzy said, regretting every unkind word she had spoken of him. "He is reserved by nature, but sociable with those he knows well."

Mary nodded a moment. "Then we must extend to him the balm of human sympathy, and open our hearts with Christian charity and filial affection."

"Oh, lord," Lydia said with a roll of her eyes, flopping back against the sofa cushion.

"Lydia," Lizzy warned, "I must ask you not to blaspheme

around your new relations. Such speech is undignified and marks you as a vulgar country girl. In two days' time, you will meet Darcy's aunt, the Countess of Matlock. She will not hesitate to scold if you behave in an unladylike manner."

Both Lydia and Mrs. Bennet opened their mouths as if to protest, then closed them again.

Aunt Philips came and shared the latest gossip from Meryton. Lizzy had never been so happy to experience the familiar rhythms of home. The idea of leaving Longbourn for Pemberley was bittersweet. It brought a heaviness to her chest even while her stomach fluttered with delight.

Once aunt Philips had gone, Lizzy's father called her into his study for a private interview. The familiar scent of books and wax candles hung in the air. Her father sat at his desk wearing a sly expression. She took the chair opposite him, unable to suppress a grin.

"Well, my dear," Mr. Bennet began, "I hope Mr. Darcy is worthy of you."

"Oh, Papa, I admire him above all men—except you, of course."

"You need not flatter me. I do not expect a woman in the first flush of love to give a thought to her old papa. But you must assure me that it was the man who won you, and not his fortune."

She squeezed the arms of her chair, disliking her father's suggestion. "As you may recall, I did not care a fig about Darcy's fortune last autumn. My stay in London did not change that. I only gave him my heart after I discovered him to be an honourable man. He has a tender side he rarely shows in company."

"I would not have guessed it." Mr. Bennet shook his head. "If you are certain he can make you happy, then you have my blessing."

She said gravely, "I do not believe I could be happy without him."

That evening, the Bennets went to Netherfield to dine.

When the men retired to the drawing room after finishing their port, Darcy joined Lizzy on the settee. The wooden back was honey maple and the thick seat cushion upholstered in green silk moiré.

"I have been thinking about what to do for a honeymoon." Darcy took her hand. "Since travel to the continent is out of the question, what think you of a trip to Scotland this summer?"

She bestowed a soft smile on him. "The poetry of Walter Scott has enticed you, I see."

"Perhaps. We could stop at Pemberley for as long as you like, then make the rest of the journey from there."

She sat up straighter, a new thought sending a tickle to her belly. "Can we also see the Lake District?"

He brightened. "Of course. It could be a poet's tour of the North."

She chuckled. "I admit I *am* curious whether the countryside is as beautiful as Wordsworth describes it." She pondered a moment. "What of Georgiana? Shall we bring her with us?"

"That is a fine idea. And perhaps Lady Cressida Marlowe as a companion for her. Lady Cressida once expressed a desire to see the Scottish moors when the heather was in bloom."

"Oh, I do like Lady Cressida. We will have great fun together —I shall write to her mother and propose the scheme. But in the meantime, could we not go to Pemberley directly after the wedding? Will the roads be passable?"

He nodded pensively. "There is the chance of a snowstorm, but I am well acquainted with the inns along the way. We should be able to travel there in three days' time, weather permitting."

"We will have to return to London after Easter. I promised Lady Matlock to help chaperone Arabelle."

"Normally the activity of the season is not a great draw for me. In this case, however, I shall enjoy showing off my wife to the *ton*." He kissed her hand. "You are a true original, and I shall be the envy of the single men."

It seemed likely to her that most single men would rather

have a bride with a substantial fortune. Preferably one from a titled family. But she did not argue that point. Instead, she met Darcy's eyes and basked in the love she found there.

∞ ∞ ∞

The Gardiner and Fitzwilliam families arrived. They occupied all the spare bedrooms at Longbourn and Netherfield. The next days were a whirlwind. Nearly every moment before the wedding was filled with planning and entertainments. Lizzy was so busy she could barely think.

Before she could catch her breath, she was standing at the front of the church in Meryton with Darcy at her side. Fulfilling his hopes, they were declared man and wife within a week of their engagement.

Wishing for privacy for their wedding night, Mr. and Mrs. Darcy rented rooms at an inn. They took the entire floor for themselves. Lizzy would have been loath to allow the extravagance under any other circumstances. On that occasion, however, it seemed appropriate.

The suite they occupied had two bedrooms with a sitting room in between. The valet and lady's maid unpacked the clothes the bridal couple would need for their stay. Waiting for them to finish, Lizzy stood at the window.

In the garden below, early spring bulbs were coming into bloom. Crocuses and snowdrops and dwarf irises. Beyond was a line of trees and a field planted with winter wheat. Above, the sky took on a pink hue as sunset neared.

After the servants had gone, Darcy came and took her hands. He kissed her temple. "Do you have a preference as to sleeping arrangements? Would you like your own room?"

She looked up at him, surprised by the question, unsure how to answer. "That is the way of the *ton*, is it not? But my parents have always shared a room. I assumed we would do the same."

He grinned. "I was hoping you would say that." He nibbled

her ear.

A knock came on the door, and the servants brought in a bath. In the spare bedroom, Lizzy washed away the day's travels. Darcy followed. After the bath was taken away, supper was served.

The newlyweds dined in the sitting room, wearing their dressing gowns. It was wonderfully intimate and a little bit terrifying. Lizzy tried not to think about what was to come, but it was impossible not to.

Her mother had been of no help whatever in instructing Lizzy on what to expect. Fortunately, aunt Gardiner had stepped in to fulfil the lack. Lizzy was nervous of course, but she loved Darcy and trusted him.

When at last they went to bed together, he showed all the tenderness she had anticipated. A hot flame of passion burned between them, far surpassing her imagination. She would have been happy to explore more of the pleasures of the married state. But the exhaustion of the day overcame her.

She awoke in his arms the next morning and nuzzled his stubbled cheek. Without opening his eyes, he pulled her close. "Mine," he murmured in a voice gravelly with sleep.

"Your possessiveness quite frightens me," she teased.

"Why?" he asked, opening his eyes. He rolled towards her so that his body half covered hers.

She suckled his earlobe. "Under the law, I am your property now. I took a vow to obey you."

"And I took a vow to worship you with my body—a pledge which I intend to observe diligently." He trailed kisses along the curve of her neck. Then, he turned onto his side and rested his weight on one elbow. "If I had wanted a submissive wife, I would not have chosen you. I want a wife who is my equal— one who will challenge me, and whose judgement I trust." He kissed her temple. "You are not truly worried I shall turn into a tyrant?"

She shook her head. "No," she said aloud to reinforce to the gesture. "I trust you—more than I have ever trusted anyone.

You have my best interest at heart, which has been true of very few people in my life. Jane, of course. My aunt and uncle Gardiner." Emotion swelled her throat as she realized the list ended there.

Her father favoured her over his other daughters. Perhaps over any other living person. But that love had not spurred him to provide for her as he ought. If she had not found Darcy, and Jane had not found Bingley…

But Lizzy would not think on that. She had made a spectacular match, and Jane would soon be wed as well. Her family's future was secure. Her younger sisters were as silly as ever, but now at least they had no need to fear poverty. They might even come to find husbands as eligible as Mr. Collins.

Lizzy snuggled up to the man who had made her happier than she had ever hoped to be. She remembered the first time she had seen him. How stunningly handsome he had been. And how quickly her admiration had turned to disdain when he insulted her. That night, she had little thought that within six months, she would find herself in his bed as his lawful wife. How strange life was!

She ran a fingertip along his muscled arm. The sight of his athletic physique still astonished her. Paintings and sculpture had not prepared her for the delights of flesh and bone. "I am glad Sally and I got caught in the rain outside the bookshop that day."

"And I am glad I had the presence of mind to hoist you into my carriage." He threaded his fingers through her long, loose tresses. "I look forward to introducing you to the staff and tenants at Pemberley. They will love you as I do."

"Perhaps not *quite* as you do," she said suggestively.

Pulling the covers over them, he tickled her neck with kisses until she squealed.

Epilogue

"Please, Mama, one more story," asked three-year-old Will. His sweet voice was drowsy and slurred as Lizzy laid him down to bed. His eyes were half closed. She stroked his dark, wispy hair for a minute, and he fell into slumber.

She rose and turned to Darcy, who stood holding their infant daughter. With a warm smile on his handsome face, he rocked the sleeping babe. Lizzy's heart filled with so much love, she did not know how her body could hold it all.

She smoothed the skirts of her ball gown. "We must go," she said in her husband's ear.

"Must we?"

"I am afraid so. The incomparable Georgiana Darcy awaits her chaperones. Someone must beat off the young swains who follow her like a mother hen with her chicks."

"None of them are worthy of her."

"None will ever be to your mind. But she is twenty now, and able to judge a man's worth. Do you not wish to see her well settled?"

"One day."

Lizzy took the babe from his arms. She gave her daughter a gentle kiss and laid her in the cradle. Then, she snuffed out the candles and led Darcy from the nursery. Noiselessly, she closed the door behind them.

Walking with him down the corridor, Lizzy said in low tones, "All Giana's closest friends are married now. Even that goose Priscilla Peabody managed to snare an army captain."

As the story went, the young man had been Rolf Peabody's commander. He had broken the news of Rolf's death at Waterloo to his family. Priscilla had been as heartbroken as an innocent sister should. Lord Wayne, though grieved, seemed to find peace that his brother had died a hero.

Aside from that loss, the Wayne family fortunes were looking up. Thanks to Lord Matlock, an investigator had tracked down old Wayne's secretary in Boston. The Prince Regent himself had taken an interest in the case. The stolen funds had not *all* been recovered. But the viscount and viscountess were no longer living on the brink of ruin.

News of Wickham had also reached them from Waterloo. Apparently he was forced at gunpoint to marry the daughter of a Belgian tradesman. Lizzy hoped he would never again darken England's shores. Some whispers about him and Georgiana had swirled about her during her come-out. But they had quickly faded. She was now the toast of the *ton*.

Darcy laid his hand at the small of Lizzy's back. "Is it wrong of me to want to keep Giana with us a while longer?"

"Not at all. I do not wish her to rush. I want her to marry for love, as we did."

He stopped, and she turned to face him. An impish smile lit his eyes.

"Darcy," she warned, "what are you thinking about?"

"Just this." He placed a tender kiss on her lips. "You still make me the happiest of men. Every day, I love you more."

She wished she could wrap her arms around his neck and kiss him deeply, but her gown would wrinkle. "Perhaps tomorrow," she suggested, "we could start on baby number three."

"Perhaps we could find a dark corner of the garden, and start tonight."

She looked at him in mock horror as they headed towards the stairway. "What? And ruin my reputation?"

"If I ruin your reputation, I promise to marry you."

"You have already married me."

He furrowed his brows. "Then there is nothing to stop me from having my way with you."

"Why Darcy, what about the proprieties?"

"Hang the proprieties."

Georgiana looked up at them, hands on her hips, as they descended. "Are the two of you flirting again?" she asked with a gleam in her eye.

"I am afraid so," Darcy said gravely.

"Married couples should not flirt," Giana teased. "It is unseemly."

When they reached the ground floor, Darcy took Lizzy into his arms and kissed her. "Are we unseemly?" he asked his wife.

"I believe we are."

Giana gave them a happy smile. "The two of you are enough to make the *ton* lose their cynicism."

Lizzy laid a hand on Giana's shoulders and looked into her eyes. "Promise me you will only marry for love."

"After watching the pair of you these four years," Giana asked, picking up her wrap, "how could I marry for less?"

They headed out into the cool April night, potted hyacinths on the front landing scenting the air. Lizzy said a prayer of thanks for the happiness she had found. She had not been content to watch life happen from the front parlour at Longbourn. Instead, she had taken control of her destiny. Now she was reaping the rewards.

Soon it would be Georgiana's turn. She had matured from a shy girl into a beautiful and confident young woman. Still gentle by nature, she was kind to all, but knew how to stand up for herself. She would make a brilliant match.

Looking up at the sky, Lizzy spotted the first star as it began to twinkle. She thought to make a wish, but she already had everything she wanted. She took Darcy's arm and snuggled into his warmth. With him by her side, she was ready to take on the world.

∞ ∞ ∞

Thank you for reading! If you enjoyed this book, sign up for Andrea David's newsletter to receive information about new releases, special offers, and exclusive content.

About the Author

Andrea David is a women's fiction author in Raleigh, North Carolina who writes stories of romantic love and family dynamics. She enjoys gardening, scuba diving, and hiking active volcanoes with her husband. To learn more about her books, visit her website.

Your words are priceless
Leave a review to let other customers know what you thought of this book. Reviews help readers find quality books and authors find their audience.

Get free, exclusive content and never miss a new release
Sign up for Andrea's newsletter to find out when she's got a new book out. Subscribers also receive special offers and exclusives like excerpts, deleted scenes, and short stories.

Read books for free before they're published
Join Andrea's ARC Club and receive advance review copies.

More by Andrea David

Darcy's Fair Lady

Fake engagement! Can Darcy convince London society that

Elizabeth will become his wife—while persuading his heart that she won't?

In London after quitting Netherfield, Darcy must convince Lady Catherine that he's betrothed. It's the only way she'll let her daughter Anne marry her beloved. When Darcy receives a sudden windfall from one of his investments, he comes upon an idea. He offers Elizabeth Bennet a substantial sum to pose as his fiancée.

Lizzy is shocked by the impropriety of his proposal. Yet she and her sisters desperately need the funds to stave off genteel poverty. Plus, while she's in London, she can help reunite her sister Jane with Bingley, her former suitor.

Living as guests under Darcy's roof, Lizzy and Jane receive lessons to help them fit in with fashionable society. Lizzy discovers a new side to the Darcy she once despised: his kindness to his staff, his devotion to his sister, his concern for her wellbeing. Is there more to this handsome and fascinating man she once considered so proud? Could their faux betrothal turn real?

This sweet Regency romance is a 57,000-word standalone novel. It includes kissing but no on-page intimacy.

Darcy Comes To Rosings

Elizabeth Bennet is enjoying a visit with her newly married best friend in the idyllic countryside of Kent. Her pleasant holiday is interrupted when the arrogant Mr. Darcy appears at nearby Rosings Park. During their frequent meetings, her spirited retorts do nothing to deter his attentions to her. In fact, they only seem to encourage him.

Realizing Darcy is in love with her, Elizabeth is torn by an awful dilemma. With her father's estate entailed on a male heir, she and her sisters face the prospect of poverty if they do not marry well. Darcy's wealth could save them. But how can she marry a man she does not esteem simply for the material comfort he can offer?

Fitzwilliam Darcy is determined to forget the lovely Elizabeth, who stole his heart during his autumn sojourn in Hertfordshire. So naturally, when he learns she is spending the spring within walking distance of his aunt's estate at Rosings, he goes for an extended stay. He finds Elizabeth even more enchanting than he remembered.

When Darcy discovers Elizabeth's rightful resentments against him, he seeks to make things right and court her properly. Can he convince her of his worth? Or have his past sins—and the machinations of an old enemy—sunk him in her opinion forever?

This sweet Regency romance is a full-length, standalone novel. It includes kissing and a fade-to-black wedding night scene.

The Darcys' First Christmas: The Disappearance

After a blissful honeymoon, Elizabeth Darcy is thrilled to see her sister Jane again as the two prepare to spend their first Christmas with their new husbands. But when distressing news arrives from their family at Longbourn, it overthrows their plans. With the shame of her sister Lydia's elopement still fresh in her mind, Elizabeth fears the worst—and worries that this new proof of her family's folly will test Darcy's attachment to her. Can their love endure this new challenge? Or will their first Christmas together be their last?

This is a clean and wholesome Regency novella with a happy ending and no cliffhanger.

∞ ∞ ∞

Mr. Darcy's Secret Stories

Want to know a secret? We do, too! What happens behind closed doors between Mr. Darcy and his Elizabeth? Find out in our shared series, *Mr. Darcy's Secret Stories.*

Each steamy, heartfelt book in this series can be read in one afternoon (or evening!) as each author imagines new ways for Mr. Darcy to show Lizzy his eternal devotion. And maybe how he looks in a dripping wet shirt. You know, both are good. Discover all of Our Dear Couples' secrets in this new series of *Pride and Prejudice* variations.